BENDING the BOYNE

Bending the Boyne
J.S. Dunn
© J.S. Dunn 2011

Seriously Good Books
Naples, Florida USA
www.seriouslygoodbooks.net

ISBN: 978-0-9831554-1-6

Cover and interior design by Deborah Perdue
www.illuminationgraphics.com

Cover photo courtesy of Declan McCormack,
county Meath, Ireland © 2008

Cataloging-in-Publication Data

Dunn, J. S.
Bending the Boyne / J. S. Dunn. -- 1st ed.
p. : maps ; cm.
ISBN-13: 978-0-9831554-1-6
ISBN-10: 0-9831554-1-0
1. Cian (Fictitious character) – Fiction.
2. Prehistoric peoples – Fiction.
3. Boyne River Valley (Ireland) – Fiction.
4. Ireland – Fiction.
5. Historical fiction.
I. Title.

PS3554.U469963B49 2011
813'64--dc22

First edition: March 2011

BENDING the BOYNE

J.S. DUNN

• SERIOUSLY GOOD BOOKS •

For Jack and Leonie,
who brought laughter and love

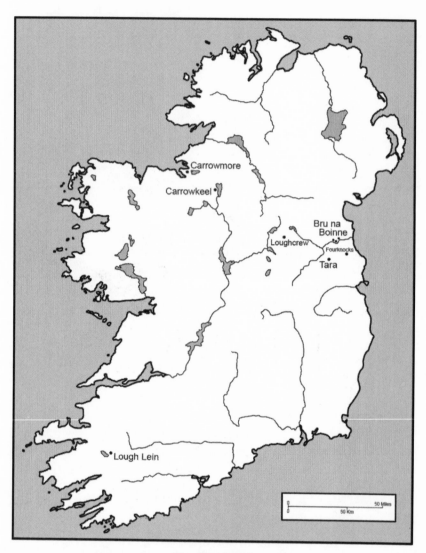

E R I U
ca. 2200 BCE

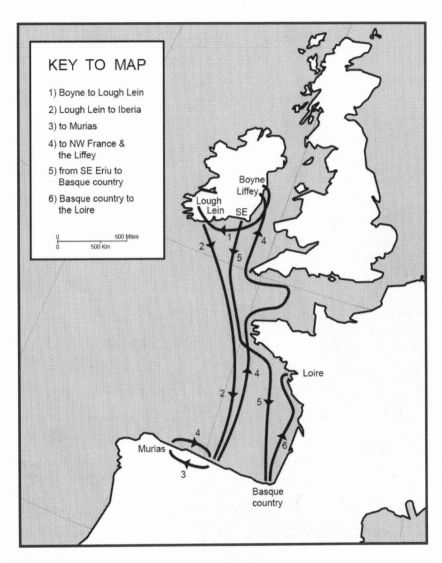

KEY TO MAP

1) Boyne to Lough Lein
2) Lough Lein to Iberia
3) to Murias
4) to NW France & the Liffey
5) from SE Eriu to Basque country
6) Basque country to the Loire

0 ___ 500 Miles
0 ___ 500 Km

SCHEMATIC MAP of CIAN'S TRAVELS
North Atlantic ca. 2200 BCE

Let us cease from the stories of the Gaedil,
that we may tell of the seven peoples who took Ireland
before them.

Lebor Gabala, *12th century CE*

What is startlingly clear is that the Atlantic zone was now
closely bound up with the changes gripping the whole of central
and western Europe.

From: Facing the Ocean:
The Atlantic and its Peoples,
Barry Cunliffe, 2001

Prologue:

Present-Day Dublin

T RAFFIC CHURNED THE fresh morning air to thick yellow. A glut of vehicles, their noise, the fumes, assailed his broad shoulders. His face brightened when he passed through the lofty portal with arriving museum employees. Already the museum visitors formed a queue.

He tracked the visitors' steps throughout the ground floor exhibits. He could point out that Eire's first copper daggers lay juxtaposed with smuggled guns used for the 1916 Rising, but he refrained. The museum authority had decided to remove the tangible evidence of that uprising to a new venue, a different building altogether. Too violent for current taste perhaps, or simply too recent for comfort, its heroes neither forgotten nor forgiven.

Dressed in a guide's navy-blue suit, he presented himself when visitors wandered into the elegant tearoom, where he smiled and held the heavy door open. A presence with authority, the tall docent hovered while the visitors lingered at tables with coffee or tea or apple tart. They looked up as if expecting him to bring the exhibits, Ireland's earliest weapons and stunning gold jewelry, to life for them while they rested. Modern feet they had, unused to much walking or standing. He took a seat and he obliged his audience by reaching back to the beginning.

"The people living here followed an obsession: they watched the sky day and night, sunrise and sunset."

Eons before them, in the time before time, giant plates of rock collided, superheating and leaching out minerals and metals laid down as beds and veins. Ancient glaciers formed and advanced like tides to scour out ridges and glens, then retreated during warming and flooding. Mighty forces severed Eire from the larger island to the east and the continent beyond, as inrushing seas submerged coastlines and thrust up cliffs. The island lay apart in the west. Their ancestors arrived from the sea, to hunt and gather food and find sources of flint.

Recumbent, safe from the Continent, their island luxuriated in balmy currents flowing from far to the southwest and up through the cold northern ocean. The island appeared serene, verdant in its innocence. Birds wheeled above its gentle granite shoulders and thick forests. The valleys teemed with animals and leaping fish silvered its rivers.

Thousands of sunrises later, new settlers straggled in on hide boats, hauling with them new animals: sheep, cattle, and goats. Those people brought innovations; the growing of cereals, pottery making, and methods for observing the sky. Using just the naked eye, they excelled at their astronomy. They proudly called themselves Starwatchers.

"For millennia this island lay beyond any grasp while its people observed the sun by day, and the moon and dazzling array moving far above them by night. They built imposing mounds that spoke to the light from above.

"The Starwatchers transformed the island's landscape with their great stones, the megaliths. Boann, a young woman in that time, was learning her people's secrets." The docent, his face grave but his manner amiable, paused to stir milk into his tea. His audience moved closer.

"At the beginning of all the struggles that forged a fierce independence, lived the Starwatchers." He would tell their story, how the Bronze Age swept to Eire at the western edge of known waters and almost engulfed Boann and her people.

His tale would be long. After one sip of tea he resumed, deep cadences taking his listeners to a place of mist and stars and myth.

"The east held dark blue, sky indistinct from waves. Then a wisp of lighter blue revealed the startling edge. The pale swath intensified and turned to gold before her eyes. No matter how many times Boann had seen the sun rising, the spectacle thrilled her. She lifted her arms in welcome where she stood on Red Mountain, above the massive passage mounds along the river Boyne."

PART ONE

DAY

I search with my mind into the multitudinous revolving spirals

of the stars.

Ptolemy

Starwatchers, circa 2200 BCE

THE FLAMING HEAD of the ancient one tipped above the horizon. The rising sun took Boann into its warm, golden embrace. She stayed until the rays hid the glittering void, ending her vigil of the stars. All in her village would be stirring and she should return to her father's house. With longing, she glanced back toward dawn over the waves.

She saw it then, a speck out on the vast ocean. With her hand shading her eyes she could see the large boat, crammed black. Sparks of light glinted from metal: the fearsome long knives.

Boann scrambled down the mountain slope to warn the Dagda. She soon found him, a dignified figure herding sheep and lambs on the grassy plain.

"You're sure that it is an intruder boat?" He cast a wary look to the east.

She nodded. "I am sure that I'm sure."

"What can this mean? Arriving with equinox, the cursed warriors!"

The Dagda raised his staff, its red stone macehead gleaming. "I'll rouse the elders and send our scouts."

He sped away on his long legs, leaving the surprised flock milling around her.

Never had she seen the Dagda swear, or run as he did now. His news would cause turmoil in their village. She had better fetch water before returning there. Feet flying, she hurried north to the smaller river.

Mist hung thick over the stream. In the grey stillness, she thought herself alone. She retrieved her clay pot among ferns, lifting their damp scent with it. Auburn hair cascaded over one shoulder as her torso leaned toward the water to fill the jug. Another time she might have glimpsed her face on the stream's placid surface but now she paid it no heed. A bird twittered and flapped in the copse and her head jerked up, alert.

Behind her a twig snapped under heavy footfall, then another. She felt the noise, she heard it to her core: danger. She spun around, eyes wide, and a pungent odor struck her nostrils. A bulky shadow lurched from a stand of hazelnut and her every muscle leaped into action. His knife sliced at her net shawl but she pulled and ran away from the smell, away from the intruder. She outpaced his shadow, leaving branches whipping behind her in the mist.

She gripped the fragile pot while her legs raced through gorse and bracken and over rocks, this way and that. Only a fox could have pursued her. After a good distance, Boann broke her stride, sank into dense undergrowth, and listened. Other than her ragged breathing, a strange quiet smothered the woods.

Shaking, she rose and stared down at the water jug in her arms. *My mother's favorite.* Head spinning, she fought an urge to be sick. Her legs stung from nettles. Water blotched her soft skin tunic and thorns had scraped it. Her good shawl lay somewhere behind, ruined. She'd have another, Sheela could make her another shawl but not by this sunset.

Sure that no one followed, Boann turned and found a path that led to the dwelling shared with her father. She slowed to a walk, heart still racing.

Glad she was to reach their home, its old but solid walls of drystacked stone. She left the wood slab door open behind her and slipped inside. Hearth smoke furled up through the roof hole in the thatch, silently reminding her to appear calm before her father Oghma. Ever since her mother had passed to the spirits, his temper could flare. She heard Oghma fussing with his mallets and stone chisels behind a woven willow screen, already up and about.

She swallowed hard; what could she do to distract him before telling him about the boat, much less her attacker? Her quick hands took pieces from braids of drying flowers and potent herbs. She plunged hot stones into a skin water bag to set it boiling and snatched up a clay cup incised with chevrons, the symbol for the Swan stars. As her father appeared, she was admiring the cup.

"Is it herbal water you're having? Are you taken ill?"

"It is close to my time with the moon. The brew eases me."

She stepped in front of the emptied water jug. Not even a sharp look came her way. She took a deep breath and told him. "Another big boat arrives. Just so, with spring equinox." Boann stood still as a deer, deflecting scrutiny.

"Yes, the Dagda stopped here in haste. More of them, it hardly seems possible. Perhaps now Cian will return to inform the elders. He is long overdue." His mouth set in a hard line.

So the news of another boat shook Oghma as well. He did not speak of Cian to her, had not mentioned him during all the winter. She would not tell her father that she had been on the mountain with Cian through the night. Now that seemed long ago.

"We must go on as we have done. Why would these intruders bother us on the equinox?" She hadn't meant to sound defiant, the wrong note with him; she exhaled slowly.

"The Dagda and I agree that the people should gather to celebrate. With Cian, or without him."

With or without you.

Before she could bring herself to tell of her attacker at their stream, her father said he must be going. His expression softened. "We'll just have to be ready for them. Our scouts left for the coast." Oghma patted her head as if she were still a child, and set out to join the Dagda and the other elders. At the open door, dust motes swirled in the early light: her bits of hope dashed to the floor only to rise and float again.

Her people must hold their ceremony. Their village at the river Boyne led the starwatching, the center of a network whose strands connected all the tribes on the island, tensile yet strong like a spider's web. *A tear in the right place could bring down our web*; she shivered and moved closer to the hearth fire. They must hold their spring rites and mark the equinox stars. All the elders would have to agree on it, though. Estranged from the elders as he was, Cian might not return that evening.

The elders including her father supervised at the immense stone-lined passage mounds set in clearings, three emerald mounds spaced in a rough triangle along the wide river plain.

Their Boyne starwatching complex had been active for centuries. The ancestors who dreamed and planned these mounds were long deceased. Their descendants completed the work in stages and returned to older villages in the northwest, or began new villages elsewhere. Final alignment and carving of the stones proceeded bit by bit.

Many Starwatchers declared that their grand mounds at the Boyne would never be duplicated. And, replied some, these mounds would never be finished. Their banter belied an unspoken fear. Fear had arrived with the intruders and their long bronze knives.

She crouched by the hearth in the room's center, arms hugging her knees and one hand suspending her cup over its warmth. Her mother's water jug lay by the hearth, safe again. Boann traced its grooved designs. She tried to not think about intruders. Taking this herbal water would erase that stranger's smell. This was the first time she smelled one of them up close. She might have told Oghma of the assault, yet why upset him further with another armed boatload arriving. He would only worry more when she went out at night. Her mind's eye saw muscled limbs streaking through the forest, a lone figure quick as a fox, coming to meet her under the stars. Now her tryst with Cian seemed unimportant.

Again she remembered the shadow striking at her, the flashing dagger.

She had avoided her destiny as that stranger would have fashioned it. Slowly the hair on her body lay down and she felt the muscles easing in her neck and back. Best that she not mention her scare to anyone. They all needed a rest from troubles with intruders, they needed to enjoy themselves. But that one's intent at the stream could not be mistaken. The heavy footfalls resounded: *another moment on the breeze and it would have been far worse for me than that man's smell*. Her soothing cup had gone cold.

She stood, her legs still shaking and with pink welts rising from unheeded nettles. Boann crossed the room, a flagged living area around the central hearth. Its dim, cool interior was fitted with bed platforms along the sides. At dressed stone shelves against the far wall, she searched for her shawl pin. Her father had carved the pin, a white length of antler with precise chevron grooves and polished smooth. It would calm her to roll its spiraling texture in her palm. She had not worn her pin since the solstice feast, or had she? Disoriented, she felt upset for not remembering, and for her lost shawl. What use was the pin without her good shawl? So many losses since these intruders arrived, and creeping uncertainty spreading like that man's shadow over all that she held dear.

She fumbled in leather pouches and wood boxes on the stone shelves and threw open the willow baskets on the floor. Her father was slipping at his task as master stonecarver; Boann knew it better than anyone. Oghma wouldn't be carving another faceted bone pin.

The loss of Oghma's apprentice had not helped. She quarreled with Cian before he left their village. "You are favored in this. You are the brightest among us. If you hear something once, you have it. But of late you've taken to learning all the wrong things, and little or nothing from Oghma."

"I've learned the sky symbols. But I lack the patience to be picking them into stone. I don't want to be out watching the heavens! For me it's time wasted, sighting in the cold for a constellation or fixing the sun's angle at a post."

She pressed him. "You spend more time among the intruders. What can they offer you?"

"Novelty," he replied. "Action. New weapons. The intruders play war games all day."

"Yes, and they feast all night using food they raid from our people. These warriors scorn our starwatching, do they not?"

"They appear to be ignorant of our symbols. They call us 'quiet ones.'"

"So is it down to Oghma to finish the carving at our mounds, alone and worn away himself and his age written on his face?"

"Boann, I discussed my leaving with the elders. There is nothing more to be said about it." He rose from their hidden place in the meadow where they had played as children. Within moments, Cian could not be seen in any direction. No sign of him, and no swift fox.

Ohma repeated to her, the elders' long and serious debates caused by Cian. His reason for leaving that he gave the elders, for him to study the intruders' ways, offended them. They could see that other young men might take Cian's path over time, dazzled by the intruders' metal tools and attracted to bold new ways.

Boann saw the hurt in Oghma's eyes, but she believed what Cian told the elders. Surely Cian stayed among the intruders for more than making sport with their shining weapons.

As the nights lengthened into winter, father and daughter drew apart across her mother's empty place at their hearth. Boann overlooked Oghma's short temper. Say what they will, and some in their village thought him too stern, or overly proud, but her father did not give in to despair. He continued his work, and she could only admire his sense of purpose. She searched the stars for some sign to guide her. The reply, the sign, came clear and simple. She would study the stars in order to replace Cian, the reluctant apprentice.

She petitioned the chief astronomer, the Dagda, for his tutelage of her.

The Dagda heard her out, then he questioned her. "What about your healing skills?"

"Airmid shows great promise. In time she can replace my mother."

"That may be so. —When our astronomers meet to watch the skies, only those women attend who can be absent from the hearth or have no young children. You must devote many sunrises and sunsets, whole seasons, in order to succeed."

"I am determined to succeed in starwatching."

He peered at her as if seeing her for the first time, his eyes blue beyond the telling, a breeze lifting wisps of white hair around his sage face. "You need to know all of our carved notations and much more about the sky's paths, to truly assist Oghma."

Recalling the Dagda's penetrating look, Boann forgot her search for her shawl pin and her shaky, stinging legs. She had not realized the extent of her people's astronomy.

She had so much to learn at the start that it almost overwhelmed her. The Dagda warned that he would condense her instruction and he had. He skipped explaining the basic movements in the skies, the facts all Starwatchers learned as children. Their carved stones recorded solstices, when the sun slowed and almost halted in its movement along the horizon and then the sun reverted back along its path. They understood equinoxes, when sunlight equaled darkness. He reiterated that the sun's basic cycle of four seasons, and that of the stars, lasted over 365 light/dark intervals and then the sun's pattern with the star cycle began again.

"You will see that the night stars behave differently from the sun," he told her.

The Dagda and other engineers made field trips with Boann to the older mounds, high on adjacent mountains. She stood out in harsh winds up at the old carvings to study the sun's range along the horizon and its arc overhead. She began to fathom how the astronomers oriented the mounds' dark stone passages to capture sunlight as the great sun moved through the four seasons.

Boann studied with the other apprentices, watching the skies and checking each other's observations. She discovered the poetry in what had seemed to be chaos in the skies. Passion for their astronomy consumed her. It compared only with how she felt about Cian, since they were children. Of late, she could not be sure of his feelings.

Seduced by the astral bodies, she spent increasing time at starwatching and that annoyed her friend Sheela. She tried to placate Sheela, with little tricks used to spot individual stars among the multitude in the night sky. For example, the Bright One could be found at four lengths of her thumb from the far left star in the belt of the Hunter, whose outline was always easy to find. This rule of the thumb delighted Sheela, who asked to learn more. They spent much time out in the dark and cold, then soothed each other's chapped faces with meal paste.

With a start, Boann saw the sun's angle across the flagstones. "The time! No need to find my shawl pin this instant." She had almost forgotten their meeting to groom each other's waist-length hair for the equinox. She quickly applied a salve to the angry scratches on her legs. She'd have to find more water to wash her face, maybe at Sheela's.

She hoped that her good friend would not ask again about Oghma's slow progress at the kerbstones, nor ask what happened to scratch her legs so.

On this equinox Boann looked forward to having few duties, a rarity. She helped with harvesting medicine plants with those of the women who specialized in healing, particularly young Airmid. Their herbalist lore they absorbed easily, since they had been children following their mothers through billowing grasses taller than their heads and deep into the green shades of the forest. Boann recalled her own mother from the faintest smell of a leaf, or in giving cool comfort to the suffering. Neat stocks of perfectly prepared medicines graced her mother's shelves. Airmid's medicines looked like that, perfect and all in good order.

If Airmid could take over the healing, then she would have more time for astronomy. Boann eyed the heaps spilling from her baskets and the mess she had made on the shelves, and sighed. She had let the house get into a muddle but she held her own at starwatching; her mother would be proud of her. She would tidy the living area later, and look for her shawl pin.

The loss earlier of her good shawl brought another shiver, and not from cool air. Steady, she told herself, but the intruder's assault would not let her go. If only she had her mother to ask for advice. She might yet tell the elders about it. Then again, that might jeopardize Cian, living among those warriors as he was. Perhaps she would tell the Dagda, before the ceremony.

The Dagda would present her as an apprentice astronomer on this equinox. She should make an effort with her appearance and she wished her mother were there to help her, there to see the ceremony. Oghma would be judging any young man who came within arm's length of her at their bonfire; she gave that a wry smile.

She made her way to Sheela's, skirting the bustle of their village but keeping watch for movement in the budding foliage. The woods no longer seemed a friendly place.

Nothing should mar this important dawning. As one of the elders, Oghma meant to sort out any confusion. He turned decisively onto the central path through their cluster of stone dwellings.

Children shouted and ran to his side. "Oghma, Oghma! When may we go to the river?" They looked up at him, faces open and excited. The elders gave prizes and treats on the equinox for things the children did: gather reeds for torches, find eggs in the woods and meadows for the evening's feast, run footraces, and the like. Oghma put the eldest two in charge, a lyrical boy and a brown-eyed girl. The two would keep the other little ones busy, and with merely a ripple of concern he watched the children scamper off.

The village hummed with talk of more intruders arriving. A community of herders, basketmakers, netmakers, toolmakers, scrapers and tanners, and not one among them who'd fought in battle. He saw his people working with a new urgency. He nodded at the bowmaker who was steaming pliant yew for bows, and again at the young man close by hewing hard ash for tool handles. The latter put down his flint adz and caught up with Oghma.

They had gone but a few steps together when the toolmaker asked, "Is there any word from Cian?"

Oghma shook his head.

"I don't mean to trouble you."

"It's no bother, Tadhg."

They stopped and faced one another, the toolmaker visibly tense. Oghma placed his hand on the younger man's shoulder. "Some wood has flexibility and some has strength. Let us hope that Cian has both qualities."

The two men regarded each other. "If he lives," Tadhg said. He clasped Oghma's arm briefly, then Oghma moved on.

His people had little use for making weapons. Stacks of hides, rushes, willow stems, wool and bast, sinew and bone, awaited their artful hands. All, even scraps, would be made into useful items. He saw a woman, hair greying at her temples, bundling rushes to make a broom. It would have a sleek wooden handle, welcoming to the touch. He blinked hard, flooded with a vivid memory of his wife sweeping the flags around their hearth, and turned away.

He looked to see that livestock had been secured inside holding pens. He checked stores of cereals and roots, and hid his dismay at their depleted food supply in this young season of the sun. That meager amount would have to suffice in the event—

Villagers interrupted him with whispered queries about the boat sighted at dawn.

"The scouts will tell us where they landed, and how many of them." Oghma reassured each person, making his voice sound confident, and not mentioning Cian.

He ordered a few young fellows to break from what they were doing and help Tadhg make pikes, wood poles sharpened into a spear point. "We may need those, and soon."

At the far edge of the clearing around their dwellings, he came upon the open pit fire where their potter fired her vessels. Her ritual acts with fire transformed raw clay into ceramic. Pots held water and food essential for life, and pots enfolded their death-ashes. The wet smell of the clay and the coals' peaty aroma mingled and reminded him of women, of good things cooking, of the hearth. Transfixed, Oghma watched the potter's agile hands.

From the pliant brownish-red clay, she shaped a bowl with wide shoulders and squat body, then smoothed this pot with a curved bone and set it aside to cure. She was young and pretty but focused on her work, like his Boann.

"A pot created on this dawning holds good luck," he said.

She looked up and smiled. "May this equinox favor us all, Oghma. Your visit honors me."

He smiled in return, putting on a glad face for her. "Fair lass! Have you decided yet on a marriage?"

"Has Boann chosen, and is there any man left for me?"

"You'll both be spoiled for choice this evening," he teased her back.

She picked up a cured pot to decorate its leathery surface, and he caught his breath. If the vessel were less than perfect, the potter must discard it and begin again. Using a bone comb, she made intricate grooves meet flawlessly around its girth. The master potter showed her well—before taken by the fever, and now who could she take on as her own apprentice? He helped to stoke the kiln then wished her luck again, secretly humbled. Unlike her firing of clay, he didn't have to risk putting his handiwork into hot coals.

He hurried on toward the river, to their sacred landscape of mounds that proclaimed the Starwatchers' beliefs. These huge mounds stood taller than a tall tree and spanned many trees across. His carving with stone chisel and mallet gave meaning to the slabs lining the passages and to the boulders forming the high kerb around the outside. His painstaking labor suited Oghma, it contented him.

But on this equinox, the impending boat loaded with men and deadly weapons from afar irritated him like a thorn. The foreigners' small camp on the southwest coast of Eire, far from the Boyne, had not seemed a threat. For a time, Starwatchers accepted the intruders' seasonal presence and their odd probing in the earth. Upon seeing copper, the Starwatchers hoped to learn how these strangers turned red-hot stones into a material that shone like the sun and cooled to the color of a shadow moon. They allowed the miners to come and go in peace at that far coast. Then with the past summer, armed intruders appeared in their bloated ships at the Boyne's mouth and traveled inland.

Starwatcher scouts followed the strangers who searched along the Boyne, poking at outcroppings and leaving behind piles of shattered and scorched rocks. Scouts monitored the dirty smoke rising from inside the intruders' new camp. The intruders wandered ever farther from their camp and began to take cattle and game as they pleased, despite the coming winter.

Starwatchers avoided contact, fearing the metal knives—and fever. His people suffered. The strangers brought the death of his wife and others, too many others. Then Cian quit his own people to live among the warriors, a thing almost unthinkable. What should be done to protect their children? Should the Starwatchers confront these intruders? The elders deliberated and watched the intruders' comings and goings.

Will we tolerate another boatload of armed strangers, Oghma asked himself.

His green eyes were clouding, his stone chisel slipping in his hand. Over his seasons, he buried two wives, and of his children only Boann survived. Twice as many Starwatcher men survived beyond the age of twenty-five suns than did women; his people cherished their scarce women, and all children. He had lived a long time and only the Dagda counted more suns among those at the Boyne. While a young man, Oghma measured in the night skies and tracked daylight with the astronomers. Led by his mentor who was descended from the revered ancestor Coll, he learned to style the stones at the great starchambers with crisp precision, completing work on each stone at fairly regular intervals. But that was decades ago.

Through that dark winter, he grieved but continued carving at the mounds, as resolute as the raindrops wearing down the island's granite slopes. Pain shot through his joints in the damp chill, his shins stuck to the freezing soil as he knelt. His lean shoulders became stooped, and his thick dark hair whitened. Oghma toiled on in order to finish carving the massive kerbstones, with a quip to the Dagda that the stones might finish him first.

All his hopes rested on Boann. In time, he might see his grandchild. He was glad enough to see newborn lambs and the promise of flowers on this bright morning of the spring equinox.

When he learned from the Dagda's lips of the untimely boat, he told the Dagda, "We people of Eire want for nothing. We have mastered the rhythms of the soil, of the salmon from the ocean, and especially those of the sky. Even the least clever among us know how to prosper here. From sun to sun, we produce enough to sustain us while we study the heavens. We should celebrate spring equinox, our time of planting signaled by the Seven Stars."

The Dagda agreed. "Despite our trials, we can show gratitude for spring's arrival. Never mind what the ocean brings to our shores. On land these intruders cannot travel any faster than Starwatchers."

How many warriors arrived this time? They trusted in their scouts and the Starwatchers who lived at the coast, to alert the Boyne. Oghma hastened along the path to the mounds, his brow furrowed.

The Dagda told him that it was Boann who sighted the new boat bristling with more intruders and weapons. She'd rushed from Red Mountain to tell the Dagda, then she rushed to bring water from the stream, Oghma told himself. That would explain why Boann looked so rattled, something amiss. He did not want to pry. She returned with little water, but he brushed that aside, a trifling thing. At least she'd had a fine sunrise to watch. It did trouble him that she watched many a sunrise and sunset, more than her share. She displayed little interest in any of their young men.

"She secludes herself more and more with the astronomy. That's not a healthy state of affairs for a young woman," he told the Dagda. "Often when I speak to her she doesn't hear me."

"Don't you see it? She takes after you, she escapes in the stars and her work," the Dagda said. "She's had the same losses, after all. Give her time to recover, let her spirit heal."

He heard the Dagda's kind and good advice like a thunderclap. So that was it, Boann still grieved for her mother, as did he. As to Cian's absence, Oghma saw little reason for Boann to feel any loss. He had but faint hope for his apprentice, an indifferent pupil of stone carving, a dreamer. But surely Cian would respect the equinox, rejoin his people at their starwatch.

The young people would dance in the firelight and pair off in the ritual of spring. Perhaps a young fellow from another village would catch her eye. But not Cian, that one would never do for Boann. Oghma tutted disapproval.

Cian once asked him, why did the ancestors build their great mounds? Not "how," he recalled the question, but "why." Oghma did not answer. It was better for young Cian to find his own answer to that question.

The ancestors' history told Oghma precisely why they built their mounds. To ready himself for the equinox, he recited their tradition now on his way through oak woods to the passage mounds. He recited verses of their deeds and lineage as they would have been told to Cian, and all Starwatchers. Back to Griane, our first astronomer, he thought. Griane, who set the first upright marker stone to show us the seasons of the sun and freed us from hunger. Oghma offered a short invocation for the spring sunset that all Starwatchers would observe that evening. "May the coming season bring us bounty, thanks be to Griane."

He waved away a cloud of midges under the oaks' emerging yellow-green canopy. From the corner of his eye, he saw a red fox flash through the undergrowth. "It is an honor to carve the stones!" he called after it. *Could Cian change his shape into a fox?* Oghma snorted. *What nonsense these intruders do believe: shapeshifting.* He swiped at the midges. *Fox or not, Cian could have warned us that more foreigners would arrive.*

There stood the warrior camp, visible when he approached the central mound's clearing, and he frowned at this affront on their landscape. He liked to rest beside the Boyne at twilight and gaze at the central starchamber, at its shimmering white quartz around the dark granite entrance. These days his view was partially obstructed by the intruders' camp: a banked, circular earthwork topped with a crude palisade of unpeeled logs. The camp's size and fortification spoke a threat from a hostile presence, a threat that his Starwatchers had yet to assess.

The Starwatchers' pikes would be useless against those high walls. Oghma knew it, sure as the sun made little green apples. He implored the ancestors for wisdom to guide the elders.

At the standing stone to the southeast of the central mound, he spotted the elders talking and laying out sightlines for that sunset using cord stretched between wood posts.

"Once in every generation was often enough to receive visitors from far across the waves. These haven't brought any women or polished axes to exchange. Just what have these latest blow-ins brought to us?" Oghma heard the question as he joined them.

"We'll find out soon enough," came the Dagda's reply, calm and deliberate.

"We made the right decision to go forward with the equinox feast," Oghma added. He saw the children playing in the clearing, laughing and running in the misty morning. With a premonition, he saw it all as if held inside a chunk of clear quartz: his villagers bent to their tasks, their precious children beside the flowing river, their carefully constructed mounds.

Oghma would make sure that the children assembled enough reed torches before dusk. After watching the stars in utter dark, the people took up torches so that no one need stumble on their way back to the village. He would supervise stacking the wood for the great bonfire to be lit after their vigil, the signal to Starwatchers at distant sites. If the adolescents collected wet or green wood, their beacon fire would be smoky and its effect diminished.

He would see to it that the Boyne fire blazed when it should with the other fires, lit first at the island's center, its navel, and then to the four sacred directions. He would see Boann enter into the ranks of their astronomers. He raised his head in pride.

"Let these intruders see our fires, and hear our pipes and dancing."

"And if their warriors venture forth?" the Dagda asked.

No one had an answer.

Legs stinging, Boann found long-eared leaves coming up along the path and rubbed them on the red welts from her flight through nettles. Relieved, she let her thoughts meander in the heavens.

She learned to track the moon, like the sun, as it moved in its phases through to full moon. Her people needed to know when nights would be bright under the full moon and their methods of observing the moon were old, "old beyond our time on this island," the Dagda told her at the rich carvings outside the great mound called Knowth.

"This stone shows us that the moon completes its entire cycle in the sky once for every nineteen cycles of the sun. That's time enough for you to have married." She felt her cheeks reddening. He ignored her blush and went on, "The arcing paths of the moon and sun intersect from time to time. We know when, from certain stars." She memorized those star patterns. They compared the carved symbols at Dowth and Knowth, the Dagda coaxing understanding of the moon's phases from Boann with a speed that surprised each of them.

Next came the stars. In visits to the old stone markers at Loughcrew, and Fourknocks, he demonstrated that certain stars' positions had changed compared with their notch on the standing stone. How could this be? It was a crawling, infinitesimal shift, not visible to them in only one solar cycle. The Starwatchers called it Northshift, because the bright stars had moved which showed them true north. Even greater prestige would accrue to the Boyne if they deciphered the Northshift and predicted the next equinox constellation. The Dagda said they would be the first people to do so.

In all their lessons, he made no comment about the intruders. She checked the woods and hurried along.

The Dagda decided when she had learned enough of the movements and cycles in the sky, to accompany Oghma to the kerbstones. Her father wouldn't allow her to carve with him, saying he did not want her to ruin her hands working stone, but she knew he admired her progress with astronomy. Boann stayed at his side, helping Oghma position the symbols on each boulder's unique surface. They planned how and when the sun's light would strike the varied carvings: star shapes, waveforms, lozenges, arcs, and spirals.

"Our great stones cannot be rushed to completion," he told her and she saw that it was so.

Her friend lived alone since the fever took both of Sheela's parents. The dwelling was simple but solid, like the others. As Boann arrived, she smoothed her tunic and retied her old shawl at her waist so that it swung down covering her legs. The sun's radiance warmed the entrance, where Sheela gave her a welcoming hug, then seated herself on a rush stool.

Boann began plaiting in the way her friend preferred, to make braided swags over a central bun. Their conversation flowed easily, but Boann tugged at the heavy strands.

"Your hands are tense, what are you thinking about?" Sheela tilted her head back, concerned. Boann concealed the thoughts clouding her face.

"Nothing, it is nothing. You look wonderful from this angle. Truly lovely."

"Then tonight it's upside down I'll stand!" Mischievous lavender eyes looked up at hers. They began to giggle. She'd only half arranged Sheela's black hair and it swung freely with her own auburn hair as they laughed together. She scooped up the bone pins that escaped, and started braiding again.

"When I finish pinning this, you can stand however you like," Boann said, then cringed with regret. Sheela only flushed and reached back and patted her hand. She leaned forward and their eyes met again.

"You'll have an offer, I know it," she told Sheela. "Such gorgeous hair, enough for three women gracing your head."

Boann wished she had more words of encouragement. Like her, Sheela was old enough to marry. But Sheela had one leg slightly longer, one ankle badly formed. It impaired her gait, and gave her suitors pause: would the children of Sheela have that ankle? It was a hard truth of their ways though there were plenty of men. Yet Sheela does have her admirers, Boann thought, she defies adversity living on her own, and has boundless humor. If not for Sheela, and the stars, she might have lost her wits in the past dark winter. Boann knew that one man who had good sense might step forward to marry Sheela, and she hoped that would happen on this equinox.

"Do you remember when we pulled burrs out of my hair?" Sheela asked.

"That I do," and Boann smiled. On a warm night in early autumn, a night Sheela spent pleasantly in the fields with that young man, her friend's hair had been strewn with thistle heads. She sought out Boann, looking much amused, and together they removed thistle after thistle caught up in the dark tresses. Sheela exclaimed how the tiny needles had hooked and enmeshed her hair.

"When I'm older, with my vision failing and stiff fingers, it will be difficult to tie patterns fine as a spider's web. So I'm trying to knot my fibers using a slender bone shaped into a little hook at one end."

Clever Sheela perfected the knotting of fibers, an art learned from an uncle who made nets for fishing in the river. Others copied her delicate knots all over the island, for everything from fringes to webbing that made an entire garment.

"And where are you getting these bone hooks? From anyone I know?" Boann asked though she well knew.

Sheela grinned. "It seems Tadhg can make anything. We've already tried bones from birds and even a big salmon bone, but those were too thin or too weak. Now I'm trying a young sheep's bone that Tadhg worked. We'll see how long it lasts."

Smiling, Boann finished pinning the looped braids. She avoided talking about the progress on the stones until Sheela's cautious question, "How is he? —Oghma, that is?"

She kept her voice casual. "The carving is sure to be going better. We're over the frosts, and have the longer light ahead."

Sheela nodded as she touched her hair. "Perfect."

The friends changed positions and moved the rush seat to follow the sunlight. Boann tucked her scratched ankles underneath it, out of sight. They chattered while Sheela pulled up and dressed her hair, complimenting its reddish-brown gloss like hazelnut shells. In high spirits, Sheela weaved the village gossip into the plaits.

Under caring hands, Boann relaxed. A chance encounter, and she wouldn't worry her friend over the stranger who surprised her at the stream. Neither spoke of more intruders arriving or what dangers their scouts faced at the coast.

They washed their faces and smoothed each other's brow with hazel tonic.

When she made ready to leave, Sheela hugged her again and tried to give Boann one of the best of her knotted overtunics. "You can't wear that old shawl for this equinox!"

"No, I mustn't take this. I'll snag it on a branch or trip over a log in the dark."

"Go on, now. You should wear fine feathers on this evening." She hesitated until Sheela said, "It's all right, I understand. Who knows if Cian will show himself? But I'll be there with our people and proud of you. Take this, and off you go." Sheela forced the supple netting into her arms. "The starwatching shall be your rock and your refuge."

"You are a true friend." Boann relented and went on her way.

"Good luck to you," Sheela called.

Her steps quickened as she turned to wave at Sheela, whose smile in reply shone to rival the sun. Boann's thoughts returned to how she might detect the tiny but crucial shift of the equinox constellation above them. Perhaps Cian would return for this evening's ceremony. *With or without you.*

The river wound past in its banks, reflecting the uncertain sky over the mounds.

Let grief be a fallen leaf
At the dawning of the day
Raglan Road, *Patrick Kavanagh*

The Crime

THE SUN'S RAYS sloped from the west when Sheela inspected her water pots, numerous but all of them empty. She wanted to set out a little brimming jug of water, an old custom to reflect the spring moon inside her door. She stepped into the early evening where the air was fresh again after becoming close under sunshine. Tadhg smiled as she passed him with her pot and her gear. Tender plants sprouted in the rich soil of the meadow along her way to the stream. She wished for children in her season, like the fecund earth.

When she reached the watering stream, the young grass and ferns along its shore showed no trampling or disturbance. A pair of swans drifted along the banks for her to admire. Sheela strolled there, looking for the bluegreen plants she used to make an excellent fiber. She would return in summer to harvest their tough stems with her sharpest flint blade. Purple evening shadows were gathering under hazelnut and willow trees beyond the grassy banks. Out in the open, nothing moved or shimmered except the first small white flowers at her feet. Birds called softly as they would before the hush of darkness that follows sunset.

Sheela had no warning of the assault.

She tried to slip from his clutches but she was not fast enough. She had only a sideways glimpse as her assailant came crashing onto her, taking advantage of her slowness. He was one of the intruders. Her water pot dropped from her hand and smashed into shards. Heavy hands caught at her waist, grabbed her arms and raised her tunic to pin them behind her. He flipped her over onto the sweet riverbank grasses.

His right hand ruined her looped braids to pull her head sideways facing away from him. He did not speak. She caught a sickening smell from him as he lowered himself onto her. He breathed fury, this was no caress. Her fear rose exponentially and she could only voice a strangled scream under his weight. Her muscles spasmed as his knees, clad in rough leather leggings that had been too hastily cured, scraped her inner thighs and knocked her legs apart. His bulk shifted and she felt him pushing to enter her. Bewildered, struggling for air, she convulsed, her insides clamping on him like the intruders' cruel metal.

Taunts she didn't understand sounded from his companions in the shadows, watching his clumsy and interrupted attack upon this woman they surprised by the stream. "Look lads, will you look? He can't!"

She sensed his rage at being observed. The bronze dagger rang out of its sheath and Sheela felt his left forearm sliding up to her neck. With a keen instinct she bit deep into his hand as he, half propped on one elbow and wielding his knife, was closing on her neck.

The sight of his own hand bloodied from her bite enraged him further. He almost took off her head when he applied the dagger.

They decided not to take her head as a trophy. The murderers fled. They left Sheela sprawled on the grass, red streams flowing out from her body over the tiny white daisies low in the grass. Horror, pain, and fear were frozen on her face. Her lavender eyes, it was later said, resembled infinite pools of the sky upon which they were fixed.

A lone bird called as darkness and mist shrouded the still figure.

When the body was found at the next dawning by Starwatchers searching for Sheela, the hideous scene wrote itself indelibly upon their memory. No one had ever done such a deed on their island. They had no word to describe the crime against Sheela. Scouts gathered up her remains tenderly after the elders had seen that place of death.

At Sheela's dwelling, Boann waited. She looked up to see Airmid bringing a basket of herbs and soft skins for preparing a body. Airmid shook her head. Her red curls looked out of place in the still and grim space. Gentle Airmid told her, "You shouldn't do this alone. Let me help." The body arrived and the two women looked at each other, aghast. The scouts left them reluctantly, one man staying outside the door.

The women silently set to work. Hands trembling, Boann redressed Sheela's hair to its state before the murderous attack, after washing it with aromatic water to rid it of the choking smell, the smell of the intruders. Airmid, white-faced, repaired wounds as best she could.

They chose to dress Sheela in a soft skin tunic bleached in the sun. They added the most delicate overtunic made by Sheela, the knots too fine to be seen at arm's length. Then the two women wept to see beautiful Sheela lying dead in her garments meant for her wedding.

The Starwatchers kept the body in the coolness of a small cairn with an honor guard of women and men until the ceremony. After lying in the great eastern mound of Dowth, Sheela's cremated bones would be interred in one of the smaller mounds to the southeast. The elders delayed the first interment while runners brought the news to other villages, so that as many Starwatchers as possible could attend.

Hundreds of Starwatchers gathered to mourn. They walked to the Boyne mounds, some traveling for the better part of one sun, and in lowered voices made arrangements to share food and set up shelters. The crowd converged at Dowth mound.

The horrific deed overshadowed the death itself and skewed the focus of the burial ceremony. The Dagda spoke first in benign phrases about the fragility, the gift, of life.

"He said nothing of the intruders," one elder whispered angrily to another.

Boann spoke briefly. "Remember our friend Sheela. Remember Sheela for her life, her joy, her contributions to our community, and not for her death."

Family members were too stricken to speak, and the singers' chorus was muffled. A cold wind arose and bowed the grass, it shook the young barley, as the people stood together in the wordless shock of what had happened.

Tadhg hung his head and when he looked up at last, Boann hardly recognized him for the new emotion showing in his eyes: hatred for the intruders.

Late sunlight glittered on the white quartz around the entrance to the north passage in Dowth. The wrapped, slender form lay upon the grass. The mourners filed past, bereft of flowers to cast down in this early season. Then four young men stepped forward. They locked arms under the body and carried Sheela across the entrance stones and along the narrow passage to the innermost chamber. They tripped on three low stone sills in the dark passage but none cursed or drew a breath. Inside the chamber, the men carefully lowered the body to the flagstone floor. Behind it in an oval stone basin, dried sweet herbs were burning, Boann's last gift to her friend.

After the others withdrew, Boann stayed inside the mound, seated, with Sheela's body. She looked vacantly around this inner chamber. Its ceiling was lintelled and flat rather than corbelled; that was a mark of its earlier construction. Sparse carvings of rayed sun circles, spirals, and chevrons would guide Sheela in the spirit world. Starwatchers treated the body with respect. The sealed mound kept out animals while natural processes cleaned away flesh. The bones would be burned and later arranged in a small cairn nearby. The bones of Sheela's family who preceded her in death lay in smaller cairns around Dowth, and now Boann served their memory by thinking of each name and reciting their lineage. Other than cousins, the death of Sheela ended her mother's line.

Boann remained motionless in the silence of the old starchamber. Sheela must lie here alone and in darkness. This north passage inside Dowth, and its second passage to her left, both faced west where the sun would soon set. She spoke to the spirit of Sheela.

"You have repose here. The moon visits on its standstill. When the sunset penetrates the darkness of Dowth in winter, then we shall return to honor and remove your bones."

She sat, numbed with pain, staring at the great grey stones. She thought of all the mounds built by her people. Carved stones from smaller old mounds at the Boyne had been reused to build newer mounds. The one had been destroyed to build the other, reshaped and renewed. She placed more herbs into the small fire in the bullaun stone. What will come of this death, she asked it.

Some events were immutable, final, like a flame extinguished. Death appeared to be one of those. The spirit left the body. Was anything truly permanent? Boann pondered the contradiction of the slow shift in the stars.

If the sky's dome itself changes, then nothing we Starwatchers know is permanent.

Anxiety seized her in this sanctuary for their dead. "What is happening to us?" Her cry reverberated against stone.

The weight of the surrounding mound seemed to bear down, threatened to crush her like the terrible mistake she had made. How could she have failed to protect others; she should have told Sheela, or her father or the Dagda, about her own attack. What if she hadn't used water at Sheela's, or if she had walked with dear Sheela for more water at the stream. If only, but now the result lay before her and could not be undone. Her mistake must be buried in this chamber. Her friend would want it so. Sheela would have forgiven her, and she must find her way forward.

The Starwatchers must find their way forward. Disgust surged in her against intruders; how could Cian bear it living in their camp?

The surrounding stones chilled her. Her flesh needed warmth and she must leave her friend in darkness. She left the cold body and dried her tears, squared her shoulders. Beyond Dowth toward the river, rose the central mound. From the narrow passage where Boann stood, she could see its white quartz glowing in the distance. As she exited the stone portal of Dowth, the setting sun flung deep reddish tints across an unusual lavender sky. A dark bird crossed it above her. She would remember that sky, and her friend Sheela, and unutterable grief.

A select council of elders convened on the next dawn at the central mound, elders from all of the Starwatchers who had learned of the crime. The council rarely unsealed this mound to withdraw inside, preferring to meet openly in fresh air and light under the great oak. Their seclusion signaled the elders' intent to link with the ancestors for guidance. That brought rampant speculation by the assembled community and visitors, while the elders debated out of sight.

Tethra of Carrowkeel, almost as old and his frame as knotted as the Dagda, spoke first within the council. "The intruders committed this abomination. The nature of Sheela's wounds, the blatant state of the body, and the smell left on Sheela's clothing; these all point to the intruders. We have no precedent and indeed we have no name for this mutilation of Sheela."

Slainge spoke next. The sun had tanned his face while he cleared and plowed his plain, but he looked at the others with clear eyes, in his prime. "The strangers are small in numbers here, but large grow our troubles with them. This boat brought warriors with more weapons. No livestock and but a few food baskets and supplies, the scouts tell us."

A woman elder added, "We see their invasion of us, of our island and now Sheela's murder. This terrible deed must be punished! These foreigners cannot be ignored, with their long knives and scavenging ways. Our women will not be taken like beasts."

"They do call themselves Invaders." The voice was Cian's.

The elders exclaimed to see Cian in the chamber. The Dagda held up his hand for quiet, and commanded Cian, "Stand and tell us more."

Cian rose and told of the intruders' boasts. The intruders had encountered mounds and carved symbols on stone as they traversed the Continent's coasts, but the fierce progress they made using their long knives did not lend itself to studying carvings, they said. At their Boyne camp, they dismissed his native skills. They needed Cian, and wooed him, solely for his manpower. He saw that young recruits were a necessity since their rowdy war games routinely injured many of their men. "They have baited me with tall tales of exotic places, at their big feasts with drink and with song. They claim the future lies to the east. They encourage me to travel east with them over the great ocean to see the vast Continent, its wonders and strange animals and snakes. These Invaders have seen it all, they say. They came looking for the sun metal, gold, they call it; like the copper in the southwest.

"These Invaders see and they take. They know little of our ways yet assume that we are ignorant. These are my observations from the winter spent inside their camp." Cian sat down after this long speech, his hazel eyes serious in a compelling face.

Oghma's voice arose, angry. "Now you appear before us. How is it that we had no warning from you before one of us suffered violence and death?" Harsh judgments echoed from other elders.

Before he could answer, the Dagda calmed the elders, saying, "Cian has returned with this sunrise and we shall hear him." The Dagda added dry twigs to the coals in a warming pot.

A murmur of discussion followed around the low fire and they put more questions to Cian. "How many will come?" And, "Why would they want our sun metal?" Cian supplied the elders with much to consider.

The Dagda asked, "Invader, that term they use for themselves. We call them intruders, implying that they are guests here, temporary. How long do they intend to stay?"

"They do not give me a straightforward response, and I must be careful of asking this too many ways, too many times." Cian looked as unhappy as the elders, but there it was. "They think we worship the sun. I gather they came here to the Boyne because of our mounds."

Oghma retorted, "That makes no sense. These intruders seem fully unaware of starwatching, they show no interest in it, none at all."

Other voices rose. "Invaders—boatloads of drunkards and rabble, more like."

A woman elder said, "These foreigners practice evil." She placed astringent herbs in the fire pot to cleanse the air of the word she had used, their word for deeds unspeakable, beneath humans, an offense before the ancient ones.

All the elders held their breath for Cian's reply.

He spoke carefully. "Their making of metals is foreign to us. It is a thing not done by Starwatchers. Yet we use fire and clay to make pots. Fire and stone can make metal."

The Dagda said, "Our making of pots and our carving in stone do not serve to kill other peoples. We do not need their long knives! Time will show us these Invaders' true nature." He raised his polished mace before the elders. "We see the effects of the intruders, their fouling of streams and the noxious fumes. We must convince them of proper ways on this land rather than merely scold them.

"And, for the murderer of Sheela, a fair remedy must be agreed. Women shall be respected. If not, these Invaders must leave."

The elders spoke in turn, and some called for vengeance for the murder. Cooler heads asked Cian to assist in negotiations. "You have a grasp of the intruders' language."

Cian looked doubtful. "I cannot say whether these Invaders will negotiate. And they have very different views from us about women and children." He did endorse the elders' goal of avoiding violence. "But we can do more than wait until the Invaders leave." He offered suggestions but the elders resisted his ideas, their mistrust of him as palpable as the granite chamber enclosing them.

Tethra cleared his throat and the elders turned to him. "What you are saying is our island is now connected and no longer protected, by the great waters to other shores."

"That is the long and the short of it," Cian said. His elders sat in uneasy silence.

"When will you return to us?" asked Slainge.

"I do not know." He sought Oghma's eyes but Oghma turned his face away.

Cian took his leave from the elders and vanished from the Starwatchers' council. He blended into the Invaders' camp, a disappearing shadow as the midsun reached its zenith above the Boyne.

Tethra of Carrowkeel shifted his gnarled shoulders to look at all the elders. "We thought they would leave us, like other visitors over the generations. It appears these guests intend otherwise. Starwatchers have little means of stopping them from coming onto our island. Cian says more boats will arrive. We must remain calm. So far we do not talk of doing battle with them. But the time is ripe for us to present our grievances to these Invaders—before the summer solstice, before their metalmaking blinds the sun and leaves this land barren. We have long discussion ahead. Something must be done."

Outside, all the Starwatchers waited at a respectful distance from the mound. Tadhg paced with the other young men, inflamed by the horrible murder. "We should have prevented this atrocity. We must fight back!" Those scouts made ready to attack the intruder camp with stone axes and stout pikes, thirsting for vengeance.

The elders deliberated further. When the sun made long shadows from the west, they appeared before the assembled people. The Dagda stood before the Starwatchers in the mound's clearing, his whorled red mace raised for all to see. The crowd listened.

"We place restrictions on your movements though we have grave misgivings at doing so. These measures fall more to the women's disadvantage in that we discourage all women and children from going out alone to gather herbs, nuts, or any foodstuffs. Even our strong young apprentices, male or female, must travel in pairs as they go about their work or to the mounds."

Slainge the elder held up his hand for quiet, then added that cultivating crops or grazing livestock must be done only within the walled fields to the north of their village. A man protested that their flock wouldn't have enough grazing area.

"We can put up longer walls," he answered. He added that a permanent watch would be posted at the stream where they bathed and drew water. "These safeguards will be lifted when we establish better relations with the intruders," he told them.

The Starwatchers heard these things from their elders and returned to their homes. Beyond the pall from Invaders' fires, they contemplated their future on this, their island.

Above them, the sky shifted almost imperceptibly.

We'll sing a song, a soldier's song, with cheering rousing chorus,
As round our blazing fires we throng, the starry heavens o'er us.
From: *Amhran na bhFiann*, national anthem of the Republic, 20th Century CE

Invaders

CONNOR STOMPED AWAY from the Invaders' camp and the carousing, the feast, the false warmth, the sullen captive women, and stale mead. The tall Elcmar dared to tell him over the feast table and in front of the warriors newly arrived from overseas, "That crowd at the mounds haven't left. I think we're going to have trouble with these Starwatchers."

He returned Elcmar's stare. "What is it you want me to do about it? Bollix!" Connor slammed down his cup. "I'll be having a look for myself." He stalked from the great hall.

Dull eyes in a heavy bulk, Connor halted and sighed. It had been three nights but he was unable to lie again with any woman. His swollen hand ached.

He labored to recall the vision, the young woman he beheld for just moments on a bright morning. That beauty got away. He had made a show of it for his companions. "Quare natives, disappearing into mists, this fecking climate. Sure, I'd break that one, what a fine filly." And that other woman they found later at twilight, that was all an accident. She bumped into them along that stream, so she had. Like your woman walking into a door, he decided.

He sat down on a small outcropping above the encampment. *Sunset! These eejit quiet ones are after watching the sun go down again. Their tedious ways, this backward place. My task here is to find metals, exploit the locals for trade. And so I shall. Great mounds of clay and stones, is it. Where's their gold?*

Invaders had found copper enough in the southwest and camped there, mining and smelting. His band of Invaders came to the Boyne eager to find gold and feed it to the new appetite for gold on the Continent, return in triumph with it. Connor wanted to go back to the drier, warmer coasts and plains to the south from where he journeyed a few seasons ago. It ate at him, his desire to be somewhere else.

He felt sick. The throbbing in his hand increased. The gods must have abandoned him. If something were physically wrong with him, a blemish, then he could not remain *ard ri*, the warriors' champion, in this place. All his trekking into strange territory and pillaging for new trade and slaves would have been for nothing. Connor listened for the voice of Lugh, to whom he seldom prayed and offered sacrifice. His hollowness told him Lugh wasn't listening. Possibly there was no Lugh nor any god here, not in the whole of this island.

Just infernal mists, and the quiet ones disappearing before your very eyes—when they aren't trying to take off your manhood.

His emptiness beset him, as stars came out above. He choked, then the awful sobbing of a grown man escaped from him.

Connor's companions found him delirious, prostrate upon the grey rocks and with an advanced fever. His left hand swelled and from it red streaks radiated up his thick forearm. His hand festered from deep within and attacked him; the very bulk of Connor could be destroyed.

A poultice made from dried leaves carried to this island from faraway forests had no effect. His hand darkened ominously.

Warriors clustered around his bed, where he was tended by a slave taken from the Continent. "Woman! Have you any medicine for his condition?"

She looked blank. "Isn't it Bresal you should be asking?"

The men exchanged glances. Their shaman Bresal had discovered small mushrooms on this island which induced trances. Bresal would be almost useless to deliver any treatment, given the mushrooms and his experiments with various brews.

No one commented on the strange, quarter-moon-shaped puncture marks on Connor's swollen hand, almost obscured by livid purple streaking up his forearm. A few doses from Bresal of the prized fungus balls culled on far shores also proved ineffective. Connor's fever continued. An invisible enemy worked deep within and his red festering hand threatened his life.

Without warning, a cloud of grit swept in and covered the face of the sun. Leaves and sprouts withered in brown air that blew cold as if winter had returned. The likes of this storm had never been seen on all the island.

The camp lay low until the worst of it passed. Warriors sent out to hunt returned with dazed, thirsty animals that let themselves be captured for slaughter. The hunters reported that the Starwatchers still congregated at the easternmost mound, where a great fire blazed nonstop. Bresal the shaman sequestered himself to meditate, as he said, since it appeared to him the world was ending in darkness. The Invaders demanded that their shaman take action about Connor's hand if nothing else.

Leery of the natives' powers at their mysterious mounds, Bresal had the quiet one Cian brought to him. "How have your people caused this affliction of dust and winds?"

Cian looked at him in disbelief.

Bresal asked what Connor's condition might be, why would that hand not heal. Cian suggested that a Starwatcher experienced in healing should look at the injury. That appeased Bresal, who immediately spoke to the warriors.

To quell the speculation and rumors in their camp, the intruders' leaders put their heads together. "Bresal says there is nothing for it but to bring in a healer from among the quiet ones, someone who might be able to diagnose Connor's sickness and give us a remedy."

One of the beefy warriors spoke bluntly. "This is our champion. But if Connor loses his hand, that would make him unfit to lead us here and establish our foothold."

Elcmar, an intense contender for *ard ri* and noticeably unblemished, stood apart. His rival's predicament only improved his own chance of finding the stores of gold that Invaders believed to be hidden at the Boyne. Elcmar's face disclosed nothing.

Another warrior spoke up. "Your man must perform with the horse to become *ard ri*. He can't be lying wrecked for that."

They all frowned. Already their men grumbled and took fright at the sudden turn in the weather. The process of choosing a new champion would throw their camp into more disarray. Petty battles would erupt between various *tuatha* for the right to be crowned champion at this fringe outpost. Connor had fathered a son here and there, but none was old enough to fight beside him. In any event, a warrior became *ard ri* by strength, cunning, and material advantages. Their process did not turn on hereditary succession, nor did they decide it by voting. And, they had with them no lawgiver who would normally supervise and resolve disputed claims to the position of *ard ri* by means of the tribal laws. That lawgiver had not accompanied them to this island, as he disdained forays into such rough surroundings. In his absence, brute contests and long metal knives would inevitably be used to force the choice. Bresal would hide in his cups until the matter had been decided.

Schemes hatched and spread through the camp like the poison visibly moving up Connor's forearm. The teams which regularly played in the war games had been assembled for skill and not along clan loyalties. Now the teams split along the lines of *tuath*, and they fought in earnest despite the foul wind—or because of it.

Cian, the defector from the quiet ones, aligned himself with different teams, trying to disappear in their ranks or confuse everyone so as not to be maimed in the escalating competitions. Lucky he was for having a broad chest, and strong arms and legs; a big fellow.

Dust swirled high above, creating a fog of half light when spring should have been bursting around them. Starwatchers inspected the damage to blossoms and cereal stalks.

The Invaders began spying nonstop. The influx of quiet ones to the Boyne plain made the fortified camp nervous. Parties of warriors on horseback rode close to the Starwatchers' clustered homes, but they avoided altogether the high mounds dominating the bend of the river.

Starwatchers remarked that the latest intruders arrived with the strange cloud. At night, incessant drumming echoed to their village from the intruders' hide-covered hoop drums, and it took on a menacing quality. The songs of the Invaders seemed louder to the scouts sent by the Starwatchers. Their scouts observed the commotion in the camp from trees in soft wet places where mist provided cover. Not one of the scouts was detected. The Starwatcher elders were made aware of the escalating struggle and the Invaders' war games. Still Cian did not return to his village.

Rain fell, cleansing the air. Clear drops hung in arcs along leaf stalks and dripped like peace into parched roots. The nights stayed cold. Starwatchers tended the fire at Dowth and their big signal fires stayed burning in all directions from the Boyne.

Boann heard the knock at dawn and heard Oghma speak quietly at the doorway before turning to her. She feigned sleep while he paused before telling her why Tadhg stood waiting at their door.

He stroked his fingers across her forehead. No one awakened another person by shouting; that was not done among the Starwatchers. When Boann was sitting up among the furs on her sleeping shelf, he motioned awkwardly.

"We sent a strong message about Sheela's murder and summoned these intruders to meet in a council and they have responded. But now what they want from us is an herbalist to heal their leader. He has a grave injury. The elders have asked for you, and Tadhg has come to take you straightaway to the intruders' camp to give medicines. —This will not wait while you bathe at the stream, I'm sorry to say. To make a long story longer, are you willing to go?"

Boann smiled at his subtlety. "Is there a choice in this matter? Our people have asked me and I am well able for it. I have taken the healer's oath and sharing medicine is our custom." She read concern in his eyes: did she understand the dangers of entering these intruders' high walls to tend to their wounded leader?

"Good. I will prepare hot grains stirred with milk just as you like it, while you dress." He knelt at their hearth but his stirring of cereals in the pot slowed as he fussed over her breakfast. She stood dressed and ready, after rummaging her baskets and stone shelves, before he poured out the food for her. Oghma fed Boann what might be her final meal. She ate carefully, to please him, conscious of his troubled eyes on her.

She pressed her hand on his heart as she left him at the open door. "Wait for sunlight to cross our threshold and bring me back." Boann nudged him gently toward the hearth, then she stepped out into the early, blue light.

Oghma released her to Tadhg's protection. He crossed again to the hearth, sat upright on rush mats by its warmth, and closed his eyes as the sun rose and arced slowly through the sky's dome.

Boann feared for her father if she should fail to return. His spirit mirrored the light and dark of the sky dome. As a young man he fought alongside the Dagda, against other intruders long ago. After that hard-won battle he struggled with inner darkness, her mother said. His work became his testament. He carved in deeper relief than anyone before him, emphasizing the play of light and shadow over each kerbstone. He wanted others to experience his joyous interpretation of the sky and their ancestors' knowledge. Even now Oghma fought off darkness, the trials brought by the new intruders. He inspired many who faltered on their way.

Except Cian. Where is Cian on this dawning? Boann could taste the acrid smoke of the Invaders. Soon she and Tadhg would be surrounded by warriors armed with metal knives.

The walled camp stood a fair walk beyond the mounds. Its walls loomed higher with each stride. Tadhg described the intruders' volatile nature and instability, all observed by scouts since Sheela's murder.

"Some of us are saying we should have killed the intruders when they landed here."

"That is not our way!"

"Shall we join them, as Cian has done?" Tadhg threw her a look. "He's a misfit, that one."

Birds circled and dove on light breezes. Boann felt strangely lightheaded, as if she too were floating above the earth. She reached again for her sectioned herbalist's bag, on a loop knot over her plaited belt. She checked its contents at least five times as they hurried along, though she had herself packed the medicines before leaving Oghma at their dwelling.

They passed a swath of nodding lavender blossoms, spring flowers the color of Sheela's eyes, and their perfume hung in the air like a charm. She glanced at Tadhg, his firm jawline, a sensual mouth, straight nose, and dark green eyes. A mass of dark brown hair framed his appealing face and neck, his body strong and well proportioned. She wondered whom he would turn to for marriage, then it struck her with bleak humor that Tadhg would have to survive guarding her to worry about marrying anyone.

And then whom might I marry? How can I pledge myself to a fox, a shadow... a rebel. She kept those thoughts to herself.

To their left in the distance, the main starchamber glimmered, an emerald hill ringed in white and set in a smooth lawn. Sparkling, fist-sized quartzes girdled the mound in a thick layer of white that rose higher than a tall man's head, above dark grey kerbstones circling its base. Throughout this white quartz bank, the builders scattered smooth grey cobbles gathered from a bay to the north. Grey stone slabs defined the entrance set deep into the white quartz revetment.

"We hold the greatest treasure of astronomy lore of any people known to us," Tadhg said, his eyes on their great starchamber. "Invaders—Cian can learn nothing from these Invaders."

"You cannot judge that!" Boann softened her tone. "Perhaps Cian will learn what we do not know that we don't know. Why the great cloud of dust blackened our skies."

He made a derisive sound but stayed at her side.

Each footstep took her closer to seeing Cian. She said nothing of it; Tadhg would not understand her feelings. Again she mourned the loss of her confidantes, her mother, then Sheela.

They had almost reached the camp. Tadhg spoke hurriedly.

"Mind yourself. No telling what they have in store for us."

An Invader sentry met them as they neared its high walls. A crude earthen bank higher than a tall man surrounded the camp. They crossed a bridge of wooden planks leading through the bank. Inside the camp's wooden palisade, more sentries stopped the two Starwatchers and checked them for weapons. Their eyes met. Neither Tadhg nor Boann carried any weapon such as these warriors carried, and given the nature of their mission in the camp they found this precaution amusing.

The smell of sweaty warriors blended with that emanating from the intruders' horses, animals unfamiliar to the two Starwatchers. Smells of cooking, and retting fibers, and a choking smoke from charcoal pits, assailed the two. Tadhg and Boann silently followed the sentry into the camp.

Boann was surprised to see that the camp consisted of small wooden buildings, made of vertical oak planks rammed into the ground and topped up by wattle and daub walls. Their roofs were roughly thatched without much ornament in tying down the thatch such as a Starwatcher might have added. Not all of them had a hearth, she judged, from the lack of smoke. Or maybe the occupants neglected their fires, or were still sleeping. She saw that the intruders hadn't bothered with flagstone paving or grass, and muck suctioned each step inside their camp walls.

Here and there, curious pairs of eyes followed the two; she could feel them staring at her back. She wore a simple tunic of soft leather whitened by the sun and realized with misgiving it was similar to the tunic in which Sheela lay buried. Her knotted shawl was draped loosely over her head, crossed over under her chin, and its ends hung down her back. Small carved bone weights, slipped over the shawl's ends, ensured that it would stay in place behind her shoulders. She still had not found the grooved antler pin carved by her father. It didn't matter, this visit merited no special costume. They came here under duress.

Couldn't even let me bathe for the stampede to get us here at first light. Why do these people travel and camp where they can't take care of their own?

Her chin rose in defiance. Tadhg matched her steps, close by her side.

The sentry and the two Starwatchers progressed through knots of people; men with tattoos at their joints and ankles and down their backs, and women with tattoos on their arms and legs. She saw that both men and women had a fondness for their hair to be bleached to an unnatural color and then stiffened or spiked up from their heads. These men and women appeared equally fond of wearing jewelry, and it was hard to see how they could move for all their bracelets and necklaces and ear and hair ornaments.

The sentry brought them before the largest wooden structure. Center posts supported its wide roofspan, where smoke curled from an interior hearth. Carved doors were barely visible under the uneven thatched overhang from its roof.

The intruder sentry spoke. "We have a tradition of hospitality. We would serve you food before you see the ill man. Do you understand me, or should there be an interpreter?"

The two looked at each other. Neither spoke the Invader language.

Cian stepped forward from a tangle of observers. "I would like to interpret."

Boann turned to him, and hid her emotion to thank Cian and ask what had been said. Once she understood the sentry's offer of food, she refused it. Her words tumbled out, "No Starwatcher would leave their hearth without the morning meal, tell him it is simply our custom to eat before leaving our dwelling."

Cian cautioned her, "Refusing the Invaders' custom of hospitality might be seen as an insult."

Tadhg offered conciliatory phrases to tell the Invaders, but his manner toward Cian was curt, cold.

"Tadhg of both sides?" Cian turned back to the Invader sentry. "The Starwatchers wish to see to the ill man immediately despite your good and generous offer."

The sentry stiffened and scowled. Boann and Tadhg were more or less ordered to take a beverage before they could see the ill champion. "They won't be disturbed for the rest of the day, so," he told Cian, "and that filly with her glorious little nose in the air, wait till the champion sees her—and his wife sees her!"

This interval of serving broth to the visitors provided an opportunity to impress them with the interior of the large building, its sleeping dogs, exotic textiles, and carved wooden beams and posts. It was a long hall. They had an uncomfortable cup of scalding brew while seated on oak stumps at the entrance.

Then the two Starwatchers with Cian stepped after the sentry through a trail of drinking cups and bones still lying about on the floor from prior feasting. Sizable polished bronze daggers hung along the walls in the only orderly display to be seen. Rush mats under the banquet debris emitted a dank odor over the packed earth floor. More than a few men were sleeping noisily along the walls and in the far corners, some openly lying with women of varying descriptions. Scruffy workers minded the flat bread baking on stones at the hearth fire, one of them a maturing girl with a hungry expression when she looked up at Tadhg.

Boann focused on the sentry's back rather than exhibit her curiosity about the dimly lit structure, the shining weapons, or its disheveled occupants. By the time they reached the rear of the hall, she knew that Tadhg had memorized its height and dimensions, the position of every human and dog in it, how many weapons hung on the walls and how many steps to reach the weapons, their distance from the entrance, and every possible route of escape.

At last they reached the sleeping chamber of the would-be *ard ri*. Its door was flung open by a woman somewhat taller than Boann. She had hair almost the color of the bronze daggers and it hung in untended clumps over her large shoulders. She was straight through the waist like a man and the belt cinched tight over her bright drapery did not help to dispel that impression. Her breasts drooped oddly to each side, under a necklace of thick lumps of amber. Her square arms and square hands hung at her sides after flinging open the door. She looked them up and down with cold blue-grey eyes, then stood aside, going to seat herself upon a stool of wide leather slung between wood supports joined by an X frame. She sat down on this stool with her tunic raised, her knees falling open, and gave a daring look at Tadhg.

Tadhg turned to look at Cian and not at this woman. The woman spoke sharply to Cian.

Cian stated in their language, "This is Maedb, wife of Connor, the champion of the intruders. She greets you and asks that you please attend to her husband straightaway."

The sentry motioned and Boann approached the bed, a wooden structure lined with furs and soft fabrics that she did not recognize. An unforgettable smell overwhelmed her from the man who lay in this bed. Boann froze. This was her attacker, from the morning that became Sheela's final sunrise; Boann was sure of it. Tadhg at her side urged her to step forward.

Can he not smell it as well?

She had no opportunity to ask Tadhg for she was at the bedside and now she could see the Invader and his discolored hand and arm.

His infection has been cooking for some time. Whatever shall I do with that hand!

Without flinching, she lifted his grossly distended hand to examine it. The broad sweaty face of Connor swiveled toward Boann and he stifled a groan and gnashed his teeth while she turned up his forearm. On the outer flesh of his left hand below the wrist, she saw the wound: a dark crescent impression, the size exactly of a human bite. She planted her feet and tried not to retch, her mind whirling with revulsion. *Sheela!*

Tadhg kept his back to the wife of the *ard ri*. Whatever distraction Maedb wanted to provide, Boann saw that he would have none of it. He watched Boann's face and movements. She disguised her deep apprehension, for clearly this champion of the Invaders lay dying.

She asked for hot water in three bowls, and Cian told her request to the sentry. The sentry then relayed an order to a woman slave. Boann filled the ensuing delay and took out a small, sharp porphyry knife from her herbalist bag. Her hand hesitated in the bag, then took out several medicines: fresh green needles and leaves, shavings of a dried root, and a black powder.

When the bowls of hot water arrived, she mixed the medicines into one, and had the intruder drink some of its contents. He drank with difficulty and Boann forced herself to help him drink the medicines. Into the second bowl, she began to deposit fluids from a deep cut she made in Connor's hand. The sentry muttered and stepped toward the bed. Tadhg moved not a muscle. Cian stood firm between the sentry's knife arm, and Tadhg and Boann.

Maedb complained from her slouched position on the leather stool, "Why isn't she chanting? Our healer would be chanting while the blood drained."

Without turning her head, Boann told Cian to explain. "I am not merely drawing blood, but removing the bad fluids from the hand. The liquid medicine will also be applied to the open wounds for quick intake, in addition to that which the champion has drunk hot from the bowl. And tell her that by after mid-sun, if this hand is not better it must be cut off if this man is to live."

Maedb began to wail in a contrived fashion. Connor shouted for the sentry to remove Maedb from the sleeping chamber. That done, with extreme effort Connor turned his head fully toward Boann, whom he had been watching sideways through slits of eyes rheumy with fever. She never returned his look. His breathing changed, and the intruders' champion appeared to sleep at last.

Boann's eyes adjusted to the gloom in the sleeping chamber. Earlier when she quickly looked for a stone shelf on which to mix the medicines with hot water, she found none. She was not accustomed to the wattle and daub walls, nor the lack of stone niches and shelves. Now she took in the features of this chamber while the wounded champion slept. The tamped-earth floor had scattered skins on it from darkhaired sheep, comfortable beneath her feet. Although, it appeared the sheepskins could all use a shaking. A mouse scurried from one.

She saw small tables and coffers made of wood placed around the sleeping chamber. She had never seen wood so thinly cut and joined and polished. It had a reflective surface like water. Perhaps the intruders' metal tools did that to wood. Wood, taken from living trees, filled the space of the room. Boann wasn't sure if she liked the effect, and how many trees had been felled to make these strange furnishings? These intruders had already cut down a large area of trees around their camp, not replacing any of them. A huge boar's tusk, and horns from an ibex, hung from great colored cords fixed to the walls by the bed. Oddities carried from far shores, she surmised.

Someone entered the room during her ministrations, a man better groomed than any she had seen among the intruders, straight and tall and handsome from his feet to the top of his head. He stood to one side watching her. The construction and stitching of his leather shoes, leggings, and tunic looked meticulous and she would have liked to closely examine his clothing.

Boann's gaze settled on his face. He had the most amazing eyes, slanted and honey brown yet cold and predatory like those of a forest animal, and fringed with thick lashes. She nearly shuddered from the shock of his cruel eyes, but he smiled with those eyes flashing sparks at her. A heat rose from deep within her and she flushed all over. He saw her color rise, but his eyes went hard and cold once more, and abruptly he turned away. This tall man was the only person who frightened her in the intruder camp and she did not understand why. She washed her hands in the third bowl, in clean water, and set it aside.

When the sun reached an oblique angle in the west, Boann met Cian's look. "The intruders' champion must lose his hand."

He translated it, and the sentry stepped out to tell those in the long hall. A great cry arose outside in the camp while warriors left the hall and brought back the intruders' own healer Bresal and his helpers.

Bresal the shaman barged into the sleeping chamber. He bent his large girth and balding head to look at her work on Connor's swollen limb and at the contents of the wooden bowls. The medicine that Connor had drunk from Boann rendered the champion unconscious, too drugged to move or snore and still in the grip of a high fever.

The shaman felt Connor's face, and shook his head. "Nothing more to be done but to remove the red hand."

As soon as Bresal said this, the tall intruder with feral golden eyes left them.

Several witnesses pushed into the sleeping chamber but sentries led the Starwatchers through the hall and outside. When the woman Maedb caught sight of them, she shrieked what could only be insults.

"Don't look at her," Cian whispered and disappeared from them as quickly as he appeared when they arrived.

The sharp point of metal wielded by a different sentry escorted them into a small wooden structure without any openings except its door that the sentry barred with a thud from the outside. Here the two Starwatchers were confined while the amputation took place. They listened intently. Maedb's wail carried throughout the Invaders' camp, but brave and stupefied Connor gave out not a sound.

Time passed and any indication of sunlight vanished. A mostly male assembly around the great hall gave a series of rumbling shouts as Bresal spoke to them, then the two Starwatchers heard the throng dispersing. Still they were held fast inside the small, dark cell. At length, the two smelled food preparations from the west area of the camp, and heard the clink of earthenware cups brought together. A wooden pipe sounded a slow but reassuring tune. Maedb's keening had ceased.

Boann said, "He did not suffer."

Tadhg raised his face to find her still standing in the darkness. She had not once sat down on the ground while they were confined, but he had. His thighs would ache from being crouched for so long, the place pressing itself in on him. Being held inside walls was anathema to a Starwatcher and she detested being imprisoned here as much as he did. He appeared thankful for her lack of chatter or speculation while they were trapped in this dark hut among scores of warriors outside. Motionless, her back against the rough wall, her escape from this ordeal had been to think of every detail earlier and where Cian might now be waiting.

"The Invader champion must be dead," Tadhg said. He stood up to her eye level. "Perhaps the long knives made a quick job of it."

"We are to live, Tadhg. Their champion lives, or they would have swiftly avenged his death on us." Mouth dry, she managed a whisper.

He inclined his handsome face close to hers. "Two deaths for the one, and all three would miss this evening's meal. Then again, might they be trying to starve you and me?"

She returned his faint smile, and they leaned on each other's shoulders. They waited for a sound, a word, a sign, from Cian or from any of the warriors plodding around the hut.

At last a stumbling drunk sentry with a torch opened the door, growled at them and motioned them into the cool night air. The tall Invader stood nearby watching her and Tadhg. She returned his look, caught up again by his long legs and his bearing. He was like one of the intruders' tawny stallions, powerful and disturbing. His eyes scorched over her body and she turned away, confused.

Under the starflung sky, sentries with torches accompanied the pair to the gates and over the plank bridge, leaving them at the forest's verge without ceremony or thanks. The sentries provided them no part of the intruders' evening meal, and no torches for their journey home.

It was new moon and darkness swallowed the two. They waited at the edge of the forest while their eyes adjusted. Tadhg pointed to where a planet had already traveled below the horizon. They quickly located a star pattern in the east and checked its position against the

North stars and bright stars in the west. Tadhg and Boann passed north through the woods and bracken and safely into their homes.

They eluded warriors lurking at a marshy clearing adjacent to the three brooding starchamber mounds. The Invader warriors sent by Maedb to kill Boann and Tadhg waited until first light to route themselves back to their camp and without so much as a glimpse of their prey.

'S a chomharsana cléibhe, fliuchaigí bhur mbéal / So, my bosom
friends, drown your thirst
Mar ní bhfaighidh sibh aon bhraon i ndiaidh bhur mbáis / As you
won't get a drop at all after you're dead
From: *Bunan Bui*, Cathal Mac Ghiolla Ghunna, 17th Century CE

Punishment

THE SUNRISE ROLLED north along the horizon. Soon it would be
the time of long sunlight and heat, called Brightsun. Slights and
injustices sparkled in the ripples on the Boyne, flashed from the
white quartz on the mounds, and rose in dark plumes from the
intruders' fires.

The Invaders ignored offers to meet in a solstice council with the
Starwatchers. More warriors scrambled to shore from arriving
boats, carrying long knives and the new halberds armed with shining
battle points.

The Starwatchers stayed well away from the intruders' camp
while their scouts monitored its activity to see if the camp
absorbed the newcomers or they departed with their boats. A
swift fox darted between river and woods under the drifting
stars. However, the scouts had no report of Cian and this worried
the elders.

After Boann's safe return from the intruders, Oghma waited for her to speak. Several sunrises passed before Boann released her cares to him about being held inside the walled camp.

When she finished, he asked only, "Are you certain you could not have saved the murderer's red hand?"

She almost told him about the assault on her before Sheela's murder, her worries for Cian; everything. But that might be too much for him. "I went among the Invaders on behalf of our people. Sheela lies dead. It would do no good for her or the living if I neglected my duty as a healer."

"You mean you had enough medicine to kill this man Connor and you chose to let him live." Oghma nodded approval, the hearth's fire highlighting his face so that it appeared carved in granite, ageless. "Their camp has calmed for the time being. You prevented great violence all the way around."

At full moon Slainge had a meal prepared for Tadhg and Boann, at which the people offered thanks for their return unharmed. After the feast, the two shared with the elders their insights into what they witnessed within the intruders' camp. The elders mulled over certain details and questioned the intruders' motives, saying, "There is no metal here at the Boyne!"

Two moons passed after Boann's mission inside the camp. Quiet ones watched the Invaders' every move. They sent a warning to Starwatchers living at mountains to the southeast, and waited for their scout to return with strong axeheads of hard greenish rock, an expression of solidarity from the Starwatchers there. Boyne scouts traveled the length and width of the island, gathering intelligence and oaths of loyalty.

The skies brought no rains and the sun's light seemed dim. To harvest what they could of medicinal herbs, Boann and Airmid trekked in a wide area around their village with the other women. As various plants came into maturity, they took the root or leaves or flower heads according to the known properties of that plant. Scouts accompanied them, especially into the woods, where the women also picked berries, leaves and bark for tea, and mushrooms and shade-loving greens. There Airmid stopped to talk with her lover Ardal, who was hard at work in a coppice of hazel and ash. Boann watched the two lovers parting, Airmid's hand outstretched until Ardal disappeared among green leaves.

Since Sheela's death, the two women grew closer and shared confidences. Now Airmid told Boann through tears, "We postponed our marriage ceremony. Perhaps we can marry after summer solstice. For now, Ardal must serve day and night with the scouts." By day the scouts surveyed the bogs for dry ridgelines, and they tended to coppiced trees in the woods, all hidden from view. By night the scouts watched the intruders.

The two women went out at night, following the healers' custom to gather certain herbs only during greatest potency at full moon. Airmid met Ardal in clearings, and rejoined Boann before dawn to return together to their village. If Oghma worried when Boann slept late into the mornings, he said nothing to her.

She continued working with her father at the mounds, going to her lessons with the Dagda, and attending the starwatching and discussions. The apprentices including Boann regularly checked the path of the sun's light along the inner walls of the starchambers. They carefully recorded the stars' nighttime positions, using the mound kerbstones and standing stones, to be sure that the carved symbols functioned as intended. Maintaining their vigil at the three major mounds gave them much to accomplish during the long days and short nights while the sun lazed as it neared summer solstice. She slept late after these nights as well.

High in the sky, a haze swirled. The astronomers waited for it to dissipate. On some nights the lingering dust made starwatching impossible. Nevertheless, the Dagda called for the summer retreat at Carrowkeel. Boann eagerly attended with novices from across the island, who walked to the ancient mounds at Carrowkeel. There lived Tethra and the respected tribe that descended from Griane, the Starwatchers' first astronomer.

"We want you to focus on the erratic celestial beings whose cycles elude us," Tethra reminded them.

That first evening proved frustrating. They attempted to track a bright object rising far from where they expected, then it crossed low in the night sky and disappeared. As dawn approached, the students assembled with the elders, who waited for questions from them. Signal fires glowed from one, and then another, of the mounds atop distant heights from where they sat.

"Dagda, why are some of the night beings never following paths?" asked an adolescent, a muscular, brown-haired fellow named Daire.

The Dagda waited several moments for someone to offer a reply. At last Tethra the elder spoke. "Perhaps they do follow paths but we have not yet determined what those paths are, my brother?" The youth brightened and nodded.

The Dagda addressed young Daire and the assembly. He spoke slowly and seriously. "It is your job to observe. You must avoid making assumptions. Only after many generations of observations have been confirmed and reconfirmed, can we describe the motions in the skies, day and night. Our ancestors have given us this precious knowledge in stories and stone carvings left to us, and we hold the privilege of adding to it."

As the Dagda finished speaking, first light illuminated the east. Below stood the stone dwellings of Doonaveragh, almost a hundred of them perched on a plateau. A gauzy smoke rose gently from hearth fires rekindled for the morning meal. Far below the village plateau, the dense forest and patches of cleared plains stretched to the horizon where light tinted the sky. The Starwatchers' imposing mounds punctuated the high places, visible to them now across the landscape's deep green expanse. The long arrow-shaped lake below them glistened with the sun's early rays. They listened, enthralled by the beauty of their island and the deep cadences of the Dagda.

"Some day your task might be completed, but that would occur many generations into the future." He described a number so large that it defied their comprehension.

Daire spoke up again. "Our people would have to live forever!"

The Dagda smiled. "If we keep the star knowledge alive, that will be true." He raised his shining red mace to the north. "The celestial cycles comprise decades, or even hundreds, of suns. Some cycles number in the thousands, reaching back beyond the memory of our people and forward to unknown generations. We needed a way to record this knowledge for everyone to see and use over time. We have chosen the most durable medium: stone. The stones of our mounds contain our past, present, and future."

He pointed his mace at stars fading in the east. "We shall see a new constellation signaling each of the four seasons, the solstices and equinoxes. Our entire calendar of constellations will shift from its current sequence. That much we know from the ancestors' chants. These chants tell us to choose the next star pattern to mark each season." He paused. "We must not treat this cosmic shift with panic." All knew that star sightings had been compared at the marker stones, hundreds of times, exactly on the equinoxes and according to the ancestors' chants. Over their generations the line on the standing stones appeared to lose accuracy. Worse still, the sky dome's shift appeared to move backward to the sun and moon.

"It is clear that our stones do not move," the Dagda said. "The Northshift is one of many riddles that make our work interesting." He urged them to figure out precisely how much the stars moved in a given time frame and obviously, to confirm the direction of the shift. "We have only so many equinox observances until the shift is complete. We must choose a new equinox constellation and choose a new North Star. Each equinox observation is essential.

"We will succeed. Wise people will voyage to the Boyne from great distances—using new boats or old—to learn from us and share with us just as those daring few have done for generations. They will help us persuade these Invaders to leave."

The time of heat arrived, when they expected to see cereal grains ripening and calves fattening. One midsun when the golden-rayed orb climbed to its peak angle, Boann ventured out to gather herbs in the north meadow. Deep in thought, she quite forgot she had passed by the Starwatcher sentry some time ago at the weeping birch trees leading to the stream.

Her eyes swept the tall grasses and flowers. She could not see their scout but all appeared quiet around her. She lay down in the meadow, a sprig of mint on her tongue. A tiny butterfly with orange striped wings settled nearby. It vibrant wings opened and closed atop the bloom that it probed. The warm sun stroked her face, the bees' humming around her faded, and soon Boann dreamed pleasantly among the scented stalks.

At a distance, men scuffled. A horse's hooves drummed the hot clay in crossing the meadow toward her bower. The noises failed to wake her, but the butterfly darted up and away.

The abrupt cool of a shadow covered her face. She drifted back to waking, then with a start she saw above her the face of the tall intruder, the man with eyes the color of dark honey. She had not allowed herself to think of him after she was held captive in the camp. He let his horse eat the grass and held its reins loosely across his right arm, his other arm cocked with hand on his hip as he peered down upon her. Still half in a dream, Boann heard the small shiny pendants tinkling on his horse's gear. The smell of his horse was very strong. She heard the heavy beat of hooves, more horses coming with more warriors.

She jumped up to run away, but in her tongue he ordered, "No!" She stood before him uneasily, locked in his searching gaze. He shifted the reins and drew his long knife with a motion as fluid as running water and lifted it above his head. The light glinted on the blade as he waved it high and she saw fresh blood smeared down the blade.

She waited for that foul blade to descend on her. *Ancient one, Shining One, witness my death and may it be swift.*

Instead the horse riders arrived, among them Cian. The Invader turned and exchanged terse phrases in his language, then all the men looked at her. The riders had their bodies bared to the hot sun but Boann met their eyes with a steady gaze.

The amber-eyed Invader grabbed at her, throwing the reins around her neck, his arm across her shoulders. Cian swung off his horse toward her but the tall Invader's knife grazed his abdomen. Beads of red formed in a thin line on Cian's taut flesh. He halted.

The Invader's horse reared its head and Boann slipped away but she stayed in the circle of stomping, snorting horses. She would not run while this man threatened Cian.

The tall Invader watched her face. The others waited, deferring to him. He sheathed his knife and gave a sardonic smile at Cian, then at her.

Furious, she reached out with leaves to press on Cian's wound, and asked in their own tongue, "Why do you come to me here?"

"Why are you here?" He motioned her to pick up her trug of herbs and return to the Starwatcher village, "Don't be out alone again during the day. Or at night."

He stepped back to his animal and she noticed a short dagger, bloodied, hanging from Cian's belt. Was she dreaming this, a bad dream?

She watched them turn their horses and ride away, especially the tall man with the strange glowing eyes. His striking male beauty unsettled her, just as when she first saw him in the intruders' hall. He moved with the animal, his long legs wrapped over its stout middle, his feet tucked off the ground. He was not tattooed or painted like the others. His skin had an even fawn color that almost matched his animal eyes. She had no glimpse of the man's spirit behind those eyes. He stared back at Boann as he rode away, without expression, but her shoulders burned where the Invader touched her. This had been no dream.

Boann obeyed Cian and made her way home, worried anew for his safety among the warriors.

She went over the hazy moments when she awoke, the tinkling gear and the horse's sharp hot smell. Suddenly she realized of the tall Invader: he does not smell like the others. Her mind swirled with the heat. What did this Invader want, what did he know? Had he seen the bite on the man Connor's hand, that red hand she failed to save?

Boann remembered Sheela's injuries and began to shake. These Invaders live as savages, and Cian with them; had she really seen him wearing a metal dagger and what had he done with it? She gagged. Dizzy, she reached her doorway and fainted onto the flags. This time she woke to see Airmid's face coming into focus.

"Boann, you must tell me what's wrong. You who brave all kinds of weather for starwatching and herb-gathering, lying here in a weak pile!"

"It's nothing. Too much heat in the meadow. I should have drunk some water at the stream. You know that I tend to get lost in daydreams. That's all, too much heat."

Airmid's hands explored Boann's head. "You should have gone with me if it's the stream where you've been. Och, what a great lump coming up on your head! You'd better be lying down."

She glanced at her trug of herbs spilling across the stone pavers.

"Don't worry, I'll take your share of herbs with mine to do the infusions or the drying, whatever is necessary for these." Airmid helped her to her bed platform and settled her into its furs laid over sweet hay.

Boann acquiesced; her latest brush with intruders exhausted her. As she closed her eyes Cian's stern words echoed in her head: Don't be out alone again.

Five suns passed. Early with the sixth light, Tadhg came to her door. She was always glad to see him, reliable fellow that he was. Since their captivity in the walled camp, Tadhg treated her differently. No words were spoken but she could feel him and smell him at twenty paces' distance, and saw discreetly that he reacted the same way to her. But she knew Tadhg grieved for Sheela and she did not encourage him.

He looked as grave now as when they were confined in the dark cell, and he returned her welcome and offer of food with a blunt command.

"You are called by the elders to the council oak. They await us there."

Tadhg would not tell her the reason she was summoned before the elders. He led her toward the council oak, then detoured slightly and they walked the cursus, a path between earthen banks adjacent to the central mound. The Starwatchers used the cursus path on only the most serious occasions. Boann's stomach fluttered. A large group congregated at the oak, but she did not see her father among them. Her father had already gone to his carving, alone, and until she saw him arrive, she feared that he had been attacked. Slainge indicated where they should stand together, Oghma beside Boann.

More Starwatchers arrived from the village. Airmid and the other young women fairly ran the cursus before seating themselves where they could see the council. Tadhg seated himself apart with companions, off to one side. He looked ashen in the face. He crossed his arms over his broad chest, waiting. Boann felt another flutter, to see Cian sitting there with Tadhg. Cian had not attended the elders since the violence against Sheela. She swayed slightly to see two Invaders watching her, one on either side of him.

She couldn't think why the elders wanted to single her out. She wanted to sit down, not have all eyes on her. Oghma let his shoulder touch hers briefly and she knew he understood. Tears sprang to her eyes; she willed them back and brushed his rough hand, next to hers.

The Dagda arrived, carrying the red stone macehead. Would this council make peace with the Invaders? Did the Invaders seek to punish her for the man losing his red hand?

The elders came straight to the point, Slainge speaking for the panel.

"Beloved daughter, welcome. You know there have been serious problems for our people during the past moons. We maintain our ways without disrespect to the intruders, but we cannot say the same of their ways upon this island. Hear us, but note, we do not require anything from you in consequence of what we shall explain to you, Boann. You may refuse this latest request from the strangers among us." A murmur arose among the Starwatchers and Slainge waited for it to cease. He went on in a voice that carried far.

"The Invaders tell us that soon they shall hold a ceremony to honor their new champion to whom they give the title of *ard ri*. This man has no wife, they say, and there is no woman among them whom he wishes to marry. Yet they say he must have a wife for their *ard ri* ceremony. He has chosen from among our women. He wishes to take you as his wife."

Boann could not assimilate what the elders were telling her. She felt Oghma take her arm as if to lead her away before he heard any more of this.

"They claim this man met you in the Invader camp when they asked for a healer for the one called Connor. And this new champion relays to us that he recently saved your life in our meadow by the watering stream. Do you recall this?"

She could think of nothing but those predatory golden eyes. The bloody knife blade above her under the sun. Her mind reeling, she tried to plant her feet.

"Do you know the man of whom we speak?" Slainge asked.

She must answer. It seemed she had endangered all her people though she couldn't think what she had done to arouse that

Invader's interest. She made her nod without much enthusiasm but could feel herself reddening from her neck up to her hairline. Cian would see it; she wished the earth would swallow her.

"You may address this matter while you stand before us, or you may counsel with your father and we would hear later what is your decision." The elders did not inquire further.

She could feel Airmid and Tadhg watching her, and Cian. She could not think.

Oghma remained beside her and touched her arm again, his lips set firm. He waited for her to speak, she knew, ever mindful of what was proper to do, when to speak and when to be silent. She must consider carefully before she would reply. Words could not be taken back.

In the long pause that followed, Boann heard their childrens' clear, high voices responding to questions put to them from the star teacher, coming from the smaller old mound of Dowth. She could see Dowth's top across the brilliant green grass scattered with tiny white flowers below the pristine sky. Sheela's voice came to her and a vision swirled before Boann. The mounds decrepit, forgotten. Women scorned and children neglected. Great battles, the Boyne red with blood. She felt faint again.

The Dagda brought Boann a sip of water from the river, a sacrament during this season of long sunlight. Her legs steadied after she drank from the Boyne.

She answered clearly. "What did these intruders tell you that is more than what you have told me? This man could have come to me himself for a marriage."

The elders were equally direct with her. "He is too proud for that, Boann. We have told you everything we know. These strangers talk in circles. They say that your life is in danger. Their new champion says that he offers you his protection through a marriage. We infer that he and his warriors intend to remain at the Boyne.

"We see many trees falling beside their camp and rising as smoke. The Invaders tell us they will be taking even more animals from the forest and the river, food for their great *ard ri* ceremony. There is one more thing that we know from our own scouts: the Invaders busy themselves with making more long knives."

The two intruder guests perked up their ears when the elders pointedly used the term, Invaders. Long knives gleamed in thongs tied at these warriors' waists.

So they won't leave us. Do they mean to harm us at our council oak? Do these Invaders mean to slaughter us all? Boann wondered, seeing their weapons. She stood as unmoving as the stone foundation of the island. What was the way forward, she asked herself, the way to avoid the terrible future in her vision.

The warm sun climbed in the east over the oak's wide branches and struck all of them with pure light. The sun's power flowed into her. Taking more time to decide, even to the following sunrise, would not help. She would decide it here and now.

"What would my name be with this man, their new champion?"

One of the elders looked away as if ashamed. Slainge said gently to her, "*Bru na Elcmar.* Their champion is called Elcmar."

"But what of my name? What is *Bru na Elcmar* to me? Did they say what *Bru* means?"

"Your question is very important, Boann. We considered this and we think it has something to do with their concept of a woman, or that it means a mystery or hidden place. We are not certain. These intruders speak at length, but they discourse in riddles.

"He means to take a specific woman from us in a formal marriage. He has identified you. We ascertain that you would not be a captive. And these men promised that under their laws, as with ours, any property you bring to Elcmar—rather, all the property that you now hold, as we pointed out to his emissaries— shall remain yours."

The two Invaders scrutinized Boann for her reaction. Cian translated to them all that had been said, then he focused upon some point in the distance. All were silent.

So the tall stranger whose eyes could read my thoughts has not come for me himself.

The haughty Invader offered a difficult path yet his very arrogance intrigued her. She sensed in him a will as strong as her own. She looked over at Elcmar's emissaries, at their long knives. Their new champion offered his protection, they said. These Invaders intended to remain among her people. Bitter smoke from Invader fires drifted to the council oak: the telling sign of making metal weapons.

Like the rest of the Starwatchers, Cian appeared to be choking on the smoke. His face gave no clue for her choice. For one heartbeat— two heartbeats—she despised Cian for leaving her no matter what was his reason. He failed to attend their equinox rites and join openly with her. Perhaps her father was right about Cian. Then she remembered him leaping off the horse, the knife's careless slice to his flesh. Cian would be willing to die for her. There he was, unarmed but proud, between the brutish warriors. If she refused this marriage, the man Elcmar might retaliate, he might well kill Cian to make an example.

That sank in, as bleak as the vision she had seen. *We are trapped like fish in a river weir, you and I.* She couldn't trust herself to look at Cian again. She must choose the way that offered the best outcome for all the Starwatchers, not just for herself.

The childrens' distant voices reached her once more. She felt herself shifting, inexorably, like the sky. There was one point she would not concede in this bargain with the long knives.

While steadying her father beside her in his growing agitation, she replied to the elders with great care, "I have heard what the intruders propose for this formal marriage between our people. The covenant I make with the man Elcmar says that I, Boann, and my people, shall complete our work at the starchambers. Regardless of how long that may require."

Elcmar heard Boann's speech, her condition for the marriage to happen, from his men who demanded her from the Starwatchers. He consulted with the shaman.

"I don't give a damn about her starwatching," Elcmar said.

Bresal the many-talented shaman recited a version of the Invaders' marriage laws from memory, burping once or twice, then he approved this contract since Elcmar agreed to it in full. The shaman announced the deal under an oak tree to all those who jostled forth from the Invaders' camp. Let it be known: Elcmar would marry one of the natives as his first wife. Bresal forgot her name so he cut his remarks short. She would have all the rights of a first wife, despite coming from the quiet ones.

Long knives were hurled into the ground by disgusted warriors who had hoped to send for a woman from their own tuath to be joined with Elcmar as first wife. Others said he might just as easily bed a slave after he performed as the new *ard ri*.

Bresal himself had commented to Elcmar, "Sure, it wouldn't be essential for you to take a wife immediately after the ceremony of the white horse. The point is what the *ard ri* accomplishes with the horse, and not the woman. There 'tis."

The camp's approval of him dropped. Young and restless warriors wondered aloud if Elcmar had already proven to be a bad choice for their champion. They were ready enough to attack the village and Maedb's contingent encouraged them, but in stepped Bresal at Elcmar's behest. The shaman dispensed some of his supply of mushrooms. Soon the young Invaders became weak from the emetic effect followed by hallucinations. They forgot all talk of a coup.

The Invader camp languished and gossiped in the midsummer moonlight. Elcmar set up informers to bring him all the rumors. He learned which warriors visited Connor, who gladly accepted brown packets paying for his favors while he still acted as *ard ri*. The deposed Connor plotted with a small party to take the Invaders' two boats to survey the land farther north. He lusted after gold, and used the unreliable weather as his mandate to search the north for it now, before autumn. He had no wish to interfere with Elcmar's marriage plans, he said.

"I refuse to go with Connor, off to forage in the north," Maedb announced. "Elcmar to marry a quiet one, and to have chosen that shortish, darkhaired woman. Why, she looks *old*," sniffed Maedb. She referred to the tender age at which a slave could be violated by a warrior without any punishment or damages owed.

"Shouldn't he know better?" she huffed. "Ach, sure. Elcmar isn't really one of us." Maedb reminded her companions how Elcmar arrived on a far shore, a few moons before they voyaged to this island. "We should have known better."

Elcmar's informers reported that Maedb paced the great hall, greatly affronted by this turn of events, keeping Connor and Bresal captive while she ranted. She complained that Elcmar had brought no retinue to them except one male slave, and few possessions, nothing Maedb was interested in except his wondrous and tall body. Traveling groups like theirs took in well-formed fighters like him, Connor reminded her. Elcmar claimed no tuath and thus he was neutral. It had been easy to choose him for *ard ri* since that avoided choosing between clans. Maedb flung a pot at Bresal when he reiterated that the blemished Connor must relinquish authority. Elcmar now had the advantage in their competition to find gold and tin on this island. He would have first pick of the warriors and boats and Connor would have the leftovers, according to Bresal.

Elcmar noted it all with satisfaction.

Maedb roared orders at the slaves. She and Connor must move precipitously from the great hall to smaller quarters in the camp. Maedb's new quarters in this outpost would be the same size as her slaves'. On her way out she took items from the great hall which were neither her property nor Connor's, but were in fact tribute to the Invaders, valuables taken by force or as gifts from other peoples they had encountered. Maedb even stripped the furs and drapery from the bed.

Elcmar learned from his spies that Cian moved like vapor inside their walls, absorbing all the rumors and intrigue. He did not trust this Starwatcher, a lad too clever by half again. With their ceremony of Lugh at first harvest, Elcmar would be made *ard ri*. He vowed that along with certain others in the camp, Cian would mark that occasion forever.

Elcmar enjoyed the new innuendoes that Maedb circulated, a terrible rumor that it was Cian who murdered the Starwatcher woman, and he did nothing to dispel that rumor. He made sure Cian knew that in the blink of an eye he could be confined or set to hard labor or dispatched to the spirits, at Elcmar's whim. Elcmar had seen his hunger for Boann and understood him in this matter. *Probably better than your man Cian does himself, sure. Boann saw that red hand... Does she know the truth about that woman's murder? I'll soon find out.*

Boann entered the Invader camp for the second time, this time as a bride for the champion, and Elcmar compelled Cian to watch the spectacle. There had been a small conflict as to her exact arrival, Bresal suggesting that the bride should arrive with the sunset that began the Invaders' harvest festival. The Starwatcher elders replied that Boann would arrive at sunrise with the light, or not at all.

The flat drums and wooden pipes announced Boann. She looked very fine indeed on that sunrise. Cian's heart must be swelling, Elcmar thought, smug. The sentries led Boann, chin held high, through the crowd. Elcmar towered over all from a platform outside the great hall where his men grouped around a white mare.

Perhaps some common ground between their differing customs would be found through this alliance. Although, Elcmar observed, we Invaders do not honor their concept of common ground. It would be tough going if more Invaders arrived, each wanting a piece of the Starwatchers' island. But he could outmaneuver them all with this marriage at the Boyne. And, find the gold.

He would use this marriage to control the whole island. Elcmar let the smug look settle into his features.

Slaves installed Boann inside the feasting hall on a proper wooden chair with a seat, back, and sides; they placed a rolled fur pillow behind her back for posture. She leaned back in wonder. No more sitting on a stump for her, said one of them kindly. Boann heard the remark but did not understand. It appeared that the intruder women ignored the ceremony outside in that most of the women filed into the great space to inspect her. She judged their comments to be curious if not friendly.

From outside she heard the buzz and drone of the males clustering around Elcmar. Bresal made a short speech that she could not construe. There followed a stomping of hoofs and the horse's strange noises, and odd shouts until a robust cheer issued from the men.

Elcmar strode into the hall adjusting his tunic, flanked by warriors slapping him on the back and exclaiming, gesturing. Detached from the men, his eyes searched ahead until he found her and he approached Boann. The unmistakable smell of the intruders rose from him. In spite of herself, she shuddered. He gave her an icy glare.

Bresal followed Elcmar inside, cleared an area among the witnesses, and motioned Boann to rise and stand beside Elcmar. Using Invader speech, the shaman married the two before the assembly. Oghma, the Dagda, and Airmid attended her, but those guests were all that Boann expected. Cian appeared but she only glimpsed him through the crowd of intruders. Their marriage ceremony was brief, shorter than what transpired outside in the muck to have Elcmar declared the new champion.

With a stiff flourish, Elcmar seated her and took his tall chair beside hers. At his signal, slaves rushed to lay wood planks over trestles, then spread fragrant ferns on the tabletops. Invaders found seats and the banquet began. Smoked fish from the great river still covered in delicate silvery skin, red meats from forest animals oozing blood and fat, and roast fowl stuffed with herbs and grains were set before them on wood trenchers. Bresal paraded, sampling this and that from different tables and sending slaves for more brew.

A slave brought them dark liquid in a tall cup and Elcmar motioned her to give him a drink from it. She did so, then he indicated she must drink it also. The viscous liquid looked as though it might contain honey and had an odor like roasted nuts. She tried this beverage to wash down the rich foods. Perhaps it would also mask the strong smell from Elcmar, a musky smell like freshly dug earth but fast turning rank. She recognized the stink unique to this camp. Did Elcmar carry that sharp smell from a horse? Boann dismissed her thoughts before they led to dark conclusions about the *ard ri* ceremony: surely not. But she smelled a horse.

Late summer berries in cream clotted with pressed mint, a digestive brought with Boann, finished the meal. Across the seated diners, her father's eyes met hers. *That would be from your mother,* his eyes said. *Yes,* her eyes smiled back at Oghma. They savored the minted berries and in that way her mother's spirit comforted them at this Invader wedding feast.

A small distance away, Maedb and her party including Connor feasted at a plank table. Theirs was the loudest group, due in no small part to Maedb. At length the two wafted over to Elcmar and Boann, to offer good wishes to the newly wed pair. Connor insisted on kissing Boann's hand and as he did, nipped at it along the side. Just so. She jerked away her hand and Connor threw back his head and laughed.

This man's behavior is grotesque, unspeakable; to openly mock me with the death of Sheela, and at my wedding feast. An immense anger surged, but she controlled herself except for a flicker across her face.

"Do you like my necklace?" Maedb was asking her, laughing. "Ach, you don't have our language. So sorry!" Maedb wore a huge necklace, hammered circlets of bronze strung on cord reaching to her nonexistent waist. She overlooked Boann's adornment, the gold disc earrings, a gift from Elcmar. Maedb, and Connor Of The Red Hand as he was now called, waved exuberantly at the crowd and turned their backs on Boann and the new *ard ri*.

Elcmar waved Bresal to his side and snapped, "Post a watch at the seagoing boats."

Bresal lurched away with his task and stopped for another full cup of dark brew.

Her head began to ache in earnest when the piping tune and bursts from the flat drum picked up in tempo. She tried to relax. Their music was lively and followed a similar scale of tones that her own people used to make music. Intruders rose and made toasts with tall cups and she listened while Elcmar returned many speeches. She saw that he ate well, he appeared to be in great form throughout the banquet. Still he exuded the smell of a horse.

Despite the festive mood, Boann felt more unwell. Every odor in the hall assaulted her and she fought nausea. She suspected the rich foods and the heavy beverage. Unsure of the Invader word for water, she was afraid to ask for water and wanted no more of the dark fermented brew.

A commotion erupted, a loud challenge between warriors at the rear of the hall. Connor shouted and followed the contestants outside, and with him many ducked from the hall to watch the fight. Elcmar rose also. He turned to Boann without showing any trace of affection.

When he saw her upturned face, she earned one smile and light flowed into his eyes. He reached for her hand but she shrank from him. His warm expression died. He announced that they were going to retire from the banquet. An awkward pause was followed by strained clapping and calls, words she did not understand. Elcmar gestured for her to rise and take his arm.

She resisted, she was not feeling well, and her eyes searched the hall for Cian to explain for her, but he had disappeared and with him Oghma, the Dagda, and Airmid. She was alone.

Elcmar pulled her to her feet and half dragged her to the sleeping chamber. Rude shouts followed them all the way inside and continued while he secured the door. Boann took one look at the wide bed layered with clean drapes and new furs. She forgot Elcmar and their strange ceremony and fell onto the welcoming bed. The noisy feasting and music lasted well after sunrise, while Boann slept through it all.

Her new life in marriage began when she awoke. Her head ached. The sun raced high above, well past the time for bathing and breaking the fast. Someone had hung up her beautiful knotted overtunic and for that she was grateful. Her undertunic was mussed from sleeping in it, and she quickly found a fresh shift from belongings brought with her. Boann's cheeks flamed to remember the scene at the causeway into the camp; Tadhg's silence, his distaste when he handed her packs and baskets over to slaves. He would have waited through the dark, to escort the two elders and Airmid home after the wedding feast, or so she hoped.

Going to bathe outside these walls was uppermost in her mind. Soaking in the cool of their lovely stream, even one sip of its water, would soothe her. Her village could welcome her and there she would take berry-leaf tea with Airmid and Oghma—. In the midst of her leaving the room, Elcmar blocked the doorway.

A smile curled the corners of his hard mouth. A dagger, ruddy like an eclipse of the moon, hung in a thong looped at a leather belt around his waist. Covered only in a loincloth held by his belt, one hand on the knife, he stood proud and naked before her.

He smelled better than after the horse ceremony, but Boann choked. She entreated gently with posture and gestures, proposing that he permit her to exit. She could see very well what he wanted, but how could he not prefer that she first bathe at the stream? Although it did seem that Elcmar had not bathed. Was that to annoy her? Another doubt to be pushed aside. She must try to communicate with this man. Her husband! *It seems he carries a weapon at all times. I cannot help my people if I were killed here.*

"I must learn your language. It sounds pleasant enough, like rushing water," she said to flatter him. She tried their word. "*Uisce.* Water! Will you ever let me by you?"

His eyes went flat and cold, the stare of a forest animal. He purposefully closed the door behind him and slid the heavy wooden bar across it. He looked very handsome, but his thin smile faded. He threw the loincloth to the floor.

"*Macc,*" he cried the Invader word for horse. "I am sovereign here!"

He didn't care what he had done with the horse, didn't care that she needed water. He advanced, chanting, crazed. She covered her ears, and backed away and onto the bed.

Boann attempted their new language. The shaman Bresal claimed theirs was the language of the gods; what gods, she knew not and he did not specify.

Bresal took her on an early tour of the camp and she remarked to him, "Look at the mist over Red Mountain. The mist lying on the mountain means bad weather comes."

He looked oddly at Boann. Later she found that he misinterpreted her remark to mean that she could divine the weather. She meant her comment as a simple observation, but soon the entire camp repeated it and misconstrued it.

Elcmar confronted her. "You're after upsetting Bresal. It is he who predicts weather from omens."

"Then I must watch what I say, Elcmar, until I am familiar with your Invader speech. But any one of you can look at the mountain with dawn if you wish to see about the weather." She pointed. "Where the sun rises, in the east."

He motioned impatiently. "I leave shortly on a journey. By boat."

"Where are you going?" She understood: a boat. But his leaving surprised her.

"To the south," he pointed, and added, "Cian shall accompany my warriors."

Then Elcmar gave her his flat, hard stare; unfathomable. Elcmar's sudden journey irritated her, and she bridled that he presumed to take Cian with him. Starwatchers had their liberties and Cian was no slave.

They spent one moon together, each cautious and unbending, before Elcmar left. His demeanor hardened when she told him the Starwatchers well knew who murdered Sheela. Boann kept her temper even, if rather cool, with Elcmar observing her constantly while his men prepared to travel.

She wanted to ask Cian to remain at the Boyne but in the crowded camp kept her distance from him during the sun's light. Except when Cian brought a girl to Boann to meet her, a young woman of fine features and black billowing waves of hair to her slender waist. An undefined jealousy stung Boann but she spoke well to this Cliodhna, a potter.

"She taught me much when I came to live inside this camp," Cian told Boann. "You may rely on Cliodhna. Of course I have told her the same about you."

After sunsets, Boann had no opportunity to leave Elcmar's side. On the eve of his leaving, he pressed his hand between her legs as they lay together. Her thoughts in turmoil, she failed to respond.

He grew cross. "What's wrong?"

"The drums, too loud, so much noise. Must this camp have so much noise?"

"Must you answer every question with a question?" He drew away, turning his back to her.

She could only watch Elcmar's party leaving through the walled bank, unable to speak with Cian among the tumult of men and burdened horses.

The dust and smell of the horses had not cleared before Bresal repeated to her the vile accusations by Maedb against Cian. She eyed

Bresal so sternly that he retreated from the great hall. Perhaps Cian's absence would calm troubled waters here, though now she was entirely on her own among the Invaders.

The shaman left her in peace for a quarter moon, and Boann meant to resume starwatching. She also wanted to learn the intruders' ways and practice their tongue. A slave girl, Muirgen, worked in the great hall. Boann tried speaking with her and found that Muirgen understood her sufficiently. She did not know whether to leave the great hall open or bar it to the continual visitors and supplicants. Boann helped some persons, and sent others away to find Bresal for his counsel.

Under the ever watchful eyes of Maedb, and Muirgen and other slaves, Boann had little privacy in her quarters. No intruder woman knew how to dress her hair and because she was embarrassed to teach any of them, her hair hung in tangles much of the time. Still she did not ask for help, but Muirgen offered to braid her hair.

"Many thanks, but sure isn't it enough you're after doing for others." Boann refused, using Invader phrases. She ignored Muirgen's bewildered look, to tussle with her heavy auburn hair unaided by any slave. For Elcmar she had tried the unguents and paints used by intruder women, but disliked their feel on her skin. Freed of pleasing his taste while he was away, she threw the tiny wood pots into the hearth's embers. Maedb came upon the smoldering remains and threw up her hands, screeching how rare and difficult to obtain these were.

Even before he left the camp, she defied Elcmar and bathed every morning at the stream. Despite cooling temperatures, Maedb and companions took it up but to her dismay, those women insisted on bathing in the Boyne, the Starwatchers' sacred waterway, where they taunted the warriors with their nakedness.

The intruders neglected the sacred river in other ways. The muck inside the camp walls, mud mixed with refuse and animal wastes, appalled her. She raised their negligence with Bresal, while he sat eating.

"Invaders dispose of animal waste carelessly. It could be set aside to enrich the fields. The trench for human waste, that is located in the wrong area and drains too close to the river. That waste should filter through a reed bed well before it reaches any water."

"These are your concerns, not mine." He looked bored and continued eating.

"Can the Invaders not see that bad practices make for sickness? Your camp brought illness to our green plain along the Boyne. We must all avoid more sickness and death."

Bresal eyed Muirgen, standing back of Boann. "No changes while Elcmar is gone. To be sure, I could have some men dig latrine pits wherever you like. But I don't care about muck." He waved his arm, bedecked with a wide bracelet of jet. "A fine armpiece, taken from the Continent. Would you like to wear this?"

Not sure whether Bresal agreed and the waste would be moved, Boann saw Muirgen hungering for the shiny black ornament and she led the slave girl away from him. But she did not let the matter rest and reminded Bresal until he did have the pits re-dug in a suitable place.

Night and day, smoking fires inside the camp walls obstructed any starwatching for her. She missed working with Oghma at the mounds. And Boann yearned for a simple outing by herself to gather herbs before hard frosts would wither them away. Bresal said her outing was not permitted though he didn't say why. She was followed by the slave Muirgen or by Maedb and intruder women, in the great hall or outside. Accustomed to being out in the open air much of the time, engaging her mind, this new life forced her to remain inside the great hall and be subjected to endless chatter. She lapsed often into thinking of what her Starwatchers would be doing during the sunlight and the starlight, outside in the natural rhythms and stillness. She missed fresh breezes whispering through grass and branches, insects' humming and bird songs. Her sense of time blurred; she took naps and awoke feeling sluggish and queasy rather than rested.

Maedb invited her to practice their sport with those few women who were not slaves, in the clearing outside their banked walls, but after watching them Boann chose not to participate. These Invaders' war games shocked her; the fervor, their love of combat. They seemed to mock her: why don't your Starwatchers fight us? More and more, she shied away from the camp's inhabitants.

She did take in a stray puppy found in the camp, underfed and wobbly, and her sole comfort was her little dog Dabilla. Each rising of the sun found her more restive. The camp boundaries squeezed her even when she could not see them. She detained Muirgen for taking walks with Dabilla around the palisade, then after a brief interval inside the hall she called upon the girl to take yet another walk. The slave at last gave her a quizzical look.

"I prefer your company to being followed by a guard, you see."

"Would you like to watch at the cooking pits?" Muirgen asked.

Boann wondered if she could bear the smells, but the girl looked fidgety herself. Muirgen pushed on a loose section in the high wall and it opened, a door of sorts. Surprised, Boann followed her out to the cooking site where slaves prepared feasts for the great hall. She stepped gingerly around the *fualachta fiadh*, long pits lined with wood. Meat cooked there in greasy steaming water heated by red-hot stones. The cooking pits and all the surrounding area reeked of spoiled fat from repeated use for their big feasts. The cooks simply heaped the cracked stones to one side of the rancid pit. Boann's nausea returned on the spot.

Dabilla nosed at a bone; she threw it and the puppy chased it. No one followed her going after him. Tossing the bone here and there, she scouted with the puppy. Anyone could come and go in the area of the cooking pits, set into a sheltered dip outside the gap in the high log walls. She ambled back to the pits, unnoticed. She told a slave, a cook, "Be sure that my food is prepared at its own covered fire," and pointed to the rise behind the sunken troughs.

The older slave woman nodded, expressionless, busy grinding grain at a quern stone.

The camp bustled with producing supplies and feeding everyone at frequent banquets—usually with food stolen from Starwatchers, Boann saw it. She hadn't cared so much about food until she lived inside these walls. Invaders ate huge joints of sheep or cattle and rarely ate salmon or any fish from the river, saying fish suited the slaves. The camp let extra milk go to waste, seldom producing yogurt or cheese. She craved fruits and greens, largely absent from the intruders' diet. Scurrying about at the whims of many, Muirgen had no time to search for late produce and greens for her and she doubted the slave knew what to select.

Food was a regular topic inside the walls, with Maedb whining that no supplies would reach the Boyne in winter, and the slaves saying that crops hadn't ripened, the heads on cereal stalks empty and only small hips and fruits on flowering plants. Boann needed to see the crops for herself, but sentries barred her way out of the camp's gateway.

Airmid brought Boann the mixed grains for stirabout, but despite the warriors admiring Airmid's red curls and her face and form, they did not allow her inside the camp to visit. Boann heard of it sadly, from Muirgen, and felt the more isolated.

Baffled, suffocating inside walls, Boann sent a brief message to Oghma that she hoped to see her people soon. She scratched the message on a rock beyond the cooking pits. No one but a Starwatcher would understand the symbols she used.

Will the sea ever waken

Relief from despair?

My *Grief on the Sea*, Douglas Hyde, from the Irish

Transportation

Connor purloined the scarce Invader boats for his trip to the north. While Elcmar readied to voyage south to the mining camp, he discovered Bresal's failure to guard their seagoing boats.

"Bresal! We won't be taking you with us on this trip, sure. No trader goods for you either. Not until Connor returns those ships safe and sound." His look bored into Bresal. "I'm leaving you at the Boyne, in charge. Do not disappoint me again."

Elcmar rejected the skin and wicker-framed Boyne boats as too small and not seaworthy. He conscripted the largest hide-covered vessel that he could find. It came from the coastal Starwatchers living at the river's mouth east of *Bru na Elcmar*. That community monitored the sun's range between the solstices using two offshore islets as fixed horizon points. Elcmar took the Starwatchers' only oceangoing boat without offering so much as a stone axehead for it. One man tried to stop him, asking, "Why do you take from us?"

"Why? Because I can!" Elcmar drew his knife and the man backed away.

This ovoid boat, framed of steamed oak ribs with yew bindings, was covered by tanned cattle hides joined by stitched seams and smeared with pitch. For this trip the boat must carry eight men. When the intruders packed all their gear, weapons, ropes, and food stores into it, to Cian's eyes it looked overloaded. He told himself, *my ancestors traveled using a hide boat*, and he made himself climb aboard with the warriors.

The *currach* set forth headed south along the coast. Elcmar's band rolled and pitched through that rough strait bounded by the larger island to the east. From comments by the men, about a place visited by some that had a great stone circle, that other coast lay closer to Eire than Cian had realized. Elcmar saw him looking east.

"Over on the Big Island, the locals rearranged their great stone circle. To suit newer beliefs, so. Those people don't be standing in place with stargazing and decorating rocks."

"Why don't you set up camp on that eastern island?" he dared ask.

"Metals," came the gruff reply. "Eire has copper, so. And gold, to be sure."

If Elcmar wanted to needle him, he paid it no attention. Cian knew of the rugged Channel that divided that larger island from the Continent to the south. His ancestors received visitors from far southern shores who bore tribute in exotic pots, fine axeheads, and yellow flint. Those items in turn made their way from the Boyne to distant passage mounds. That his Starwatchers had long maintained broad contacts, exchanging knowledge from the Continent with tribes east across the strait and north among scattered islands in colder waters, Cian kept to himself. Faraway tribes looked to the Boyne as their center, a center for starwatching. Innate pride, and caution, combined to seal his lips.

When at last they turned west into open water, the broad sea rolled smoother. Cian looked at his hands. The boat's hemp rope that he hung onto left a ruddy stripe across his palm, a mark of his first travel on the great waters.

His journey introduced him to new beauty from the ocean vantage point. He had no idea until this sea voyage, of Eire's majestic eastern and southern coasts. Sheer, dark cliffs rose from headlands and along inlets. Small islets rose vertically to assert in stony heights what they lacked in girth. The waters washing the island's shores showed every imaginable shade of blue, from light aqua in shallow inlets blending to brilliant lapis depths. They passed the place where the three sister rivers flowed together into the sea, all the way from sources at the island's navel, the midlands not far from his home.

Flocks of crying gulls circled above the boat. Cormorants soared and plummeted for prey. He saw golden-headed gannets plunging from on high, and for the first time the migrating curlews, their trilling cry lingering above the boat. Jets of water lashed up through holes in the rocks and crashed back out into the ocean. Placid crescent-shaped bays with golden sandy shores beckoned. Sloping green meadows rose behind the cliffs and beaches up to deeper green forests on the flanks of grey-green mountains. Cian longed to be showing the island's beauty to someone he knew would appreciate it with him. But the bobbing *currach* carried him ever farther away from the Boyne.

Despite crowding and rigors on the boat, he enjoyed every overnight camp with the intruders: making shelter, and then cooking what they caught in water or hunted after coaxing wood into flame. All in the same boat, or warmed by the same fire, the warriors acted more equitable toward him. Their taste for adventure, and gifted storytelling and music, were not lost on Cian. He observed their strengths and weaknesses. They constantly took fermented beverages and acquainted him with various brews.

"You do not trust any fresh water," he commented.

One of the warriors chuckled and held out a cup. "Try this to ward off the evening air, Starwatcher. A concoction made in a warmer climate. We call it Water of Life."

The Invaders said that drink gave them relief from the northern chill and darkness. Cian took the new beverages in moderation only after he suffered due to overindulging. He ate sparingly of steamed mussels and oysters offered by the intruders; eating seafood in the shell tended to sicken him from the richness of it, he said. The other men snickered, assuring Cian that on this voyage he would get used to strong drink, seafood, and the rolling waves.

He found out how greatly these intruders depended on their possessions. One of the warriors rigged a bone hook on a fiber line and caught a trout. The man stood while it thrashed on his line, flummoxed at having nothing to hold this trout while he fished for more. Cian leaned over into the long soft grasses along the stream and deftly wove an arched basket of grass with one hand, then deposited the trout with his other hand. The warrior looked amazed but still he bemoaned not having a proper basket. By the time they finished fishing, five more trout waggled inside the moist grass cradle. Cian rolled them in a skin and all arrived in the camp in good condition, their silvery gills still reflexing.

At the embers of their camp fires, Cian tried to see the island's future. He had seen more of the beauty of his homeland and had little desire to see it changed. Patiently he waited for an opportunity to escape, chafing that he traveled against his will. Any misstep, and out came a shining knife against him. Cian neither patronized nor avoided Elcmar. He merged into the men, keeping his eyes open.

After less than a half moon, including stops to look for gold or to wait out rough weather, the men arrived at the island's southwest coast. There deep fingers of land jutted into the ocean. These men knew a specific landing place, he saw, and marked that place in his mind. After tucking the skin boat beyond reach of tides, they all journeyed inland, up gorgeous red sandstone mountains and through deep valleys thick with animals and fish. Cian stopped to admire the breathtaking scenery of this headland, the distant blue waves below steep cliffs. Elcmar charged past him on the trail, pushing him to the brink: Invaders did not pause to admire the view. So Cian kept up their pace and silently tracked their route using the sun and shadow, and the stars.

They marched along over two sunrises until reaching a spot overlooking a group of azure lakes surrounded by dense woods of elm, birch, and oak. Lower mountains to the north backed the calm blue lakes. The warriors indicated the northeastern shore of the larger lake as their destination. They rounded this lake and came upon the mine at midsun on the third day.

Cian heard the mining activity from a distance, the sound of many hammers. Heavy smoke filled the air. They halted at a gash made in the earth. In its recesses, fires blazed against rock walls where men struck ringing blows, gouging out the hillside. The mine looked like a red eye in a seared face.

A warrior elbowed him. "Impressed? Invaders found this treasure lode of copper ore. We returned here, bringing masters at smelting and pouring it: smiths, the shamans of the metal," the warrior boasted.

Elcmar stepped apart to speak with one of the smiths, a powerfully built man, and Cian overheard him order that man to guard the Starwatcher at the camp. Elcmar would then be free to inspect the mines and inventory the camp.

The smith Creidhne scowled, but he took Cian with him over the next suns.

As Cian followed the smith, he learned the copper miners' routine. The miners accessed the ore by digging horizontal caverns. They lit big fires to fracture the limestone, then hammered the rock loose with stone cobbles, grooved and lashed with leather cords onto wooden handles. After hammers freed chunks of copper-laden stone, other workers smashed the large pieces into usable ore. When a hammer broke, the miners discarded the damaged cobble and their discards littered the caverns and the mining camp.

Everywhere lay pieces of copper-bearing ore, streaked with grey or purple veins when fresh from the mine. This substance mystified Cian: the streaks turned color to a bright blue-green if the rock had lain exposed long enough. From sunrise to sunset, the miners fractured ore and gathered it inside the mines by light from burning resinous switches, then hauled the ore out of the horizontal tunnels in split-wood baskets or leather bags. They hauled the ore-laden rock some distance to the smelting area, where workers used shovels made from cattle shoulder bones to shovel it into piles at the smelting pits.

More workers sorted the copper-bearing rocks by hand, and used stone hammers and anvils to separate the richer bits. At charcoal fire pits, the pulverized ore transformed into copper droplets. Cian counted more than a dozen smelting pits where workers crushed the ore and melted it into irregular drops of shadow moon metal. The workers consolidated the copper droplets using heat again, then took the lumps to Creidhne and the other smiths at a different charcoal pit. The next time Cian saw it, the copper had been smelted into irregular, flat ingot cakes or into finished axeheads.

The smith was a big, bear-like man who disclosed next to nothing about how it was that stone changed into shining, malleable copper. Creidhne gave him small tasks at a distance while the smith produced shining tools, mostly axeheads. When Cian tried to work close to the smelting pits, the smith sent him away.

Cian felt no embarrassment to be working near the women and the sleeping huts. Huts dotted the work area. Tens of workers, including but a few women, toiled at the copper mine and cut trees. The women ground grains and cooked joints of meat to feed workers hungry from smashing and hauling copper ore. The miners had a mix of languages; few dialects were native to Eire. The most common dialect was that of Seafarers, a people familiar to the Starwatchers. Despite the workers being of childrearing age, no children lived at this mining camp, he noted. A woman explained that many workers stayed only during the warm seasons, then traveled the great waters to spend the cold moons with their families.

"You mean to say they have been here more than once from your shores?"

The woman chuckled at seeing his surprise.

From the litter of cobbles and depth of the caverns, it appeared to Cian that miners had been extracting copper from this place for many cycles of the sun; that also surprised him. Intruders didn't freely exchange those copper axeheads or Starwatchers would have them at the Boyne by now.

Rather than any smith's magic, what most impressed him was the repetitive nature of the mining and smelting—and the debris. No smith's magic could repair the shattered rock faces, the volume of spent ore and litter of broken cobbles that mining left behind, defacing the area by the lake. For all that, he found only one drop of shining hard copper overlooked on the soil.

The smelting of raw copper ore produced a choking smoke, by now familiar to him but even stronger here than the intruders' smoke at the Boyne, and these pits burned nonstop. Everyone at this Lake Of Many Hammers picked up the distinctive smell. He suspected the smelting fumes to be toxic. He scrubbed, but could not get the smell out of his hair and skin. It clung to his leather tunic and leggings. Out of aversion to that smell, Cian traded his making of stone tools to have a new set of clothing made for him by the women, who did fine work with needles made of the shining metal. Making stone tools and scrapers kept him occupied away from the charcoal pits and seemed to please Creidhne.

Cian observed the camp activity until his mind boiled. Over a shared evening meal with Creidhne, he tried some questions.

"Much labor goes into felling trees and hauling wood." He gestured toward an area naked of trees.

Creidhne grabbed for a slab of cattle ribs, and eyed him. "You are a quiet one, at that. So in honor of your asking me, I'll tell you:

it takes tens of trees to produce one copper axehead. That's from the start of it, burning roundels of oak and ash inside the tunnels to shatter the rock. Then as you've seen, the rock is transported to the charcoal pits. If we carried wood to the mines and smelted ore there, we'd have a lot more work than we have carrying ore to the smelting pits, believe me. To make copper uses wood amounting to hundreds of times the weight of the finished copper. It's easier to transport the mined rock to the fire pits, rather than carry all that wood to the mine, so."

Creidhne traced symbols in the dirt that counted sun cycles, to show him how much wood the fires consumed to make just one axehead. Still the smith said nothing about the smelting process itself.

Cian took his meals with Creidhne and other miners, seated on cattle skins. The miners ate boiled or roasted meat of cattle and pig. He found the food well-prepared: they used a grated root that made his eyes water, different herbs than he had tasted, and ocean salt. Their women foraged for nuts and produce in the woods. He liked their soup of forest mushrooms and herbs pureed under a pestle and heated. They had supplies from the rare boat, like dried beans from over the waters, in varieties new to him.

The miners traded locally for beef and cereal grains, and they were aware of the harsh growing season after the dust storm early in that spring. Here, unlike warriors at the Boyne, men did not go raiding for foodstuffs; or so it appeared to Cian. If the winter ahead looked bleak and short of food, these workers would want to go to their homes. No one spoke of boats coming for them. He wondered if this camp would keep peace with the locals on empty stomachs.

The women favored him with a meat that melted in his mouth. These Seafarers raised their pigs in enclosures and fed them only acorns, then lightly smoked the meat until pink and tender, at the ever-tended charcoal pits. Cian fairly well gorged himself on that succulent ham.

He took another bite from his chunk of ham and asked Creidhne, "Why aren't the men here using copper axes to fell trees?"

Creidhne pawed at his beef and answered offhandedly, "Cost. You've seen that it takes a great amount of wood and many men to produce copper. The traders decide what copper stays here and what they send off, east to the big island and farther beyond."

"The copper axes wouldn't do the work faster?" Cian persisted.

The smith shrugged his broad shoulders. He was massive, but from those hands Cian had seen delicate work, finely etched lines decorating copper tools made by Creidhne's sure fingers. "We make copper axes for trade. But for these ordinary workers to use, we have a good supply of hard stone axes. These men know the proper stroke with a stone axe."

Cian thought of Connor's trip to the north: did Connor want the blue-grey stone axeheads that Starwatchers there made in great quantity? No, he decided, it would be foolish to journey north just for those axeheads, and it would be more foolish to ruin those ceremonial axes at felling trees. Those famed axes came from fine-grained rock quarried on the slopes of Tievebulliagh, a mountain far up in the north. The highly polished, ovoid axes had long been deemed valuable for exchange. His people had an exchange network for axes that included other coasts and they didn't need Invaders for that. More likely, Connor sought copper or the sun metal, gold, on his sudden trip north with his men. If they found ores, the Invaders might quit the Boyne and move north. He kept his face impassive while Creidhne continued speaking.

"Your axes on Eire—the polished flint axe, and those made from hard green rock found along the east coast—take down any tree well enough." Creidhne looked to see if his answer satisfied Cian. "This island is awash with stone axes, so!"

Cian saw that the smith did not bother himself about the enormous amount of work and wood to produce just one axehead of the metal that Starwatchers called shadow moon, the exact color

of an eclipsed moon. Of necessity, Cian compared the intense labor
at the mines with the Starwatchers'. Building their immense mounds
at the Boyne had required hundreds of Starwatchers working over
a long period—when the fields, or the animal breeding and birthing
and grazing rotations, did not occupy them. But he did not see the
reason for so many workers brought over hazardous seas to these
Lake mines, working throughout the light and dark, and felling vast
numbers of trees, to produce so few axeheads of this copper. It must
be possible for Starwatchers to make copper and pour axes. Cian
wanted to try using a copper axe to see how well it felled a tree,
although he had seen that the smiths kept the copper axeheads and
ingots under an alert guard.

What power does this shadow moon metal have over the
Invaders, he wondered.

He decided to take another approach. "The workers know how
to fashion a stone axe, also stone hammers. They know how to
make charcoal to heat the copper ore. What is to stop them from
going off to mine the shadow moon metal from other places?"

"Right you are, Cian. Nothing stops them from mining ore
themselves. Except that Invaders control the copper trading. And the
big boats! These workers want to go home, back to their peninsula far
over the waters, to their women and children. They have to get there
on a big Invader boat. For example, that *currach* your man brought
you lads in on from the Boyne, won't hold up for another sea journey."

So that was it, Invaders controlled who received a metal
axehead. They drained copper from the earth and sent Eire's copper
over the ocean. No exchange, no ceremony; he sat stunned. It didn't
appear that Elcmar alone controlled the copper, and if not, who did?

Creidhne's last remark referred to the Invaders' boat called the
naomhog: a high-sided *currach* that was larger, swifter, and less
likely to be swamped in tall waves. None were to be had on this
coast at present, but Cian heard the rumor that Elcmar was
considering using the currach in which they arrived to cross the great

waters to the Continent. He had seen it was not well suited to the ocean. It was madness to consider using that currach again, even to return to the Boyne.

His grip tightened on the drinking cup he held. Its blossom shape reminded him that he carried messages from Cliodhna and others at the Boyne camp, for delivery here at the Lake mine. The crescent moon sparkled over the sooty lake surface in the distance. Before this moon was full, he would find all the trusted persons and deliver those messages.

Creidhne sat chewing, and Cian saw that the brawny smith did not want more questions, that he stubbornly withheld the details of the smelting art. Cian finished the last bites of his meal. *Creidhne follows Elcmar's directions, to keep me busy around this camp, but not show me their magic of pouring shining metal from rock.* One of the workers had told him that it took a long time, much practice, to smelt copper correctly.

He put one more question to the smith. "It is said that gold is the best metal, the easiest to work."

Creidhne yawned. "Gold is warm, soft like a woman. Copper is more temperamental than a woman. If only tin were to be had here we could use it with this slick copper for making a good malleable bronze." The big smith sighed, and his fingers twitched as if touching a woman, or gold, or both.

"What is tin?"

But the smith arose from Cian and went off to his cold bed of sheep skins, alone, in his hut like the others, a domed wicker enclosure roughly plastered over with mud. Despite knowing some star cycles and using them to communicate numbers to Cian, Creidhne rarely looked up at the skies. This night was no different.

That one has journeyed far away from his ancestors, thought Cian as Creidhne lumbered off into the darkness.

Before Cian would sleep, he withdrew himself from all in the camp in order to look at the moon and certain bright stars. Seeing the mining camp shook him to the core. How much longer there could be equilibrium on Eire given the intruders' ways, he did not know. He saw no reason for the Starwatchers to adopt Invaders' ways. And there were not enough island women for these intruders to steal for wives, certainly not if they murdered women in the process.

This Elcmar was no fool. It would be easier to make friends through a marriage than to battle the Starwatchers, who greatly outnumbered the Invaders. Cian himself could see both sides of things better, after living among the warriors. Hadn't his people, Starwatchers, fought to establish themselves, clear areas of the land, and build their mounds? Of course, that conflict happened generations ago; things improved and his elders had forgotten days of battle. The tribes on this fertile island kept relations peaceful, trading polished axeheads and brides. They lived in relative equality, uniting for projects like building the mounds. All the people engaged to some degree in starwatching, proud that their island had become a destination, a place of pilgrimage to their Boyne mounds. Complacent, his elders had no idea how vulnerable they now were.

Invaders would not tolerate equality; it appeared they had no word for it.

He should have explained himself better to his elders after Sheela's murder. We cannot defend ourselves unless we understand these Invaders, he should have said. Not that it would have done any good. His elders could not, would not see what was happening to their island, despite the murder. Invaders had not turned over the man responsible, nor made amends.

His fists clenched now, to recall armed warriors bringing him before his elders so he could translate Elcmar's demand to have Boann, long knives on either side of him. The elders' disbelief changing to consternation with Cian. Then, the look of scorn at him from Tadhg when Boann made her fateful choice. He'd considered leaving the Invader camp at the first opportunity, on that very night if possible. He would have changed her mind, or left the Boyne.

When his head cooled, he stayed on inside the camp walls to try to protect Boann. She must remember their precious nights together; maybe she wouldn't go through with the marriage to Elcmar... He looked for an opportunity to kill Elcmar at the warrior games. But your man Elcmar was too clever and skilled with the long knife for that.

He recalled Boann being led by sentries to the great hall. *If it were a Starwatcher marriage, she would have been accompanied by joyous women, not armed guards. She must have been choking, for the smells coming off those lads.*

How he strained to follow Boann from the crush of onlookers, catching sight of her russet hair shining in the sunlight, caught up and beautifully braided. Airmid and her friends outdid themselves in presenting the bride, though this day pained them all. The overtunic she wore could only have been made by Sheela of the spirits; its fine knotting molded every curve of Boann. To him, she was perfect, nothing to be changed. Gold discs shone at her earlobes, a gift from Elcmar. Elcmar barely noticed her during that long day and Cian despised him all the more. For all that these Invaders occupied themselves with boasting and ogling, they lacked the most basic skills with women. In fact they brutalized women; a knot formed in his throat.

He regretted his silence, how he stood suspended among the Invaders shoving to see the Starwatcher bride. He never could manage to say much to Boann, even when they were children; her presence made him awkward, shy. If asked whether that was why he had left Oghma and carving the kerbstones, he would have denied it. Yet there she was and there he stood, tonguetied and inert. She would become first wife to that bounder, Elcmar. Cian wanted to carry her away, fly away together like mated swans. Instead he stayed at a distance while she passed by and into the intruders' great hall, unable to assert himself.

Constrained by long knives in light and darkness, here in this mining camp just as he had been at Boann's wedding. He stared down at his tight fists, shook his hands to get feeling back in them. He would fight his way out of this camp, make it back to her at the Boyne after taking revenge on Elcmar. As Creidhne said, his people have stone axes enough.

He'd need only one axe for the deed.

He shivered in the first autumn chill at the Lake mine. Killing Elcmar would accomplish nothing. More Invaders seeking metals would take Elcmar's place, more boats and yet another swaggering *ard ri*. Courage alone could not win the battle against bronze.

Cian's spirit ebbed so low that it frightened him.

Through that night he watched the skies as he had been trained to do. He would find the plan for what he must do, if he kept himself receptive to seeing it. He would keep his thoughts about the future to himself. The eyes and ears for Elcmar were all around him, he knew.

He continued to make scrapers and tools, placating Creidhne when the smith was about. But while that smith dozed, Cian moved closer and closer to the smelting, sitting nearby as workers toiled into the night. He offered them interesting comments about the stars, hearing in return bits of what these Seafarers knew. They had but brief exchanges, for the men at the pits dashed like fireflies with the red-hot ore under a shower of fiery sparks from the smiths' hammers.

Lir, a mariner whose trading boat had foundered at the rocky coast, sat close by and perceived that Cian could not be observing the dark skies while seated so near to the glowing coals. Lir could tell that the youngest smith, Lein, did not want this Starwatcher watching them at their smelting. It might well lead to trouble with Creidhne or Gebann, or worse, Elcmar. The smiths resented Elcmar's dictates but he held sway as *ard ri*.

Before the testy Lein picked a fight, Lir told Cian in a quiet aside, "You should spend less time at these pits. We'll row out on the lake and you can ask me your questions."

Cian replied without turning his head, "Yes. I'd like to learn rowing."

Their friendship began. Lir's word was sound. Over the following lunate, Lir managed to show him basics of the smelting process. They strolled past the pits after dark without lingering or attracting attention. On the lake and out of others' hearing, Lir told him the smiths did more reliable smelting at night when it was easier to see the color of the flame and monitor the pit's heat to obtain a smooth, uniform copper.

"It takes an artisan to finish metal: knowing how many tempering blows until a tool is ready and one more blow would only serve to smash it. Knowing when the copper will take more heat or when it would split with more heat."

A smelter had only one blink of time to move the glowing-hot stone crucible off the charcoal and pour out the molten copper. The worker handled the smoking crucible with tongs made of green wood. Another man stood ready with the stone mold. Very swift movements were required whether pouring an irregular flat ingot cake, or pouring into the stone mold for an axe. When the copper was ready to pour, the smelting workers seemingly danced in the darkness as rainbows of molten fire issued from their hands, a smith close by.

The smelters' use of wood tongs and their dance with fire resulted in mishaps so that a number of pit workers had disfiguring burns on face or chest or arms; some had lost fingers.

Cian confided his horror at these burned workers, during one of his jaunts with Lir over the lake. "Why must those injured ones continue to labor at the mines?" He used Lir's Seafarer dialect that resembled his own language. "I first saw persons treated as slaves by Invaders at their Boyne camp. Again, here at the Lake of Many Hammers, the numbers who struggle and toil for these few Invaders. How can this be?" He tried to express himself, aware of his own tenuous position under Elcmar's thumb.

Sunlight reflected dappling waves onto Lir's somber face. "It looks like an endless task, Cian. Many tribes have been foolish in this regard, to be ensnared by the traders. These Invaders decreed mining as a way for certain tribes to pay off debt. At least during the winter, the work slows here at the mines and many workers are allowed to return to the Seafarer peninsula. That is, if seagoing boats can be had to take them back. My own ship, the Sweeper of the Waves, broke up as I landed at this coast or I wouldn't be stuck waiting here for another! But I agree with you, this mining is like living at the entrance to the Otherworld. Perhaps this is the entrance to their Otherworld, one of darkness and fire." Lir gazed at the rippling lake, his long arms dipping the paddle. "I know firsthand the dangers of traveling the great waters when the autumn stars portend storms. The rumor persists that Elcmar will travel on to the Continent, after it is deemed wise. To risk a long voyage after equinox is inconceivable. Yet I would myself risk it to leave here and return to my Seafarer coasts."

"Is there no way to be free of these Invaders?"

"Ach, sure. We'll see. There, did you ever see such a fine great fish as that!" Lir skillfully turned the hide coracle toward widening rings on the lake after a resounding splash. They sped over the lake's pristine blue under a clear sky.

Cian let matters rest for the time being. He did not understand "debt" and tucked away that word to ask about it later. He had seen the blazing hot pits and the brutal pressures of pouring without accident, that even a drop of copper wasted on the ground would result in punishment for the whole crew at a pit. He was glad that his friend Lir could enjoy being on the water on this sparkling day, even as he vowed to find out what Lir meant about the Invaders' snare.

Cian remembered the messages he brought from the Boyne. To deliver Cliodhna's message, he must approach the mining supervisor, Gebann, her father. Gebann was a solid block of a man and sure of himself. The older man's proud profile, a high forehead and straight prominent nose above a firm jawline, resembled the strong features of Tethra and more than a few of his own elders at the Boyne. Gebann's demeanor reminded Cian a great deal of Oghma. He took his time delivering her message to her father, waiting for the best moment.

The smith looked piercingly at Cian with deepset brown eyes as the young Starwatcher first approached him, Gebann returning from the mine along the pleasant but smoky lakeshore. He saluted Gebann in dialect. They stopped. Cian nodded at an isolated rowan tree where the late sunlight shone on bright berries remaining on its branches, and he told Gebann an old tale of the Starwatchers to see how this Seafarer would respond.

Gebann answered with his own ending, an ending similar in form and meaning to Cian's.

"We share this tale of the rowan, and long tradition between Starwatcher and Seafarer," Cian said. Gebann grunted in assent. He voiced Cliodhna's message to her father. "Cliodhna sends you her love, and that she is keeping well among those women living at the Boyne. She hopes to rejoin you soon."

"Among those women living, she says? What does she mean?"

Cian hesitated. "There was a woman murdered, a Starwatcher. We Starwatchers shall miss her." He added tersely, "A sharp knife killed the woman Sheela."

The two strolled toward the smoking pits and workers' huts.

Gebann had been impressed with what he had seen of Cian since the lad's arrival at the lake. Elcmar took him aside and implicated this Starwatcher in a slaying at the Boyne. But Gebann saw for himself that Cian kept apart, worked as he was told, and observed quiet ways. *What threat does young Cian pose to Elcmar?*

Then he wondered if this young man were too clever by half again, positioning himself to ask for marriage with Cliodhna, who had come of age and no man failed to notice. Gebann wanted only to have his daughter return safely to their homeland. He saw no future for her on this island. Since she had been taken to the Boyne camp, her personal safety among those reckless warriors kept him awake nights. That Invaders looked upon Seafarers—and her—as expendable, despite his own importance to mining copper here, he knew from bitter experience. Cian's remarks heightened his concern. So it was true, a young Starwatcher woman had been senselessly murdered at the Boyne on the sacred spring equinox. Cliodhna's message reassured him for now, but among Invaders she could never be truly safe.

The young Starwatcher maintained a respectful silence, waiting for the elder smith to speak again after hearing Cliodhna's words.

Gebann considered what he could use as leverage with Elcmar. He thought again with satisfaction: I am the only person on this island who knows where lies what Invaders want very much: tin to mix with copper for bronze. And, gold.

The ore of this Lake mine made a good slick copper that poured well, but he knew how much more valuable it would be given a local source of tin. The Invaders could then opt either to smelt the two metals together for export as bronze, or to export tin and copper in separate ingots. Booming trade could be made in the new metal, bronze, along northern coasts. Many communities had never seen this stronger alloy, bronze, but they had heard of it. Sources of tin to make bronze were very rare on the Continent. Tin had yet to be found in quantity over on the big eastern island, or anywhere along the channel and northwest corner of the Continent. Traders craved tin. The powerful trader Taranis craved tin.

Here on Eire, the Invaders had copper in good supply at this Lake mine but they had not found tin. Only a small amount of tin, one part tin to ten parts copper, was needed to produce bronze, with its superior qualities. If Elcmar wanted to make bronze here, his smiths had to re-smelt it from bronze scrap, costly and imported. *Elcmar searches Eire for gold when he should also be looking for tin. And he fancies himself a trader! Mighty Taranis will have his head...*

Gebann retraced his negotiations since Elcmar returned, newly made *ard ri*, to the Lake Of Many Hammers. That Elcmar insinuated himself into the penultimate position as chief warrior did not surprise Gebann, who had known the tall Elcmar since he scrounged and fought his way as an orphaned boy. Even then, the young Elcmar boldly hitched passages along the coasts with Seafarers while he assessed trading and trade routes with a fierce intelligence. Elcmar was aloof but disciplined, Gebann gave him that much; but the man operated according to only his own scruples and for his own ends.

The smith, feeling his age, wanted a definite end to his supervision of the mining here, when he would return to the sunkissed shores of his home to the south. He could almost smell and taste its luxuriance. He missed his wife, his second wife who raised Cliodhna after her mother died giving birth to her. That woman would by now be frantic that they had not returned, or worse: she might give up and throw herself from the cliffs thinking they had been lost at sea, as some women did.

It was probably better to be pressuring Elcmar than Connor, for the latter's attention span was short and that man showed a base and depraved nature. Gebann had guessed who in fact murdered the Starwatcher Sheela.

Disappointment stung him when the tattered currach arrived from the Boyne without his daughter. Elcmar blamed Connor for taking their seagoing boats north, stranding Cliodhna. *It may have been for want of a good boat. Oceangoing boats are not to be had here. Not unless another trader soon happens to put in at the coast below. Could I count on anyone here to assure Cliodhna's safe journey to me?* Gebann's steps dragged.

A heavy feeling slowed his legs and arms. He dreaded spending a winter in this colder, damper climate than on his own coast far to the south. He reflected on what might happen if he departed Eire, bolted for good. His people at the Lake mine would miss him sorely, for he led them in the ore extraction and ensured their spiritual well being on this island far from their home.

Their common beliefs made it easier for Starwatchers around the mining area to accept these Seafarers who came onto their island to dig ore. There had been no violence over the many seasons of miners coming and going from the Continent, and the Invaders did not fortify this mining camp against the natives. Over time, the local Starwatchers traded fish and beef to the miners; some even worked at felling trees for the smelting pits. We grow careless about our secrets here, Gebann thought, and he glanced at Cian.

"Is it curious about the metal making that you are?" he asked in the Invader tongue.

"You could say that," Cian said. "Curious about many things. Your land, that of the Seafarers. Your customs." He again replied using their old shared dialect.

Gebann told him, "My people have long marked the sun's seasons and the constellations, like Starwatchers. In fact, it would be hard to say which people influenced the other more. My own ancestors navigated all the way to this island. We tell the story and we still have the axes," he said with pride. "Seafarers exchanged starwatching knowledge for many generations, north along the great bay of the Continent and south along our Seafarer peninsula. In those times, the building of mounds and other ideas traveled slowly over the great water. Not like these boats full of Invaders with strange ideas." He checked the lad's expression.

Cian asked, "How did your people come to know Invaders?"

"Same as here. They arrived searching for the stones to make metal."

At the clipped answer, Cian wisely resumed his silence.

Gebann thought, these traders set up camps and they do not leave. Not if these marauding sons of dogs find out where ores lie waiting. Rather, where experienced men like me find metal ores for them. We Seafarers rue the day that Invaders counted us in their debt from trading and brought our miners—using our own mariners—here to Eire to toil for them. It is I, Gebann, who can see where solid earth has boiled up or been thrust and folded, and locate metal ores. It is I who select a deposit, then supervise pulling it from the earth. It is I who roast and smelt. I turn formless rock into shining metal.

He'd been stuck here more seasons than he bargained for. When he first arrived on the Starwatchers' island, he chuckled. The sun and stars told these people of Eire where to find anything. They used natural boundaries, the mountains and rivers within the four corners of its lush wilderness, to delimit one tribe's area from another. It would confound the Invaders no end trying to locate anything on this island.

He went prospecting when he could, periods when the Invaders left the mining camp and he had the run of things. He ventured all the way to Eire's east coast with a Starwatcher named Sreng guiding him there and back. He noted but a few stone carvings marking a valley's entrance or a high place but for those Gebann memorized the landmarks and place names.

He wanted to explore more in those eastern mountains, but he had Cliodhna to consider. When Cliodhna begged to come here with him from their peninsula, he should not have agreed to it. They'd made it here despite the mariners saying a female brought bad luck on water. A girl then, she matured rapidly, and now only his power as the master smith prevented any of the men taking her to husband.

A fine new boat arrived from the Continent carrying Connor's party including the jumped-up Elcmar. Gebann asked to leave Eire with his daughter but Connor ignored his request and made sure Gebann had no boat to take them. Connor made him search the rugged southwest mountains with them for gold, without success. That at least kept those two away from Cliodhna.

Then those two rascals left the Lake of Many Hammers on a misguided quest for gold at the Boyne. Connor now wandered farther north seeking gold. Gebann wished Connor all the luck that man deserved. And still Elcmar would keep him at the Lake mines, holding Cliodhna hostage at the Boyne for good measure, but to no avail.

Gebann grunted. *I have seen it in swift mountain streams, sun metal in shining chunks. There is gold on this, the Starwatchers' island.* He hid well the gold he found on Eire, small flat ingots disguised by a thin coating of copper, his own idea. Only another smith would know those were too heavy to be copper. Gebann kept those stashed for transport home with him. That gold could solve his own tribe's problems with these traders. His people would be free again.

Elcmar arrives without Cliodhna, relishing his power over me. At least he forced a different woman to marry him, that's small comfort. Gebann fumed, wondering what his escape plan must be.

The mariner Lir predicted a difficult winter and offered to get them back to the Continent. Lir foretold that the spring dust storm with drought and unseasonable cold threatened the food supply in these isles, and it would be best to get on a boat for home while they could. With every sunrise, the chance of any vessel landing from the Continent shrank. They might be trapped here.

Gebann looked at the young Starwatcher keeping pace, a big fellow, and had him repeat Cliodhna's message. "I appreciate your care in this. Take a drink with me and we'll toast her using her cups. She made pottery here."

"Few women at the mine," said Cian, adding, "She makes pots at the Boyne also."

"I should never have brought her across the sea." The smith rubbed his face, frustrated.

The two men seated themselves upwind from a smelting pit, able to have its warmth but evading its fumes. Gebann favored light mead made with fermented grains and honey, and had the same brought for

Cian. Miners, grimy and stooped, returned in the gathering dusk to the settlement huts beyond. As Gebann greeted passing men by name, Cian related messages to certain weary miners.

Gebann asked if the cloud of dust covered the Boyne at the past spring, and they talked about its aftermath, the brilliant sunsets and stunted growth. When he asked about the Starwatcher woman who married Elcmar, it was the lad's turn to give clipped answers. Gebann glanced over at the smelting activity. "We could sit farther away from the smoke. I see it doesn't agree with you."

Not knowing if he might have private access to the great smith again, Cian risked asking questions. He asked first about the stone molds he'd seen used to pour copper axeheads and simple tools.

"You know that I carve in stone. The molds for the axes—how are those made?"

Gebann sat back, big hands splayed on his knees, and eyed Cian. This was probing of secrets, the deep secrets of the metals known by very few in all the world. *Information that this Starwatcher is not privileged to have. Not just yet. But the time may come. This quiet lad's got the fire in him, as sure as the sun will rise again.* Perhaps this Cian had a fight coming; let it be with Elcmar.

The smith reached for an axe mold, its flat hollow for the axe carved into solid rock. His stocky forefinger jabbed at the smooth, symmetrical outline for the axehead. "See that? We trace the shape of a folded leaf onto stone, that way the axe is exactly the same along both halves east to west. You would know how to do it yourself, lad. Now heft this axe in your hand. It's heavy for the size, isn't it?"

Cian nodded as Gebann gave him a new copper axehead to hold.

"We can adjust the axe size with different molds. The crucible holds what a man is capable of pouring while the metal is hot. Once the mold is filled, we quickly lay on the cover." He handed Cian the mold cover, flat on both sides, then Cian noticed slight tunnels routed into its ends.

"Those holes let out impure spirits from the hot copper that could flaw the axehead. The copper cools, and then the axehead falls right out. If you're lucky, you can make a hundred axeheads before the mold receptacle breaks." Gebann did not mention that a good smith would preheat the stone mold for a better casting of the copper so that it required less forging and hammering on its release from the mold.

He did add that itinerant brokers carried these molds and a quantity of copper ingots on the Continent. "The brokers travel and pour an axe on site. That's much easier than having only one location to which all traders must come for a copper axehead."

Before Cian could ask why the Boyne elders had not received copper axes as gifts, they heard footfalls.

"Very interesting, I ought to have myself a lesson."

Both men stood quickly at Elcmar's assertive voice as he strode out of the darkness.

"Don't get up, Gebann, I could use a chat. You sit also, quiet one, and learn some more."

Cian could keep a stony face as well as Elcmar and did not react to the slur. He gave up his seat for the *ard ri* and got himself another oak stump, of which there was no shortage at the charcoal pits.

"So what shall we talk about? You're wanting to go home, is it, Gebann?"

Gebann nodded and looked eager to hear more.

"We'll all be leaving soon." Elcmar didn't disclose where they would be going.

Gebann frowned. Then he asked, "Did you like the earrings I sent for your bride?"

Elcmar had demanded a pair of gold earrings sent to him at the Boyne for his bride, and that Cliodhna must deliver them. Gebann swiftly sent along earrings already fashioned by Creidhne from placer gold on the Seafarer peninsula, not that there would be a visible difference in any gold. The speed at which Gebann produced the requested earrings left no doubt that the gold had not been found on Eire. Creidhne styled earrings as a thin disc, with lines dividing it in a central quatrefoil and delicate etching around its circumference. Another such disc made by Creidhne had been lost, and if anyone had found it that lucky person was not telling. Gebann had hoped that the showy discs dispatched to Elcmar would ensure his release with Cliodhna from his duties at the Lake mine. They dared not refuse Elcmar. Now he had her trapped.

"The earrings were grand. Just like a pair from the Continent." Elcmar stared at Cian.

Cian wondered if he were being sent to the Continent. That had seemed a good idea, not long ago. He wanted to learn all that he could of these Invaders, their trading and the metals. Such a voyage would confer great prestige on him. His throat tightened at the thought that the unwieldy currach on which they arrived might attempt a winter voyage. For a fleeting moment, he remembered the starchambers, the texture of rock under his hands and the simplicity of carving all day in one blessed spot by the river. But he had left all that behind after heated discussion with the Dagda and his elders. His life lay before him in blank now and he groped to find the tools for shaping it. He must not allow his head to spin nor let Elcmar see or feel any change from him. Cian sat upright and unmoving next to the *ard ri*, even as sweat broke out under his tunic and rolled down his back.

"Lir will command the boat. That gives your ocean journey a better than even chance," Elcmar added.

Cian took a sip of his drink. It tasted of ashes.

The *ard ri* carried a new bow, shorter and curved. Cian saw that this curved bow was made of yew fused neatly with another wood along its length. A quiver of new arrows hung over his left shoulder, and Elcmar wore showy red jasper wristguards on plaited leather cords. A copper dagger with a carved bone handle shone at his waist.

Gebann spoke up. "Why could Cliodhna not return to the Seafarer peninsula with me before the storms?"

Elcmar briskly replied, "Cliodhna shall spend the winter where she is. Do you get my drift, Gebann? If you go overseas for a winter visit then you must come back here to stay for another six moons at least. We'll see then to increasing the copper produced here, and finding gold.

"Three years in a row of bad harvests like this harvest, here and on the Continent, would bring disaster. But that is what Bresal reads in the omens. We may need copper just to eat."

Cian followed most of this dialogue but not all. It sounded like talking in circles, as always with Invader talk. Schemes for things far away, and omens one could not see.

Gebann understood from Elcmar's new finery: a trader boat had arrived. He'd be forced to leave on it without his daughter. He tried to digest the latest disappointment.

I must send someone to the Boyne camp. He eyed the Starwatcher. Can this lad be trusted? Sure, he isn't so much younger than your man Elcmar, maybe younger by six transits of the sun. He took a long drink, then belched irritably. *Cian appears to be fully as intelligent as the Invaders' new ard ri, and not so full of himself. Too inquisitive for his own good here at the copper mine. We'll see if Elcmar means to banish him to the Continent. Or if Cian can slip back to the Boyne.*

The time had come, he must rescue Cliodhna. The harvest equinox heralded cold and storms. He could do little if trapped here through winter.

Gebann went off to find Creidhne and Lein, for in his absence the two younger smiths would take charge at the Lake Of Many Hammers to wrest more copper from the earth.

Night of the Dead

That harvest brought the worst yield in living memory, after lingering dust blocked light needed for crops. The sun hastened toward the autumn equinox above the river plain the Invaders had begun to call *Bru na Boinne*.

Boann needed to speak with her elders; they would know how to survive the coming winter. She looked for excuses to be outside of the dingy hall, with its rows of cruel weapons and clusters of people waiting to consult Bresal while Elcmar was away. She sought out Cliodhna, the potter Cian had introduced, whom she had seen working at an open kiln.

There she found Cliodhna making drinking cups. Boann stood watching at her side as the potter started with a small lump of clay that she kneaded into a flat circle on her palm. Her nimble hands turned and pinched the circle up to produce thinwalled, uniform cups in the shape of a spring flower. Each cup she smoothed and set aside without decoration.

The potter motioned Boann to be seated, inviting her to work the clay herself.

By adding tiny amounts of water while pinching and turning the clay, Boann found she could work it up from the palm of her hand. She felt good to be doing something productive though she had no potter's skills.

"I fear you'll have to redo my efforts."

At that Cliodhna smiled.

Boann chose her next words with care. "Starwatchers decorate our pots with great complexity. Perhaps this is because we constantly watch the heavens. We do admire rare pots from over the ocean. We value those pots, for they teach our potters new ways. Starwatchers hold knowledge from other shores in high regard."

Coals sizzled in the kiln. Cliodhna replied to her using the old dialect that Boann might understand. "At first, I had problems understanding the clay of your island, how it should be worked, what could be added to it. Other material, ground stone, or bone, must often be added to temper the clay or it will slump during firing or later the pot cracks. But add too much foreign material and that ruins the clay." Cliodhna looked at Boann's hands forming the clay cup.

Boann nodded, a smile playing on her lips. "It can be difficult to learn foreign ways, and so many all at once."

"You are doing well among these strangers while Elcmar journeys in the south. I see that you have not cracked or crumbled."

Encouraged, Boann described her people's richly decorated pots, but in her halting use of the Invader language. When Boann offered to give her pots from her village as a gift, Cliodhna leaned forward over their work.

"Be careful what you bring into this camp." She leaned back, smiling.

Boann paused in turning her circle of clay in her palm. "What do you mean?" She reverted to the Starwatcher tongue.

"They value only pots made in their Invader style."

That puzzled Boann. A Starwatcher artisan could freely fashion pottery, or a stone axe or basket, as they wished, as a medium of expression. How could any pot be special if it must look just like the next pot? To Cliodhna she said, "Is the ritual more difficult to make these intruder pots?"

"They care little about how the pot is actually made, and told me not to waste time decorating their flat beakers. To them, a pot means status. Only warriors can own the tall drinking cups, one way these Invaders show off."

Boann nodded slowly. She'd seen the Invader etiquette between free persons and those called slaves. Slaves were not allowed to wear daggers, awls, or jewelry. Metal items in particular were forbidden to slaves. Bresal spoke of a *geis*, a ban on long knives for any hand but a warrior's. No slave dared to touch the knives hanging in the great hall. Invaders shunned most of the work tools handled by their slaves, and treated ordinary tasks as beneath them. Frequent quarrels over assigning work ended up before Bresal, with varying results. It was clear this camp had too few slaves to cater to warriors who refused to grow crops or herd animals.

She pointed to a large cooking vessel, straight-sided with a flat bottom. "But why are their pots like this?"

Cliodhna shrugged. "The old rounded pots represent eating while seated around the hearth. A roundbottomed pot can be set on soft earth, or in a pot hole, but it will not rest on a table. For the warriors' table, they demand flat bottomed pots and cups, many vessels and made quickly. They care little if I decorate the surface with cords, or grooved designs."

She began to show Boann the coiling technique used to form an Invader pot, then her posture abruptly changed to a submissive curl over her work. Boann's eyes rose to see that Maedb approached with companions.

The woman Maedb sniffed as she passed them, "I guess a quiet one only talks to slaves while her husband is far away." Maedb's entourage filed by, eyeing Boann as she sat with Cliodhna at the potting hearth.

Boann saw herself as they would see her, kneeling in dust and ashes, hands smeared with clay. She ignored their reproach and could have laughed but held it back.

"That woman is your enemy," said Cliodhna. "Beware."

"What will she do?" came Boann's urgent whisper.

"That one! What wouldn't Maedb do, there's the question." Cliodhna rolled clay between her palms, and whispered back, "Do not discuss anything known by your people with her. Already she blames the Starwatchers for the bad harvest."

Boann looked closely at Cliodhna. She had the stature and coloring of people from far in the south, whom the elders spoke highly of in old stories. She admired her wavy black hair, wide brown doe's eyes, and skin like autumn grasses; slim-hipped but strong body, and charming smile like Sheela's. As the working potter for this camp she should be held in great esteem, yet Maedb and others treated her badly, as badly as they treated their slaves.

"You come from a land to the south?"

"My people live far south where the Continent curves into a large peninsula, many times larger than your island. I come from an important settlement overlooking the ocean." Cliodhna spoke proudly. "We are Seafarers! For generations we have fished and we have traveled between coastal peoples." Her expression darkened. "Some of us labor on Eire now, in the southwest at the copper mine. My father, the smith Gebann, waits there for me to return. At the summer solstice, Elcmar ordered me brought from the Invader mining camp, here to this river plain. I carried the gold earrings Elcmar gave you, from my father. That Invader boat left with Connor. I have had to remain in this camp." She bent close and lowered her voice. "My people carve in stone also, star signs and other symbols. I understand many of your star signs.

"Invaders oppose the star knowledge, they fear it. You must not reveal what you know of the stars' movements to any Invader, not to Bresal or even Elcmar. Let them think Starwatchers worship the sun. Your people are in great danger."

"But why? And how many sunrises is it to reach the mining camp by boat?" Elcmar told her he would return at winter solstice, or as he said it using his fingers, the moon after three moons passed. "Cliodhna, what news reaches you from your father? Do you know if the Starwatcher Cian arrived at the mining place?"

Cliodhna's averted face told Boann that more intruder women were approaching them. She bowed the upper half of her body as Boann stood.

There and then Boann insisted with her guardians that she go at last to gather herbs and late fruits outside the gates. These women could follow or stay inside their walls, she told them.

Turning from the potter's hearth, she alone distinctly heard the lovely young Seafarer say, "Take care for your baby."

She felt a rush of gratitude for Cliodhna's perceptiveness and warmth. For Boann knew that she was both shunned and minutely scrutinized by the intruders, as first wife to Elcmar. Their marriage still caused the camp tongues to wag. Hard feelings remained against her from those who favored Connor. The hostile Maedb treated Boann as an outsider in her own land, for reasons she did not yet understand.

It further annoyed some, that Elcmar absented himself from the Boyne. The Invaders wanted Elcmar's contest with Connor to find gold on the island. But to leave Bresal in charge at the camp! Intrigues simmered among the Invaders, some saying they should send for Connor before Bresal's neglect ruined them altogether.

She had little protection with Elcmar away. If the warriors chose another champion, what would become of her?

Lacking battles to wage, as the days grew shorter the idle warriors harassed Starwatchers as they tried to go about routine tasks and attend to their mounds. Warriors raided cattle, then released it to the Starwatchers, then caught the animals again for sport. Bresal did little to intervene. So far her marriage to Elcmar had not improved relations between the two groups.

Talking with Cliodhna confirmed that the intruders derided her ways, those of the "quiet ones", as inferior. She must be vigilant or she would find herself caged like a bird inside the great hall, and of little help to her Starwatchers. She met with Cliodhna again, and often. Boann needed a friend inside the camp, for she was indeed pregnant.

The nausea subsided and her vigor returned. She must do something useful. She could learn how the Invader laws would treat this child, ascertain her status and her child's.

She approached Bresal with a show of deference to him. "I desire to understand my duties here. As the wife of the champion."

Bresal puffed, shifting a wide etched copper bracelet. "It's happy I am that you seek my advice. Very wise of you."

Effusive, he began by explaining her status. "The champion and warriors hold the top, then artisans and musicians, then herders. Slaves have no status, they are property. Invaders have formalized all this into rules, our laws. Mind you, I spent a great amount of time memorizing rules and rituals, to be sure. So it I who assist Elcmar as *ard ri*, to dispense the laws."

"And women?" she asked him, her manner casual.

"Women can, by right of their birth or by a good marriage, belong to any of the upper orders. You have been fortunate to marry this *ard ri*, Elcmar, who undertook the full ceremony with the white horse," he simpered. "Under our laws, as first wife you also enjoy more status than a subsequent, additional wife."

"What says your law about a woman having multiple husbands?"

Bresal did not seem to follow her question. "The child inherits from the father," he answered as he dipped a finger into shaved bits of mushroom.

While affecting an interest in his mushrooms, she questioned the shaman on their complicated laws. He enjoyed delivering pompous speeches while nibbling this or that for a divination. Boann abstained from ingesting anything Bresal offered, his herbal lore serving only as her pretext to have more audiences with him.

He preened and lectured, satisfied apparently to believe that she listened in awe of his considerable magic. Bresal was only too glad to indulge himself into trances while Boann questioned him at length on the Invader laws of kinship, property, and inheritance.

Boann spent what time she could in Cliodhna's company. They each waited for word from the Lake mine. The moon waned, and then it was new moon again and dark by night. She urged Cliodhna to accompany her outside the palisaded camp to the mounds. Bresal had let it slip that as an artisan, Cliodhna was not a slave. Boann treated her as her companion and they became bold enough to leave the camp together, suspecting that the sentry would report all to Bresal.

Toward sunset on the equinox, the two women attended an observance of the autumn sky at the mounds. The Dagda spoke, recalling Sheela of the spirits and the prior spring equinox. Tadhg muttered an oath from among the scouts. Unruffled, the Dagda reminded the astronomers of their important task of detecting the Northshift.

Boann stepped forward with the astronomers to mark the equinox constellation's position above the old stele that stood near Dowth. They sighted on the well-known figure of the Swan, its four stars clearly winging against the deep night sky. Swans returned with autumn to the sheltering Boyne marshes. The Starwatchers all had enjoyed a good meal of roast swan, and would be drying the extra meat for winter. Airmid gave Boann a feathered cloak of swan skins, saying, "I knew you would be here with us."

Thanks to this warm cloak, she felt the chill air only a little as she carefully aligned the position of the Swan with the ancient notch on the stele. Daire assisted, standing to one side with younger apprentices to show them exactly what Boann and the Dagda were doing. He held the glowing tip of an apple rod pulled out from a covered fire many steps away. This ember enabled him to point at stars for the others without ruining their night vision.

It pleased Boann that Daire immersed himself in their dilemma of the shifting constellations. He had traveled from Tethra's village to the Boyne to study and already he had learned a great deal at their newer and larger mounds, and from the richly carved stones.

The Dagda confided, "Daire is quick to connect what he sees. He reasons well in the abstract—and without my having to explain much. Rather like Cian."

She had not heard Cian's name aloud for some time. What did the Dagda know of their attachment? His face unreadable, he continued.

"For example, Daire noticed that unlike Carrowkeel's layout, our mounds stand well apart from our dwellings, from cooking fires and torchlight." About heavy smoke from the Invader camp, the Dagda said only, "On this sunset our luck holds. No smoke drifts here."

Aware that she had been unable to stop the Invaders' rude ways from encroaching on her people, Boann said, "The skies shall clear for us," as much to convince herself as him.

He nodded. "We understand the difficulties of your position. Mind yourself and the child you carry. You are what is most important to us."

One by one, the apprentices stood with Boann at the old marker stele to help judge the distance the Swan constellation moved. She laid each one's polished bone strip over another at the stele. Many did not see the minute difference from the preceding equinox. Daire stepped forward with his bone marker strip and did the same.

The astronomers conferred after the sighting. They could agree on the direction of the shift, but not its size. Some said the Northshift would be complete in another twenty autumns, and some said, in one hundred autumns.

Boann held up a collection of bone strips holding scores of notches. "Daire amassed these markers from different elders and studied them. Starwatchers have been checking the equinox constellation for generations. Daire and I," and she gestured to include him, "compared the observing sticks, those made here and at older stones. We estimate that over forty sun cycles or so—roughly, the life span for most of us—the shift of the autumn constellation equals the width of the full moon. We know the ages of our mounds. Here at the Boyne, the constellation has moved the width of several full moons. At the oldest stones it has moved beyond the stone's shoulder."

Under a torch held by Daire, they compared the markers side by side, oldest to newest, inciting comment and questions.

"How can we know if the change is the same amount from equinox to equinox?" asked a woman, a visitor from Fourknocks.

"Again, we know the generation of each mound. Based on the differences between markers, the change in position looks to be a constant. Going forward our astronomers can verify this using the total shift over five suns, and then ten, and then twenty suns. Our children will verify that the amount is a constant."

On that night, the astronomers came closer to understanding the Northshift.

The Dagda retold the ancient story, their chant about choosing the next constellation. "Our ancestors lived in a different land when they observed the shift," he reminded them. "They used the stars to reach this island. Their generations prospered down to us, the keepers of their knowledge. We will find a way to deal with the intruders and reclaim the future."

Their troubles with Invaders seemed distant as the Starwatchers lit their signal bonfire and celebrated the equinox under the river of stars.

After that equinox, Boann openly left the camp with Cliodhna during sun's light. The two gathered roots and nuts before heavy frosts would spoil those, and dry moss and bark for medicines and kindling; and brought those to share with her village.

Another full moon waxed and waned above the Boyne. Unnatural cold gripped the island and no one knew when it might end. Still no message came from the Lake mine, from Elcmar.

Maedb continued to drop in on Boann in the great hall. She gave out, from a bench by the warm fire, that neither Connor nor Elcmar had found gold on this island, and how very cold and wet was Eire's weather. Boann finally responded, "Yes. It must be very cold for the men, those men who are working out in the cold. But sure, faraway hills are greener." Two slaves working close by turned away to hide their laughter.

"You must cease wandering outside this camp in your condition. Bresal agrees with me. Or, he says I could accompany you." Maedb flashed a triumphant grin.

A rumor began circulating in the camp that Elcmar had gone to the Continent. In a toast overflowing with malice, Maedb wished for his safety on the high seas. Boann only touched her lips to her cup then put it down, having heard that Maedb used strong poisons. Just when she thought she might understand the Invaders, their actions confused her again. She could see no reason for Elcmar to visit the southwest, much less undertake the killing voyage to far shores. And where was Cian?

Will this child have any father, Boann wondered, but in Bresal's fogged eyes she could read nothing.

On the sunrise that brought the Invader feast called the Night of the Dead, Boann woke feeling the child lying dormant, waiting. The intruders' holiday had little importance to her. Instead she looked forward to a starwatch on this crossquarter, midway between autumn equinox and the coming winter solstice. It gave her another chance to detect the elusive Northshift. Excited, she ate little on waking and left the hall to seek out Cliodhna.

"At sunset the Starwatchers have an important observation."

Cliodhna exclaimed, eyes wide, "But this sunset begins a time of feasting for these intruders. It is their Night of the Dead!"

"How to get out of the camp and to the mounds, without a guard or chattering intruder women following?" Boann wondered aloud. "I have my liberties—if anyone tries to stop me.

"Cliodhna, put aside your pottery making if you would. We shall wrap up foodstuffs, some hazelnuts, dried apples and herbs, to bring as gifts to Oghma. If you could come out with me that ought to appease Bresal."

It did not take Boann long to find Bresal, surrounded by an entourage at the cooking pits. He had commandeered a cooking trough and supervised as a quantity of imported cloth was dyed a rare blue, fussing with his male slave over whether it was vivid enough and evenly dyed throughout its length. The women slaves who normally did the cloth dyeing stood back in disapproval: men should never be allowed near the dyeing process as that would bring bad luck. Also the dye had spoiled that *fulacht fiadh*.

Bresal looked up and nudged his slave. "Wonder how she's keeping, with her man away? A woman on her own!" The shaman leered. "If they are all breeders, we won't have to bring in many women here a'tall."

Boann heard all this and saw at once that he was in rare form. "Good sun to you, Bresal. I'm after having my bath and breaking the fast. I shall be joining my father Oghma, the Dagda, and others to observe the sun set. With your consent, Cliodhna shall accompany me."

Bresal swayed indecisively over the dripping cloth, as if not sure why tonight's sunset would be so important. "Should Elcmar's wife be absent as we begin celebrating the Night of the Dead?" His face struggled to evaluate all the portents if she were away and specifically any negative results for him.

To her he inclined his round head. "Are you aware of our feast tonight?" he asked.

"I am not familiar with this Invader custom. Please explain more to me if you would." She waited for Bresal to go off on a tangent and he promptly did so.

"The Night of the Dead is a major feast, the beginning of the new year for us Invaders. It might have significance for the quiet ones as well." Boann stiffened at his using that term quiet ones for her people but he babbled on, heedless.

Bresal described the presence of the dead walking among the living. Huge fires would be lit so that the spirits could see and thus not disturb the living. He detailed how he selected the animals to be slain and how he would publicly examine their entrails in order to predict the coming crops and success at various endeavors. Bresal ended with a flourish. "Your presence is highly necessary for all this as the *ard ri's* wife, and notably so in Elcmar's absence." He looked at her extended midsection and up to catch her eye. "We can make you a new tunic but not in this blue fabric, I'm afraid. That color is reserved to shamans, and to Elcmar. That is, if Elcmar were here with us. Alive, to be sure. For this feast." He hicupped and swayed again.

"I quite understand. Thank you, Bresal. Whatever color would suit me."

She diverted Muirgen with an errand and when the girl had left the hall, Boann filled a leather pouch with a few belongings. She found Cliodhna waiting at her pottery hearth, lit as if the potter would be returning. As they started toward the gate, Boann suggested that Cliodhna bring her clothing and personal articles, "just in case we are delayed." Cliodhna left, quickly bundled her things, then returned to Boann. They moved between the plank huts and passed unnoticed by a sentry dulled by cold and the prior evening's drinking.

Once underway through the forest, Boann spoke openly to Cliodhna. "Night of the Dead! Already most of the slaves are frightened out of their wits from talk of spirits walking among them, great bonfires or not. These slaves have enough to fear from the living." She could only imagine the mayhem that would occur upon poor animals. She had seen enough of the murky approach taken by Bresal and his followers.

Invaders divided the sun's seasons into only three instead of four, and for them this night marked the beginning of the new year. The shaman Bresal hinted to her that he could halt the sun. He dared to say that Invader ships brought the great dust that ruined the past growing season. He seemed to have little idea of either the sun's or the moon's movements. She had not risked inquiring whether he knew about the erratic planets, or had names for constellations. She found less and less to discuss with Bresal despite his cloying attention.

Free of the camp's environs, her boldness grew. Maedb, she wanted nowhere near her labor pains nor this child. It would be far safer for this baby to be born in the fresh air of her own village, among her own people. She need not return to the intruders' stronghold for their feast, and she decided not to return to the Invader walls until after this child was born. *Elcmar cannot hold me inside their camp, it is part of our marriage contract that my starwatching shall continue!*

Elcmar's offer of protection with their marriage rang hollow. For a moment, Boann recalled Sheela's brutal murder. She told the surprised Cliodhna, "Stay with me in the village. The shorter days and cold will keep the warriors penned into the intruder camp until spring and with little to do. You need safeguarding from them."

Boann stayed on with Oghma at the Starwatcher village and they sheltered the young Cliodhna. In the lunate following the Night of the Dead it rained frequently, more rain than usual. What food remained in the fields for late harvest, soon went bad in the damp. The Starwatchers gathered and counted their animals. Their remaining livestock would need to be fed over the winter and not be consumed. Oghma and the elders worried that game would become scarce with more people living along the Boyne. "If these intruders will scavenge for their food, must they kill everything in the forest closest to our village?"

While Airmid was entertaining Cliodhna, away, Boann had a private audience with the elders in the plain comfort of Oghma's dwelling. "No doubt this weather stops the warriors from fetching me back with Cliodhna," she told them. The elders confirmed the two women should remain in the village. Pikes and stone axes awaited the Invaders if they came looking.

Cliodhna made a temporary outdoor hearth for firing pottery, but it sputtered and lay cold, the wood too wet for building up coals. "The dirty smoke for making metal in the intruder camp rises no more. We hear their hoop drums and songs, perhaps louder now? I am grateful to you and Oghma for sheltering me."

They spent increasing amounts of time indoors with Airmid and others, as numbing gales swept in from the surrounding ocean. The women taught Cliodhna the intricate knots tied by Sheela of the Spirits to form garments and shawls.

Cliodhna in turn offered to show the Starwatcher women how to use a loom for weaving. "I wish that I had thought to bring linen fiber for weaving, but we can substitute hemp."

Boann smiled. "Oh, I'm afraid the smell and mess of preparing hemp won't have much appeal here. But I'll help you with that. Our women do want to learn the new weaving."

Oghma and Tadhg hastily built a bark shed away from the village, down from the prevailing winds, where the mass of hemp fiber was put to soak and dry. Then, tempted by making larger textiles than they had previously been able to weave, all the women spun thread to give the new loom a try. Eventually they produced a lumpy but serviceable length of cloth using Cliodhna's loom. As pleased as the women were, they knew it would be many lunates before more fibers could be harvested and spun for weaving, and they carefully stored the new cloth.

Boann and Cliodhna looked at the clouds blown about in the harsh grey skies. Cliodhna sighed. "My father Gebann and I long to the return to the Continent, to our people."

"The season of storms has arrived. Elcmar sends no boat here for you. He would keep you hostage at the Boyne."

The village faced a hard winter and would be competing for food with the warrior camp. The elders confided to Boann that the disastrous weather affected all of Eire's crops and no doubt ravaged crops on far shores. There was little chance that any Starwatcher tribe could help oust the Invaders from the Boyne.

Boann thought, this new weaving loom arrives even as the Starwatchers' lives unravel beside our great mounds. She crossed her arms, defending the life in her swelling body.

It was then they made the sun stand still
to the end of nine months—strange the tale—
warming the noble ether
in the roof of the perfect firmament.
From: *Metrical Dindshenchas*

Month of Two Moons

DUST CONTINUED TO smudge and distort the skies. Two of the nocturnal orbs shot past on irregular paths, ignoring the stars and moon. Then on a rare clear dawn the astronomers observed the glowing, reddish planet rising up before the sun, an event that they understood.

The Invaders saw the eerie dawn also and it caused panic in that camp. Bresal and his helpers set to work sacrificing swans, rather than watching the skies or asking the Starwatchers about the angry red planet. "It's angry because you've let the *ard ri's* wife and the woman Cliodhna escape," Maedb scolded Bresal.

The Starwatchers prepared for their solstice ceremony that would occur in less than one lunate. Boann used this solstice event, in which the moon's arc would play a special part, to record with Daire the lunar rising on the horizon each night. He knew that the moon rose on the horizon where the sun would rise in six months. Daire followed the moon's path overhead and found the nodes, where the moon crosses the sun's daylight path twice as the moon waxes and wanes during one lunation.

Daire tracked the moon and the Dagda confirmed with him that the moon reliably spends half its time above the sun's path and half below. "You are closer to understanding the mysteries," and he smiled approval at Daire. As the moon phased into the quarter preceding the solstice, Tethra and more astronomers from other villages joined them. The air in the village vibrated with purpose and anticipation.

Falling stars streaked silver through the dark above. Boann mentioned it at a meal, that this star shower occurred every winter while the sun approached its standstill.

Cliodhna shook her head, amazed. "How can you keep track of it all?" she asked. "I would enjoy attending a solstice watch with you. My father will be most interested to hear about the great Boyne solstice."

When the two arrived, the Dagda showed Cliodhna what the astronomers were doing. "For generations, Starwatchers observed the moving light. Our ancestors were building small passage mounds long before we attempted to direct sunlight into a narrow passage. After many generations we engineered the great mounds by this river.

"That central mound, that one admits sunlight only at winter solstice. Our builders calculated the angles and where to place the passage to the inner chamber," and swept his arm along the clearing to show Cliodhna. "During the solstice the directed sunlight enters the passage for a brief period each dawning, on around ten sunrises. Perhaps future generations can build a monument that captures only the exact solstice sunrise. And our weather does not always cooperate! But you see that our astronomers relish their tasks.

"The small change in the sun's rising position when it slows at the solstices is hard to observe reliably with just the unaided eye," and the Dagda energetically lifted her hand to show her. "The variation from one sunrise to the next around the solstices is a sliver, it is no more than the tip of your fingernail."

"How do your astronomers keep from looking into the sun?" Cliodhna asked. "My Seafarers have this difficulty as well, in tracking the sun above the great waters."

The Dagda nodded. "To find the point of sunrise, without staring into the sun, we made ever more precise refinements in how we track it on the horizon. Watch that man, he is going to take a careful stance at that standing stone, to sight beyond it to a distinct point in the landscape."

Cliodhna watched. Round balls in different stones' colors, made of worked granite and chalk, were used to position the engineer at the stele and the other astronomers so that they were standing exactly at the proper place. "So slight is the change at solstice that as we near the actual event, only one astronomer takes all the sightings. Using different observers could affect reliability of the measurement."

An apprentice lay on the ground holding the engineer's heels firmly in place during the delicate observation. When the sun's first rays appeared and created shadows, a chant started: the astronomers were counting in a steady rhythm. Some held stones tied to cords and they let the stones fall to the ground, and others pounded pegs along the cord's shadow line. When the counting ended, apprentices cut notches on lengths of bone. The Starwatchers conferred with the engineer at the standing stone. It was Daire who showed her, on a strip of bone, a tiny space for how far the sun had moved south from the prior sunrise, and a large space for how far it had moved since equinox.

"My father would understand these things far better than I, Dagda," Cliodhna said.

"You may tell him what you saw here but in these dangerous times, tell no one else," the Dagda said.

She repeated solemnly, "No one."

He stood still as a standing stone himself, or like a gnarled tree tipped with white in the winter morning, thinking. The Dagda asked her, "In this season on your peninsula, the Seafarers' home, have you more daylight than we have here?"

"We have, yes. But our light shortens in winter as it does here in northern waters."

"I thought so," he said. Cliodhna's gaze turned to where his blue eyes like infinite sky looked south. "Starwatching links our people. I would have liked to meet your father and your Seafarers and study your skies. But I am too old for that journey. —Mind yourself on these new boats, for the ocean remains unchanged."

"What do you mean, Dagda?"

"Patience, fair Cliodhna. You know that the fickle seas hold more peril in winter."

Cliodhna and Boann passed Daire on their way back to the village after the dawn sighting. He sat on the spiraled entrance boulder at the central mound, working bone using a flint awl and scraper.

Boann indicated the mound entrance to her. "Our engineers placed the opening to the southeast, to align with the winter sun. On this solstice the sun and the full moon shall each enter its long passage. If the weather favors us, that is."

Daire made a gallant bow to them but hid his work behind his back.

Cliodhna reached out to touch the necklace of varied beads that swung from his neck. He explained to her that from his apprentice time with the Dagda he would have the memento of this marked leather cord. It held small stone beads of different colors, knotted into place. "These can be used to remember the sightings I made at the Boyne starchambers. All the apprentices have beads strung on a leather cord. The older astronomers' beaded cords are long enough for them to use as belts, from their many observations."

She admired the beaded necklace, an object showing his personal achievement and study. "May I have this?" Cliodhna said in jest.

"Oh, no! I—well, I couldn't—" The request and her dimples muddled his young head.

Boann teased him. "What is it you're holding behind yourself?

May we see?" She tried to reach around him but her protruding middle made that impossible and they all laughed.

The two women bribed him, they said, with hazelnuts and smoked salmon for him to eat, so he would show them what he was carving. In his spare time, he told them blushing, he crafted a new set of moon markers in cattle bone for a special friend. Daire carried his own set of observing sticks, marked with one moon width up to seven moon widths. This simple device aided him to measure the visual distance between points of interest in the stars, and to follow the moon through the night skies. When Boann and Cliodhna guessed which young girl was his special friend, he blushed again but remained at his work.

Amused, Boann made her way with Cliodhna back to the stone dwelling they shared with Oghma. The child she carried kicked and rolled low and heavy inside her, ready. She patted the defined mound, sure that this child was a boy and feisty at that.

"How good it is that Daire studies with us, despite the troubles here with the intruders. His spirit is free."

"He has a hungry mind, like Cian," said Cliodhna without guile. She had assured Boann that Cian behaved like a friend to her in the camp and she with him; nothing more.

Boann shivered, anticipating when Elcmar and the men he had taken away with him might return, and with them Cian. She didn't miss Elcmar, nor living in his camp. Here her child could be born in safety away from Maedb and Bresal. She wouldn't worry beyond the coming birth and Elcmar's return.

As light faded in the west, a messenger arrived for Cliodhna. A Starwatcher named Sreng, saying he traveled all the way from the southwest, appeared at their door with a Boyne scout who then slipped away. They all sat at the hearth, where Sreng surprised them with items carried under his sheepskin cloak.

Oghma exclaimed as Sreng handed him an axehead, "The shadow moon metal, such a ruddy color it has! And it is heavier than stone."

Sreng told him, "This axe was made far to the south at the Lake of Many Hammers," and he described the hole in the earth there being plundered for copper. Cliodhna nodded as he talked. Sreng showed Oghma how to keep the copper axe tucked away in an oiled skin until it might be mounted on a handle and used. Then Sreng gave the women thin copper armlets. Cliodhna saw the bracelets had the distinctive marks of Gebann and put hers on with a smile, her eyes shining.

Their visitor had traveled long and hard, and they made sure that he took food and warmed himself by the hearth. Sreng shared the news that Cian might not return to the Boyne until after the lambing time or even longer. Oghma sounded his displeasure. Boann took that information without comment. She asked politely about the return of Elcmar.

Sreng shook his head. "While I lived among the miners, I worked at felling trees and had little access to information about the *ard ri*, until I left hurriedly for the Boyne." He turned to Cliodhna. "You and I will talk now, before warmth and good food put me to sleep."

Sreng and Cliodhna left Oghma's snug hearth. They walked together on hidden paths along the north stream's icy banks and Sreng explained all in secret to wide-eyed Cliodhna. When they returned, Cliodhna said she had heard her father's wishes from Sreng and she agreed. Oghma fretted and he questioned Sreng while Boann and Cliodhna packed foods and herbs for a journey. Then Oghma found him lodging until the next sunrise, when he gave Sreng new hide footcoverings with a padded grass lining.

A scout stood waiting. Cliodhna pressed her hand in goodbye on Boann and then Oghma, all their faces saddened to be parting.

Oghma gave her a stone amulet carved by him and he took her hands in his for a moment. "You'll find a way home. May you have many children, Cliodhna. Teach them our ways, the old ways. Remember that not all change is for the good."

She gave him a brave smile. The visitor Sreng left swiftly with Cliodhna, a heavy mist closing around them and Gebann's daring rescue for his daughter.

The Invader camp fermented with affront at Boann's prolonged absence, and Cliodhna with her. Maedb took it upon herself to harass Bresal, demanding their return, and Bresal heard whispers growing loud in the camp.

"Your woman Maedb blathers about needing a village to raise a child—maybe she means the slaves' children who resemble Connor and it's all of us who must feed and raise those children of his. Maedb won't, so. And your woman giving out, saying the father of Boann's child is a Starwatcher."

"Sure, won't Elcmar be pleased to hear that. It's a bad brew our Maedb has started."

Bresal tried to ignore the aspersions about Boann's child. Maedb's incessant tongue was Connor's problem, not his. But he did want the camp to be placid for Elcmar's return which was surely imminent, around the solstice, though Bresal was not sure precisely when winter solstice would occur. It would not do for Boann to have gone missing, that much he knew.

The soaked warriors refused to bestir themselves to go looking for the *ard ri's* wife, their bark-fiber rain capes and hats having disintegrated in this damp. The slaves claimed they didn't know how to make more rain gear, and none went looking for suitable bark in the soggy forest.

Wet and grim darkness, and the thin peace between Starwatcher and Invader stretched to breaking. Horrified Starwatchers found spoiled carcasses of swans littering the Boyne marshland. Their revered swans, decimated. Starwatchers took swans just at the equinox and only a set portion from the total flock. The Invaders' massacre of winter-sheltering swans was incomprehensible.

"Inexcusable!" The Dagda and the elders sent a scout to Bresal, demanding the groups meet at winter solstice.

Since Sheela's untimely death, their village waited patiently, past the summer solstice and longer, after Boann's marriage and then autumn equinox; but the council with Invaders had yet to happen. The Starwatchers were willing to meet with whomever the Invaders might send.

The rains continued, occasionally as sleet. Starwatcher hunters had to go farther afield to find game and fish than before the intruders' camp. The elders worried that hunger would be upon them all before spring. To protect food supplies and water over three seasons until the next harvest, these intruders must cooperate, must act responsibly.

The Starwatchers' grievances had been thoroughly discussed among themselves. Scouts determined the extent of felled trees and habitat loss along the river and surrounding the Invader camp. Dead swans, and plants and fish found poisoned, had been stored inside cairns, to show the Invaders if they denied their drastic impact. In the event a cold summer or heavy rains damaged the next harvest, then there was a real risk of starvation for all—especially if bad stewardship reduced the food available by foraging, fishing, and hunting. The densely encamped Invaders must change their ways if they wish to remain here, the hunters insisted and the herders agreed.

The most pressing issue was the Starwatchers' personal safety, particularly of their women. Restrictions on all comings and goings since the murder of Sheela had been a great inconvenience. The people had lived freely on this island since before living memory. This last item, their liberty under the skies, they would not negotiate.

Bresal arrived by surprise with his Invader delegation. He meant to find Boann, and swept up to the village clearing with an armed party on stout horses. The Dagda's lips pressed into a hard line as the intruders approached, and he pointed his red macehead toward the mounds. Scouts led the way. Bresal decided his warriors should dismount, but he misjudged the distance. It was a fair walk to the council oak for half-clad Invaders while leading skittish horses over grasses slick with frost. Bresal looked annoyed well before they arrived at the oak and more annoyed when he saw that the only seating provided was cattle hides placed over chill ground.

He spoke first without preamble. "Boann must return immediately to the Invader camp." He watched as his translator told the quiet ones.

Elders turned to look at the Dagda and Tethra, who each acknowledged the shaman with a blink. They made no reply. Tadhg began to state their grievances.

Bresal waved a pudgy hand. "Quiet ones! We have not come to discuss these other things. The omens are—are ominous! You have observed the unusual skies, and the flooding rains and bad harvest. The gods are angry." Bresal attempted eloquence, but these Starwatchers looked impassive. He pulled at his bronze neck piece from the Continent, and drummed his substantial thigh with a holly switch. To his translator, he muttered, "These people have not even offered us a beverage. How can we proceed without comforts, including a drink in hand? Sitting here in the open during winter— it could kill a man." He tried a different approach.

"Maedb, esteemed wife of our Connor, raises concerns about the child carried by Boann, that this child should have proper attentions at birth and our protection, and the inheritance due to it. As befits its station in life. Our village must raise this child. That is, unless Boann wishes to state that this is not the child of Elcmar?"

His accusations puzzled the Starwatchers. Tadhg, dumbfounded, translated to the elders who broke into questions. Boann's hips had deepened, that was so, but unobtrusively. She might be midway, or she might be in the final stages of pregnancy. Everyone knew a pregnancy lasted around ten lunates. Didn't these Invaders know that much? It would be indecent to quiz Boann or speculate about the child's father.

Did the intruder shaman refer to Boann's practice of gathering herbs under the sun? Surely these intruders no longer believed, as in the oldest myths, that the sun could impregnate a woman. The Dagda signaled that Tadhg should reply. He looked for one of the women elders to explain things rather than him, but none did, so he continued speaking in the Invader tongue.

Tadhg said, "Yes, Boann is rising with the sun in the east."

Bresal sneered at his attempt. "Are you saying that this Dagda fathered the child?"

Tadhg groaned inwardly. This Bresal mistook him, thought that he named their Lord of the Light, the Dagda. "I say only that it is a blessing for this child to come forth with light, with the returning sun and coming spring." Tadhg spoke as if he were telling young children about basic and universal facts.

The Dagda chuckled, and the Dagda's son Cermait sat beside him holding back laughter.

Tadhg tried again. "We Starwatchers do not understand any concern for whose child Boann carries. Our experienced midwives shall attend to this birth. For the duration, Boann is able to take exercise and she continues in her astronomy, weather permitting. She would be happy to receive Elcmar again, whether that is before or after the birth of this child. Everyone on this island can welcome the return of the sun and Boann's child."

Bresal's interpreter whispered to him. A long pause followed. Bresal perceived that an abyss of differences between Invaders and Starwatchers threatened to swallow them all. Not only did their casual approach to this coming baby irritate him, but the arrogance of Boann in removing herself from the camp. He should have brought more warriors with him. He shook his head, frowning.

The scouts including Cermait took offense at the shaman Bresal's pained expression. Children were a gift. Starwatchers did not glorify paternity, for them any such custom had receded like long-forgotten glaciers. They reckoned kinship using the mother's line.

"Tell them we accept children in the natural course of things!" a woman elder urged. "This is the child of Boann."

Scouts reached for wood pikes, warriors for gleaming long knives.

The elders urged Tadhg to press for an apology, and he saw Bresal's sneer change to tentative, hesitant. The intruders were outnumbered here.

Rather than defend a situation that needed no defending, Tadhg said, "We take the marriage contract seriously, whether before or after the arrival of a child." This time the shaman kept silent. He confronted Bresal to list the Starwatchers' grievances and concluded, "Your numbers on this island are small but in a short time you have caused many changes.

"We live uncrowded and we live free. We, ourselves alone, we decide how this land shall be used!" Tadhg rose gracefully and raised his arms, the sun held between his hands.

"Our gods, if you will, travel the sky in observable patterns. They are neither pleased nor angered by us. These gods teach and we learn from them. Just as the sun gives light and wisdom freely to all, we have learned to be patient and tolerant of each other. We would like to exercise tolerance of you. But we must protect this island's health in order that we and generations after us may enjoy life here."

Bresal perked up at the hint of what he considered to be theology coming into their exchange. On the Continent, backward peoples could be tricked into fearing that the sun would not rise, not unless they did what Invaders demanded. He had himself used omens, colored smoke and twisted guts, to coerce such people. It might be possible to trick these self-assured Starwatchers out of their gold. Simpletons, worshiping the sun. He must tell Elcmar all about this discussion. He might even have their gold before Elcmar returned! —For now, sure wasn't his own arse freezing; he shifted position.

Bresal said only, "We would be glad to observe the sun with you in order to understand each other better." He heard sharp retorts from the Starwatcher elders that the man Tadhg did not repeat.

The groups agreed that Bresal with his chosen Invaders would attend the forthcoming solstice sunrise at the central starchamber. At the solstice when the sun began its return north, leading them all toward spring and renewal, the two groups would formally confer. Bresal insisted, signaling with stiff hands, and the Starwatchers promised him, that they would meet inside shelter warmed by a fire until they reached an accord. The shaman and the elders exchanged touch and flint tokens and promised again to meet in council. They would find their path toward co-existence on this island.

Boann remained out of sight, and that vexed Bresal long after his meeting with the Starwatcher elders. He had forgotten to demand Cliodhna's return to the camp, and for that Bresal endured the wrath of Maedb.

The first dawn glowed red. The mariners saw it as they embarked from the southwest coast to voyage across the great water to Gebann's homeland. They set out in a trim, large *currach* that had been commandeered by Elcmar, along with obtaining new finery for himself, from the trader who blew in late at the mining coast. That trader now rowed with the crew, grumbling, for Elcmar gave Lir charge of this voyage. By midsun following the red dawn, the sky hung low and black and horizontal rain drove the ship. Up and down on monstrous swells they rode.

Cian thought this *currach* would be blown off the huge white horses of waves carrying them to the Continent. Soon they might be forced to the ocean's very depths. His stomach heaved.

Gebann stood laughing as Cian released violent seasickness into the salt spray and lashing rain. "Sure, at least you're kind to the rowers. Grab on and keep leaning out over the side, lad, we don't want that back on board."

Cian felt too weak to be embarrassed. This ocean sickness overcame him worse than the worst of what he experienced after too much taken of the intruders' brews. Elcmar, Gebann whispered to him, lay ill under the skin-tented area amidship.

If the *ard ri* is too sick to show himself, thought Cian, then I am keeping well to be standing.

The sleek barque, covered in hides but with a longer and higher profile than the currach in which Cian reached the mining peninsula, held more rowers. The mariners called it a *naomhog*. The vessel had more height above the water line by means of wood planks lashed along the top through holes lined up with cleats in the framing. Lir said the higher and more pointed ends, where the upper planks met, fortified the hull against the immense waves. Cian did not see how wood and skins might withstand waves like these, but this boat carried them through the storm. He woke, terrified to see nothing around them but open water.

"The currents shift with treachery in the narrow waters between Eire and first landfall," said Lir, then added they had missed the first landfall due to the storm. Lir calmly watched the waves and wind, and sun and stars. Cian hardly slept, as if willing the vessel to stay afloat. They traced the strange coast of Big East, then the crew cheered to see familiar islets to the southeast.

Gebann said that Cian was getting his sealegs now. He told Cian stories about the peoples who inhabited these little islands near coasts. Most of them watched the skies and built small covered mounds, and since ancient times they ventured onto the sea and traded polished stone axes. Gebann quipped, "Look sharp and you might meet some distant cousins, Cian."

The *naomhog* landed on one of these islets for fresh water and provisions. Cian eagerly left the rocking boat. It was then, upon landing, that he did not see Elcmar among the men leaving the boat. He turned to Gebann, who revealed that Elcmar was not on the ship.

"Elcmar has not come on this voyage." Gebann swallowed, and crossed arms over his chest. "The champion desires to pursue gold before he returns to the Boyne. Understand, lad, I had to keep it from you. I have sent your man Sreng on to the Boyne ahead of Elcmar, for the good of Cliodhna."

"You sent Sreng! I would gladly have gone."

"Elcmar wants to keep you away from the Boyne and off the island. He's determined to find gold on Eire before Connor or anyone else—including you. And he has reason enough to fear what you learned about making metal at the Lake Of Many Hammers. You're not to be harmed, since Elcmar perceives you might be useful to him in the future. He said he might make a mariner of you." He saw Cian's clenched jaw. "Elcmar thinks that his holding on to Cliodhna will force me back to Eire. It's true, Cliodhna's life is more important to me than my own. That's why Sreng is now on his way to take her out of Elcmar's clutches.

"Sreng brings my warning to the Dagda to protect the mounds. These fool Invaders think your mounds contain hidden gold!" Cian looked ready to strike him so Gebann spoke fast. "In the event that Sreng can get Cliodhna away from the Boyne, he'll see that she keeps the right company through the mountains to the southern coast. The problem for her will be, as for us, to wait until a ship can be had to the Continent."

"In this season of storms, isn't that unlikely?" A vein pulsed in Cian's forehead.

"Lad, it's important for us to go on, to appear to follow Elcmar's orders. These men want to go south, to their homes. They won't give us passage back to Eire from here." The lad looked like he might try to swim back home and Gebann took him by the shoulders. This wasn't the right time to tell Cian about the Starwatchers' gold, close to the route that Sreng would take south with Cliodhna. "We'll take our time going along toward my village. You can study the mining and the trading with me on the Seafarer peninsula. When a ship returns to the Starwatchers, you can come back."

Cian pushed him away. "How many moons will pass? When Elcmar finds that Cliodhna has escaped, do you really think that you or I could ever return to Eire? And what will he do to Boann and my people?" Cian swung but in stepped Lir and blocked his punch.

The Starwatcher stood panting with rage, held back by Lir. The scuffle drew stares, from their crew and from strangers. Lir gave Cian a quiet warning and let go of him.

Gebann had no easy answer for the white-faced Cian. Whether he intended to return to the Starwatcher island once Cliodhna was safely home on his Seafarer peninsula, he could not say. He felt his creeping illness, legs heavy and a tingling in his arms.

"We'll find a way back to Eire for you," was all he could offer.

The *naomhog* continued south over endless swells. Lir and the Seafarers used the sun by day and stars at night for navigation, skills learned over countless generations along northern coasts. Lir ran close to shore when possible, or camped until the worst of wind and rain let up. Thick ropes bound all the bundled goods, and each of the men, firmly to the craft. They had already lost one man overboard along the way. No one would sit where that man had been sitting.

Cian's seasickness abated and he passed the time learning to navigate. During light, the mariners used familiar landmarks along the coasts to position themselves on the great waters. They chose two points along the shore backed up by a prominent landmark. "It's much the same as sighting between points on land," he told Lir, who gave him a nod.

He felt he might as well be navigating to the moon, given the limitless water surrounding them. Tossed and battered, Cian grabbed at his ropes while their boat rose high upon waves then plummeted into troughs. Gebann had broadsided him, swamped him. His anguish grew at Gebann's mischief, grew to be as deep and wide as the waters tossing him. He woke from terrible dreams: whirling and bobbing through a void, the skies no longer recognizable.

They stopped at another island farther south. Cian found a place to flop down on solid ground, away from the crew who strolled easily and looked for water and foodstuffs.

Lir came to stand above him, looking at the sea. "Those who do not fear the waves do soon be drowned, for going upon the sea when they should not." He leaned into Cian's view. "But I do fear the waves, as you do. My men are drowned only now and again."

The sunrises passed; he lost count, to his chagrin. Two quarters of the moon it had been since they left Eire. Lir indicated they were nearing the Seafarer peninsula. Here the great bay's flat coastline held lengthy sand dunes, with few trees or settlements. Lir explained to him how wind and currents interacted, and that at each river estuary or inlet the tidal flow varied. Lir appeared happiest when he traveled water applying his considerable skills, and Cian felt glad for his friend at least. The large currach traveled steadily south, then veered west with the curving coastline.

A light fog closed around the *naomhog* as it reached the Seafarer coast. Cian thought he must be seeing things, deprived of sleep as he was, for far above the damp mist he saw mountains jutting impossibly high into the sky.

Gebann clapped him on the back. "Those mountains run west along my peninsula, lad. When I see those gigantic peaks reaching into the sky, I am home!" With a mighty heart, all the rowers put on fresh speed.

Cian saw that these jagged mountains—grey and devoid of trees on their sharp peaks and higher than he thought the earth could rise—ran steeply to the sea. Here and there golden beaches stretched in inlets or dark cliffs filled this coast; that much looked similar to his island. But these mountains! He had only a few hazelnuts remaining in his food pouch, but he opened it and cast the hazelnuts into the waves as an offering of thanks for letting him live to see this sight.

Lir chuckled behind him. "You should have eaten those and not fed them to a salmon! It's a good while until we reach the landing and food, lad."

Cian smiled, his first in a long while, to hear that salmon swam in this place. He cast a finely knotted cord net he had made on the journey, pleased to see that his net held open in the drag of the boat through waves. The crew pointed out patches where the water dimpled as if raindrops were pelting the surface, schools of fish. They trawled Cian's net expectantly.

Soon he had taken numerous small fish and other creatures in his net, to cook over the little fire-pot on board for a quick and tasty meal. These slim little fish were new to Cian but he saw that the crew welcomed his contribution. He tried a cooked piece of a many-legged sea animal, and found it chewy but delicious. The Invaders control the landing area, Lir told him as they ate, and any food on offer there cost dearly and was not half as fresh as Cian's catch.

As they neared the place to land, Gebann stood beside Lir, their voices too low for Cian to make out words. The number of arriving boats surprised him, many with foreign shapes. A bump and scraping, and they landed amidst hustling, shouting men and pack animals. The smith Gebann was first to wade onto shore. Shamans rushed forward chanting and waving holly branches at the smith and the arriving vessel. Cian hung back, evaluating the strange scene before his eyes.

While the crew unloaded the ship, he observed that Lir handed over a sizable portion of its copper and other cargo, to a well-fed man wearing a copper neckpiece and armlets and speaking the Invader tongue. Lir took Cian aside to explain.

"The payment to these officials, we must call them, is exacted on all boats for the privilege of landing here." As if reading Cian's mind, Lir added that if they were caught landing elsewhere, "All the cargo would be confiscated. They'd take your eyes and come back for the lashes."

Cian tucked away this incident to ask about later, for this levy impressed him as much as did these steep mountains. Stumbling onto shore, he helped with unloading of the naomhog but stayed out of the way of Invader officials. His legs rolled as if still on the pitching boat, more so than after his short voyage to the Lake mine. *Will I ever be any good at sea travel?* He waited to get his land legs as Gebann said that he would, not sure that he could rely on anything the smith told him. Gebann's walk looked none too steady, and not from drink.

The Invaders directed the men to unload the copper cargo into a storage area. It tripled the inventory on hand. The biting smell struck him, of scores of copper axeheads, daggers, and raw ingots stored in a guarded hillside passage. Cian eyed and tallied the stacked haul brought with them. The bulk of the copper produced at the Lake mine that season had in fact been shipped off to the Continent.

Fury welled; he wanted to reclaim the copper cargo, take it home. Why should others far away have the use of it? But an unarmed foreigner must not create a disturbance. *I am here to see and learn all that I can learn, not get myself more troubles.*

Gebann let all the crew depart to their wives and homes, admonishing the men to return quickly when summoned by Lir.

Lir stood by, hands at his waist, a bemused expression. "Mind yourself, Starwatcher! Keep your head." Cian gave him a slow smile; the friends touched with the sign of farewell and Lir strode off, pack slung over his shoulder.

Lir would be getting himself another boat; the one they arrived in must return to the north, Gebann said, "To Taranis." That name meant nothing to Cian.

"Follow me," said the smith. Gebann bargained for two sturdy animals, mules he called them, from a sun-wizened trader of animals. Gebann said they would be leaving on them. The animals appeared bad-tempered, teeth bared and long ears twitching, even compared with Invader horses. Cian got up onto one but as Gebann handed him the hemp strap controlling its head, something closed around his wrists. He looked down. The crafty Gebann had slipped a leather thong about his wrists in a slipknot that tightened when he tried to pull free. Stunned at being bound, he struggled to handle the mule and keep his balance. He resented the smith now as he had no one else except Elcmar.

They ventured into the peninsula, into more land area than he thought existed. They threaded narrow valleys through towering mountains, Cian following Gebann's lead. The animals carried them and leather packs on each flank. In the roughest terrain they walked the mules. Cian took greater care to count sunrises than he had on the sea voyage. The jumbled, high peaks made noting the direction they traveled difficult.

After almost a quarter moon, they crossed a high pass in an area that Gebann said was unknown to intruders. "The few people living here do not grow crops. Nor do they mine metals."

Below them forested plains went south into a deep green unbounded by mountains. It occurred to Cian that endless forest could swallow him, hide him.

"I have heard that farther inland, some of the tribes practice cannibalism," Gebann told him. "In case you are thinking of giving me the slip." Gebann indicated that they would be traveling west from this pass. It was then he took off the binding from Cian's sore wrists.

They continued to travel west. The inland air seemed warmer, spicier, than on Eire. Cian marveled at drier, yellow soil. Plants he had never seen bore grey-green, thick leaves like fingers. Shrubs had glossy leaves covered in a waxy substance protecting them from the hotter sunlight. He sampled new herbs, strange but wonderful, and he wanted to bring these to Boann and Airmid. A native healer would know of their medicinal uses and the best way to take them, root or cutting; he would find such a person to show him. Gebann jolted his thoughts back to the here and now.

Along their way, the smith showed him gold. How to separate placer gold from gravel in streambeds. They climbed ridges and he showed Cian how to find gold veins in quartz and other rock types, and to examine the layering of an outcropping or an entire mountain. Cian found himself eager and grateful to learn.

They arrived at a mine after having to urge their mules steadily upward on narrow trails, Cian not sure whether Gebann took him on the most convoluted route to reach this area. He saw men digging out shadow moon metal, soft and malleable. The miners carried out ore in thick leather bags.

"Leather bags spill less ore than hauling it in open sledges on these slopes. Every drop of metal must be squeezed from the rocks," Gebann said.

At a different spot, men sluiced water through a dugout log to capture sun metal. Cian wondered what power the sun metal conveyed, new to him as it was. He saw gold carefully assessed, portioned into equal piles using the amount of water it displaced in a vessel. Only then was a weight of gold turned over to a smith who worked it into jewelry—a finely crafted ear disc, or gold wire, or hammered sheets. He saw many items unknown to him and wondrous in their craft. The copper jewelry worn by Lein and Creidhne in Eire exceeded any ornament he could have imagined. Here the master smiths wore even thicker copper pieces, and a very few of them flaunted jewelry items made in fiery gold.

He saw that Creidhne's talents were underused at the Lake mine so long as that smith lacked sun metal to produce stunning gold adornments like Boann's gift from Elcmar. The competition between Connor and Elcmar to find gold on Eire took on new meaning to Cian.

They traveled on. Gebann pointed out standing stones carved with rudimentary symbols: rayed suns, and grids of lines and slashes. He said the metal traders' search for ores from their very first contact disrupted the Seafarers' ways.

"We learned to use subterfuge. Axes carved on our stones, or patterns of lines, or a shepherd's crook, meant little to illiterate Invaders. They couldn't tell if a marker stone showed a boundary or the sun's path or where to find metal." Cian laughed aloud for the first time since he left Eire's shores and Gebann went on with gusto, "We had more than a few skirmishes when Invaders couldn't find any ore deposits after getting bad directions. That's how we protected our gold and copper from pillage." He sighed. "I hope you're listening, Starwatcher."

With Gebann, he visited several old copper mines, the rude huts in bad repair and the rock barely producing enough metal to justify the labor. The miners dug inside lateral tunnels, going after ore that was readily available, just like they dug for it at The Lake Of Many Hammers. Mixed forest of black poplar, ash, and conifers had disappeared around the mines, cut down for making charcoal. Cian saw the telltale sediment of erosion filling in nearby streams, the land dead, birds and animals gone. The air stank of smelting.

"The ore always runs out. Remember that, lad. The ore supply does not, cannot, last. We journey on now and you shall meet one of the big traders," Gebann said and the two rode on.

They arrived at a much larger mining area. A few words from Gebann caught the attention of its overseer. He brought them up a hill where one larger dwelling stood among a cluster of eight or so inside fortified walls, removed from both the ore smelting and the mining. A man named Bolg stepped from the larger dwelling, and waved away the overseer. Gebann and Bolg cautiously exchanged touch, then Bolg showed the two men around at a smart pace. The fort's stone walls enclosed a cistern, a grain storage place, and huts where the final smelting and any smithing occurred. Guards stood watch over all of it. After their rapid tour of his fort, Bolg bade them rest and then return to dine with him at sunset. All had been spoken in Invader, not the Seafarer tongue.

The two walked back down the hill. Stout horses bred by the trader Bolg crowded a pen. Sheep grazed close by, but those sheep were for the fort's table, Gebann told him.

"How did one man, Bolg, gain control over this area?" Cian asked.

"The same as all traders. Traders arrived with exotic wares, new textiles and necklaces made from strange stones, which they would exchange for metal from our land. Within one generation, Seafarer tribes became indebted through trading with the Invaders. Bolg merely takes advantage."

Cian stopped him. "I do not understand this word debt."

"Just as we did not understand their ways of trading. Over time our own greed outstripped what my people could exchange: our raw ores never equaled their goods. Ore must be mined and smelted as you've seen yourself. Like your people, we had never traded in copper, bronze, or gold, or amber or jet, or foreign fabrics. Soon trading affected our farming and herding and our very landscape. Even what we drank! The traders introduced new grains for making beer, supplanting the mead we brewed. They had us fermenting beverages from all sorts of fruits—the Invaders crave a better wine, one that does not sour on long voyages.

"Our fields expanded for all this, until we actually produced a surplus of grain—only to see that food stored and guarded by Invaders to dole out to us. Invaders staked out territory as theirs for trade and now they live among us." Gebann looked up at the stone fort and rubbed a hand through his black hair shot with silver, his face showing fatigue. "Many traders come from our own people, those who learned new ways. Like Bolg."

At the setting sun, after they rested below the fortified walls, they washed and redressed. Cian rued his salt-stained and frayed tunic but it was all he had. A grateful man took a scrap of copper from Gebann for minding their mules and packs. They ascended to the stone fortress.

Inside its gate, a slave boy took them to Bolg. Every surface in the trader's dwelling held sumptuous items of stone and wood, along with patterned textiles. When he saw Cian looking at a curving tusk of white, the trader let him hold it.

"From shores far to the south," Gebann said. "Traded for a great many copper axes."

Bolg smiled serenely, then indicated they would have the meal outside to enjoy the cool air. There stood a large open pavilion, a ceiling of painted skins supported at its corners by polished wood poles. They took seats with the other diners, all men, on leather and wood tripod stools around a hearth pit wafting fragrances from burning rosemary and apple branches. Their host took up a translucent marble cup. The burnished black cups passed to his guests with a flourish were of thin-walled ceramic.

All these things were new to Cian and his senses whirled.

Their host and the other men seemed to ignore the serving girl. She wore a thin linen top that ended above her navel, and a short skirt made of twine cords looped through woven binding at its hem and waist. Every time she moved her thighs showed, or her bottom, through her string skirt. This display made Cian nervous. She had flaxen hair dressed in braids pulled tight around her head, dull blue-grey eyes, and a square look to her body. Overall, she looked not unlike Maedb and he guessed she came from the same land as did that rough lady. She filled their cups without care for the rare objects he understood them to be.

The serving girl brought steaming food courses of partridge, wild boar, and rabbit. The men ate with their fingers from polished wooden bowls. They used bread made of pounded acorns to clean the bowl between courses and Cian imitated this while enjoying the new bread. He was relieved that his host did not adopt sitting at a table to dine, although he could have done without having the serving girl's breasts served up under her flimsy top—and her privates served up, close—while he was trying to follow the conversation. All these men skillfully used the Invader language.

Bolg had moderate height, with curly black hair, high cheekbones, and smooth skin of even color like bronze. He dressed for the dinner in a tunic that Cian guessed came from far away and cost a pile of copper. Bolg's tunic was made of white fabric like mist, finely woven, and pleated all over, even its joined sleeves. A patterned woven belt in many colors circled his waist, cinched by a bone hook carved into an animal head. He wore a gleaming dagger.

The decoration of Bolg's pavilion dazzled the eye. The diners were seated over colorful rugs made of joined cords and with tasseled ends. How comfortable their host seemed in his expensive tunic and lavish tent—while dirty, hungry miners worked the ore tunnels a stone's throw down the hill. Cian sobered and poked at the food in his polished bowl.

Bolg saw his discomfort when the swaying skirt neared Cian, and laughed. "Starwatcher—never seen that? I guess we men of the bags can show you men of the bogs a thing or two!"

Cian felt shame for these men. A Starwatcher would not refer to any woman in that way, much less in her presence. He waited to see, would she slam the wood tray she carried down on his host's head, but the serving girl appeared oblivious to Bolg's remark.

Gebann intervened. "I admire this Starwatcher's reserve with women. A bit of reserve is a fine thing in a young man, don't you think?"

The men stopped talking to listen. A few nudged and winked; her string skirt meant this girl was available, no less and no more. Cian sensed ridicule of him.

Bolg arched an eyebrow and quickly turned their conversation to the safe transport of ingots and the metals trade. And he complained,

"Production declines steadily here. I should have set up my camp along the southern coast where copper streams from the earth."

Gebann eyed their surroundings. "Production might be declining—but that needs more study."

A trader who came from a great fortress in the south, who wore a bright saffron-dyed tunic and a wide bronze armpiece, bragged, "I have speeded up mining. We burn off the forests to get a ready supply of charcoal for smelting. That means I need fewer laborers in the woods and I put the extra men to work in the tunnels. And fire clears off the land for fields and grazing. In one shake of a lamb's tail!" He pointed at the serving girl's bottom and laughed at his own pun.

Cian's hand stopped midway to his mouth. This trader spoke casually of putting the torch to whole forests. The other diners exclaimed approval, that burning away trees was a grand idea to get things moving at their own mines. Cian put his food bowl down, his appetite gone, envisioning a huge conflagration and then silent, scorched earth. Did even one of these men think about how many suns it took to make a forest? He glanced at Gebann.

"Steady, lad." Gebann spat it over his shoulder. "Not here. Too many long knives."

The man wearing loud colors waved his jeweled arm. "At Zambujal we'll be pouring bronze and not just copper, when we get our hands on enough tin. Mind you, despite our success, this erratic weather and lower grain supplies could tighten all our belts."

"Keep your friends close, and Taranis closer!" cried another.

All the party toasted to that, their mood buoyed by the serving girl who refilled their cups. She stepped among the men as if pushed at them, hips forward, dangling the jug.

The diners' exchange of words tantalized Cian. He needed to work out what the word credit meant, and debt. From being immersed in their tongue of trading, Cian did not think the mystery to him of "credit" and "debt" to be merely semantic. He had much more to learn about trading in order to protect his people from enslavement to anyone.

Later, before they retired, Gebann confided, "You handled yourself well at the trader Bolg's dinner." The smith pointed up the hill at the stout walls. "This fellow Bolg lives and eats so very well at the expense of other traders far away, those whom he thinks cannot see the ingots disappearing."

And at the expense of those who labor below his walls, thought Cian.

"When Taranis finds out about missing copper and gold, the sun will set for Bolg!" Gebann's thick forefinger stabbed up at the fort, and Cian nodded that he understood. Except who was this Taranis?

That night he dreamed of a gold disc earring divided into four equal quadrants, the four cardinal directions given to his people by the sun and taught by the Dagda. North, south. East, west. He dreamed of navigating through dark waters using the star patterns that shone brightest. Cian dreamed of the Swan drifting through the milky stream flowing in the heavens, and of Boann.

It was almost sunrise along the Boyne, and the chorus stood half to either side of the entrance to the central mound. In the approaching dawn, a faint glow emerged from the white quartz revetment with its random dots of smooth grey stones. Starwatchers waited at the speckled gate. The entrance gaped wide and dark, framed by the grey stone forming its portal and the boxlike aperture above. The great stone slab covering the passage entrance had been moved to one side.

The mound's inner chamber accommodated around twenty persons. On this morning the Dagda chose the group to be allowed inside, with the guests. Bresal and his entourage of five warriors stepped cautiously into the narrow passage. They had never gone inside one of these mounds, here or on the Continent. The rumor among Invaders that this mound concealed a hall of solid gold gave the shaman courage to enter it. Bresal hadn't taken any drink before they arrived, so that he could later recall this event with clarity for Elcmar, but he was all the worse for being sober.

He groped along the passage as it seemingly closed around him. Someone ahead of him carried the only torch. Above his head, great slabs overlapped to form the long passage ceiling. The long passage transitioned upward with the ramped floor of wide flagstones. The tall passage uprights were thicker than two men around and Bresal wondered how these giants had been set into place. Here and there, carved symbols leaped out at him as he passed and at the first of these, he stifled a cry. The warriors scoffed and pushed him forward.

They continued into the shadowy, tall passage. The construction that Bresal could see was meticulous. Unseen by him, a secondary roof of stone slabs protected the passage. The mound engineers positioned these secondary slabs to be supported independently of the inner ceiling stones, and this hidden upper layer kept the great weight of the mound off the corridor and the inner chamber. The passage uprights stood independently from those of the inner chamber as well, all built to stand for eternity.

Tense in the dim passage, Bresal counted off twenty-two slabs along the west wall and twenty-one along the east. The group filed silently around slabs that angled slightly into the passage.

The shaman panted with nervousness as he followed the rising passage floor. His fingertips brushed a carved triple spiral and he squeaked. Then he stumbled into the great height of the main chamber. In flickering light from the Dagda's torch, his gaze followed stone layers up and up. Neatly corbeled slabs overlapped inward and rose to a single capstone at the height of three men. His mouth slacked open in surprise. Two smaller ovoid spaces lay east and west from the inner chamber, but in the low light Bresal could not see these recesses clearly. In one, he glimpsed a big stone basin that held cremated bones.

The Dagda indicated that they should stand lined around the walls of this inner chamber, and extinguished his reed torch. They waited in darkness. No one spoke. He had not seen Boann among the assembled Starwatchers outside, but she might have filed into the chamber after him. When he strained to look it was so dark that he became dizzy, and stopped for the effort. Bresal stood awed by the stillness and absolute blackness of the inner chamber.

A sweet low humming began from the chorus, carrying along the passage, and upon hearing it his skin prickled. The hosts and guests stood under the lofty corbeled roof, listening. This inner chamber felt neither cold nor damp, he realized.

Hidden to his eyes, above the capstone lay a cairn of water-rolled stones. Over this cairn lay alternating layers of clay, and sod turves, and pebbles, covering all the passage and chamber. As an extra barrier to dampness, the builders caulked between the drystacked roof stones with sea sand mixed with burned earth. The layers of the great mound and its carefully slanted inner roof slabs, grooved for runoff of water, had already kept the long passage and interior chamber dry through hundreds of solstices.

Starwatcher masons carved the hidden, reverse surface of some of the passage's upright slabs although this work remained unseen after the outer layers covered the passage. A removable slab over the entrance roofbox had a reverse, hidden side, carved by Coll himself.

Aware the place was some sort of temple, for Bresal this mound held little meaning. Though, he had marveled at the carvings on the outer kerbstones. His fingertips tingled from the carved spiral in the passage. Its artistry eluded him. None of these carved symbols looked to refer to gold. A few reminded of sun and stars. As an Invader shaman, he abhorred writing of any kind, it weakened the memory. Bresal's skin prickled again as he waited in utter darkness, the chorus growing louder. He could not remember ever feeling such anticipation.

The quiet ones stood waiting for the sunrise, for their stones to speak to them.

They had hidden their knowledge in plain view. Their symbols covered these stones and reached an apogee of complexity and execution. Oghma carved the kerbstones with sensitivity, following the contours and overall shape of each stone. On many he laboriously pick-dressed around each symbol over the entire kerbstone, and the raised symbols swirled over the textured background like living tendrils wrapping the boulder.

Two of the kerbstones held the most symbols and relief picking, an entrance stone and the kerbstone opposite it on an axis running north through the mound. A prominent vertical line on these massive kerbstones emphasized this north-south alignment. On the entrance kerbstone, unseen to Bresal and his warriors inside the mound, the solstice display began.

Slowly the rising light cast a shadow from the standing stone up onto the entrance kerbstone, crossing the eloquent spirals to touch its deep vertical line. The expectant Starwatchers saw the shadow, a finger, with satisfaction. Griane and Coll returned with all their ancestors, Starwatchers who harnessed light and dark into their calendar.

The deepest voices from the chorus reverberated into where the guests stood. The sun peeked above Red Mountain. The moment in time arrived.

Bresal heard the surging chorus. A young woman's clear voice soared, the others responding. A quiver ran up his spine, he sensed the shaft of light before he saw it creeping along the passage. Dazzling light burst into the inner chamber and gilded the carved stone at the rear north wall. Light bounced into the side recesses. Bresal and his warriors gasped at the rich decoration now clearly illuminated in golden warmth.

The Dagda spoke, and Bresal's interpreter delayed, intent on the words. Bresal nudged but the interpreter waited until the voice no longer rang in the vaulted chamber. Only then did the interpreter repeat the Dagda's words:

"Almighty sun, you alone give us warmth from above. You alone remove darkness from the sky. With this rising you return to us. Soon you will bring forth the fruits of the earth to all. We honor you here and consecrate our deeds before the eye of all knowledge. We wait upon your blessings, and we are thankful. Let us all go in peace."

Bresal deflated with utter disappointment. What was so remarkable in this speech? He would have made a prediction for the masses, exhorted them, lectured them. These are really such simple people, he thought, these *culchies* hiding from the sun inside their mound. And where is their gold?

While the light retreated from the inner chamber, that clear voice soared again above the chorus. In the chamber, all the people craned their necks to watch golden light fade in the side recesses and from the high vaulted ceiling. The singing blended into final notes as the light seeped out, until they all stood in total darkness and silence. They filed back through the passage and out onto the forecourt.

The warriors looked stunned as they came out into the brisk morning air. Early sunlight gleamed on the silver Boyne. Bresal felt unnerved, or overly stimulated; whatever it was, he craved a drink and something to eat. To his amazement, large steaming pots of food and drink arrived and the quiet ones distributed the pots' contents. He looked over the choir, trying to ascertain which of the young women had done the solo, to see if her face and body matched that voice. *Perhaps I too should take a Starwatcher wife...* He definitely felt on edge.

Bresal stared at the magnificent triple spiral chiseled in relief on the entrance boulder: light and darkness and infinity. He lost hold of it, his one insight, for at that moment his interpreter came to his side and while bestowing on him a small joint of roast fowl, steered his gaze toward the standing stone casting its shadow.

"Tairdelbach tells me that they knew sunlight would reach the inner chamber and strike its back stone. They direct the light so that it penetrates this mound only at winter solstice. He claims tonight there shall be another ceremony these Starwatchers haven't told us about—to bring the moon into this mound with the Bright One."

Bresal winced at this ludicrous assertion from his informer. "These people can hardly feed themselves. Bowsies and cute hoors! How would they know to make the moon and the Bright One appear together inside this mound?"

His interpreter smirked and leaned closer. "Tairdelbach tells me the quiet ones also will bring another full moon, before it is time."

Bresal frowned. This smacked of outrageous heresy: to claim that Starwatchers controlled the heavens. He stayed long enough to appear polite and make full use of the food, then hustled his group off to their horses tethered east of the mound. There a Starwatcher boy, evidently posted to watch their horses, stood up from the winter grasses. His obedient but proud appearance provoked Bresal.

"What's your name?"

The lad told them, *Dubh*. It sounded like the name for the dark mound.

Bresal heard the bold reply and inspected the young Starwatcher. He had good height with a strong build, and an angular face and jawline under thick brown hair. His growing hands and feet appeared too large, but when he grew into himself he would be quite the specimen. A potential fighter, thought Bresal, like that big fellow, what's his name. Like Cian.

"Do you want to come with us and learn our war games, so?"

The boy shook his head and said something firmly about the Dagda.

Bresal laughed. "Lord of the Light, is he?"

Still laughing, the shaman and his group rode away, back to the Invader encampment and their pasttimes within its reeking walls.

With nightfall, Bresal and two of his men returned to the mounds. They tied their horses at a different spot, and sauntered back into the level area surrounding the main mound. A small group of Starwatchers stood at a covered fire, their backs to its glowing embers.

The Dagda stepped forward courteously and inquired of their mission, and he did so using the Invader tongue, noted Bresal.

"We wish to see the moon with you tonight. The full moon may be viewed inside this mound. Am I correct in this?" he inquired of the Dagda.

"You are correct. As you wish."

Ah, thought Bresal, *this Dagda is indeed the man of few words, a quiet one. We may have surprised them. I might gather something of value to us here.*

The Dagda left them standing apart from the Starwatchers for what seemed like a long time, on the bright side of the fire, then motioned Bresal and his group to follow along into the main mound whose tall entrance stood open. None carried a torch in the darkness, but the ground around the great mound was smooth from tending it. They entered the looming, silent mound and lined up midway along the passage, and waited. Outside, a damp frost blanketed the ground as freezing mist floated in the air. The moist chill clung to Bresal's clothing as he waited inside the mound, flexing his stiff arms and legs.

The Starwatchers stood with eyes fixed on the entrance, ignoring the cold. Bresal began to feel uneasy inside this mound once again.

The brightest star appeared. The shaman trembled. The full moon glided into view, framed in the opening above the entrance, shining there in the deep night sky together with the Bright One. Intense silver moonlight struck them exactly where they stood in the passage.

On seeing the moon framed just so by the stone box over the portal, Bresal quaked. How was this possible?

His men stirred and muttered, and bolted. The Dagda approached as if to speak to him, but the sage of the Invaders retreated to the outside with his men, across freezing rime on the ground and into the moonlit night.

As Bresal ran for his horse, he thought he heard the crying of a newborn child. Luminous mist curled around the riders and they had trouble finding their camp, lost in a milky haze from the river Boyne.

On the next morning Bresal sent formal word to the Dagda that negotiations, the council with quiet ones, would not occur.

This breach came with no explanation from the Invaders. Starwatcher scouts reported normal activity in the intruders' encampment, considering that it was the cold season, and they all waited for further word from Bresal.

During the solstice moon the Starwatchers attended another evening ceremony. As was their custom, the cremated bones of Sheela would be removed from Dowth as the sun set and reburied at a minor mound a small distance away. Boann had not fully recovered her strength from delivering her son, Aengus, on the solstice, and she was thus accompanied by Tadhg and Airmid to the ceremony.

On that setting of the sun, preceded by noise from their horses, a party of Invaders swept into Dowth's clearing in a raucous frenzy. They surrounded the Starwatchers who convened for the solemn reburial. Those who could run, dispersed quickly from the scene. Tadhg and Daire sped away, helping Boann, with Airmid protecting them all under the cloak of swan feathers. The Invaders tilted the standing stone at the dark mound's north entrance, and rode their frenzied horses around and over the mound as if to destroy it.

The Dagda emerged from the north passage, guarding a large pot and waiting to complete the rites so that Sheela's ashes could be re-interred. He stood without weapon or recourse while jeering, shouting riders displaced stones that contained centuries of observations. Bresal intercepted him and with warriors he took the Dagda into the intruder camp for questioning.

Bresal allowed the old man to be seated and planted his rotund frame close to the Dagda. "Where's the gold that lies here, the gold in the mounds?" He queried the stoic Dagda several times with little reply made. The Dagda's arms wrapped a large clay vessel and Bresal got an idea. The sweating shaman put his face up to the old man's. "What is it you have in this pot?"

"The bones of Sheela, the murdered woman," said the Dagda.

Bresal set the Dagda free at once.

The waning moon backlit the low clouds. All was white cold surrounding the lone figure put out from the camp. No Invader would walk with him and help carry the burden of Sheela's ashes. The bent form slowly made its way back to the mounds where the Dagda deposited Sheela's urn with her ancestors, and on to his village.

The Invaders had disturbed burial rites and riled the Starwatchers. Bresal cowered in his dwelling inside the walled camp, drinking whatever he could find.

Foolhardy warriors threatened to tear apart the mounds looking for gold. The warriors came and went as they pleased. Over the next sunrises, one, then several, warriors went missing from the camp, their bodies found frozen but without signs of injury or struggle. The swaggering Invaders had reason to fear the long dark nights at the Boyne.

Starwatcher scouts armed themselves with long flint knives or stone axeheads lashed to stout ash handles. The carrying of battle weapons alarmed the elders, but they did not speak against it. Frostbitten, the Dagda recovered painfully, healed by Airmid's good care.

Heavy sleet intervened to quell the troubles. Both sides waited out the icy storms.

To Bresal's consternation, at the end of the Invaders' lunate a second full moon arose, dark bloody red in the east on a bitterly cold night. With it, Elcmar returned to the Boyne camp.

PART TWO

NIGHT

Aengus, The Youthful Son

ELCMAR WATCHED BRESAL hurry into the great hall, no doubt hoping to find a feast laid out by bustling slaves and to claim a share of any spoils. Instead the hall stood dark and the pots lay cold, no serving women in sight and no toasting warriors. A damp dog lay at Elcmar's feet, one loyal companion but even so it was Dabilla, Boann's puppy. Halfway into the gloom of the great hall, the shaman's pace slowed.

Elcmar smoldered with anger. "Perhaps you should have taken greater care to anticipate my return," he said, his eyes accusing Bresal.

"But you return now, many nights past the solstice." Bresal stumbled backward but Elcmar pulled him forward again with his piercing look. The shaman groped and took the first bench he found, not the closest seat to the champion. Lacking the feast he had hoped to enjoy, Bresal's stomach gave a loud rumble and he cursed it.

"Where! Where is she? And where's the child?" Elcmar's questions bounced around in the rafters.

Bresal's voice shook. "There's a snapper—ehm, a fine new son for you at the Starwatchers' village, and Boann there with him, awaiting you."

"And how many warriors have been killed here at the Boyne?"

"A few, only a few. Well, five. None injured, so." A long silence underscored Bresal's absurd statement.

"Are Starwatchers getting our weapons? Who is trading in weapons?"

"To be sure, I don't know that a'tall."

The air roiled to midnight blue in the hall. Only Elcmar's eyes glowed in the chill space. "You had my instructions on these matters, Bresal. To be sure to be sure."

Even Bresal had the sense to not reply. He lingered, eyes roving.

"Why are you sitting here?" Elcmar snapped, tempted to draw his knife.

Twisting a bronze armlet wedged onto his wrist, Bresal babbled about a party that had just arrived from the Continent. "Ten in number, all warriors save for a shaman, Ith. They brought only a few provisions for us and no horses or livestock. Their boat had been swamped several times and some of these lads are half-drowned and half-frozen."

Elcmar rose. "I'd say Taranis sent this crew for an inspection. We must ready some hospitality. The men have been shown to quarters for now and their injuries tended, no thanks to you, Bresal. Warm some honey mead and have that served while you keep them waiting. Tell the slaves to make a feast of smoked fish and stewed fowl and dried apples, whatever can be readied quickly. Bring in torches and have fresh mats and rushes laid in here. Stoke the fire. When this place is aired and warm, if anything on this island can ever be warm, only then bring in the guests. Make sure they eat well, get drunk, and have a selection of women. And—don't wake me." He wondered if Bresal would remember half of these instructions, and sent for a slave and repeated all to her after the shaman left the hall mumbling.

Elcmar strode to his sleeping chamber, where he slammed the door and barred it. *Sure, it's a grand welcome for me here, their champion. Bru na Elcmar, is it.* Safe inside walls, he let his leather leggings and shin guards and tattered shoes fall from his body. He swayed with fatigue. Inspecting the Lake mine had been easy enough, but not the trip back to the Boyne.

After sending Gebann off with Cian held hostage, Elcmar searched for gold in the southwest with Creidhne. Then word reached him of distant troubles with Starwatchers at the Boyne and he departed quickly for the north. The only good boat at that coast, he had already sent to the Continent with Lir and Gebann. Elcmar loaded his men and gear into the battered currach that they used to arrive at the copper mine before autumn, but that boat barely held together for a few days of pounding by winter swells before it had to be abandoned, banjaxed. They had to travel over land for the rest of the journey. His small party made their way north slowly against heavy rains and fierce winds. Starwatchers attacked them in the mountains before they descended to the Liffey river plain.

Blood that had dried on Elcmar's worn tunic caused it to stick to his skin. As he struggled to peel it off, sharp pain doubled him over. He had killed the Starwatcher who dropped onto him from a tree and broke his rib. After grappling with relentless adversaries, his warriors left only two dead Starwatchers along a mountain stream. Every breath tortured him but Elcmar bound leather strips around his ribcage and kept walking, barking orders. He focused on getting out of those mountains alive while the rain turned to sleet needles and then pelting snow.

His men's wounds made it tough going. Elcmar and his warriors detoured off Starwatcher trails and followed the streams, their knives drawn, eyes scanning the trees and ridges. They salvaged scraps from their soaked, dwindling food supplies. Pain and hunger slowed their descent, the men needing to rest often. One complained loudly, "Your man Elcmar wouldn't give you the steam from his piss."

Elcmar marched on, leading them all away from danger and death. Cold, hunger and pain clawed at him. He discovered a desire to see Boann, to keep moving until he was safe at her side and warm, a home for him there and it drew him on like a small constant flame in the storm.

Then he saw it, shining nuggets of sun metal in the swift waters they followed down toward the plain. Gold, but in a remote and hostile place. Elcmar saw again the dead Starwatchers' faces: a worthy opponent protected this gold. He couldn't stop to search for the gold's source, not with his injured men and the weather. He carefully lowered his body to the stream and picked up the largest nuggets while he pretended to scoop up water to drink. Elcmar trusted no one well enough to leave a man posted at the gold-bearing stream. He chose distinctive rocks and trees, he tried to remember that very spot and that stream for his return, as he drove his warriors on through the snowstorm. Low clouds obscured the mountaintops and pressed close around them.

His find disappeared behind him in the white-shrouded valleys.

Now he rotated his knifewielding arm and grimaced. *Taranis, sending collectors here from the Continent! Why else would they travel all the way to the Boyne in the dead of winter? I'll say we found no gold here—I'm not sending these few nuggets! We have little of anything to send back. The almighty Taranis will have to accept hides, pine marten or fox or the like. I must deal with that on the sunrise as well.*

He stared at the chamber's plank walls, more hollow than from just his empty gut. Traveling suited him better, he understood how to do that, how to survive. This Boyne camp had fallen apart in his absence, and Bresal with it. How he had looked forward to seeing Boann, and the stolid natives crisscrossing between their tidy village and the mounds and mountaintops to endlessly watch the skies. Like bees they were, always busy, and he knew it was best not to provoke the hive of quiet ones.

Instead he found his hall dark, his wife gone missing, her with her soft voice and pliant limbs. He had no comfort here, no reward, no constant flame. Elcmar did not like anything about this place now. So far he had refrained from dismantling the Starwatchers' mounds to look for gold. Bresal and the others learned nothing of their gold in his absence. *Eejits.*

He threw his long knife into the plank wall and watched it hit exactly where he wanted it to hit. He knew how to tend to himself, he had seen worse times. This bad night like all the others would bring the dawn, bring a new sun for him.

A new son? He fell onto the wide bed. He could smell Boann in the furs as he sank into deep sleep. Through the songs and feasting resounding from beyond his chamber, he slept until the full light.

He took his time before seeing to the guests lying about in the hall. He ordered heated water for himself to do a bit of bathing, and shoved some slaves in the guests' direction in case they should awaken. Other slaves, he sent out of the hall with orders to heat stones and boil quarters of fresh beef in the cooking pits. One of the slaves whinged that Bresal had fouled all but one of the cooking pits with dyeing of cloth, and brewing beer.

Elcmar glared at the slave. "Then use that one clean cooking pit, so."

The slave ran from his hard eyes.

His irritation grew when he stepped outside. "Where is Cliodhna?" he shouted. No one answered. The last slave in sight, he sent to bring the new shaman Ith directly to his chamber. Back in privacy, Elcmar dressed with difficulty over his bound ribs, and waited. He desired to gauge this newcomer's reaction to Bresal, and more importantly to question his new advisor about the marriage laws. He soon got to the point with Ith, a lean grey blade of a man.

"I can see how it must have been for Boann, dealing with eejits while I was away. But that's no excuse for the state of things in the hall, nor her absence. She has left this marriage, for all intents and purposes. The marriage agreement says she keeps her property. What are my rights?"

He listened to Ith's impeccable discourse on their respective rights, given this novel situation. Ith summed up then added, "Of course, we are outnumbered here."

Elcmar quickly made his decision. Yes, Starwatchers greatly outnumbered his warriors, but that concern was dwarfed by his desire to find gold before they would quit the Boyne, or Eire. Gold awaited them, or wily Gebann wouldn't have stayed on Eire so long. And Elcmar had seen gold, touched gold in the mountains. He would talk about this later with Ith, and try to appease the men sent by Taranis. There was little chance that his overseers would soon depart.

They were interrupted by the arrival of Bresal, whose commotion awakened all the groggy guests. Elcmar stepped out, inquired of the guests and their rest, and made arrangements to humor their wishes for awhile. He placed the new shaman Ith in charge of things while he, Elcmar, would ride out for the day. He had heard enough for his purposes from Ith. He ignored Bresal; that fool could stew in his own juice. On this morning Elcmar's concealed injury made his temper short indeed.

He eyed the cold, untended smelting pits on his way to the horses' pen. Several warriors followed their champion clamoring to ride out but Elcmar waved them away. This errand would be taken solo. He chose a horse and mounted it stiffly, guarding his side. He wore a new soft leather tunic, under a short fur vest belted by a glossy strap that closed with a conspicuous gold loop. All around the tunic's neck opening shone small plaques of gold sewn on with linen thread. He wore supple leather boots lined with fur over well-stitched leggings. He'd bought up most of the trader's fresh finery from that last boat at the Lake mine and no mistaking the cost, he paid dearly for it from his champion's share of copper. No bother. He could afford to be *flahool*. Hadn't he located a mountain stream of gold?

Elcmar knew he looked impressive that morning, washed and fairly well clean shaven, his eyes and gold ornaments and long bronze dagger all glowing. No man on this island could best him; Boann would see that, so she would. Off he rode. The sky held a pale wintry blue and for the moment he wouldn't have to worry about lashing rain.

He felt gratified to be riding again rather than walking, and with care he cantered his horse across the river plain to the shimmering emerald mounds and the Starwatcher village beyond. As he neared the area now frosted and sere where he had found Boann lying in tall scented grass of the past summer, he felt a sharp longing. Or was that his sore rib? He dismissed his pain. His anger whetted itself on his memory from the prior night, of Boann's faint, herbal scent left in their marriage bed.

He did not dismount at the cleared lawn that marked the village entrance. Heavy silence met the advancing hooves and closed behind Elcmar's insolent back as the animal carried him through Starwatchers interrupted in their morning routines. Elcmar rode his horse right up to the house of Boann's father. The trespass or disrespect to the quiet ones from this act, he ignored. It was time for him to exercise possession, to show his dominion here. Sunlight flashed from the gold adorning his person and from his metal weapon.

Let these Starwatchers see me coming here to take my wife and child, so. He slid expertly off his white horse, and hid the stab of pain. He waited only the shortest interval to enter the dwelling when the door slowly opened to his shout. Elcmar immediately found the infant and snatched him aloft.

"*Lugh!* What a beautiful son!" This burst from his lips before he could stop himself. Boann was not there, only the woman Airmid, and she did not take the child away but put his hand under the baby's head. Airmid smiled at his expression, encouraging him.

Elcmar unwrapped the tiny bundle and examined the infant all over, then gently put him down upon the wrappings. "He is perfect.

What is his name." He spoke to her as a command in his language, and stared at the child.

"Aengus Og. It means, 'the youthful son.'" She tilted her head, watching Elcmar. Perhaps this shining child shall bring peace, her look said. "Boann is having her swim at the stream. You might like to join her there?"

He closed his face into its proud expression again. "Yes. I will go to the stream to find Boann. Stay with the child, with Aengus."

He caught up with Boann as she returned, skin glowing. He used the Invader tongue. "I see you're after taking your bath without a companion, or a sentry. Will you ever follow the rules here, Boann? It's a guard you must have, someone with you at all times."

"Whose rules would that be? And welcome back, husband." Her tone softened. She tried to touch his face but he stopped her hand. She stiffened. "Who would attack me? It wouldn't be a Starwatcher, sure, and your people don't bathe here with us. And which rules are you after mentioning? Our marriage agreement says that I am not your captive. I like bathing, and I will bathe on every dawning. We have already had this discussion, so." She used the Invader language.

"I have reconsidered." It disconcerted him to see Boann after seeing the beautiful boy child, Aengus, but he would not tell her that. He would not show any injury. Elcmar looked off into the distance, not at Boann. His anger hardened and took shape in words. "I have reconsidered many things. In fact, given the conflict for us with Starwatchers, the troubles caused during midwinter sun by your Dagda, I shall ban all use of the starchamber mounds."

It vaguely amused him to be married to this little Starwatcher, but his attachment unsettled him. Never mind that she drew him safely home, a flame in darkness. If Boann could not prove useful as he had intended, then changes would be made. He turned away from her.

Boann took a step after him. What could he mean by banning use of the mounds? To retaliate for lost and frozen Invader warriors who had harassed her people?

"You cannot be serious! Your warriors ruined one of our mounds! There have been troubles enough, that is true. Both sides need to sit in council together."

She tried to tell him about the winter solstice ceremony; that for her people, the solstice sunrise streaming into the passage or the full moon seen through the portal, were no more nor less than revered truths. "The stars tell us all that we need to know. We don't put on a show with incantations, or cut open animals to rummage their intestines."

Elcmar stopped. He turned, but his eyes avoided contact with hers.

She picked up two shrunken apples from the cold ground, showing him how the moon crossed the line of the sun's ecliptic on a regular basis. She tried to explain how the position of the Bright One had lined up with the moon at winter solstice. "It's nothing to fear."

Elcmar stared directly at her now.

She faltered; Boann could see that he understood neither the sun's movements nor the moon's. He might not understand the import of the solstice. Did Elcmar know that the equinoxes set the cardinal directions of east and west? It was useless, even dangerous, to explain anything more to him about the movements in the sky. She tossed aside the apples.

"Right, so. Have you no limits on what you do?" She seethed.

He stared, his eyes cold and smooth as flint.

"My people's starwatching shall continue at the mounds as before. That is part of our marriage contract."

His voice came harsh. "You are mistaken. I own this land. And the mounds on it."

"You own it, Elcmar? No one person owns this land. It has always been so. If anyone does own this island, it belongs to all Starwatchers!"

He took her arm roughly. He had not let her touch him in welcome, and now this. She restrained herself, seeing icy anger in his eyes.

"You keep only what you brought into this marriage. As you say, none of you Starwatchers own Eire. You don't believe in ownership of land. This island is, therefore, ours. We have taken Eire and I hold all authority over it." His words drove a dagger crueler than any metal into her heart. "Listen carefully, Boann. I never loved you. I want only this island. For my son. For Aengus."

She twisted her arm from his grasp. Bresal's lessons on the Invader concepts of property and inheritance came back to her. She thought of the seeds of doubt sown by Maedb. Elcmar would hear the gossip soon enough, if he had not already.

She struck back. "You cannot prove that Aengus is your son."

He lunged for her but clutched his side.

She outran him though she could hardly breathe, her heart like a stone. She was lengths ahead, more fleet on foot. Had she looked back, she would have seen Elcmar drop to his knees, folded over in agony. It took him a long time to rise, alone, and fetch his horse that he found staked at a distance from the Starwatcher village.

Boann reached cover, a thick stand of yew trees where she could catch her breath. Her thoughts raced. She had known that leaving the camp to give birth to Aengus would be difficult to explain, but Elcmar pushed their argument well beyond that. All his words stung as if he had slapped her like he would a slave.

She leaned back against the smooth trunk of an ash, its bright yellow spears of new leaves furled tight in wait for spring, and tried to make sense of their quarrel. She had been glad for his return but saw him now all too clearly. Their intimacies and quiet moments, their pleasures as man and wife, meant nothing to him. *What, then, could he want with a woman?* His Invader concept of ownership and that it carried the right to abuse and discard land, things, and persons, was a lesson she did not want. She would not give way to tears though some slid down her cheeks. *I have simply been wrong about him. He wants only to exploit me, as he intends to exploit this island.* She must think what to do.

Elcmar asserted that he owned this island; that was ridiculous. No one could own or carve up the land any more than one could own or carve up the sky's dome or the ocean. That Elcmar desired to have authority over Eire was a different problem. The Invaders must not be allowed to impose their ways at the Starwatchers' expense. He showed no remorse for the destruction of Dowth.

Anyone could observe the skies' movements, yet not one of the intruders could see them. Elcmar was quick and cunning about many things, but he hadn't studied the skies. The Starwatcher facts which she took for granted were to him deep secrets. Worse, he was capricious as weather: sunny, then raining before one could blink. Perhaps that resulted from his chaotic early years, always scrabbling for food and shelter, on the move as he said it. Rarely sitting engaged with a task for his mind or free to play, unlike a Starwatcher child. Her child.

She drew her cloak tighter. She must protect Aengus, and deal with Elcmar and his hard-edged people as they were in the here and now among her people. She longed to talk with Sheela of the spirits, and closed her eyes to imagine their conversation.

You thought Elcmar would change but it is you who must change, wise Sheela said, sighing with the yew boughs.

Boann opened her eyes. Invaders could not grasp the Starwatchers' way of life; so be it. She must be cleverer than Elcmar. She would not allow him to overwhelm her, nor use their marriage to claim this island. She understood now what Cliodhna warned her, what Sheela's spirit was telling her. She must pretend to accommodate the Invaders, no matter how rude or ignorant she found their ways. I can be cunning, dissemble, and use guile if I must, she told herself; I can say yes when I mean no and no when I mean yes.

From now on she would react in strength rather than from fear. She lifted her face to the winter sun. If these Invaders interfered with use of the mounds, they would see dire consequences. No more compromising; she would convince her elders at the earliest opportunity.

Whether her child had a preassigned status or what he might inherit from Elcmar, did not matter. She would raise Aengus as a Starwatcher. Not as a warrior, to wander strange lands and compete for the absurd privilege of mounting a horse to appease invisible gods, or if he were scarred to then be scorned as blemished and not fit to lead. None of that made sense to her. Aengus would have a very different sense of himself and the world and his place in the world, than any of that. Aengus descended from the mother, in her line, like any Starwatcher.

She would guard little Aengus' future. Elcmar only mentioned the child to her at the last, when he claimed ownership of Eire. Had he seen Aengus? The ash tree's bare-limbed shadow on the frozen ground showed to her surprise that it was past midsun. She rushed back to Aengus at her father's house.

The Invaders' *geis* began that very nightfall. Elcmar acted discreetly, sending armed warriors in the dark. One restrained Oghma while they took away his daughter and grandson before his eyes.

"Wait for word from me in our signs—" Boann called to Oghma in their tongue.

She refused to ride the horse offered to her. They traveled back to the Invader camp, a warrior sullenly leading two horses and another minding the *ard ri's* woman who insisted on walking. She hugged little Aengus close to her.

On Boann's arrival at the great hall, dimly lit and quiet, the slave Muirgen took Aengus from her arms. She anxiously followed the slave, who carried Aengus back to the sleeping chamber. Boann saw that a nursery area had been prepared for the infant there, where

Elcmar waited. She sat away from Elcmar, in the shadows, tense while he held Aengus. She did not speak. It did seem to her that he handled the baby with care.

After a time, he indicated that the slave must withdraw from them and watched Muirgen leave. He turned to Boann. "You must also occupy the sleeping chamber in order to be near the child."

Elcmar did not bolt the door and he wore no weapon in his belt. She relaxed enough to sleep in the bed beside him, but lightly, and she rose quickly whenever Aengus needed to nurse.

When she woke in the morning light, she found that Elcmar had left a white gown of cloth woven finer than any she had seen, and a belt woven in many colors, draped over her clothing baskets. Soft leather shaped to cover the whole foot, her first shoes, lay close by. His gesture touched Boann until she comprehended it fully from the slave girl, who returned to her and Aengus. Elcmar wanted a grand show of her arrival in the camp, as if to say that Boann returned of her own volition now that the *ard ri* had returned. Muirgen brought tepid water for a hasty washing of hands and face and neck, and secured the gold discs at her earlobes.

Elcmar paraded his wife in her new clothing together with little Aengus. The camp's newcomers acted polite, almost servile in their attentions to mother and child. When Boann met the new sage, her skin crawled. Ith had dry cold hands, sunken eyes, and his thin mouth turned down at the corners in a narrow face without color; an altogether humorless apparition of a man. She hugged Aengus tight against her soft new tunic.

Boann chose to stay in the camp despite having been brought to Elcmar in darkness and against her will. If she aided Elcmar to save face with his people, he might reconsider his ban on use of the mounds. She would privately remind him of their marriage contract, that he needed their marriage to make any claim on her or Eire or Aengus. I can be as merciless as Elcmar, she told herself. And Elcmar has no other home but the Boyne and no boat to leave it.

Some days later, Boann hosted Maedb and her retinue. She refrained from comment while the gaily dressed and painted women bounced and jangled Aengus. Instead she signaled and the slave girl quickly brought aromatic water of Boann's own blending, and served it to the women in the fine blossom cups of Cliodhna.

"Aengus Og!" Maedb toasted. "Aengus the young son." Maedb held out her cup to be refilled and inquired pointedly about Cliodhna.

After an awkward pause, Boann answered her truthfully, "I do not know of Cliodhna. She has disappeared from this place."

Maedb searched Boann's face but it was smooth of concealment.

The slave Muirgen tactfully withdrew little Aengus from the women's excessive handling, but not before Aengus spit up on one of Maedb's companions, on a rare gown bordered with hundreds of tiny stone beads sewn onto it. Muirgen leaped to dab at the stain, and the intruder woman managed to be gracious about it to Boann.

Almost one lunate passed. In the camp an evil atmosphere hung like the oppressive winter skies. The intruders still chattered about their month of two moons and the portent of the second, dark red moon. Elcmar set the warriors and smelters and slaves to furious work, and made Bresal's life grim by ordering no drink served to him before darkness fell. Bresal swore he would make darkness without end and challenged Ith to help him. Ith replied that he would leave that feat to Bresal's own magic, perhaps another cloud of dust would suffice?

Whenever any issue concerning the Starwatchers arose, Boann made it appear that she deferred to Elcmar. Her relations with him remained polite, but they no longer coupled as during their first lunate together. He questioned her several times about Cliodhna, then abruptly dropped the topic. Even the slaves seemed to blame Boann for Cliodhna's absence.

She dodged the new advisor Ith, no matter how he tried to flatter her. Ith sidled close to her at feasts, or while she potted herb seeds in a sheltered sunny space beside the great hall. To her ears, his words came out hissing like releasing bad air from a bloated sheep.

"You could become a celebrity with us, Boann! A woman of status. Just like Maedb."

No, never like Maedb. Not a'tall like that woman. She gave him a cold shoulder.

"These passage mounds surpass anything I have seen, even the famed stone circle on the Big Isle. You Starwatchers cover your great stones with carvings! We must discuss these carvings soon." He hovered, almost whispering.

Distressed that this shaman had set foot at their sanctified mounds, Boann forced a smile and replied, changing the subject. She saw that unlike Bresal, Ith had a mind sharp as a dagger.

Despite rebuffs from Boann, Ith pursued the Starwatcher knowledge. During sunlight, he tried to decipher the kerbstones' carved symbols. He aspired to learn their astronomy secrets as much as Elcmar desired to find gold. He had seen megaliths along the Seafarer peninsula and he saw megaliths on the Continent's northern edges that piqued his interest. He found more mounds on these islands. All these tribes who build mounds know something weighty about the skies, he surmised, and at this *Bru na Boinne* complex their observations carry on day and night. These quiet ones organize their lives completely around the starwatching, they revere their astronomers: why, he wondered, what indeed happens here at midwinter solstice.

"We have only to overcome their elders in order for us to gain ascendancy on Eire. Elcmar has done well to camp here at their power center," he told the pouting Bresal.

Ith tried to glean from Bresal what occurred at the solstice, an event so impressive that the warriors who were there swore that these quiet ones captured the full moon with the Bright Star inside their central mound. Soon after arriving, he had a sit-down with

Bresal over an array of drinking cups in his cramped hut littered with animal bones, feathers, and mushrooms. Ith brought his long face close to Bresal's.

"Howyeh—" Bresal giggled and drew back. But at Ith's insistence, he fatuously described his sessions with Boann during the moons leading up to the Night of the Dead. "That was before Boann fled from the camp. I never laid a hand on her!" he added.

Ith tried not to sneer. "Bresal, we are shamans. We are guardians of the holy festivals, we Invaders who keep track of the moon. We count from the last light, that is to say, from nightfall as the beginning of a new day. For us the day is measured from darkness to darkness. Surely you have seen that our concept of time differs from that of the Starwatchers?"

Bresal flushed and his hand shook in raising his cup.

"Our Invader year begins at the festival we call the Night of the Dead, when the sun is leaving us. Would it be safe to say that Boann knows this much about our counting of time?"

Bresal nodded. Then, he shrugged.

Ith cajoled him. "That's fine. Our Invader time, our day, month, and year, begin with and are defined by darkness. We divide a lunate by the moon's phases into halves, a dark fortnight and a bright fortnight. Our system gives a year of thirteen moons, more or less.

"But we must adjust our count to keep up with the sun. Since we rarely linger in one place, we don't record each rising of the sun. Yet we see that these Starwatchers go to great lengths to observe the sun's exact path, and that of the moon. Every nightfall and every daylight. Can you think of anything a'tall since you've been on this island, anything these Starwatchers know or use, that could help us in counting time?"

Ith examined Bresal's full moon of a face. It reflected light but gave no heat of knowledge from within, not on this subject anyway. Clearly, your man had not used his time with Boann to learn how these Starwatchers could accurately track solstices and equinoxes, much less the stars. If indeed they can do so, Ith wondered.

Slowly the sunrise moved north on the horizon. Invaders raiding cattle met new resistance and serious injuries occurred to men on each side, Starwatchers and Invaders. Smelters used copper ingots from the Lake mine, acrid smoke filled the walled camp, and more long knives and halberd points hung in the great hall. Boann suggested that it was a mistake to not hold a council of the Starwatchers with Invaders, but her opinion merited Elcmar's harshest glare. She refrained from open comment to him when others were present in the great hall.

Cian, said to have journeyed to the Continent, had not returned to the Boyne. Boann inquired about this voyage from slaves who might know about the Seafarers' coasts, but she gathered little and the questions gnawed at her.

She felt Elcmar's anger simmering just below his tight surface as he supervised the camp. His temper flared occasionally, but he kept it in check when holding little Aengus. Elcmar searched for the sun metal, with added pressure on him from Taranis' men and the new shaman Ith. He sent three warriors south to the mountains to seek the stream bearing gold, but those men did not return. Elcmar kept silent about this loss but she knew that he could not spare those warriors.

It was still the season of storms and no boats arrived. Boann waited for news of Cliodhna, and Cian.

Ith caught Bresal fondling the slave Muirgen in a fiber drying shed, and with contempt dismissed Bresal on the spot and in the young slave's presence. Ith then avidly questioned the girl. He allowed Muirgen to be seated while he asked her about herself—and Boann. Cowering before him but openly glad to be rid of Bresal for the moment, she told him enough to make herself appear useful. When he recruited her to befriend and watch over Boann, Muirgen readily agreed.

Rumors in the camp to explain Aengus' mysterious birth while Elcmar journeyed, had it that these Starwatchers stopped the sun. Ith viewed that as nonsense, but he repeatedly circled their high mounds and examined their odd carvings. *What do they mean by the Red Eye Of All Knowledge? Have these Starwatchers discovered a way to meddle with time?* He entertained that idea. No people had a system that accommodated the moon with the sun's annual cycle. Time was a fluid concept and each tribe known to Ith used a different method to fix a date. Mistakes, delays, and misunderstandings resulted; these disrupted trading. An accurate calendar followed by all tribes would give a shaman, namely him, dizzying heights of power. If he gained control over such knowledge, over time itself, for him it would be a better discovery than gold. He could appear to control the sun and moon and possibly the stars, he could coordinate the whole cosmos!

He would invent a religion that went beyond mundane matters of when to plant and when to cross the ocean. The Invaders could conquer the world with Ith's powerful new creed. That is, as soon as he figured out from the Starwatchers what that new creed would be.

He tried several more times to ingratiate himself with Boann. She engaged him as well as she could converse—and her command of their tongue improved rapidly—but still she told him nothing meaningful, nothing useful about her people's starwatching. He sought Elcmar for his aid with breaking down Boann.

"Can we learn the Starwatcher knowledge from clever Boann? If so, I have arrived here at a propitious time. Perhaps you were wise to marry this little Starwatcher."

The champion looked preoccupied. "Connor has not returned nor sent any metals from the north. My few Invaders camped here along the Boyne do not have time enough to search for gold. Particularly if we indulge ourselves nonstop in astronomy."

Ith clasped his hands behind his back and had his say. "These Starwatchers put extreme effort into building and maintaining their high mounds. These mounds hold more than burials, to be sure; the quiet ones attend at their mounds every sunrise and sunset. We should find out the meaning in this, their practices, their astronomy. It could be very valuable to us especially for trade."

"And Bresal tells me there is no gold inside or out of these mounds. He claims that the quiet ones fail in their sorcery with the skies. Somehow, these natives' simple ways need to be redirected. Can they ever be made to produce a surplus of anything for our trade?" Elcmar added, "Taranis wants payment and he won't wait long. There are harsh ways to make these Starwatchers work for us, but so far we have spared them. If they spent less time at their mounds and more with cattle and crops, then..." His eyes bored into Ith.

"They do produce a surplus of babies," Ith said. The *ard ri* scowled at him. He spread his hands wide to show he had nothing to hide from Elcmar. "You know that I do not agree with putting a *geis* on their mounds. I would prefer us to be more subtle in order to learn their skywatching secrets. But we can try banning use of the mounds, as you say." He could spend more time studying the detailed carvings if the quiet ones no longer could gather at their mounds.

They shared the objective of dominating the Starwatchers, and the two men agreed that the slave Muirgen may prove useful toward that end. Elcmar and Ith kept a close eye on Muirgen.

The lambing time drew near, and this moon brought a feasting time for the Invaders, Boann learned from Muirgen. For Boann it brought the crossquarter starwatch between solstice and equinox. She practiced speaking to sound both submissive and determined, in private with Dabilla, who licked her face with friendly joy no matter what. Then she approached Elcmar about her attendance at the mound ceremony.

He was firm, dismissive, with her. "There won't be any ceremony for Starwatchers to attend. You and I discussed this when I returned to the Boyne—don't you remember, Boann?"

The same words she had used with him when they fought. Undeterred, she devised a way to attend the starwatch. Slipping away was much more difficult than before, when she left the disorganized camp as Bresal prepared to glorify darkness and she shuddered to recall his oration about their Night of the Dead. She was again determined to slip out of these walls. Thinking of the slave who admirably protected little Aengus from Maedb so far, Boann thought to bring Muirgen with her. The pretext would be gathering whatever hazelnuts remained in the woods along the river. The nights were still long and the sun would set early. She could hurry back from the mounds, back to the camp for the Invader feast that would not begin until full darkness. She was certain that her plan would succeed.

That morning of the crossquarter, Boann came upon Elcmar while he was inspecting a young warrior. He barely turned his head during her speech.

"I and the slave Muirgen shall leave the camp after midsun to gather hazelnuts. Surely you see that our food supplies are short due to the rains during the late harvest?" He seemed indifferent to her excuse to leave the camp. Soon a sentry took her and the slave girl to the plank bridge and let them go off on their own.

They walked to the northwest, Boann thinking along the way that Elcmar had taken a natural interest in Muirgen. Boann had pointed out Muirgen to him as being quick, and protective of Aengus. She was pleased that Elcmar would show an interest in anyone other than his warriors and his new shaman from the Continent. This slave girl deserved a better life.

With Muirgen's help, she filled two large netted shoulder slings of the nuts that remained in a hazelwood stand. "We'll have to see if winter frosts have ruined these nuts," she told Muirgen. The nuts they cracked open looked edible. Muirgen cast the meat of one hazelnut into the stream for thanksgiving, and Boann nodded approval. She held up a hazel rod to check the sun's angle, then turned to the girl.

"We go beyond the hazel trees now. We shall have to go quickly," and the two skimmed through the forest to the distant mounds. Boann's mass of auburn hair swung and caught in twigs along their way and Muirgen offered to braid her hair. Though short of breath, she declined. "We must hurry. The observation is more important than how anyone looks."

As they entered the clearing at the mound, Boann saw that there would indeed be a starwatch, albeit by a small group. Only a few astronomers stood watching while the sun met the western horizon. Perhaps the others in her village feared another attack with horses. Her blood pulsing, she joined them in her robe lined with swan feathers and looked with Daire at certain constellations, checking notches in stone and bone against the early evening stars.

Immediately after their observations finished, signal torches were lit and then quickly extinguished. No large signal fire had been laid so as to avoid arousing the intruder camp. The astronomers saw with gratitude the signal fires lit at surrounding high places by other Starwatchers.

In the twilight no one saw the distant retreating figure of Ith as he slipped from behind an outcropping and returned to the Invader camp.

Boann had but little time to talk with an elder or two, then she departed.

On their way back to the camp, Muirgen uttered the Starwatchers' name for their ceremony and Boann found that the slave knew it fell between solstice and equinox.

The girl had been quiet and respectful at the mounds. Boann wondered if Muirgen understood their reverent observance. The signal fires coordinated the starwatching effort all over the island. The fires were lit in a series, outward from one high place to the others. These ritual fires confirmed the amazing events seen in the sky to all the people on their island. It had been done in this way for centuries, since they began building mounds as observatories. Their signal fires bound the people to the sky and to each other.

Muirgen blurted as they hurried through the dusk, "I come from the south. Invaders raided our coast and took me at nine suns of age from my people." Muirgen's villagers were excellent mariners, she told Boann, living along the northwest corner of the Continent. They sited their mounds beside the ocean's horizon and observed the stars relied on to navigate.

Over her shoulder, Boann saw the slave girl clutching the robe of softest swan feathers, that Boann cast off to move faster. Muirgen kept talking softly, "My people assembled at our mound built on a small rise, looking out at the rolling waters. I remember sighting on stars with my mother, and hearing stories of the Swan, the Hunter, and the Seven Stars."

Boann winced. The ceremony at the mound had given the girl a taste of dignity, if not actual belonging. Perhaps it occurred to Muirgen that the Starwatchers are more like her own people than they are different. It was the traders, the Invaders, who took slaves. They took even children.

But she could not stop to hear Muirgen's tale. Boann offered a few words of comfort, seeing that little remained to the young slave of her mother's ways, scraps from the past that Invaders had ripped away. Stolen while but a child, Muirgen learned the baser appetites of her captors at a precocious age. Almost a woman now, she had large grey eyes and comely hair and figure. Boann knew: Muirgen used her body to gain advantages, little gifts and rewards, food and a warm sleeping place, and thus she survived her captivity.

Boann did not know that the girl had met several times with Elcmar and Ith, who knew from her that a starwatch would transpire at lambing time.

Muirgen kept the pace as Boann scurried over frozen tussocks and around thickets, to reach the camp and join the Invader feast. Darkness stretched fingers from the east behind their backs until it blotted out the last light in the west. The slave hastened at her heels, hands wound tight around the cloak of swan feathers, as Boann rushed toward certain disaster.

With sunrise, Elcmar took Muirgen aside and into Ith's chamber. She reached expectantly for him and he pushed her away. Elcmar had no appetite for this girl whatsoever; her fawning at him while they gained her confidence merely annoyed him. He spoke with Muirgen only when others were present. Ith stepped out from shadow.

She began trembling before these powerful men, the *ard ri* and the austere Ith. Her moment of belonging with Boann's people faded; these two had her back inside walls.

"Your opportunity to gain favor with either Elcmar or Boann has evaporated. You can be killed, or worse, if you do not cooperate." Glowering, Ith questioned her in detail about accompanying Boann to the mound ceremony. Elcmar made her describe the final moments of the starwatch, then repeat to him when and where the Starwatchers lit signal fires.

"Surrounding the Boyne, it was." She stood shaking before them.

Disgusted, Ith saw that she gave them the barest bits and pieces of information, she played the fool. "You are not to talk to other slaves, d'you hear me?"

Before that very sun set, Ith married Muirgen to a disabled warrior who had been a source of discontent. They could start a new camp close by, at the place called Teamair. There they would have to be productive, he told them, and gave the couple charge of a cumal of cattle that Maedb had neglected. Muirgen reached without hesitation for her scarred new husband and a chance to forge an existence apart from the camp. Ith allowed the couple no wedding feast and no time to lie together before he sent them away with only a poor herd onto the cold plain.

Their union solved a problem as to each, he declared to Elcmar.

After they disposed of Muirgen, Elcmar left Ith's side. He evaded the throng who sought him inside the great hall and rode alone out of the camp and hiked up Red Mountain. From there he stared at the Boyne valley and the mountains ringing the surrounding plains. Elcmar spent some time evaluating all the information he had gathered thus far about starwatching.

He gleaned several bits from what Muirgen told them. First, that the Starwatchers lit signal fires only after their extended observations of the skies. Next, Elcmar reasoned that for greatest effect, these fires were lit on the highest places. Finally, that this all happened in some sort of order. Ith told him that the first signal came from close by to the south, a place these quiet ones thought to be the navel, the physical center, of this island. Only torches had been lit at the Boyne mounds on the previous night, but Ith had seen the signal fires progress outward at high places in all directions.

Disruption of the next Starwatcher ceremony would be so simple a task that Elcmar chuckled. He allowed his horse to trot back to the camp, his rib having almost healed. After a few nights spent in solitary thought beside the hearth's flames, he sent for Ith.

Ith had never seen Elcmar so full of himself.

"I may well have divined the enigma of the fires." Those amber eyes glowed like sun metal as he told Ith his plan. It would be easy enough to carry out.

*The better the question the harder the answer. There is no answer at
all to a very good question.*

At *Swim-Two-Birds*, Flann O'Brien

Seafarers

D URING THEIR TRAVELS west from where they landed on the
Seafarer peninsula, Gebann halted abruptly. Cian had no choice
and climbed with him all that morning on a rough path up through
sun-dappled beech and oak forest. They reached a striking monument,
totally hidden from below. When they arrived at the tall outcropping,
the height they had ascended startled Cian. The ocean stretched north
and east and west, far into its distant meeting with the paler blue sky.
From this new perspective, the water's endless expanse dwarfed him,
it dwarfed even the mountains where they stood.

Subdued, he said, "Here one can see a ship coming in any
direction from where it's half the sky out from shore."

Gebann caught his breath then answered, "Yes, that's part of my
bringing you to see this high place. Now let us look at the message
of my ancestors."

The massive grey rock had a rough cylinder shape. Its eastern
and southern aspect held the most stonecarving that Cian had seen

so far on the Seafarer peninsula. He stood facing the carvings on the towering rock, the ocean glistening on the horizon beyond. He saw chiseled into the stone, above his height, a rounded solar symbol topping a tall rectangle etched with horizontal lines. This arch-topped rectangle was bordered entirely by two bands filled with lozenges, the sacred shape used also in passage tomb carvings. He had in the past carved such a lozenge pattern. The carvings here were dusted with ceremonial red ochre to highlight them, or he would have touched them.

More amazing to him, to the left of the arched plaque was carved a large upright dagger, almost the height of the arched plaque. Below the dagger, a deep horizontal line began at the left edge of the monument and ran straight to the border of the rectangle, ending in a slight cupmark. Someone had colored the dagger and the line with deep yellow ochre. He looked at Gebann, who stood watching him.

Solemnly, Gebann explained each symbol. "We stand at a holy place of those who lived before us on this coast—those who fished the waters long before my people thought to call themselves Seafarers. At this high place I affirm our traditions. Here I search myself for good and bad, and I ask for wisdom from the ancestors. Take your time here, so." He moved away a few paces.

Cian shut his eyes and conjured those who had ventured for centuries from this littoral onto the treacherous ocean. Countless generations who explored strange coasts yet whose spirits rested at this place. Those people protected their beliefs, they took care to record them on this mighty rock and carried them to far shores. His eyes stung to recall the triple spiral carved at the Boyne. In this land so foreign, but familiar with its mounds and carved symbols, he at last understood Oghma and his singleminded devotion to carving stone. He could choose a different future for himself without discarding his ancestors. Their weighty past could anchor him in shifting seas, rather than pull him under. How he wanted to talk with Oghma and his elders now!

He looked again. The entire figure made sense to him, except the dagger. The oversized dagger had been added later, that was clear. Its outline under the midday sun was grotesque, hastily incised, a warning perhaps? An Invader long knife, good only for attacking another human. He checked the deep blue horizon for trader ships, as if Invaders might appear while he stood before the menacing knife.

A cold fear gripped him under the hot sun of this peninsula. *I must return, I will return to Eire.*

Gebann sat close by on the edge of the rock plateau, staring at the ocean.

"Are you all right?" he inquired, not sure whether the older man had taken ill.

Gebann took his time answering. "I am thinking of Cliodhna and how to find her on the ocean."

They stared north at the vast undulating blue. Then Cian left the smith to ponder, and below in the musty forest he snared a rabbit and found mushrooms and laid the food on a flat stone. He climbed the cliff again and led Gebann down the steep path from the monument. They went further down the mountain to prepare their meal in the shade of beech and oak, after leaving one mushroom behind in thanksgiving.

They traveled for several more days, moving west. Steep emerald mountains enfolded them as they passed through lovely valleys. Rushing streams were bordered here by thickets of apple trees and berry vines in varieties Cian had never seen. Despite the strange yellow soil, there were good fruits to eat and unspoiled by frost. The big dust cloud hadn't come this far south along the Continent, he told the smith, who nodded in tacit agreement.

Among still sharper mountains packed close together, they hiked to several copper mining sites on the slopes. Gebann pointed out how the long lateral tunnels had been dug and reinforced, unlike the shallower Lake mine on Eire. Inside, the miners used a swinging hammer contrivance: large rocks on ropes tied to wood uprights, bashing them against heated rock faces to loosen ore; he admired their ingenuity. At the smelting pits, Gebann showed him how leather bellows clamped to the pit walls forced air in and raised the pit's temperature. The miners were polite but guarded with them. Gebann indicated he did not wish to burden these struggling men to shelter and eat with them as guests, and the two travelers left to find the coast again.

There Gebann exchanged the mules with a man who ferried in a dugout canoe to continue west, for this stretch of mountainous coast was too rough to traverse even with mules. Cian noted how the smith traded bits of metal and colored stone beads for things they needed, including food and two fresh horses when they landed; and they rode forth again.

They spoke infrequently and that pleased both, and they settled into easy companionship as they traveled. Mines and Seafarer settlements dotted this scenic coast. Always the smoky mining areas were denuded of trees and eroded soil was filling in adjacent streambeds. Where the streams ran clear, Gebann looked for gold and often picked up a good-sized piece or two under the sparkling surface. "We're too late for good fishing here, Cian. Might as well catch something."

They progressed in humid, salty air toward the place of the setting sun. We're headed for land's end, the smith teased. Along the shoreline, Gebann showed him how to catch seafood, periwinkles and squid, among the rocks. Cian's fair skin darkened in the warm midday sun as he waded for seafood and bathed.

As the two men rode or walked the horses, Cian saw the familiar shape of passage mounds along the way. Gebann affirmed that these small mounds enclosed stone chambers with burials. They stopped at stelae having strange markings. Some of the carvings resembled a human outline or a face; others were in the form of the familiar sheepherder's crook. Still other stelae had geometric hatch lines. Horizontal granite slabs had cupmarks. Cian recognized the symbolism of many of these carvings and he learned new Seafarer symbols quickly.

"It is a good system here, to show boundaries and grazing lands," he said.

"Else the traders come along and build camps wherever they like," Gebann added.

Dagger shapes threatened on some stelae that they passed. Cian felt they were being watched, shadows moving in high places along their way, but he could discern no one following. Gebann glanced over his shoulder from time to time as well, and left Cian's wrists unbound.

Traders invariably built their enclosures on elevated places where mining took place below. None of these traders lived in caves. Cian saw that the native Seafarers who lived back from the coast often used caves as handy dwellings, dry and warm enough if facing sunlight. The inland Seafarers embellished their cave interiors with reed dividers and colorful hangings, and added drystacked stone walls and flagged entrance courts.

Their travels brought them to one such dwelling cave. When no one greeted them outside it, Gebann and Cian dismounted and ventured inside. They found this cave filled with bodies, dead for some time and almost bare of flesh, all of them young people and children, some infants. None had a burial tunic or ocher tribute. The bodies had been tossed into piles, some carelessly dismembered. Cian recognized the clean slice of metal through the tangled bones. The fetid air choked him and he struggled to keep his morning meal down. This scene was the work of madness, depravity. As Gebann and Cian exited the cave, several old women and one old man whom they half-carried along emerged from the woods to speak with them.

"What happened here?" Gebann asked with a stern face.

The old ones told him in the Seafarer tongue. Gebann's shoulders slumped. "Dead, all dead, killed!" he repeated.

Cian winced in the sunlight after the darkness and horror of the cave. "Shall I burn the bones?" he asked in a low voice.

"No, lad. Leave the bones as they lie. So that all may see the poor murdered ones!" Gebann bellowed. Later he said as they rode, "That tribe refused to work for Invaders," and he spat on the ground.

The smith reached up and drew blood from his cheeks in mourning and Cian did the same.

"I must return to help my people, Gebann."

"I know that." Gebann sounded weary, and they camped prior to the setting sun.

They rode together through most of another lunate, Cian wondering if they would ever reach this land's end. At last, past a midsun, Gebann drew back on the braided hemp reins and gazed across a marshy green plain that stretched west from their vantage point, along the great sea's coast. For Cian, this place reminded of the Boyne and he had a ripple of homesickness at seeing it. Above the plain's distant edge stood a settlement.

"What is the name of this place?"

"The traders call it *Murias*." They rode down an incline and across waving grass toward the fortified settlement, located high up on its own plateau and reinforced with stones layered thick around its base.

The height of this trader settlement ensured it had a fine lookout over the ocean. Cian assessed its size and importance as they approached. Gebann confirmed his assumptions.

"Invaders control the water traffic. They keep officials posted day and night. Here, close to the northwest corner of our peninsula, this landing has become a trade node for either offloading cargo or taking on supplies. Vessels continue on the oceans in either direction. A ship continues east along this peninsula's northern coast. That trade extends up to Taranis and the Continent's inland rivers. Or, it voyages west and then south. Along the southern coast the route leads east through narrow, rocky straits and into the middle sea, warmer salt waters bounded by exotic lands." His forefinger traced it all in midair.

"It was here in this port that I first laid eyes on Elcmar." Gebann's eyes narrowed against the sun. He briefly described Elcmar's rise from a scrappy orphan without a tribe to an accepted warrior. "He's after landing on his feet again—as an Invader champion, in Eire.

"But that's not why this place is special to me," Gebann chuckled. "Here you will meet my wife, at my home!" He urged the horses into more speed to cross the plain to his home.

His wife welcomed Gebann with cries of delight, and surprise that he would return after autumn equinox. Her eyes soon brimmed with tears to hear that Cliodhna had been held hostage, and she pressed a hand to her mouth. Small-boned and darting, like a shore bird, she hurried away to fetch bread and hot food from a communal oven.

The exhausted Gebann rested with Cian. His wife flitted around them, ministering to their needs. They shared meals of flat chewy acorn bread, and little olives, and sharp cheeses, field greens laced with chopped wild garlic stems and oil, and roast squid, fish, and game birds; most of it new to Cian. Refreshed and well fed, the two men discussed all they observed on their journey.

They talked late into many of the following nights. After several jars of brew, Gebann spoke freely. "Elcmar thinks you're my hostage, but to him I say—" and he made a rude gesture. He grabbed Cian's shoulder. "Their shamans insult us, say that we lack proper gods, your people and mine. Sunworshipers, they call us. Bah!" The smith fell back on his seat. "We have no use for their meddling shamans. Creation happens with every sunrise."

The two prowled the harbor loading area at odd hours, to evade curious trader officials who might question the young Starwatcher though Cian by now wore his hair tied back like a Seafarer's. Cian saw foreign goods and people that he could not have imagined to exist. The sight of captives bound with ropes contrasted with the goodness shown to him by Gebann. How would he ever repay it? Gebann led him on narrow lanes and into dark rooms where they met with experienced Seafarers, many of whom knew Lir. Cian heard tall tales of their journeys along these coasts, of crystal islands under the sea where people lived without growing old. He was less fond of their sea monster tales. But there was no word of Cliodhna among any of these ships' crews. The smith's steps became halting as their search for news of his daughter proved futile.

"It was too late, too late," Gebann muttered at night over cups.

Cian kept to himself at the winter solstice, aching, blaming it on the damp cold that descended on this coast. He pretended the winter storms blew here after touching his Starwatcher island, as if the wind carried a trace of Boann. Spring equinox would follow the storms.

He must take his leave of their hospitality and this pleasant, busy harbor; and Gebann agreed. At an evening meal to say farewell, he looked into his cup of dark red brew. It smelled deliciously of berries and he complimented Gebann's wife on its brewing. But deep within, he was concerned about the smith's shuffling gait. Gebann had made arrangements for Cian to travel east but without him. Cian could see that the once-hearty smith might have made his last ocean voyage. He thanked the smith profusely for their journey together.

Cian did not want to further trouble his kind hosts. Yet something lingered with him, an idea forming under the sun and stars since he left Eire. He turned to Gebann's gracious wife.

"Could I see one of your earrings?"

Surprised, she handed him the small gold disc. Its shining surface was minutely etched with sets of parallel lines dividing it into equal quadrant sections. Its design spoke to Cian of the four sacred directions under the sky's dome. This disc held their knowledge passed through generations, Seafarers and Starwatchers alike and long before new ways troubled their coasts. This elegant little gold disc, etched with the four directions given from the sky, lit up Cian's mind. Suddenly his restless dreams of the Starwatchers' island and beautiful Boann and the firmament above them all, made perfect sense. He slept well that night for the first time in many lunates.

Surely Gebann knew where the sun metal could be found in Eire. On his final sunrise there, Cian induced Gebann to describe where he might look for gold if he made it back to the Starwatchers.

"Any sun metal I find might be useful to return Cliodhna to you. Lir would help. I promise on my own blood that I will inquire throughout my travels—even to the hall of mighty Taranis—so that you may look upon her face again."

Gebann studied his hands wrapped around a blossom-shaped cup, one of hers. Cian knew: smiths were shamans, keepers of secrets. Gebann would not have volunteered to tell anyone his secret, a grand source of gold waiting in Eire.

At last the great smith spoke. "I am now like your father as well as hers, young Starwatcher, and you are like a son to me. Cliodhna is now your sister. I believe what you tell me. Look for the sun metal, and our Cliodhna. It is not likely that I shall return to your island, even if Elcmar himself comes here to take me. I will be waiting here in the sunlight of our home for Cliodhna."

He retrieved a strong leather bag. From its contents, Gebann showed him types of rocks veined with gold, including the precious white quartz that signaled the sun metal might lie close at hand. Cian handled each rock to know its weight and texture, and they flaked off samples for him to carry. Gebann then scratched marks onto a thin stone plate. These etched stone plaques, the size of one's hand, were used by the elite on this peninsula, and Gebann warned that this one would attract attention if it were found in Cian's possession. Gebann's marks on this plaque for Cian showed him where to look in the eastern mountains of the Starwatchers.

Gebann took him by the shoulders. "You're traveling by water, Cian? More ocean voyages for you, is it?" and he threw back his dark head laughing.

"Isn't that at least the third time I've been tempted to hit you," Cian sputtered.

He departed from them before dusk, on his way to a small inlet where he could slip onto a boat that would take him east to Lir. Gebann struggled to walk to Cian's horse and threw an unsteady arm around his shoulders. He presented the smith with a gift, a carved walking stick.

"Safe journey, my son!" Gebann called as he leaned on the oak staff, his wife at his side.

Cian saw with sorrow that the smith had been poisoned in his limbs. Surely it was from the many seasons this good man had spent hovering over caustic, smoking metals.

Winter's shorter light and cold, foggy weather protected him. Cian met few other travelers while he steadily made his way back to the port where he first entered the mining peninsula. There he joined Lir but he dreaded another miserable crossing on the great waters. Despite Lir's best efforts to come, the stars showed that it was still the season of storms.

Lir sensed his fear and advised before they set off, "We're three times more likely to have strong winds and heavy seas than with a summer crossing. I did hand pick this crew, so. You'll have to trust in me and the crew."

Cian remembered the torment on his first crossing. Again on this voyage they spent eerie days and nights in deep fog, or bitter wind and tossing waves, when he was certain they had seen the last rising of the sun. Lir interrupted their passage several times at small islands where they rested among the people living there. He skirted along the coastline all the way up the arcing coast.

The Starwatcher kept patient and tried to hide his anxiety, and learned more navigation skills from Lir and the crew. He remarked how the north stars' position slowly changed while they voyaged into northern waters. Cian discussed with the Seafarers how the constellations spiraled around the north stars. Aware of the Northshift, the mariners looked to his Starwatchers to solve the riddle, they told him.

He thought of Boann trapped inside the Invader walls. Had she continued starwatching? His stomach churned but he willed this boat to go faster, speed him through the enormous distance to reach her. He dreamed of gold, and of freeing Boann and his people.

They saw little sea traffic during these cold lunates. That was good, said Lir, for they had less risk of encountering traders or warriors, those who might relay a message to Elcmar. Lir pointed out in the distance, the deep mouth where mighty Taranis controlled the river trade. Then Lir eased his ship west along the jagged coast, west and then north. Ahead lay the sea channel with its hazardous open water they must cross for Eire. Lir stopped and they waited several sunrises for promising skies and smooth water.

The weather held as they cleared the northwest edge of the Continent, but not their luck. Somewhere Lir scraped too close to rocks. He cursed when he saw seawater gushing into the boat. Cian scrambled between rowers, grabbed a skin, and pressed it hard where the men told him. While he tried to stem the leak, they turned back toward the south coast, a smudge on the horizon.

Leather bags, pots, and desperate hands scooped water out of the boat. They looked for a likely stretch of shore to camp and make repairs. Water rose inside the boat and lapped at their ankles. They raced against the rising water to gain the shore.

Lir threw over the side a great portion of scrap metal, damaged axes and parts of ingots that he carried to trade, with no look back as his wealth sank beneath the waves. That bronze scrap could have gotten him another boat, or seasons of ease. Cian picked up his own bundles to throw them over, but Lir stopped him. "Not necessary, lad. Keep that skin hard in the gap."

The sun's light faded. They all squinted at the coast for a safe cove to land before dark. The men bailed and bailed, until at last Lir saw a suitable landing place. Exhausted, the crew dragged the boat onto the rough shore and collapsed.

Rescuers came out slowly from the woods, then approached with ease when Lir spoke assuredly to them. "We are Seafarers. Not invading, only foundering. We'll need to fix our boat here."

Their hosts brought the drenched mariners to shelter, to fires and dry robes and hot food.

For much of the next quarter moon, the crew and Lir completed repairs using wood and hides and then pitch. All wondered if this *naomhog* would be seaworthy again. They were stuck with it. Lir had this boat built to his specifications, he owned it, and Invaders knew nothing of it and could not claim it for their trade, not unless they caught him.

Changed Utterly

THE LUNATE OF spring equinox arrived. On the equinox, under orders from Elcmar, Invader warriors hauled immense logs to the Starwatchers' ritual places. Before the sun fully disappeared below the horizon, Invaders set the logs blazing. Great fires burned where the astronomers gathered, blinding them to the skies.

At *Bru na Boinne* the fire lit by the Invaders reddened the sky and angry warriors scattered the astronomers and villagers. Enraged, but unarmed, a few young Starwatchers threw stones as heavy as they could heft, but stones did not turn back Elcmar's warriors. Warriors forced them to flee the mounds into the forest.

Invader bonfires burned through the night at the high places and ruined any starwatching at their most revered sites. It was devastating: the elders could not conduct the proper equinox observations nor make their blessing on the people. Neighboring Starwatchers could not share the important equinox.

This ceremony would have honored the spring, one of their four holy observances. They lost their hold on the Northshift, the sky was turning without them. This equinox also marked the first anniversary of the gruesome murder of Sheela. Twice, these Invaders committed an abomination on the spring equinox. The people dragged themselves in distress back to their homes.

At the next rising of the sun, they saw the Dagda's carved stone macehead displayed high atop a yew pole outside his dwelling. The people gathered before it. The polished whorls resembled a face with open mouth, a silent scream. The Dagda's macehead stayed aloft until the last rays of light, and the people laid herbs surrounding it. They sent runners to other Starwatcher villages—all the able-bodied were summoned to attend a Boyne council with the next dawn.

A hot sun rose, splitting the trees. The arriving Starwatchers walked the pattern of the cursus with its views of the silver-white river and their mounds. They met in open council with their elders. This council went on through two sunrises.

A few voiced caution, saying, "We do not have enough information from other Starwatchers. Did fires profane all their equinox skies?"

Gentle Airmid spoke up. "We all know how it was that Sheela died. The elders stayed our hand against the Invaders and see what has happened. We have not been able to honor Sheela's bones, nor remember her properly on this equinox. Our tolerance of these intruders, they misperceive as submission. We avoid violence, but receive only more violence in return."

Tadhg rose and spoke, then Cermait, and Daire; all said the time to fight these Invaders had surely arrived.

Older Starwatchers, Slainge and Tethra and others, listened then had their say. "The smell of death grows stronger than the bitter smoke from the intruders' fires. We could annihilate these warriors, but it might cost many Starwatcher lives."

A woman elder added, "Starwatchers have not made war for many generations."

The people debated. Oghma, who suffered a stroke when he saw the terrible fires, sat upright as well as he could and listened with the elders to what his people wanted. Slainge raised the delicate issue of Boann's safety with the infant Aengus inside the intruders' walls. All knew that Boann would be frantic to come to Oghma's side after the message telling her of his illness, yet she had not come. Elcmar held her trapped inside the high walls. No one offered a solution.

Oghma began to shake and he waved his good hand to Daire, who bent over him to hear what he said. Daire told the assembly, "Boann knows what she must do. She stands with us."

The Starwatchers would give the marauding intruders an unmistakable reply. The Starwatchers dispersed to gather foodstuffs and water, they fed and penned their animals, then they returned to their hearths.

That night before the quarter moon set, their scouts kidnapped an Invader warrior. The scouts held him at a place apart from their village. They made sure that this man was not a captive Seafarer or one who was otherwise sympathetic to their cause. They gave the defiant warrior a light meal laced with a root extract, and he slept soundly on that first night. The next morning's stirabout fed to him was also dosed with sleeping herbs. When this man had peacefully passed to the spirit world, the scouts lashed his body to one of the few remaining trees close to the intruders' camp. The dead warrior was soon found by forest animals.

Invaders went looking for the source of a terrible howling coming from the woods at the edge of their camp. Instead they found the carcass, one of their own men.

The significance of finding their warrrior's mauled remains was not lost on the Invaders: the Starwatchers openly challenged them. It was the first mutilation of a dead warrior by Starwatchers, although in fact animals had done that work.

Invaders crowded around the tree. One of them pointed just above their heads. There someone had carved a symbol: a figure of a woman with knees wide apart below a hag face, all chiseled clearly into the wood and highlighted with red ochre. Below its ghastly face, the figure's arms reached below her legs holding her privates open. Warriors called Ith out to the tree to examine the carving. The carved face loomed almost the same size as the lower half of the body. Ith recoiled from the sight, the first depiction of the human form he had found on Eire. The warriors gathered up the remains and fled with Ith from the hag's image.

Heavy cobbles rained on them from the woods, and Invaders narrowly escaped Starwatcher arrows in the clearing as they scrambled to safety across their plank bridge and inside their banked enclosure.

Boann returned from her stone by the cooking pits just when Ith and the warriors surged back into the camp with the body. Ith caught sight of her and rebuked her in his rasping voice, blaming her for the mutilated warrior. Angry Invaders surrounded her, but Elcmar's tall figure appeared and at his shout the mob parted. Her head held high, Boann walked through the heckling Invaders and into the great hall. She shut herself in the sleeping chamber with Aengus close by her.

The Invaders stayed out of sight within their walls. Elcmar huddled with Ith in the great hall, examining what course they should take. Warriors clamored outside the hall for battle. Elcmar meant to contain the wildest Invaders, those who would retaliate against all quiet ones including Boann. To wear out the agitators, Ith and Elcmar encouraged drinking, nonstop drumming, and contests of strength. Over the next sunrises, shouts still issued against Boann from Maedb's followers, scuffling outside the great hall.

The moon above the Boyne passed into its next quarter while the Invader camp feasted and fought. Spring was not a good time to be going hungry, nor to be slaughtering their few livestock.

Boann did not speak to anyone nor take solid food. Elcmar posted a guard at her door. The unbearable walls pressed closer upon her, trapped as she was.

She had told the elders not to spare her if ever they must act against the Invader camp.

What about Aengus? She regarded the infant tenderly. She sent away the middle-aged slave woman who cowered with her inside the chamber, out to find a wet nurse for Aengus. If she could not herself escape then that slave woman, or the wet nurse if courageous, must escape with Aengus. They could say they were taking him out for an airing or setting Dabilla free in the woods... She waited, feverish, listening to the drums and wild rabble outside.

The slave returned without the wet nurse. Instead she brought her a warm salmon. Boann sat up from her bed to smell it. This salmon was very fresh; it had the green scent of the stream north of her village. It seemed a miracle to see a salmon at all given the odd weather since Sheela's death.

The Starwatchers had sent her a message, a question: are you still among us? This message was simply the moon's exact shape on that night, carefully slit into the silvery layer of salmon skin. Daire had made this mark at Oghma's direction, then wrapped the salmon in wet leaves and twine, and Tadhg managed to have it delivered; she was sure of all this. She must reply to her people.

Are the slaves free to come and go without harm? What if this woman betrays me? Unsure, Boann motioned the slave away from her side.

She pricked out one vertical line and a shorter line under Oghma's moon sign, and retied the glistening fish in its covering. She turned to the slave. "This salmon has not sufficiently cooked. Take it out and place it exactly where you found it."

The slave hesitated, then took up the bundled salmon and left the chamber again. The shouts rose outside the great hall. Aengus' breathing changed and he whimpered.

Distraught by his hunger, Boann pulled at a fur covering on the bed, then saw that it had a morsel of salmon left on it. She chewed this bit of fish well and fed the mash to Aengus. His eyes widened and his lips clung to her finger for its salty taste.

"You shall have the Starwatcher knowledge," Boann promised. She cradled him until he slept. She rose from her bed, ravenous, and at a thin gap in the chamber's walls she drank in the moonlight. It would have to sustain her.

The slave woman slipped back into the chamber. "I found one slave who has milk," the woman said and stroked little Aengus' cheek. "She comes presently."

Loud cursing sounded beyond the plank door, along with a familiar long stride. Elcmar charged into the bedchamber, berating Boann for sending away food, hand on the knife at his waist. He stopped short. She had the fever, the very same that killed many Starwatchers; she saw him flinch at the deep lavender shadows under her glazed eyes.

The slave hastened to show him Aengus, content and asleep with round pink cheeks.

Boann stood pressed against the wall, heavy hair falling around her shoulders. Let him see her pinched and pale face. She looked at Elcmar from a distance, from near the Otherworld.

"I won't eat. It's no food I will be taking!" She told him in her tongue, then his.

Elcmar took out a small dark stone carved like the hag on the tree.

She gasped. "Where did you get this? On Eire we do not make such carvings!"

"Never mind where I got it. What do you know of the hag?"

Boann raised her chin. "Oghma would not carve a living tree with your hag of destruction. Besides, he has taken ill. He could not."

They glared at one another.

"You will bend to me, or I will break you. You, and all your people." Elcmar grabbed Aengus from the slave's arms and left the chamber.

The sentry waiting outside banged his halberd across the door.

The Seafarer slave told her, "I will fetch the wet nurse to take the child." She pushed out past the sentry.

"Aengus," Boann breathed the name, knees collapsing. "Save Aengus." Then all went dark.

Tadhg retrieved the salmon and returned it to Oghma and the Starwatchers. They saw that Boann lived, for the time being, and Aengus.

At the Starwatcher village, no one could be certain who carved the hag into the tree. No one asked the next person, who has done this thing? The intruders' fires had desecrated the equinox ceremony and their remembrance of Sheela. The Starwatchers did not need to speak of the hag. Someone had spoken for all of them.

They would resist the Invaders, starve them to death. Their scouts surrounded the Invader camp, day and night, and waited.

Inside the palisade, Elcmar posted his most reliable men to guard their scarce horses. The camp bled their remaining cattle to ration a drink of blood mixed with milk, then consumed the emaciated animals one by one, wasting nothing. The cooking pits went cold, with even the grease scraped out and eaten. The Invaders ate all of their cereals including their stored seeds. All the camp had was mare's milk, fresh or boiled down to dry curds; and broth from beef bones. New cases of fever appeared.

It required both Ith and Elcmar, and their most loyal warriors, to subdue the famished agitators. Ith took care to silence Maedb, who complained loudly without offering any viable way to make peace. Bresal looked wolfish and desperate. The warriors bickered as they drew lots for who would have to venture outside their bank and clearing for food. The Invaders' fears multiplied as they tried to predict what the war tactics of the quiet ones might be.

"No one will find gold if we are all dead." Ith's hoarse voice carried to Elcmar as they sat by a sparse fire in the hearth.

"Boann means to die first," he told Ith without emotion.

The shaman gave a coughing laugh. "Her hunger strike! Easy enough when there is no food to be had."

Elcmar shook his head. "Her slave dribbles broth into her. Boann still has fever on her." He handed Ith the small carved image of the hag.

Ith looked at him, astonished. "You carry the death-hag?"

"That image hung around the neck of my first kill on the Continent, a trader from a far shore who tried to cheat me." Elcmar took it back and stood. "I shall not be defeated. Not here, not by these people."

It was Elcmar who came out of the camp walls, alone. Remains of Ith's boat, dragged upriver by quiet ones during darkness then set afire, lay strewn in the Invaders' clearing. Elcmar passed the charred boat, its ribs pointing east toward the coast. He could bolt, escape, he could go north to Connor or south to the Lake mine. Instead he rode past the central mound and to the Starwatchers. He expected an arrow or stone to find him, but none came.

Again he took his white horse directly into their village clearing. He halted at its center and waited, proud there on his animal. A ring of strong Starwatcher men surrounded Elcmar and stood in silence.

At his bold arrival, the elders left their tasks. They refused to approach him on the horse and gestured toward the mounds. He turned his horse, and all proceeded toward the council place at the great oak tree near the central mound. The young scouts, carrying pikes and stone axes, followed in a group but no more Invaders arrived.

The elders halted at the entrance to the cursus. Elcmar abruptly dismounted to walk with them. They all filed through the cursus. A light breeze crossed the clearing as they gathered close to the oak's whispering branches.

Elcmar faced the Dagda, admiring the polished red macehead, and he gestured at it. "This mace came to you over the great waters, in trade."

The Dagda met his look without comment.

"There shall be a truce. These are the terms." Elcmar took care to speak simply. He came here to win the quiet ones over, not make a speech. One scout translated though quite a few among the Starwatchers appeared to understand his words.

The elders listened. The champion's belt carried many weapons but his arrival without warriors made the elders receptive, although some showed offense.

"There should be no more violence, nor any taking of hostages, by either group living along the Boyne. No one, Invader or Starwatcher, should be found outside of my camp or your village after sunset, except with my express permission or from your elders. Anyone wanting to be out at night must carry this sign of permission." Elcmar drew out a pouch containing a supply of strange stones, hard and glossy layered-yellow stones, saying that these stones could be carried as passes. He gave the elders the striped pebbles, tumbled by water to a uniform size and shape.

"These cannot be duplicated to supply extra passes, for this stone comes from the Continent. You must restrict who carries these few safe-passage stones," he said, ignoring their irate looks.

The elders confirmed with him that Boann lived, and Aengus. The Starwatchers withdrew from him, and deliberated. Perhaps now a peace could begin with these Invaders, he overheard one say. Dissent followed and the elders leaned together in heated debate.

Shortly the elders rose and motioned that Elcmar rejoin them. "We demand a council in order for any truce to become effective. Boann with Aengus must be allowed to freely visit the Starwatchers. She is not your hostage. At her option, Boann may divorce you. We shall continue our starwatching. The cattle raids must stop; you must grow your own food. You must have permission to clear trees. If we cannot agree in council, Invaders must leave the Boyne."

They sounded adamant and Elcmar nodded to all of it. He might yet find gold here.

The Dagda raised his mace. "Anyone accused of violating this truce shall be judged by both sides in an open hearing. Three Starwatchers and three of your people shall decide upon it and they shall decide the punishment."

Elcmar readily agreed. Their truce being complete, it was sealed by an exchange of touch with the elders. The elders set a date for the council, on the next crossquarter or perhaps during Brightsun; he didn't understand what they said fixing it on the sun but he didn't inquire. This same promise to confer had been made after the prior spring equinox and Sheela's murder, and he paid it little regard then or now.

He rode away from their council place, his rib injury taunting him. On his way he met with the suffering countenance of Oghma, barring his pathway through the grasses.

The old man shook the upraised fist on his good arm.

Elcmar gave him one slow nod and rode on to the walled camp.

Tadhg left the council place with the Dagda. They refreshed themselves at the north stream and caught a salmon to send to Boann. The two men walked back to their village, the sun slanting in the west.

Tadhg sighed heavily. "Making peace is harder than making war."

The Dagda considered what had happened. "What their champion Elcmar said is partly true. Boats have reached Eire within living memory. But those traders came for exchange in a ceremony between equals, not to despoil us and abuse this land.

"Now we are all hostages, held in their darkness." The Dagda looked at the silent, disused mounds in the deepening twilight.

But come you back when summer's in the meadow.

From: *Danny Boy*

The Time of Bright Shoots

LIR WAITED FOR favorable wind and seas, then ventured again into open water from the northwest edge of the Continent. Their repairs were soon put to the test, for a sudden gale lashed them and blew them far off course. Tension showed on all the crew, and fear. Cian watched a huge wave come rolling, curling high above into a deadly green tunnel to slam them broadside.

"Hang on!" Lir shouted at him. The rowers had seen the giant coming; they strained and pulled and the tiny hide craft turned away at the last instant. Up they rode at a sickening angle toward the frenzied sky then down, down.

Too busy to cheer or curse, the mariners watched and rowed. The storm slackened but not enough for them to make it to shore. Through that night they stayed awake, to keep their boat within sight of beacon fires atop mounds along that coast. The soaked and freezing crew checked seams for new leakage. When the low clouds broke up at sunrise, a cape and large islands beckoned far to the southeast. They could see nothing but waves to the north. More time had been lost, but they were alive.

Cian released his ropes and clambered over men and bundles to reach Lir at the stern. He meant to urge Lir to turn back again, to fires and hot food, but his friend spoke first.

"We are far to the east of where I wanted to cross open water. Should I find the north coastline and hug that up to Cymru and cross over, or risk all and head us west for Eire? By the way, in this tight channel the surface current can reverse in just a few notches of the sun." Lir's eyes scanned water and sky. Cian kept quiet, hands gripping a thwart.

Lir ran a course straight for Eire, assisted by good visibility. They had only waves leading to the horizon without any reference points on land during sunlight. The men looked for birds, monitored smells on the wind, and watched for branches carried on the shifting currents. They watched also for any vessels. At night they sighted on sunset stars, and constellations, and with that Cian could assist.

He woke with the sun's first rays, wondering if they had passed into deep blue oblivion, never to sight land again. But no, there was his friend Lir silhouetted against water and sky, as if he were back in a coracle skimming the Lake Of Many Hammers. The sea and skies remained in blessed calm. Without that, they might glide to the back of beyond on the open water over which Lir guided them.

They had scarce food supplies and scarcer fresh water. Cian rationed his own portion of water to moisten the plant cuttings he brought wrapped in oiled skins for Boann and Airmid.

The seas heaved again with heavy swells where Lir turned northerly for the Starwatcher island. Scattered islets to the northeast marked the yawning end of the channel and the men rallied to see these familiar dots far on their right. The crew compared notched sticks that tallied how many sunrises it took to reach this place, settling a bet they made when Lir set his course west. The salts, as the men called themselves, boasted about the places and distances they knew along the channel. Lir's daring had added to their knowledge about traveling this channel relying on sun and stars and currents.

Their first signs were seabirds, terns and shearwaters making steep-angled dives for fish. Cian exulted with the brave mariners when Eire came into view. Lir traced the eastern coast, keeping it in sight but not close. He looked for a specific mouth on the coastline and there used his boat's shallow draught to boldly bring them up a black-pooled river past the sheltering headland. At last their patched and reinforced ship did arrive.

They landed after the spring equinox. The surroundings seemed placid along this river.

He stood together with Lir, untying his bags from the load. The two solemnly agreed that during a set quarter of the next lunate, the boat would return for him. The crew watched the shores and the water, nervous that their naomhog might be spotted by Invaders.

Lir gestured. "This place lies not far south and east of the Boyne." He pulled Cian's dark head close and whispered. "You're home, lad—now find us the gold!"

Cian touched his friend and each of the crew and spoke fervent good wishes to all. Trouble showed on the Seafarers' faces: here the dangerous part of his journey would begin.

He dropped over the ship's side, pulling his oiled leather bundles over the shallow water. When at last he touched Eire, his legs steadied. He stood there on the shore, inhaling its cool scent of woods and herbs, hearing its familiar birds. He had been gone for over two seasons of the sun. It seemed much longer than that. Cian touched a stone in silent and heartfelt thanks.

He glanced back. Lir's boat sped from view, headed east across the rough strait to where it was safer to rest, make repairs, and take on supplies. Invaders would not bother to pursue them in the violent currents around a speck of land off Cymru's north coast, Lir had told him. "That islet has small passage mounds for its people do follow Starwatcher ways. Metal has yet to be found where I and my crew can hide!

"Outsiders came there and built themselves a banked henge and stone circle. A small circle though it was, the locals knocked it and put up a strong mound over it. They ousted those intruders' arses, so."

Cian turned and made his way south into the gently sloping mountains backing his landing spot on the Liffey. With the spark glowing in his head, he sought the sun metal.

Gebann's map sent him first to the area of Glassamucky Mountain, where he found the giant stone containing a distinctive large cupmark and several smaller cupmarks, just so, as Gebann told him. Sly Gebann said to sight from a natural notch in this giant bullaun stone to a distinct notch in the mountains. At sunset he must align that notch with a constellation and follow it to ridges lying beyond Lugnagun mountain, and to the high peak of Lugnaqilla. There on western slopes, he would find a noisy stream running through a stand of ash and oak. This stream trapped the sparkling sun metal as it rushed through overhanging cliffs streaked with white quartz.

Cian followed Gebann's directions, crossing the peaks and rivers etched by the smith onto the small plaque. He ignored hunger and thirst, checking his path against the plaque, at times choosing one way against the other as he went deeper into the mountains.

When he found what he sought, he had cause to marvel at the old smith's accuracy. Gebann guided him right to the stream. Placer gold for the taking glittered under laughing water and gold fell out in chunks with a tap to exposed veins in the cliffs. Cian rocked on his heels to see the gold, some nuggets the size of a child's fist.

He loaded two deep leather bags with gold in less than three suns and hoped that his bags would be strong enough. These bags could be carried off later, the weight distributed to either side of his body. He built a cist of flat rocks in a dry place above the stream's high water mark and there he deposited the heavy bags with a thud.

As he covered them, he decided against notching any of the trees around his hidden cache of sun metal.

Cian marked the hiding place with a carved half circle on his stone plaque. He also marked a natural stele there with the same half circle placed around a natural cup mark. It felt good to be carving stone for awhile, and he relaxed. That night he verified the orientation of the carved half circle against the sky, just after first darkness in the west. He lined up his mark with the early spring constellation he had followed. He looked at which sunset stars shone at all four directions around this tall stone. Too excited to eat, he slept well and rose with the sun. He found a sharp antler bone to carve stone, choosing to save the short copper daggers he carried.

He followed the stream down and at different points along this stream, Cian carved several more symbols on prominent slabs. He had to work fast and he marked only stones whose surfaces already contained natural cup marks. The antler tool broke, so he found a hard stone and fractured it easily into a long, thick blade. On his way out of the Wicklow mountains, he etched several elongated, hasty lines as directional markers for his return to the stream of sun metal. His right hand bled from using the crude stone blade, but he ignored it as he eagerly turned north to the Boyne.

Cian progressed invisibly over the land.

Boann moved patiently through the meadow along the stream to the north of her village. A scout, the young lad called Dubh for his dark hair, stood close by while she worked. She had evaded bringing any Invader woman or slave on her outing this morning. Elcmar was away from camp on this day, off on a short hunt. She did not care to think what his warrior party might actually be doing. The Invaders raided cattle much farther away now, in daylight and with minimal deference to the truce with her village. When they returned, stolen cattle appeared in the pens and there would be a noisy feast at which they embroidered the tale of another daring cattle raid against neighboring peoples. She must help the elders figure out how to stop the raids.

On her way this morning she visited her father at his house. Since his stroke, Oghma recovered some mobility but rarely went carving. His hands could no longer clasp his tools. Indeed, his last carvings at the kerbstones appeared to be shallow and lacked the lavish artistry of his earlier decorations. Perhaps Daire could take over the carving, quick of mind and strong as he was.

Boann thought about all this while harvesting young medicines and vegetable plants. She hungered for greens and ate tender shoots while she worked. She searched for burdock, a delicacy whose stems could be stripped and then steamed. It would be a treat for Airmid; she knew not to eat it herself while nursing little Aengus. Young nettles, she pulled to make into soup for Oghma. The nettles reminded her: Sheela of the spirits had been dead for more than one cycle of the sun. That did not seem possible.

Soon it would be the crossquarter, the Time of Bright Shoots after spring equinox. Boann wondered again if the council of Starwatchers and Invaders would come to pass. She relished being outside the camp walls alone, though Elcmar's informers would be sure to tell him about her solo foray.

Boann looked up from the thick plants. A magnificent fox crouched nearby. She blinked and suppressed her joyous exclamation. Cian had come to her silently, hiding low and watching her from the rippling grasses. She motioned and he looked at Aengus lying in a willow carrier at her side. Cian pointed toward the village, then back to the spot where he crouched in the fox skin. He angled fingers low in the west. Boann understood to return at dusk. Then swiftly Cian faded into the meadow.

She picked up Aengus and the greens, and took a different path back to the great hall. There she managed to stay calm, trying not to pace until dusk arrived, feeding Aengus then tucking him in with her trustworthy older attendant. Boann used the excuse of a sudden illness to avoid the feast planned for Elcmar's return to the great hall. She waited to be certain no one followed, and slipped like water through the camp walls. She found Cian waiting at their special place in the meadow.

He smelled different than she remembered, but not like an Invader. Her heart pounded.

They sat down among pliant young grasses. He held out a closed hand then opened his fingers to show her an aqua bead strung on a plaited leather cord.

"Cian! I have never seen such a stone, the color of sea water!" This ocean-blue bead delighted her as he slipped the cord necklace over her head.

Of even more delight to her were the numerous plant cuttings and roots wrapped in moss inside soft leather. But she had trouble eating the dried-out olives he brought and he chuckled when she wrinkled her nose and spat them out. Those got soaked along the way, he told her, but were good when fresh; and she smiled.

Next Cian gave her buttons that he carved from antler bone. Boann could see that these ovoid buttons took much time, to slice the antler and then patiently pierce with an awl from two directions, to make a shank for attaching the button.

"I have admired such buttons on intruder clothing. You have carved and polished these to be better than any I have seen." She held them, her voice low and soft.

He opened the last bundle for her. Boann hesitated, and then she accepted a small triangular knife of shadow moon metal. This weapon they deposited quickly under a heavy stone until she could hide it elsewhere.

Then he asked many questions about Aengus, and she was full of stories of her firstborn, eyeing Cian as she spoke. She spilled over, brimming with every detail about the infant Aengus. Cian nibbled the steamed roots and beef strips she had brought him, beaming at her, occasionally scanning the horizon. Early stars were appearing; no other person was about.

A look passed between them when she finished speaking of Aengus.

"Aengus was born at the solstice," she said. It was then she saw the bright fire behind Cian's eyes. His look seared her, a look of total understanding. She wanted to put him on his back and take the sweetness from Cian that she had not known with anyone else.

But she sobered, as she told him about the violence at Dowth.

He knew each of the young Starwatchers who had been killed or injured. "How can it be that I survived voyages to the Seafarer peninsula and back, but some of our companions who remained here walk now with the spirits," and he shook his head sadly.

"Then value your time among the living... and go forward with us," she said.

She posed questions about his travels. His clipped replies about the ocean crossings implied dangers and uncertainty beyond telling. He shrugged off her concern, described new things he learned on the waters, particularly for navigating. "Seafarer communities favor the Seven Stars and orient many of their coastal mounds to this constellation. They light fires on their mounds as beacons. Their mariners memorize the night skies and travel over water like we do the land. They observe old ways but have become new men, explorers of places unknown to us."

She murmured of hearing similar things from the slaves. When he assured her that the seas flowed smoother after spring equinox, Boann touched his arm. "Why do you tell me this, Cian?"

He held back his answer to her question. He changed the subject, describing new foods and herbs and the strange etiquette at Bolg's feast. "The men eat in strict separation from women, and talk of trade dominates all else." He mentioned the increasing flow of goods; that traders exchanged metals, salt, and rare beads for hides and other produce, some from far lands. Given Eire's paucity of animals and crops, he didn't go into detail.

He mentioned that all the traders he had seen wore long knives and a privileged few Seafarers carried metal daggers or long knives. Cian said, "I know the elders will talk further with the Starwatchers about these things, for I met with our elders through to dusk." He emphasized to her, "At the Lake Of Many Hammers, and on the Continent, the land suffers. That pungent odor from smelting was worse at the copper mine and again on the Continent."

At his mention of the Lake mine, Boann asked eagerly, "And Cliodhna?"

Cian could only shake his head. "All anyone knows was that she left Eire by boat from the southwest coast, not far from the mine, with a man named Iuchnu. Given all the coastlines and islands where they might hide from traders, it could be a long time before anyone learns the outcome of their journey." It was not the fault of Sreng, they agreed. There was nothing more to say regarding Cliodhna's fate and they fell silent.

He regarded her face tenderly. Would Boann ever see the Continent, he wondered, but he would not suggest that. Women did not usually make long voyages, Lir told him. Nor did Cian dwell on the array of rich furnishings, the lavish personal adornments and clothing he had seen. How could he possibly describe the serving girl's revealing string skirt? Boann had already admired his well-stitched tunic and leggings, and his light but tough foot coverings. She wore a fine linen tunic that must have been brought to her by Elcmar, and over her shoulders a beautiful robe of matched skins.

He tucked a spray of apple blossoms into her hair and saw matching pink suffuse her cheeks. Not all of their time together would be spent talking, he decided. Cian gently removed the fur robe in which Boann wrapped herself against the damp grass.

Suddenly shy with him, she chattered and showed him the robe, told him how she pieced it using needle skills learned from Airmid.

"We used the softest winter rabbit skins at hand to us. I saved the robe for this time, for your return."

The first act of vanity in her life, he knew, and his heart pounded.

Cian embraced her against the robe and she arched against him, blood racing together. He let down her heavy hair and lost himself in her. They lingered under Boann's robe while the turning patterns above went unnoticed. They made slow, all-consuming love, bodies joined in their own universe shot through with glittering, innumerable stars. Two halves of the entire, reunited, and they clung together until the morning stars showed.

They stirred, and they smiled and clasped hands. Cian leaned up on one elbow, his face serious again as he touched hers.

"I have told the Dagda, your father and all the elders: they shall receive an object from me, by and by. This thing, a disk like the sun, shall be kept hidden. It is of great value to the Starwatchers and it must be kept safe. You shall know this object when you see it. The elders will give it to you to teach Aengus, when that time arrives. This metal disk could replace our building of starchambers. It might even solve the problem of the shifting constellations."

He had more to share. The two had not spoken privately in many lunates, not since Elcmar found her lying in the meadow. Cian could feel the sun's light coming in the northeast; soon it would be time to leave her. For once, he would open himself to Boann.

She wanted to question him. What wondrous object could ever replace their starchambers? Why would Cian himself not teach Aengus with it? But he put his sweet long fingers on her lips. His least touch felt like shooting stars. He started with what he knew of the death of Sheela. Boann heard with astonishment...

On that equinox dawn, Connor discovered Cian sneaking back inside the camp. He took Cian along to guide an early hunt. "We were four or five, a small intruder party. We came along the stream on foot. There you were. Connor stumbled ahead to assault you.

The others' knives held me back!" His eyes smoldered.

Boann nodded. She knew too well this paralyzing fear of the shining, deadly knives.

"You got away—clumsy as he was and a head on him from the drink. Later with the sun lowering, we were all back inside the Invaders' walls. Connor left the camp again, but Elcmar stood watching me and so I could not follow. By next light, Sheela was found murdered. Ardal got word to me. I guessed that this mayhem and death was Connor's work even before I saw his wounded hand. I slid between the camp and our village to attend the council, to warn our elders against reprisal." Cian did not elaborate how he slipped in and out of the Invaders' camp except by saying with some disdain, "The Invaders believe that I change shape from a man to an animal and back." He continued, his words rushing against sunrise.

"Not one intruder showed concern about the murder of Sheela. They quarreled night and day over making of their new *ard ri*. They questioned me about Connor's swelling hand. I urged the Invaders to have a Starwatcher treat the wound. In that way the Starwatchers would know who was Sheela's murderer." Cian struck the earth with his fist. "Bresal agreed to bring in a Starwatcher healer since as he said, it appeared to him that Connor might die anyway. So it was that the Invaders ignored the Starwatchers' request to meet in council and demanded instead that our elders send a healer."

He choked. "Boann, when they brought you into the camp, I was beside myself. If you had been killed—" She squeezed his arm to go on.

"After they amputated Connor's red hand, turmoil continued as the warriors fought to elect their new champion. Intrigue fed upon intrigue. Maedb added me to her enemies, and claimed it was I who murdered Sheela. Elcmar no longer allowed me out of his sight. To be sure, he and I foiled several attempts on your life by Maedb's assassins. Each having different reasons than the other man, perhaps, but there it is.

"He learned when another attempt would be made, and Elcmar rode out with his own warriors—and me—to look for the assassins. We hunted down your hunters, and this time we disabled them. A warning to Maedb. But a waste of sound men, it angered Elcmar. He rode off. Shortly he waved his blade above the grass, and we followed after not knowing what to expect. He'd found you, sleeping there under the sun in the meadow, and it's alive you were. I spoke to make you heed the danger, not knowing then if you had two enemies: Maedb, and Elcmar. He kept his watch on me. So I kept a watch on Elcmar! When his position as the new champion appeared secure, Elcmar announced that he would have a marriage with the Starwatchers." About the choice Boann made and her sudden marriage with Elcmar, Cian said nothing. She stroked his cheek.

"Connor of the Red Hand remains at large in the north, as you know. And Elcmar sent me off the island. The smith Gebann thinks Elcmar banished me so he could seek the sun metal, the gold, for himself. But that's not it, not at all. Elcmar had to keep you for himself, Boann."

"Elcmar cares nothing for me! I see that Maedb resents me—I don't take food or drink from her hands." Boann sighed. "Is this all we can learn from these Invaders? Intrigues? Killing?"

Cian's voice took on an edge. "I saw a cave on the Seafarer peninsula littered with bodies of young people, over thirty bodies. It is the end of that tribe. Long knives killed their young people for not submitting to the Invaders. Now some of the Seafarers build strong camps to live in like the Invaders. Those people live inside walls on the high places, instead of using the high places to watch the stars."

He was thinking out loud. "I warned the elders. The great water insulated us, protected us from many evils. The new ships can bring good things to us, but we must be careful of what enters Eire, whether people with new ways or a new weapon."

He stopped speaking for a moment. Boann kissed his hands, his beautiful hands so strong and brown, not roughened any longer with carving stone. She rested her head on his chest, smooth skin with a mat of curls; he smelled like salt and leather, good smells. She guessed what he wanted to say, what he had never told her.

"Duty prevented me from acting on my desires, just as duty made your decision in this matter." Then he did tell her: he loved her, and he would always love her. He shared his hopes for Aengus and for the future, a future free of the Invaders' shadow.

"I know that you must stay here. I must go." There was still more to say but his time with her ran short. "I cannot stay on Eire, not at present."

Boann raised her head to see into his eyes. "You must go? —Cian, when are you coming home?"

"Not for many seasons of the sun. I must leave you at once, before the sun's shoulders clear the horizon."

He held Boann while she allowed herself to weep. The truce proved itself a sham, already the troubles resumed. Clashes between Starwatchers and Invaders paralleled her own with Elcmar. Maedb would try to kill her, or Ith. Ith tracked her like a wolf.

She said only, "It is too much to hear that you leave us again, and so quickly."

He held her until the weeping exhausted her. She drifted into a light slumber, and when she awoke under sunshine grazing the tips of the young grass and flowers, he had gone.

Her heart almost stopped. She felt at her neck for the cord carrying the seawater-colored stone. It was her only means to be sure that the night she remembered with Cian was not just a dream.

Cian traveled light. He had given away what he carried to the elders, and Boann, including all but one of his copper knives. Gebann freely gave him those knives, metal knives though he had nothing to trade the smith for them. He must retrieve the gold to return what he owed to Gebann and to Lir and others, or he could have no welcome back on the Continent, no safe haven there. Nor any here in Eire, and he felt at his belt for his one knife.

He passed undetected, cutting through woods south of the sacred river and then through the plain beyond, avoiding areas with signs of Invaders and their horses. He traveled south by southeast, keeping the mound at Fourknocks to his left. You shall not come sunwise across this plain, he could hear the Dagda's admonishment. He still wasn't sure what that meant, but now it helped him stay clear of wandering Invaders.

He crossed the dark-pooled river like an otter darting between its shaded banks. From there he headed upland into the blue-hazed mountains, his direction made sure from his own slashes on rock faces, and unerringly he found the discrete cupmarks he made on his notched stele. Up in the mountain valley, tucked under the steep cliffs streaked with quartz over a rushing stream, he retrieved his sizable cache of gold nuggets.

The extreme weight of his leather bags filled with gold soon slowed his trek to the southern coast. *A sleek naomhog coming for me, to carry me back to the Continent. The seas will be smoother in this season. The sooner I leave here, the sooner I might return*, Cian repeated to spur himself onward. He followed the sun anxiously and counted each sunrise.

His shoulder and back muscles throbbed with the weight of the bags. He sought to reassure himself, while keeping a constant watch as he traveled laden with sun metal. He cast one gold nugget into a bog in thanks to the earth on his descent to the south through green mountain valleys and uplands. The fertile valleys looked to have few people living in them and he thought about locating a new settlement there, far from Invaders. *I, and Boann and Aengus, Airmid and her man Ardal, and those elders and others, maybe Tadhg, who would come with us...*

But instead of stopping to assess the land's promise, taste a morsel of soil and rub it between his fingers, Cian pressed on, south by southwest, to meet the naomhog at the correct phase of the moon. He could feel the stress of keeping his appointment with Lir's ship as keenly as the burden of his bags of gold. *For now, it would be good if this gold rode on a horse!*

He steadily made his way toward a smaller ridge of mountains, their deep profile arrayed in successively higher steps up to the northernmost peak. Gebann told him to follow the river valley lying west of this profile, among pleasant hills. The black-stepped mountains stayed on his left in the east, while he traveled south above the river's banks on a natural path. This river shimmered, running wide and with many swans floating on it past flowers and ferns. Already the late spring undergrowth gave mushrooms and starchy roots for him to eat while walking, so that he stopped only at sunsets for a brief rest. He saw less food growing than in prior seasons and it worried him, how dangerously low Eire's food supply had dwindled.

He had one night of restless sleep, hungry. He dreamed that he hooked a berry to a thread and caught a shining trout. Boann came to him, apple blossoms in her hair. The gold disc at her ear expanded to form the sky dome where planets battled. Men warred on the plains below, the Boyne ran red. He felt a hand pinning him by the throat, saw the shadow of an intruder over him with knife raised. Cian kicked the warrior off balance and jumped to his feet, copper dagger in hand. They wrestled.

The man looked to be a renegade, disheveled, someone on the loose from the mines or a boat. Weak from lack of eating, he judged. Cian pointed at his food pouch and when the man turned to see, he leaped on him. They fell hard, and before he used his dagger, the stranger's head struck a rock.

Cian awoke with a start. He hastily gathered his things, then moved as fast as he could south along the river. His legs skimmed the earth, the loaded bags suddenly weightless.

For the rest of that sun, he tried to shake off the attack and whether he had killed the apparition. He regretted hurrying along the smooth river, framed by stepped mountains tinted purple-black at sunset, the most welcoming valley he had ever seen. In time he would return here with Boann and Aengus. A lump formed in his throat. He kept walking.

He made good progress and could hope to meet Lir on the appointed dawn. The river valley opened as it led him south and a pleasant river joined from the west, and later another. Among deep green forests edging lighter green banks, three great rivers flowed into a spreading silver flood. Cian followed the estuary along its east banks and caught sight of the ocean. This confluence of rivers with the sea brought back the richness of his night with Boann. He saw the mystery of water, water bringing forth life from soil just as new life emerges in a flood from the mother. He recalled with a thrill his glimpse of Aengus, born at the solstice.

Cian reached the shoreline where golden sand met the rich green-blue waters. He let the heavy bags fall from his shoulders and he watched wave after wave dissolve into the sand leaving only a slick trace.

Here water meets solid earth, held under the infinite sky. He felt very alive and yet very close to the spirits at this thin place, a threshold between worlds.

At water's edge he came face to face with himself. He could not be sure what he saw, a fugitive maybe, fleeing his home, and no better than the shadow who attacked him in his sleep. Cian checked his arms and legs. He wondered that he had no bruises from the attack.

The *naomhog* would arrive shortly for him to travel back to the Continent, if not on the coming sunrise then on the next. He would remain here in this thin place. Not long after sunset, he noted the constellation in the south that curled like an insect on the celestial horizon and he adjusted his internal bearings with it. During that night spent before a covered fire that cooked a small fish and seaweed, Cian watched various star patterns rising so he could help navigate on Lir's boat.

Through the night he heard water breaking on the shoreline in hypnotic rhythm. He could turn back to the Boyne; to Boann, Aengus, and his people. The truth, heavier than his bags of gold, crushed his impulse. If he returned now for a contest with Elcmar, your man would win and take all the gold after forcing him to reveal its secret source in the mountains. Then the *ard ri* would kill him, and take revenge on Gebann. *It would happen in that order if Elcmar were thinking!* He well knew that man's cold cunning by now.

Elcmar's fiery disruption of the Starwatcher ceremonies might prove to be his undoing. Cian had discussed the Invader truce with his elders. He told them of the cave containing the young bodies, of the doomed future of that tribe on the faraway peninsula. "I saw evidence of great violence, mass killing using metal weapons."

"Have the Invaders no fear of upsetting the natural balance?"

"They disregard any notion of balance. Invaders have been infected with beliefs from deep in the east, beliefs that center on man rather than on the heavens and harmony. Their Otherworld holds torture and punishment, a dark place of death that they say lies below the living world. You have encountered their hag's image, I am sorry to hear it. Their hag symbolizes chaos, darkness." Comments arose; he waited until they quieted.

"Do all foreigners have a custom of taking skulls?" an elder asked.

"Invaders have a fetish for the skull. I have heard they display skulls of enemies they respect. They practice burial of the body, the bones not defleshed and burned. Warriors get special treatment, and rarely, women.

"In Gebann's homeland the Seafarers still honor their ancestors and the stars as we do. Most keep the old ways despite Invaders, and you would feel at home among them. Inside one of their mines I saw a skull and bones that had turned dark green from the copper dust where they rested. Those miners, Seafarers, respect the green bones, bones of their ancestors who learned to make metals."

"Little green men," one elder exclaimed and the others gave a nervous laugh.

Slainge asked, "Have these intruders taken over the lands you visited?"

"Not exactly. Usually they arrive on water, but some coasts are free of their influence. They do not appear cohesive, they compete rather than act together as we do. They seek metals and in those places Invaders could not trade for metals, they have left." He spoke of hiding Eire's gold until they heard from him. Above all, that the Starwatchers must guard their mounds against the Invaders' misguided beliefs, as Gebann and others warned. He mentioned Cymru's example. "Others have told you of changes on the big island, open stone circles replacing the long barrows. But on the shore facing us, Cymru, those people continue in Starwatcher ways. They'd be allied with us. We should increase our contacts with them, and those to the north."

Again the elders broke into discussion.

He caught Oghma watching him, effects of the stroke still visible. His old mentor signaled using one good hand, a sign of welcome, making Cian's heart leap.

"Do the traders have any useful knowledge? Do they share knowledge with other people on the Continent?" another asked.

"Long before intruders arrived on those shores, Gebann's people knew the skies and navigated far out at sea to fish, and went exploring as we know. Their own artisans learned to make metals. Then these traders came along and took advantage. It appears that traders contribute little except new goods to trade. And strife." He described Bolg's stone fort and its hoarded grain, and the elders shook their heads.

Then he tried to explain how metals circulated, controlled by the very few, and the metals' varied uses. He did not have time to fully explain things his elders could not see for themselves, things Cian himself was not sure that he understood about exchanging for metal.

He warned them against greed. "Wherever the making of metal occurs, it devastates the land. No matter what enticement those men offer, you must resist those who would have you ravage the earth and burn off whole forests. The ore does run out, leaving a place that is not fit for living things.

"You trained me to observe patiently and I intend to do just that. I have tried to tell you enough so that Starwatchers might not be ensnared by these Invaders. There is still much to find out on my next journey." He thought of his full bags waiting in the mountains.

For a time the only sound was the fire, its popping bark and swish of falling embers, while his elders contemplated the fundamental changes taking place across the restless sea.

His people did not understand making war using metal, and that too must change. He took up a ceremonial stone axe, polished and perfect, never used. Serious faces turned to him. "Some of our young males must go live and train with the Invaders." He paused for emphasis. "Your best and brightest, to be shaped into fighting men with new skills. They can train others, in time. Trained killers. You must encourage this."

The shocked elders tried to understand. Voices rose in dissent.

"Butcher boys!"

"The Invaders' training need not convert our young men from our values and beliefs. Cian is proof enough of that," said the Dagda, but others grumbled.

Said another, "Already Invaders break the truce."

"Until Starwatchers across the island have trained and have the new weapons, the long knives, you should not try to battle Invaders in their style. Yet you must prepare for war," Cian told them, adamant. He didn't know how much gold, nor how many suns, it would take him to acquire enough metal weapons. In any event, Starwatchers needed to know how to use those. Meanwhile they had the shaky truce at the Boyne and his elders could attempt councils with whomever Elcmar sent. The people would watch the stars, tend their crops and animals, and they would coppice trees, hundreds of trees. They listened to his ideas.

"I will return when I can." He stirred, ready to leave.

The elders sighed to see him departing so soon. "We salute your bravery, Cian. Few would venture upon the mighty waves and for such great distances."

There were those who doubted his judgment, wondering aloud why he left them again for strange lands. Some elders did not know what to make of him, he could see that, that and their ambivalence to do battle. Would you hobble the entire island and call that making peace with Invaders, he could ask, but he'd said enough.

His eyes singled out Oghma's to make an apology: *See me as I am. I might never be the Starwatcher you wanted me to be.*

Oghma's look replied: *You are a Starwatcher.*

The waves swept the shore, relentless, clattering its shells and pebbles and dispersing his reverie. He felt in a small pouch at his waist to be sure he still carried the safe-passage stone that the Dagda gave him. He would be sending more of these very stones back to the Boyne from the Continent. He smiled, shaking his head. Did Elcmar really think he controlled the great waters to Eire?

The heliacal stars faded in the aura from the coming sun.

He stood up, legs numb from sitting watch over his bags through the night. He tried to fill his lungs, the air salty and piquant with sea creature smells. Raw fear of the ocean journey seized him: to be on the watery void again and beyond sight of land, like trying to go to the moon. Spring had arrived but mariners still must overcome squalls and shifting currents and turbulent swells.

Bitter grit rose to the back of his throat. Ready to vomit and he wasn't even on the boat; what would his elders say to that?

As he searched the sky, the sun's majesty spilled across the horizon and lit the wavetops. Cian greeted the face of the almighty.

The sun looked on with its beneficent light.

You cannot fail for trying, the ancient one told him.

The dark shadow, the fear that stalked him, dissolved. His Starwatchers depended on him, as did Gebann and Lir. He basked in a moment of peace with the sun, his ancestors, and himself.

Ready to cross the thin place between land and ocean, he walked to the surf and splashed his face and body with bracing cold seawater. He saw the naomhog edging along the coast. Pulse racing, he placed just enough pine tinder and seaweed on his fire to make white smoke showing his position. As the sun notched above the waters, Lir's sleek boat, fit for the ocean's churning troughs, pulled into the shallows.

Lir threw out a stone anchor offshore. Two crewmen jumped out to replenish supplies. They refilled skins with fresh water, and stuffed string bags with greens and roots. One man gathered seafood from the tidal pools; Cian steamed it over his fire and they would eat it later. The other fellow climbed and found a clutch of seabird eggs, a delicacy to be pierced and sucked raw from the shell. All made haste; it was best that no one, intruder or native, see them. They had supplies from the opposing coast, they said, and Lir would as usual put in at friendly islands along their way. They told Cian with a poke at his ribs that they carried the acorn-fed ham that kept well on voyages.

He realized then the hunger he had on him, an enormous hunger. All of Eire looked underfed. Their harvest had better be good if the Starwatchers were to survive another winter. The spark flared in his head. He had his own plan to outwit the Invaders.

They returned to the *naomhog* before the sun stood above the treetops. On board, he clasped each crewman and Lir, unable to speak for gratitude and glad to see each face.

"You found us," Lir teased. "What's that in your big bags? Elcmar?"

Bundles filled the *naomhog*. On Cymru, they had traded for stacks of skins and furs and for pots having feet, a new style. He helped the crew redistribute the load to take on his heavy bags. They triple-lashed those bags onto a wide plank using stout yew withies, then tied down that plank with hemp ropes leaving just room enough for two rowers seated one on each side.

Lir checked the knots himself. "The ropes should be tight yet these knots would release that plank easily to you," he said, showing Cian. "We'll hug the coasts as much as possible. But if we start to sink—then you'll be swimming for shore with that plank!"

The crew snickered but Cian knew that his friend was not joking.

Lir straightened his back, and stood a head taller than any of them. He blew out a breath long and strong enough to stir the waves. "I congratulate you on the find, lad.

"Let's be off, your bags have us wallowing as it is. Cut the rope to the anchor stone! Saves us the time hauling it in." The famed mariner spurned ritual before his voyages, but this time as they sped out from the estuary Lir cast a fragment of copper into the blue depths, and grinned at Cian.

Just like way back in the days of old
And together we will float into the mystic

Into The Mystic, Van Morrison

A Pot of Gold

ON EIRE, ALL the people made good use of the lunates of long daylight and smoother seas.

Invaders continued taking copper on the southwest coast. A trader boat came and went from the Lake mine. At the Boyne more warriors and slaves arrived to replace the past winter's losses. To rub it all in, the intruders built new stone walls at intervals around the large mounds, enclosing plots to graze their purloined cattle and small fields to grow their barley.

The superstitious intruders bypassed the ruined mound of Dowth. Bresal proposed that they rebuild this mound, higher than any other, to reach the heavens. Elcmar and Ith had with difficulty talked Bresal out of this scheme. Ith posted a sentry at the central mound in a wood and wattle hut, and went there often himself, going round and round the great mound, trying to decode its carved kerbstones.

The sun and the moon continued to light the passages and chambers at Carrowkeel, Loughcrew, Fourknocks, and the Boyne. The Starwatchers' ceremonies occurred in stealth; the *geis* made it dangerous for them to gather at the mounds, especially during darkness. The Invaders regarded starwatching as bad luck with Ith's encouragement, or so the Starwatchers heard it; but they saw that the shaman skulked around the mounds, examining their carvings. Training of young engineers like Daire had been greatly disrupted. The Starwatchers redoubled efforts to teach astronomy to their little ones. Deciphering the equinox shift became paramount for the astronomers.

Boann occasionally joined them, though occupied with her infant son. Aengus, who grew fat and strong and enchanted all who looked on him. Aengus the fair, the Starwatchers said of him, fair as our sun.

The long days bloomed, one after another. On their whole island, no Starwatcher had heard from Cliodhna. If anyone had had word from Cian, they kept it a secret.

Cian's return voyage to the Continent with his heavy bags of gold from Eire's mountains, took him to a landing place further east than where he first landed with Gebann. As the boat neared shore, he strained to see signs of Invaders.

Lir explained, "This eastern stretch of the peninsula where its shoreline curves north, and its mines, are controlled by a most ancient tribe. That tribe keeps aloof; they use their own mariners, have their own sacred symbols, and keep their own customs intact. They speak an old and complicated tongue, and they answer to no one. There's no Invader official here and so no duty to be levied on what's in those leather bags." It greatly relieved Cian to hear that his gold would not be depleted by a greedy Invader the moment Lir's ship landed.

"Come on, let's find you a place to stay among them." Lir helped him find lodging in a village along the coast, shaded by tall oaks and pines. He recommended that Cian remain there through one lunate and learn what he might of their trading and smithing. "You can inquire here about Cliodhna, whisper it like a breeze among the pines. I'll be searching as well, and I'll speed a message west to Gebann. You'll have his reply before the next moon, I swear it."

Cian held out several chunky nuggets of gold and Lir accepted them. He held out a small bag. "And here is gold to give to Gebann for my success on Eire. Tell Gebann that I now understand the meaning of debt, since I can never repay him."

"Don't be so hard on yourself, Cian." Lir gave him a friendly tap on the arm. "That's enough sun metal to keep me afloat for a good while. Probably enough for a new boat. Now enjoy the food and drink on offer here, will you? These Basques do be famous cooks—and you're after getting thin."

Lir introduced him to a mariner friend on the coast fronting the Pyrenees, and left Cian to live among the renowned metal workers for one lunate. Their smiths could show him all that he needed to know in their art. Lir's friend, who gave him the use of a hut, warned him,

"Turning stone into metal must be treated with awe by those who do not know its secrets, secrets our smiths have kept for generations."

Knowing it would take awhile to earn the smiths' trust, Cian found himself carving with stoneworking tools again so that he might be of use while he lived with these people. Now I don't mind working in stone, he thought, chastened to compare his awkward time with Oghma. For his labor, after awhile the smiths allowed him to enter privileged spaces where they cast various metals and worked each metal after casting.

Gradually, observing the smiths, he learned the finer details of smelting and casting of bronze, the alloy of copper with tin. He learned to combine the proper proportion of copper with tin, to pour a bronze that would not be brittle. The smiths listed the superior qualities of bronze: easier to cast when hot, required a lower smelting temperature, it was easier to work after casting in a mold, and bronze made harder objects even before it had a final hammering. For Cian it was all strange sounds and smells and irritating smoke but he stayed on.

While at rest, he familiarized himself with plants and animals, many unknown on Eire. A little visitor interrupted his solitude at his sleeping hut, sitting just outside the entrance. Its improbable coloring made Cian laugh in surprise: pointy ears topping a slender body with tawny red fur spotted with black, black feet and a black line down its back, then black rings alternating with tawny around its long tail. The size of a small dog, the genet sat looking baleful until he gave it some stale meal cake. It ate and ran away until the following dusk when it reappeared. For the genet's company, he gladly shared his food.

Smelting began to have a rhythm and logic for him. From ore to finished item, it took labor involving many different hands to produce an object in copper, or gold, or the other metals. As the smiths showed Cian the finer points of their art, he comprehended why these metal objects had extreme value. Copper, and the much rarer bronze, the smiths poured as tools with obvious utility: axeheads, knives, and awls. Pliable gold or silver was usually hammered, little heat required. In the case of gold and silver, and sometimes copper or bronze, those became items to adorn the body as gleaming jewelry around the neck, or the arm, or as an earring.

Unlike Creidhne and Lein at the Lake Of Many Hammers, here dwelled smiths who wrought only gold and silver, and they worked apart from toolmakers who poured and styled the sturdier metals. Sheet gold's shiny surface surprised Cian with his reflection so that he almost dropped the first piece he handled. The jewelry smiths showed him that even the smallest scrap of malleable gold could be used, whether rolled into gold wire or hammered into thin sheets. Gold could be used to overlay another substance: gold foil wrappping rare amber around the circumference of an amber earring, or burnishing the wood hilt of a dagger.

Very few persons could possess these objects, one smith told him, but their craft flourished as smiths worked more gold into finery. "The big traders lust after gold," another added. "It carries great power."

It dawned on Cian: sun metal conveys abundance. His hidden bags of sun metal gave him enormous means to barter, even among these *Euskaldunak*, the Basque people. He could have anything he desired.

Cian met with the elders. Their master smith Basajuan needed much gold for making a ceremonial object, the elders told him. For a weight of gold from his cache, he could gain access to Basajuan, said to be a goodhumored giant of a man. Cian bargained as he had seen Gebann do on many occasions. The Basque elders were to exchange the gold he would turn over toward many things Cian indicated that he would need including the use of a strong ship, a crew, and supplies for it, heavy rope and provisions and food; all that would be needed to take him far north along the curving bay. That raised some eyebrows, they saw he was no mariner, but they agreed.

After he took a ritual sweatbath, the elders introduced him to Basajuan. The man stood like a bull with an incongruous broad smile.

Cian turned over the agreed weight of gold. Basajuan labored at hammering the gold into a wide flat sheet, Cian working nearby to make a new curved anvil. The great smith wanted the anvil for just this project. Cian chipped and polished small stones into rectangles which Basajuan used to smooth the sheet gold into final shape. At the anvil, the smith fashioned a cape of gold. It spanned the chest and over each shoulder and upper arm, with its opening at the back of the neck. Basajuan bent over the anvil to finish the exceptional cape, embossing tightly spaced curving ribs alternating with curving rows of tiny raised bosses, until the gold appeared to be a flow of luminous textile and beads folding around the lucky wearer. Its underside, he would finish with reinforcing leather held with bronze strips.

This flowing gold cape astounded all who saw it; it was an unprecedented object.

"Who shall receive this cape?" Cian inquired as the smith tapped the final rows of dazzling embossed beading into the gold's arcing surface.

"This? This cape of mine is going to Taranis, the chief trader at a great estuary north of here." The master ran his hands over his delicate work. "I shall never see it again." He stared with Cian at the gold treasure that would travel far away from his talented hands.

"Will this chief know where it is that you Basques obtained the gold for it?"

Basajaun considered this, wiping his brow. "What do you suggest?"

"Let Taranis hear that this gold came from the Starwatchers. Nothing more."

Basajuan agreed with a wink.

Cian felt very comfortable among the *Euskaldunak*. They held their important councils under a great oak, much like his people. He tried to master their language, but found it took a long time to learn if one had not heard it while a child. The Euskara phrasing and complicated grammar made it similar to the Starwatchers'. In comparison with the less precise Invaders, the Starwatchers and these *Euskaldunak* expressed themselves very well using few words.

"So, both our people are quiet ones," he teased the placid Basajuan.

Glad for his safe journey and good fortune, Cian asked to visit a starwatching place as the elders might permit him and they chose a fellow his age to take him. They traveled inland on sturdy horses, then climbed steep footpaths. His guide brought him to small mounds with ancestor burials, where they stopped but Cian grew restless.

"I wish to connect with the sky," he repeated and pointed above. His guide's look changed.

"Our practices are hidden from outsiders."

"What face do I wear?" Cian replied. "I look more the *Euskaldunak* than you!"

They traveled to higher peaks in the coastal mountains and on the third day reached the sanctuary, Oianleku.

Cian thought he stood at the top of the world; then he saw that, no, to the east rose another ridged profile of equally high mountaintops. He turned slowly. From the grassy plateau of Oianleku, he looked toward the great waters to the north, barely seen across the intervening peaks and lush valleys. The smudge of dark blue led to Eire, his home, and he felt the pull as he gazed north. He turned to the west and then south, where rugged mountains filed into a hazy infinity.

Cian turned again to the east. Now he saw that the mountains directly across from him had five distinct peaks, like fingers folded over into a mighty fist. Deep notches lay to either side and divided this raised fist from the mountaintops on the left, north, and to the south.

His companion nodded in answer to Cian's question, yes, at this plateau the *Euskaldunak* recorded the sun's journey to its most northern and southern extremes in the seasons. In this breathtaking vista they unlocked the moon's cycle and many other secrets. As the two explored, the young Basque showed him how the various stones aligned with distant peaks and celestial paths. The north and south stone circles lay snug against the landscape, intriguing him. The plateau was like a disk marked for the sky. He went apart to reflect.

It was the same in this mountainous land as among the Starwatchers: the ancients used the high places to build their observatories. But here their burial mounds stood strictly apart from this sacred plateau. He could see the tribes of this area kept to themselves, the mountains almost inviolable. Was it from them that building of stone passages to capture and direct sunlight first crossed the water up to his people? He felt linked with this place and these people just as he had farther west among Seafarers. This isolated site to watch stars in peace, the place of the raised fist, captivated him.

The high plateau held such beauty that Cian wanted to stay for a time. The two made camp there with sunset. Wait for the stars in the Hunter's belt, his guide told him. Through that night they sighted star patterns and planets in its cool and clear air. The sun rose, steadfast with its warm blessing—and a reminder. He had forgotten to honor summer solstice, while helping create the fabulous gold cape; the realization stunned him. Without explaining why, he asked and his guide agreed they could remain that sunlight and another starwatch at Oianleku. He fasted and followed sun and stars, circling the stones with care. His vision of the sky dome upon a metal disk burned brighter than ever. He went forward restored from his mountaintop sojourn.

When they returned to the coastal village, his guide who had become his spiritual brother told the elders of their journey. Cian's reverence for their sacred site and his knowledge of the skies so impressed the *Euskaldunak* elders that they honored him with a feast before he would be departing.

He would long remember the line of merry girls who approached benches where the guests were seated, eating. Some girls already wore the fertility apron of womanhood, stepping self-consciously as a doe. Each girl carried a slender pitcher and tall pottery cup. Cian gaped as these laughing maidens poured fermented cider in an arc streaming overhead from the pitcher and into the cup held outstretched in her opposite hand. Their pouring made the cider sparkle in his mouth.

At this feast Cian ate with gusto from all the hearty and spiced fare. These *Euskaldunak* had a flair for preparing bounty from the sea or the earth. He overindulged in that meal and the strong golden cider, laughing if a girl splashed him while she was pouring. He was hiding deeper concerns. At length the feast concluded. He drank the last toast with his hosts and weaved along the path to his hut, alone, a lamp pot wobbling in his hand.

He needed to think. Before the feast, he learned with sorrow from Lir's messenger from the far west coast, that Gebann was all but paralyzed in his legs and that Cliodhna had not returned to her people. Not one among the mariners knew of her whereabouts. He rubbed his forehead. *It is time for me to leave this shore. I can inquire north along the coast, perhaps traders detained Cliodhna or she has had to hide... With this gold surely I can find her.*

To sober himself, he examined the plaques marked by Gebann and sent back with the messenger. He would add his own marks later and send the directions on to Eire somehow. On to Sreng, somehow. One step at a time, he told himself. Then he thought ruefully, one grueling voyage at a time, so. He needed sleep and stretched out on his narrow bed of sheepskin over hay but it seemed to pitch and roll in the dark and he slept badly.

On the following sunrise, his head aching and his stirabout left untouched, Cian paid a visit to the elder woman who was said to have the special sight. She might at least give him aromatic water, herbs that could quiet his head and his insides.

The woman had high cheekbones in a striking face, sleek hair black as a raven's and held back coiled around a long bone pin, and golden skin. The woman's deepset brown eyes seemed to take in everything and nothing. When he told her his name, she told him she did not need to hear it. She waved him to where he should sit, opposite her. Between them rose a cloud of smoke from her hearth fire, its scent heavy but pleasant. She said nothing further.

He shifted, restless and queasy, then told her about Cliodhna and his search.

The woman inhaled the smoke and sighed, dark eyes glinting in the low light. "I cannot see anything of this Cliodhna." She gave him a sharp look. "You would leave on a sea voyage?"

"Yes, soon I leave this coast."

The woman's body tensed, though her eyes took on a dreamy expression. "I know the reason that you seek my vision. You need not worry about the waves! The caul was on your head when you were born, Starwatcher. You cannot be drowned."

Hardy young Basques volunteered to travel with Cian, north to where traders met in the fabled hall of Taranis. From there, it was said, cargo went inland to far corners of the Continent, and they wished to observe this trading. The Basque elders readily consented to send these young men with Cian. All had grown fond of this quiet, respectful Starwatcher who bartered without undue haggling, and paid in gold.

With Lir's mariner, who promised to come straightaway to the Loire when summoned if Lir could not, Cian hired the use of a stout hide boat outfitted with hemp ropes and supplies. The jovial crew took him up the coastline of the Continent, north by northeast. Once more he traveled using an unfamiliar vessel. He had not chosen the trees felled for this boat's frame nor the hides, nor known the hands that shaped it nor those men who launched it into seawater; all this gave him pause. Still, he had grown to trust these *Euskaldunak*.

He gave the crew control of their boat and let them try out a novelty, a small square leather sail. The Basques treated the great waters like a familiar lane between villages. They respected but did not fear the ocean as he did. Like Lir, they wasted no time making sacrifices before each voyage although in early times that had been the custom, they told him; but they made hasty offerings when they saw a storm coming over the water.

They stopped at islands and inlets where starwatching peoples lived and where a boat carrying Cliodhna might have put in to hide from Invaders, but learned nothing of her. He could not accept that she must have drowned in the sea, and that no amount of gold could find her.

Cian remained in charge of his and the crew's fate. Another long journey, and he continually stepped onto a shore where he could not be sure of the welcome. His gut-twisting anxiety out on the vast ocean did not leave him, despite the words of the Basque seer woman. Intent on his mission, he paid his fear little attention. The waves' ceaseless motion still made him green and that he could not ignore. Their journey north held no special torments for they traveled while calmer seas prevailed. The Basques fed him tidbits, jesting and rolling their eyes, trying to ease his all too evident seasickness.

He pieced together from all he saw and heard in the settlements along this great bay, that Invaders squabbled here over trading as well and any people in their path knew little peace. His gold gave him power but he circumvented men wearing elite trappings, metal knives and jewelry and fine tunics, wary by now of their limitless greed. The crew gladly avoided busy ports even when that meant camping in rough grass and sand, rolled in a hide against chill night air.

More often than not, a humble local vendor rejected his sun metal. Gold being a rarity, it could not be exchanged for simple goods like food. Cian learned to take on goods he did not want, then trade them at another spot for other goods, eventually striking a deal for items he needed. Trading in goods also attracted less attention than his gold, or even copper and he had but scraps of copper.

Have I become a trader, and what does that mean? Gaining confidence, he eagerly pushed north to the river where one man, the chief, reputedly controlled trade leading into the wide Continent. *I hope that Taranis is enjoying that stunning gold cape from Basajuan...and that your man has an insatiable appetite for sun metal.*

They progressed to where breezes blew cooler, the land smelled more familiar to him. Cian's hired boat and lively crew veered northwest and arrived at the estuary where Lir said the Loire flowed into the sea. His men indicated that this bay and string of islands provided good shelter, lying inward from the projecting coast to the west. They beached during low tide, just short of the estuary, where a mound and small village stood on an islet.

Cian dropped over the side and waded in to speak with the young scout who watched from atop a grassy rise. They spoke using their hands and a combination of dialects. Yes, he was assured by the youth, here dwells Taranis who controls cargo on the long river.

The scout walked him past pools of brine collecting greyish sea salt and back to the pebbled shore, cleared an area and traced lines on the sand. "The river leads to two trade routes. This northern route extends over plains and up to the Cold Sea. The great river turns south and the southern route bypasses this chain of mountains running east to west and leads into hotter lands along the south sea."

"Oh?" was all Cian could manage.

That got him a strange look but the lad continued. "In the center of the Continent more deep rivers lead east through land of rich black soil. Salt and fine stone is mined at snowy mountains there and traded. Of course Taranis has a supply of salt here."

Impressed by the lad knowing so much and easily etching a map onto sand, Cian assumed all to be accurate. To thank the scout, he invited him on board for a quick meal. The Basques agreed, it was best to eat before one landed among voracious traders.

The scout relished the tender ham and tangy cheeses served to him by the *Euskaldunak*, while he advised them exactly where to put in and that they should stay on their ship that first night. With sunrise, they could go onto shore and find the market. There they would see goods arrayed from across the Continent: amber and jet from the north, and woods, pots, unusual beads, and stone axes from mountains. From the Basque coast and Seafarers farther west, came ocean-blue variscite beads, copper items, boars' tusks, and ermine skins. They might see novel goods from remote southern lands: gossamer-light linen, strange skins, scented oils, bright dyes, rare ivory and timber; the scout named them all in quick succession. Cian and his crew readied their craft with great anticipation as the scout splashed back to shore.

The tide rose, and the Basques pushed off. In a short time they steered their modest craft carefully into the harborage packed with trader vessels. They eyed an imposing wooden structure set back above the banks. Clearly, Taranis positioned himself to control this estuary's traffic.

That scout did not mention gold trading, Cian thought, anxious.

As they threw out a stone anchor and secured their vessel, a scowling official bore down on them in a wooden dugout paddled by two slaves. The official boarded showing disdain for their modest boat and unimpressed by the sail. He drove a hard bargain. Cian surprised the Basques at how well he stood up to this man. The port official left them after lightening their load, he said. No one let on by how much, the bulk of it secured where the official failed to look.

Cian made light of the exchange. "If I'm to be killed for gold, well—any one of the voyages might kill me anyway!"

After their first night spent listening to the scurry of strangers and beasts in this port, he and his Basque crew left one man on watch and went ashore to see what was on offer.

They all needed fresh clothing after their voyage, and as the lad at the coast told them, here it was possible to have any garment in the known world. Soft hide tunics, textiles coarse or fine in bast, linen, and dyed wool, and brightly woven sashes, and every sort of belt, pouch, and sack; filled wide planks set on trestles and spilled from leather packs. Shorter more flexible bows, and new arrowhead shapes, and carved stone wristguards, vied for attention.

Cian noticed the absence of metal weapons on display, and no ingots, no smelting or smiths. Natural caution led him not to inquire about metals; besides, those speaking the Invader tongue had a different accent than he had heard, and he recognized no words in their local patter. He had the sensation of being immersed in colorful new sights and smells and sounds, like being underwater and where staying too long might mean forever.

People crowded in to view the goods, many carrying packs of their own to barter. One of the young Basques, whose beard had only started to sprout, gawked at various women. The crew pulled him along. The crew and Cian studied the Loire trade, drawing little attention to themselves, until their stomachs told them it was time they had food.

The Basques tasted cheese after cheese, and fruits, and mealcakes and breads. They moved on to smoked fish and meats. To obtain food and small goods they traded copper scraps and trinkets furnished by Basajuan for this purpose, nothing showy. Vats of leftover barley mash soured the air: brew made for Invader tastes. Cian could eat and drink little, expectant and alert.

Soon enough, Taranis learned of their presence. His personal invitation arrived from a sentry bristling with metal knives: Cian and his men must appear before the chief.

The great hall and its clearing occupied a rise overlooking where river swirled with ocean. They climbed the hill, led by the sentry. At the summit lay a wide path paved with quartz cobbles, split and polished to a high gloss. Cian halted. He had never seen white quartz used other than at a sacred mound entrance and its use underfoot paving the way to the hall of Taranis struck him as extreme arrogance. The sentry jabbed at him and only then did he step forward on the path.

Yew hedges growing beneath shaped beech trees lined the approach. Halfway to the hall's entrance, he stopped again. On their left, a man's head rested on a pike; it was a few days sitting there atop the pole, he judged. Behind the grisly pike stood a tall stone grotto stacked with layers of skulls and long bones, clearly not a burial. The burly guard approached to prod him again and he and the Basques moved along.

The wooden structure appeared many times larger than the Invader hall at the Boyne. They passed beyond carved entrance doors, into a chamber and through more impressive doors, then into a narrow antechamber with inlaid beams and patterned hangings. A crowd of men waited. Strong guards wearing leather helmets stood before a heavy door rubbed with red ocher and wax, their pikes crossed in front of it. Men talked in muffled accents behind smooth plank walls on either side. From somewhere, a man groaned in pain. The Basques stood firm around Cian, waiting.

Their turn came. Guards hurried them into the commodious reception chamber. One man sat at ease behind a long table made of rare wood. His hooded, eagle's eyes locked with Cian's.

An aide standing beside the seated chief ordered, "Taranis wants to see your pass for this port!" He phrased it in the Invader dialect.

The young Basques stiffened: a Basque craft traveled without any pass for any port. Cian thought the ermine skins and hefty gold nugget he handed over to the port official disposed of the matter.

Faced with Taranis, Cian seized the moment. "With all due respect, I ask Taranis to recognize my pass for these shores." From a gap in the seam of his tunic he drew out a heavy deerskin purse and emptied it onto the table. Guards bolted toward him.

Gold nuggets large and small rumbled out, covering the tabletop. Taranis jumped to his feet. Before his eyes lay more gold than he could have imagined one man carrying, more gold than he had seen in his life. Even for the owner of the fabled gold cape, this heap of nuggets presented an incredible sight. He called out and more sentries stepped into his chamber. The brave Basques surrounding Cian drew their concealed knives, ready to spring in defense.

Cian looked steadily into Taranis' eyes.

The chief raised both his forearms and lowered them with palms downward. His guards stepped back to the walls. Taranis spoke. "My sentries will protect my guests, not harm them."

The Basques lowered their knives slowly. The trader chief bade his guests be seated and they met for a considerable time around his smooth table burdened with gold. In the end, Taranis assigned them a personal guard, the very same official who relieved Cian of the large gold nugget. The man entered Taranis' chamber and fell to his knees before his chief.

"Do you want me to kill him?" Taranis inquired of Cian.

"No!"

"Then he serves you and these *Euskaldunak* with his life. This man's already been well paid as you know. Don't pay him again," Taranis snapped. He glared at his port official and each guard. "You may all leave me now.

"Starwatcher, you return to me at sunrise. I'll have an interpreter. We have much to discuss."

Over the next sunrises, Cian held the great trader's attention through prolonged audiences while others cooled their heels, outside the chamber. He brought more of the impressive nuggets, "as a sign of good faith and for safekeeping," Cian said, as if he had access to unlimited gold.

The trader chief commanded the Starwatcher and the Basques to move into ample quarters close to his hall. They remained vigilant and kept an eye on their ship with the help of the newly meek port official.

In lengthy discussions with Taranis, Cian spoke openly. "I want to establish trade in gold directly from the Starwatchers to the Continent. I need your help. There are other harbors, other nodes on this long coast to ship gold or goods inland, but I like your routes here from the Loire. I'll pay you well for my landing privileges through one full cycle of the sun, if you show me that the gold will not be molested coming into this port by anyone, from your lowest port official to the top. And we'll need a safe place to be storing the gold."

Taranis grumbled while they determined how not to be robbed by his own men at his port. He looked down his long nose set in a sculpted face, in a manner that showed him fully aware of his good looks. He wore his hair smoothed with rosewater and formed into black curls around a high forehead. Over a simple linen tunic, Taranis flung a length of softest wool in rich dark blue; it formed a drapery that hung perfectly on his formidable frame, elegant and masculine at the same time. Taranis' nails displayed an even trim and buffing. This chief wore no bauble that would distract the eye, yet he oozed power.

Cian reminded himself to get a much better tunic, a fresh leather vest and shoes, maybe a good cloak, and a shave and haircut in the market; but he would do without rosewater curls and buffed nails.

The two men agreed by and by, in addition to the landing fee paid for ships carrying gold from Cian's agents, that more gold would be apportioned to Taranis after one full solar cycle. In four seasons hence, Cian thought, he would know how much gold the Wicklow streams would reliably yield. He placed great trust in the trader chief who seemed as sound as Lir, feeling his way through their intense negotiations until all had been decided to mutual satisfaction. Elcmar would have no share in Eire's gold.

Afterward, in his private quarters, he shook his head to clear it. The man Taranis had better prove worthy of his trust. It was only then that Cian saw how daring he had been with his own neck—and that he held the freedom and fortunes of Eire in the palm of his hand.

Taranis might send his own party looking for gold, careful as Cian had been to not give its location. Cian called for one of his Basques and sent him to the harbor ships to find a messenger, someone headed south who could fetch Lir from that coast.

Lir would bring the first shipment of gold from Eire.

Still dazed, he withdrew from the Basques and strolled to the ocean horizon as the sun set. Much depended now on the fickle waves and weather. You shall not fail for trying, he told himself. Cian prayed to Griane and Coll, his ancestors, as the mighty sun spread its fire over the waves before it set.

Taranis found their arrangement to be reasonable and much to his liking. Elcmar's recent copper shipments from Eire had been unreliable and so his credit suffered with Taranis. That bounder and your man Connor had diverted copper to the Seafarer coast to pay off their goods and travels, the chief knew. *If any trader so much as sneezes, I hear about it.* Nothing bound him to permit only Elcmar to trade from the Starwatcher isle. *Why not allow this clever lad to establish Starwatcher gold flowing to me? So much better than my having to wait for others to find it!*

In their meetings, the astute Taranis questioned Cian about his island of the setting sun, on the northwest edge of known waters and fabled for its learned Starwatchers.

As a Seafarer, Taranis had some understanding of star signs. The two men worked out a notation system for their gold shipments. They sought to verify that the gold's original weight coming from Cian's agents on the Starwatcher island matched its weight on arrival at the port and again at delivery to them. Cian showed him the stone plaques introduced to Cian by Gebann. Stone plaques were durable and portable, and copies could be made; they seemed reliable in that etched symbols on them could not easily be changed or erased. Taranis showed him small clay cylinders used to keep track of goods by those trading in hot lands far to the south, he said; but then he agreed that fragile clay seals didn't suit their purpose.

Taranis remarked, "It goes without saying that your average Invader wouldn't be able to read scratches on a stone plaque." He smiled at the Starwatcher.

He saw Cian's hazel eyes twinkle in return. "All my men handling the gold can be trusted. And they know the symbols, at least those we'll be using, so." His face grew serious once more as Cian took from his tunic a striped dark yellow stone, polished to highlight its color and grain. "Have you ever seen a stone like this?" he asked.

Taranis held out the striated yellow stone to see it better under pitch torchlight. "Yes, perhaps—and I know someone who would be certain what it is. A collector of stones, a metalsmith. I want you to meet him for our purposes anyway. I'll have him here with the sun."

Shortly Cian had a supply of safe passage stones to send on to Eire, scores of these stones, in fact.

The chief concerned himself with getting the gold flowing. The Starwatcher and his boisterous escorts served merely as a means to an end, though Taranis did wonder why the muscular young Basques remained with Cian. Over the next moon, he had the Starwatcher and his companions monitored and reports made to his ears alone. Once Taranis understood of the search for Cliodhna, he sent out word among his network along the coasts, and for that help Cian expressed utmost gratitude. From Cian's personal habits, Taranis inferred that the lad's tastes ran to women and not men; though he kept to himself, reserved if not aloof, an enigma. To the worldly trader, the young Starwatcher exhibited no sign of guile in word or deed.

If this young Starwatcher had exceptional loyalty and smarts, then he might have further plans for Cian but not before the lad proved himself. He announced to Cian that he would send the Starwatcher and his Basque companions traveling inland, save one whom Taranis kept behind as a hostage and to exploit that one's talent, an excellent hand at preparing food.

Cian adapted to this swift change. Taranis moved like the planets, on his own course and not with ordinary stars. He too must plan in advance and act swiftly, to catch up with events or make things happen far away. His new life entailed trying to outrun the sun rather than working within its risings and settings. He needed to get Sreng moving with miners to Eire's eastern mountains where they could take the gold. Soon Lir would be arriving at the Loire, but that master of the waves would know to wait here until his return.

Before their expedition inland, Cian and his Basques searched among the boats moored in the estuary for one bound for the northern isles. Their obeisant helper the port official pointed out a good ship that readied to depart for the Lake mine of the Starwatcher island, a stroke of luck. It looked to be a high-sided *naomhog* that Lir would approve. They rowed past it in a little coracle. Cian chose with care from the faces on board and singled out one man to approach.

That night under a crescent moon, the Basques tempted this crewman ashore on the pretext of selling him a portion of brined meat. "Good sea salt from this coast. That tasty meat's sure to last the voyage," they told him. On the broad landing stones they all bent to examine the potted meat. Cian stepped out from the shadows, a cloak over his features. The Basques pulled their knives, pretending to be startled, watching the mariner.

"I have a better offer for you," Cian told the Seafarer. He held up a large gold nugget while he convinced the man to deliver the pot with its contents intact all the way to Sreng at the Lake mine coast. The Seafarer's eyes glittered and he stretched out a toughened hand for the big nugget. Cian gave him a smaller chunk of sun metal.

"I can see that you are wise. You'll receive the large nugget and be set for life when you return from the Starwatcher island with the man Sreng's sign to me. Fail in that or give this pot over to the wrong hands, and Lir himself will chase you to the bottom of the seas. Safe journey to you!"

The Seafarer's eyes narrowed but he accepted the pot and small gold nugget, and good cheese that would fill his stomach on the voyage, they told him.

Cian melted into the darkness and watched, pensive, as the Basques rowed the man back out to the moored ship soon to leave for Eire. If the stone plaque hidden at the bottom of the sturdy pot made it safely to Sreng, all would be well.

It was Gebann who suggested that Sreng lead their men, for stalwart Sreng would know which miners to recruit and he had seen firsthand the mining and export of copper. The sun metal had such inestimable value that it would not take many men working with Sreng... While he crossed Eire west to east, Sreng could seek news of Cliodhna. Then perhaps Gebann and his wife could have an answer. *Ayah*; Cian inhaled making the sound that meant affirmation.

The Basques rejoined him in the shadows. Satisfied that the mariner and big pot had tucked in without awakening his crew, the men left the slumbering boats.

Several miners trudged to the coast from the Lake of Many Hammers to see what the trader vessel, arriving late in that season of high sun, had brought from Taranis' famed port.

Creidhne noticed the man Sreng giving a mariner a polished red jasper bead for a foreign pot, and interrupted them. "A Starwatcher trading for food? Why should I let you have this meat when I could eat it myself?"

"Have it then, but your man says the meat's gone off and shouldn't be eaten, so," said Sreng, glib with the Invader tongue, and turned as if to walk away. "I want only the food vessel."

The husky mariner snatched up the red bead, swore an oath at Creidhne, and thrust the pot at Sreng.

"Keep it, will you!" Creidhne moved on to inspect other goods from this shipment. He would not cross any man who dared to ride the high seas.

When this boat left, Creidhne would be sending Elcmar's spy with it, but he kept that fact to himself.

Sreng emptied the big pot that came from a far shore, its markings curious to him. Under the meat, somewhat spoiled, he found the plaque etched with signs, and Sreng rejoiced.

He mobilized select men among the miners, showing them the plaque, and his small group quickly left the Lake Of Many Hammers. As they made their way at night to Eire's eastern mountains, Sreng circulated the safe passage stones smuggled in from Cian so that those tokens would reach the Boyne. His group arrived in the valleys around Lugnaquilla well before cold weather.

Cian's plaque brought them to the steep cliffs streaked with quartz. Sreng and his men began pulling gold from the rushing stream. The gold lay accessible and in good quantity, they found.

Sreng shattered the plaque and threw the pieces into the stream. He kept the strange pot.

They built a more permanent camp in a narrow ravine at a distance from the sun metal. The local Starwatchers, who had lost men to Elcmar's warriors, aided them with scouts who showed them routes to carry sun metal to the coast. The sun sped south along the horizon toward equinox. Starwatcher scouts brought Lir from the coast up to the mountain stream. He arrived just before the autumn sun, laden with goods for the miners.

Sreng tried to convince Lir of the quantity of gold around them. "You simply pick it up. With gold there's little smelting, so we'll do little felling of trees. We can leave scarcely a footprint and live out of sight. Unless Elcmar challenges us. Then we must fight him."

Lir gloated with him over their find, but cautioned Sreng. "Cian cannot send metal weapons to you, not yet. The trader chief Taranis does not permit it.

"You must hold back your share of gold until the right time comes. Do not trade with anyone using sun metal! I bring you a few copper axes, ropes, furs and warm cloaks, and hides worked for clothing and shoes. With each boat, Cian will send items you need."

"No more spoiled meat, tell him." Sreng made a face, then laughed and told Lir about the mariner who delivered the foreign pot. "Still full of meat, it was." They savored the ruse.

"How was your man to know that he carried a pot of gold!"

Lir gave precise instructions to Sreng. "Here is how you must divide the gold according to Cian's arrangement with mighty Taranis. Use these symbols on each plaque sent back with gold."

No Starwatcher in Eire would reveal the gold source nor its paths to the ships, and only Sreng knew it was bound for Cian.

To Streng's dismay, he had no news of Cliodhna to send with Lir.

Cian and the Basques used dugout log boats from locals to follow the river east, hiking when they encountered shallows. His companions enjoyed the trip and camping. They had Cian try eating frog legs seared with wild garlic, a dish he only tolerated. The tribes they encountered proved friendly and helpful, grateful to receive metal scraps and beads since his party carried no pots or stone axes for exchange.

Their expedition could have been deemed a failure in that Cian returned sooner than expected, suffering from an onslaught of allergies the farther they went inland. However, he brought back insights having immediate benefit to Taranis' trade. He had the pleasure of placing a dark lump of alluvial tin on Taranis' tabletop.

"Tin, to make bronze." Cian tried to sound offhand. The two stared at it.

Taranis lifted his eyes from the tin. "If there's more tin where you found that, your efforts have been a huge success. Rest now, have a sweat bath to clear that head. I'll send my own slave to give you a massage." The trader chief looked down his nose, resting his immaculate chin on soft fingertips, at the Starwatcher seated across from him. "One more thing. I have met with your man Lir, inspected his vessel and sent him off. Impressive mariner. Nothing escapes my notice in this port, you know."

Upset though he was to have missed briefing Lir, Cian thanked Taranis. He could only hope that Sreng received his message and had gone east to take gold. Also he had wanted to send seed grain with Lir's vessel that would have gone on to the Boyne to help feed his people. Now he must simply wait.

Cian's favor with Taranis annoyed the chief's sons. They plotted and came to the hall for a formal audience. Taranis kept them waiting in line with all the others wanting his ear, then his guard ushered them into his presence, seated at his long table. He displayed a gold nugget on its smooth expanse, along with quartz crystals, blue-green copper ore, and the newly found tin; all from Cian.

"We hear of troubles at the Morbihan. Traders attempt to set up camps there to send their goods inland and bypass our harbor here. What are you going to do about this?"

Taranis snorted. "What is it that you are going to do about this, my sons?"

They regarded each other furtively. "Why not send the Starwatcher and his *Euskaldunak* men there?"

Taranis nodded. "Very well. When all of you return to me from the Morbihan, I want a full report. Does this pose any problem for you?"

They left him quickly.

One of the brothers informed the Starwatcher that he must leave on sea travel.

Slaves loaded much equipment and brimming food baskets onto boats, and Taranis' sons embarked with their armed guards, and Cian with his Basques, for the brief voyage west to the Morbihan. Their boats turned in at the curved bay where a jagged arm of land stretched out like a crab's pincer into the water from a marshy area backed by low rolling hills. Though the sun stood high, the entire bay was eerily still. A haze made sky and water a matching pale blue. They saw no sign of Invaders or trading vessels. They decided to pull in and go onto shore. Leather soles crunched on the wet shingles, the sound muffled in the heavy air.

As the group made their way inland, the scene unfolded. The haze thickened into dirty smoke. Fires flickered in the wind on the tops of sacred mounds, their entrances smashed and blocked. Giant menhirs lay crashed on the ground, columns of granite that had stood tall as two oaks. The tallest column lay in four pieces, another in three pieces. All around the fallen menhirs lay bodies, the coastal inhabitants, the males slain as they protected their mounds and their homes. Seafarer women and children, killed at dwellings that had been put to the torch.

As the men surveyed around the bay Cian found the area thick with stone monuments and alignments. The Morbihan venerated the sky for centuries. Now the land reeked of destruction and death. The wide scene could not have been ghastlier. Why Invaders or anyone would kill these Seafarers and destroy this place, he did not apprehend.

Their expedition turned into a burial detail. They all worked over several sunrises. A few survivors appeared from the woods and helped to cremate and bury their dead. There was no glory to be had and the sons of Taranis had little to report to him in his great hall, except that all of their men and Cian with his Basques had indeed returned.

Cian looked as if he had visited the spirit world. The slaughter at the Morbihan reminded him of the cave far away to the south filled with murdered young people. The senseless murder of Sheela at the Boyne. Worst of all, one of the dead children at the Morbihan had been the tender age of Aengus, and his image of that slain infant stayed with Cian. So close he was to snatching the gold safely away from Elcmar, but all that he held dear for himself he had left vulnerable at the Boyne. He fasted, and mourned the dead, and he spent many chill nights watching the stars of his ancestors and following the white river in the sky.

The Basques fretted and brought him special foods, dishes they concocted with their own hands, to have him eating again. Slowly Cian returned to his surroundings at the Loire and to his senses. But he could not stop his inner reality from revisiting the slaughter at the Morbihan. A large carved axe that menaced him overhead in a stone passage near to the wrecked menhirs, recurred in his fitful dreams. He woke shaking and sweating.

He recalled the long alignments, hundreds of standing stones over large areas. The Morbihan's profuse, swirling carvings inside passage mounds; he knew that style, like carvings at the Boyne and Fourknocks. A sillstone inside a passage almost tripped him, and his touch found that it was carved like sillstones in mounds on Eire. He recognized a tradition as rich as the Starwatchers' and deeply connected with theirs. Did those Morbihan astronomers know of the Northshift, he wondered. Did those bayside dwellers honor the eight year cycle of the sunset star, and the moon's long cycle? Why topple their menhirs and desecrate their mounds and standing stones? Why would anyone kill those people?

He tried to make sense of what he had seen, desolate for Boann and Aengus and his Starwatchers. He considered leaving the Loire forever and returning to the Boyne. There he could share the Starwatchers' fate, die among his own people. Traders and trading were a curse, a plague; Cian wanted no part of this life. His quest for the gold trade seemed pointless.

Cian sought Taranis and found him tallying goods in his inner storeroom: ingots, piles of fabrics, rare pots, stacks of scented wood, bright feathers, animal hides, stone beads and pierced seashells, oils, dyes, and exotic herbs. Metals, every known metal; except the gold was kept elsewhere, hidden. The glut of goods repulsed Cian but he needed an answer, now, or he would leave immediately for Eire.

Taranis dropped another pebble into a clay jar then looked up from counting. "Yes?"

"Those people were killed for their beliefs," he confronted Taranis.

The great trader did not inquire which people he meant. Taranis pouted his lower lip, threw up his hands, and shrugged.

That was not the answer he expected. Whether Taranis had himself ordered or permitted the slaughter, Cian never wanted to know. He did not ask.

He returned to the shoreline, to the sun and stars and incoming ships, and he waited. The reaping time, and he could only hope this harvest replenished Eire's supplies. He could not yet return to Boann and little Aengus. He understood now: no one could be safe. Invader violence infected every coast he had seen. The truce at the Boyne would not hold, the Starwatchers could have no peace.

He felt sullied. He stacked flat stones to form a small arched cell and installed himself in it alone at the coast, and he waited.

Before winter seas set in, he saw the first gold shipment from Sreng arrive at the port of Taranis. Cian's gold trade had begun. He greeted it with mixed emotions: what good would come of this and for whom?

Taranis had to see all the gold before it went into storage—but this time I'll not have it banged on my rare tabletop, he cried—and revelled in the sight. With Taranis' consent, Cian rewarded Lir handsomely. They feasted with Lir and his crew on a venison stew redolent of roots, herbs, and juniper berries cooked by the Basques, and they heard the tale of Lir's stormy autumn passage.

At sunrise, Lir departed to winter among his own Seafarers, but first he took Cian aside.

"Elcmar has sent an agent looking for you along these coasts."

Cian put his guardian, the port official, on watch to warn him of any stranger seeking the Starwatcher named Cian. If Taranis heard any of it, the great trader said nothing about it. Taranis had already given Cian a new name and that name was how he was known to all at the Loire.

While he had Taranis' attention over that first winter, Cian consulted his mentor on whether to hire boats rather than build his own. "When a vessel lies idle in harbor, or if it sinks, either would be a senseless loss. Let others own the boats. Even a small amount of gold will yield enormous trades for us on the Continent."

The wise trader endorsed this, saying that Cian would avoid the mistake of those who converted all their surplus into an expensive ship then swiftly lost it to the deep ocean. He encouraged Cian to ship their gold on different types of vessels. "Lir uses the naomhog, but let me show you a promising style, the plank boat coming into use to cross the great channel. My men are improving on this new design."

Taranis took him to a harbor area where three carpenters finished building one of the new plank boats inside a wattle shelter. One of the men eyed Cian with suspicion while refilling the braziers warming their workspace, but that worker relaxed when Taranis introduced him.

The woodworkers described the process: they sectioned an immense oak log into planks, two wide planks for the bottom and two for each side, those he saw already in place. They fashioned additional, topmost side planks which curved slightly. The bottom formed a Y fitted with an upcurving endpiece that would cut through waves. The flatbottomed craft, the length of a mature tree, looked to be slightly longer than Lir's vessel. The oak planks forming its sides were lashed together with strong cord made of twisted yew branches. Nine thwarts crossed the upper width of the boat, wide enough for rowers to sit upon.

He caught the distinctive smell of honey and looked for its source. One fellow was mashing beeswax with cattle fat to caulk holes around the yew withies and into seams between planks, followed by another man packing in moss held down by oak laths. The smell of freshly worked wood reminded Cian of Tadhg and his skilled hands. These men showed great skill also as they fashioned and hewed, practiced at building boats. The bottom width had integral chiseled cleats joined in mortised holes that required great precision to make. The head carpenter showed him how these cleated sections across the bottom planks held down rods passing through the cleats along the length of the planks, reinforcing the boat.

Taranis told him, "My men made it stronger, added more cleats and heavier rods, against our heavy north seas. It takes my three experienced boatbuilders around one moon to complete a plank boat from start to finish."

Cian listened but he remembered well his own ordeals on the ocean. The plank construction bothered him. He could only compare it with the *naomhog*, that flexed and allowed the ocean's awesome strength to surge through it. After they left the boatmen's work hut he suggested to Taranis, "The moss and wax used to caulk between the planks will surely give way and that vessel will take on water. And how will this long narrow boat survive the huge troughs that the *naomhog* rides into and out of like a floating leaf?"

Taranis dismissed his concerns with a wave. "This boat can carry more goods than your average *naomhog*."

So that was it: more goods for trading, always more. Cian said he appreciated seeing the new boat, and agreed to use a plank vessel whenever available. Taranis meant to produce the new type of boat and he would defer to him in this matter, he would be flexible like the currach. If not, Taranis could well bypass him once they established the gold's production from Eire. The last thing he wanted would be that Taranis assert control over the Starwatchers' sun metal. Surely Lir would not object; he could talk Lir into trying a voyage using one of the new plank ships. A man could drown using one boat just as well as another, as Lir himself might say.

Spring came and he honored that equinox, then the solstice. Through the bright summer to autumn more shipments of gold arrived, raw nuggets and worked gold, on ships coming to Cian. Sreng measured and sent an amount of precious metal, recorded on stone plaques. He never sent too much gold with any boat. One of the new plank vessels sank in the waves, but not Lir's *naomhog*; more arrived safely and before autumn equinox.

He sat down with Taranis at the anniversary of their bargain to tally up and divide the weighty stored gold. The venerable chief announced how very pleased he was at the deal they struck.

"And I so admire these neckpieces." Taranis touched the etched gold crescent at his neck, one of the better examples. "Well done, you must have stolen a smith from Creidhne. We'll order more of these." He laughed, and sipped from a polished burlwood cup. Then he leaned forward and prevailed upon Cian to make a terrible bargain.

"My own sons could not have done better for me in obtaining the gold from the island of the setting sun. But in order to continue our arrangement, you must agree to marry my daughter Enya. In doing so, you become like a son and in time I hope to see you become the next chief, the ruler at the Loire." Taranis must have seen the doom flooding Cian. He gestured, expansive. "Now hear me out. As you say, you cannot return to Eire. Why not be living well where you are; it's the best revenge, no? It's important to be earnest, but a man must have some pleasure in life, eh? All this, all that you see, shall be yours."

Taranis commanded Enya to appear and make herself agreeable.

Cian masked his shock. He lived without a woman, resigned to it just as he endured cold darkness to sight on constellations. His memory of Boann he carried like a treasured object which he infrequently allowed himself to examine, then placed back into safekeeping. He could not return to Boann, not just yet; but unless he humored Taranis he might have no gold trade and no haven at the Loire. He had climbed the highest mountains and run through fields, he had scaled Taranis' walls, in order to reunite with Boann. Aengus. His own people. He fought a black tide of despair.

When Enya appeared, Cian beheld a lovely face and form though before that he scarcely noticed her among Taranis' sons and the multitude of slaves, visitors, guards, consorts, traders, smiths, and warriors orbiting mighty Taranis.

Torn between homesick or homeless, adrift once more, he agonized under the stars. He did not wish to offend Taranis and lose his privileges at this port. Nor did he wish to have this unwelcome complication. The skies did not provide him with an answer.

Over the next half moon, Enya paid him minimal but courteous attention. In their small talk during strained meetings, he detected in her a kindred spirit.

They strolled out in the gardens behind the great hall and Taranis made sure that no sentries followed. There Cian explained himself to Enya as they walked on flagstones set among fragrant herbs. His asceticism came from a different kind of love, from reverence for women and not from scorn for women, he assured her. She listened. It turned out that Enya did not oppose what he suggested on their walk.

She told him with good humor, "What you offer me is less objectionable than marriage with any of the others whom my father has eyed for me. I perceive that you love someone else—as I do. But I find you very interesting. This undertaking for your island, your gaining control over the gold under Elcmar's nose, amuses me! I think it amuses Taranis." Enya held a late flower to her lips, covering a smile. "It would be dangerous to cross my father. For either of us, don't you think?"

He saw the deep pink petals against her luminous skin; temptation raked his body.

His gratitude overcame his doubts. "You have little fear, and show me that you are indeed wise. You give me great honor in agreeing to this marriage, Enya. I shall try to give you the same, always."

The couple talked of the coming seasons, of how to secure the gold trade so that retribution from Elcmar would be pointless. He found her so sensible and intelligent that he almost overlooked her beauty. Perhaps in time they would share common goals. Cian returned the lissome daughter of Taranis to the timbered hall with relief and a sincere kiss on her forehead.

Taranis clapped his manicured hands in delight to see his success as their matchmaker.

He ordered their wedding ceremony held within the lunate and during full moon, at an old passage mound on an islet close to the Loire. There they encamped with guests in pavilions of polished poles hung with drapery and evergreen boughs and golden sheaves. Warming bonfires and torches blazed nonstop. Cian flinched at the lavish display on their behalf.

With the deep blue ocean rolling behind them, the couple spoke brief vows that combined Loire beliefs and Starwatcher practices. Enya's brothers scowled throughout the recital of the marriage contract and stood apart during the feast, glowering and counting the jars emptied of costly brews.

Taranis' latest consort, a fair-haired woman not much older than Enya, clung to his arm. Cian's eyes searched her face. Bolg's serving girl, and she laughed to see his surprise. Whatever had happened to Bolg, he guessed she did not care. So the talk must be true, he realized, Taranis trades in certain women along the coasts, like livestock. He would have no part of such dealings.

Taranis had given his Basque chef a weight of figs, novel fruit from extreme southern waters and worth their weight in gold, and he demanded a new treat to finish the wedding feast. His chef baked the figs in thick custard of milk and chestnut flour, glazed with honey and lavender. The exquisite dish brought tears to Taranis' eyes and loud acclaim from the guests. The great trader appeared wistful to see his only daughter marrying, but proud to show off his gold cape circling her shoulders, and his newest plank vessel.

Cian tried to keep his thoughts from wandering to the wedding he last witnessed at the Boyne, lest that memory poison this feast and this day. So fresh in his mind's eye, yet it was many voyages and two complete suns since Elcmar banished him. Aengus would be taking toddler's steps... Enya stepped forward, smiling. With Taranis and the guests watching and cheering, he brushed her full lips with his. She reciprocated, just the right amount, but when he felt her healing touch his resolve left him. Then she stepped back with a knowing look at him. All will be well, her look said. Even so, he flushed.

The couple sailed to and from the ceremony with Taranis and their guests in sturdy new plank ships. Taranis amazed his guests. These new vessels had a stepped mast and small square sail of smooth leather; an idea from far southern waters he told them, failing to credit the Basques for introducing him to the concept. He had the sails edged in sheet gold squares forming a border and the gold flashed in every direction. The Basques sprinkled the boat carrying bride and groom with sweet-smelling petals and herbs, and insisted on manning that ship themselves, with dire jokes to Cian about embarking on the deep waters of matrimony.

Enya at his side, Cian watched the white path trailing the oars and that above, the river of stars leading north. He would have plenty of time to appreciate Boann's sacrifice.

PART THREE

ETERNITY

Two thirds of the progeny, the wheat, and the milk of the people
of Ireland...
Wrath and sadness seized on the men of Ireland for the burden of the tax.
The Book of Leinster, 1150 AD

The Fosterage of Aengus

THREE CYCLES OF the sun passed. When he exchanged copper
tools and ingots for what his camp consumed from incoming
boats, the island that Elcmar claimed for himself, Eire, did not
produce enough to satisfy him. He searched for gold and searched
again, without success. When his agent did not return from the
Continent with Gebann or Cian, Elcmar sent his smith Creidhne
back to the Continent, to fetch Gebann or force the secret from him
of where gold lay on Eire.

Aengus was precocious, as bright as the sun. At age five, his wide
shoulders and strong legs gave every promise of coming mass. His
face and firm jawline bore the stamp of Boann as did his thick mane
of auburn hair. The name Aengus Og stuck on that shining child.
Aengus the young, but Elcmar ignored the gossip. It pleased him just
to look upon little Aengus, well fed and safe; not at all like his own
childhood. Elcmar brought the child to visit daily with the horses.

They kept their stubborn little horses inside an oval enclosure
made of rough wooden planks set into a rubble stone ditch, just

inside the larger camp embankment. These horses had smooth-haired, light-colored coats. Elcmar stood admiring their profile, bulging cheeks set above a thick neck. The horses' shoulder level came below his own by two handspans or so, but their backs were strong enough to carry a warrior.

He felt a bond with horses that he did not feel for any man or woman. He had not had a horse or any pet as a destitute wandering child, and it was only in his late adolescence working his way along the coastlines that Elcmar learned anything about horses. When he eventually had the means to care for and ride a horse, he took great pleasure in it. Horses, especially the white horse, remained a symbol to him of power, internalized while he learned the ways of the world. One of the reasons he had fallen in with this particular group of Invaders was their love of horses, especially the *macc*, the horse tame enough for riding.

On this morning it gratified Elcmar to see that due to his efforts, Aengus did not fear the horses, their noises and smells, unlike his mother Boann and many of the Quiet Ones. The animals bared their big teeth for the soft apples offered by little Aengus, who laughed.

"Soon I'll have you leading a young horse on a hemp bridle, then try your hand at milking a mare. In time you'll be getting onto the back of a pony!" Elcmar watched to be sure the horse didn't nip Aengus. These horses could be good-natured if handled properly while young. Invaders bred them selectively to improve their short stature and shorter temper.

The colts used to start this herd had been difficult enough to transport from the Continent to Eire, the fragile legs lashed together and their eyes showing white for much of the voyage. The horses' limited numbers at the Boyne resulted in problems. The stallion foals should be kept with the mother for at least one year; otherwise that stallion might never behave well enough to breed or be much good for riding or even transport. Trainers separated the yearling males from the herd, and kept them in bachelor groups until they matured to four or five suns in age, and only then were they allowed access to females. For Elcmar, the Invaders learned only too slowly from the horses how to successfully breed and train them in captivity.

I want, I need, more horses for breeding stock. Elcmar poked at a clump of nettles with his well-shod foot. *On the Continent we'd raid horses from tribes who keep them, or catch wild foals to enrich our stock. Horses, another resource not to be found on this island, and too valuable to risk towing many on rafts behind boats... How to pay for it all?*

Connor and his party remained in the north in a futile search for gold and tin. *Your man used his severed red hand in some trick to claim land there.* Elcmar shook his head, wondering if Connor blended in with the natives. That took time, especially if the gruff Connor were no more skillful at diplomacy than he had been here at the Boyne. So far Connor had not sent any trade goods to Elcmar, setting them all back further in the exchange with the Continent. Between the new settlement in the north and that to the west where Ith sent Muirgen with her husband, and mortalities on lost ships, Elcmar saw the Invaders spread out ever more thin and shorthanded on this island. The slaves had to be worked harder to keep this camp operating and fed. The erratic climate mocked his efforts.

As he mused, he noticed Aengus playing with the apples in the morning light. Aengus rotated one apple slowly around another, casting shadows. The child was totally absorbed, ignoring the horses. Elcmar recognized something in Aengus' play with the apples and his gut twinged. Or was that the old injury to his rib?

She's been at it, so. Teaching him Starwatcher ways. He picked up the child so as not to attract attention but the child wriggled and complained in his too-tight clasp.

"We'll be going now, Aengus." Elcmar held the boy up over the planks' top and ordered him to quickly feed all the apples to the horses, then took the bewildered child, tears in his eyes, to a slave woman to watch him rather than Boann. Elcmar stormed off to consult with Ith.

He found Ith trying to explain a principle of trading to Bresal, who occupied himself eating a hunk of roast pig. These were not the same as the pigs at the Lake mines; here they were fed whatever was at hand and their meat tasted bland.

"Work away there, Bresal," he barked at the pudgy shaman, whose greasy chin glistened.

Ith raised his eyebrows. Elcmar drew Ith aside and told him, "That one is beef to the heels. Your man Bresal needs to train with the warriors and get himself fit. All the men in this camp must keep fit. That is our warriors' rule and it is my rule. But I cannot order a shaman to do that."

Ith replied, "It's no problem a'tall. I shall speak to Bresal; some physical training will do him good. How else can I help you this morning?" He exposed pointy teeth in a smile.

"I am just after coming from the horses with little Aengus." Elcmar described what he had seen Aengus doing with apples. Then he described to Ith what he recalled of Boann showing him, her using apples for the movements of sun and moon, that day they had words and he decided to ban the mound ceremonies. He spoke warily. "Do you understand what is the problem here, or are you thinking that I am away with the fairies?

"Little Aengus has spent enough time with the brood mare, I think. I won't have him growing up as an ignorant savage. Who can raise Aengus properly as a warrior?" He crossed his arms over his chest.

Ith made a rasping chuckle. "I wish you'd told me about her apples and shadows. I've said it before, we keep our eyes on the ground here when we could be studying the heavens.

"About the child, it's you who needed to arrive at this conclusion rather than me. I do have in mind the house of Midhir and his wife Fuamnach for the fosterage of Aengus."

"Fuamnach! Is she not Bresal's foster daughter, the woman who quit our camp for this Midhir?" thundered Elcmar.

Ith answered, "One and the same, but Fuamnach was not raised by Bresal and she shows some sense. As does Midhir, a quiet one to be sure, but he allows Connor's men safe passage through his territory. Together they will provide a stabilizing influence. Having Aengus there may promote an alliance with Midhir. Do you think Boann will object to Aengus' fosterage?"

"No. Boann won't be objecting. I won't tell her of it, so. Neither will you."

In a few lunates, Elcmar rode off to Midhir, where he placed little Aengus at the training camp on the plain. After his tears at separating from his mother, for which the kindly Midhir comforted him, Aengus grew delighted with this new arrangement. Here he was free to wander, ride horses, run footraces, and practice wrestling and sports with the other boys. Slaves served his food to him at a table, and as the alleged son of the champion Elcmar, the slaves catered to the child's every whim.

Boann was incredulous that Elcmar had taken little Aengus from her care. Barely weaned, to be sent off to foster parents. She thought of throwing Elcmar's belongings onto the smelly forecourt outside the great hall, then she thought better of it. She hastened from the camp to see Airmid, who knew Midhir and his people.

When Boann arrived at Airmid's dwelling, she saw Ardal and Tadhg outside it preparing a number of young game birds for a meal, their flint knives methodically revealing the tender flesh. She set her basket of herbs and berries before Airmid, then told them all what had happened.

Boann took a limp pink bird into her hands. "Is this what will happen to our Aengus?"

Tadhg put his hands over hers briefly, and took back the bird. "There's little we can do about it. And it's your Cian who encouraged us to train boys as warriors." His tone chided her.

Boann flushed and took a step back. "Cian has good reason, I'm sure of that. But this was Elcmar's doing."

Airmid's pleasant voice came from the doorway where she stood spinning thread. "She's saying that Aengus is too young for the warrior training, Tadhg. Let me go have a word with Midhir. Oghma can journey there with me; Midhir wouldn't deny his grandfather looking in on Aengus." Her movements stayed smooth with whorl and spindle, one hand stretching the bast thread as it formed.

Ardal glanced up. "If things were different, it's our child who would wear Airmid's fine cloth." He clapped an arm around Tadhg, still a bachelor since Sheela's murder. "But all in good time. Right?"

They all seemed put out with her and Boann wanted to leave. But Ardal picked up his pipe and began to play, and instead she joined them for a dance. Ardal's high spirits cheered them on the summer evening, the slanting sunlight thick as honey around them.

Airmid did intercede with Midhir. Soon enough, visits with Aengus had been arranged and certain details of his daily life stipulated to Boann's satisfaction. Midhir agreed with her: over time, Aengus would receive instruction in the finer arts and skills than just warrior training and horses. Midhir avoided consulting his temperamental wife Fuamnach, though she did not speak to Bresal or the Invaders and cared little about the arrangements for young Aengus.

The season of long sunlight passed quickly. The island faced another precarious harvest. Still Elcmar helped himself to more horses and finery brought on the rare boats from far shores. He waited with little patience for Creidhne's return.

A messenger arrived, breathless, from the coast. He fell to his knees before Elcmar and told him the news: Creidhne set out to return over the waters, bringing gold and secrets to Elcmar from the Seafarer peninsula, but that famed artificer met his end on the sinister pool. The ship, its crew, the gold, and Creidhne had all disappeared, a staggering setback for Elcmar's fortunes.

Boann turned to Elcmar. "So the ocean has claimed your smith— fair play, for the drowning of Cliodhna."

He showed no concern for either death. He stalked away from Boann and did not speak to her for a full lunate, then another, and autumn turned into cold winter.

With spring, Elcmar demanded more copper. At the Lake mine to the southwest, Lein complied. Clearing of the forest accelerated and the miners hauled wood from ever increasing distances to the acrid smelting. The copper production increased, but then decreased since it took many more men just to haul the wood used at the pits. The mine workers refused to torch the forests to make charcoal, Lein told him during Elcmar's visit at the Lake Of Many Hammers. The miners pointed out that poor growing seasons had stunted the trees' growth, as it was.

"Save the trees then. It's time for everyone on this island to pay up," Elcmar announced. He would levy a share from Starwatchers' crops and livestock. In practice, this levy proved difficult to enforce and his men could not seem to collect his share.

Worse, Elcmar sought to cull the island's finest young males to engage in warrior training or serve on Invader boats. Boann feared for Aengus, and anxiously kept messages going between *Bru na Boinne* to his foster father, Midhir, to ensure Aengus' safety there.

The sun passed through the cycle of seasons. Boann brought the Dagda herbs for tea and as they shared it he told her news: the Invaders' reach extended now to another settlement, the place called Lough Gur far to the southwest of the Boyne. The people there lived at the margin, removed from other Starwatcher communities. Their ways were not as advanced, still hunting and gathering; suddenly the group at Lough Gur began making the Invader style of straight-sided pots, and more surprising, began pouring metal axes from ingots acquired from the Lake mine. Scouts reported that the Lough Gur community had built a large open stone circle, not an enclosed starwatching mound.

"Those at Lough Gur could make war on us as easily as the Invaders. They could act against us to side with Elcmar and

Connor." The elders at the Boyne kept an eye on Lough Gur to see where its loyalties would lie. Boann relayed any information that could be of use though on occasion it meant conversing with Ith to see what he might disclose.

The Invader levy on crops and animals resulted in more clearing of land, the cutting and burning of stumps to make new fields. The weather continued its shift, cooler than in previous cycles of the sun, and areas of bog increased. The bog's encroachment made land unsuitable for growing and grazing, and the bog crept onto sites where surface flint had been easily available to Starwatchers.

Slainge told the Dagda, "We have to look for more supplies of flint, maybe dig for it. Just as we feared, our young Starwatchers want to trade with Invaders for metal tools." A flint tool had fine sharp edges when newly made, but it dulled quickly or worse, it broke. The best stone axe could shatter without warning. "The young covet the new copper tools."

The Dagda cracked open hazelnuts and chewed the rich meats thoughtfully. "We must avoid being drawn into trading and reliance on the Invader goods, against which Cian cautioned us. Cian spoke of other metals and other traders. We must wait for alternatives, for traders sent by him or Cian himself to return. For now, we can work under and around this taxing scheme."

The Boyne elders traded cautiously for a few copper axes from the Starwatchers at Lough Gur. These they buried, for when weapons might be needed against Invaders—or the tribe at Lough Gur.

Subtle changes in attitudes and values pained the Starwatcher elders. No formal council had ever been held with the intruders and reluctantly, they discarded that idea. Across the island, their astronomers met in such groups as and when they could travel and still evade the Invader sentries at the mounds.

In truth, it was not always possible to ignore either the sentries or the nighttime curfew. The elders had a limited supply of the yellow safe-passage stones and inevitably stones went missing. The notion that Elcmar could detain any Starwatcher who didn't carry the stone pass did not sit well with them. In reprisal, Ardal, Tadhg, and the Boyne scouts engaged in skirmishes with Invaders, those who ventured out after dark. These encounters usually resulted in a rout of the intruders by the quiet ones, who escaped swiftly into dark mists and forests and bogs.

Elcmar's warriors claimed that the natives disappeared before their eyes.

Then Airmid was intercepted after dark, by Invader sentries freshly bruised from doing battle with Starwatcher scouts. Mindful of repercussion from harming her, the warriors brought Airmid straightaway into their camp. Elcmar did not wait for Ith's arrival before he began to interrogate her in the great hall.

Airmid remained calm before Elcmar. "I know nothing of this. You say the Starwatchers attack the Invaders at night. But I have been collecting herbs, as you can see." She held out fresh shoots to show him.

Elcmar called Boann from the sleeping chamber.

She rushed to Airmid's side. "Elcmar! For Airmid to be out gathering medicines at night is routine for our herbalists. You well know this."

At the public rebuke from Boann, his jaw tightened. "Pull off this woman's cloak!"

The warriors smiled to do as he said, and stripped off Airmid's cloak so that it flew to her feet. All the herbs inside her cloak fell out in confusion: dandelion, meadowsweet, yarrow, water mint, plantain, wort, and chamomile. Shocked, she did not stoop to pick up the scattered herbs, nor did anyone present.

Elcmar sheltered Airmid briefly in the slaves' quarters. Ith made sure that her fate was similar to that of Muirgen; he quickly married her to an Invader warrior. They changed her name to Brighid, and compelled her to live within the camp walls with her new husband.

Boann and Airmid, now called Brighid, from that night ceased supplying medicines to the Invaders. Of this misfortune the intruders said, Brighid's cloak scattered the island's herbs so completely that since then no one knew their healing properties.

Great was the distress of Boann at her friend's plight, but greater still would be Ardal's sorrow.

Outside the camp boundaries, he patrolled the forest and waited for her. Of necessity, Ardal's duties as a scout kept him away from their village and from Airmid more often than not. I cannot rest easy on another man's wound, he told her. The lovers waited to marry with formalities until the time their island would know peace.

On that bitter night, he traveled through low marshy areas on a hidden trackway. He and the other scouts had built this trackway, extending older tracks since soon after Sheela's murder, when the elders instructed their scouts, "More trees shall be coppiced. Allow these rods to grow tall, half again as tall as a man, and thick as a strong thumb. We need thousands of straight hazel rods."

To coppice a tree, they manipulated its growth by cutting it down to a stump. The stump yielded young shoots springing up around it that were not allowed to branch, so that these shoots became long straight rods of ash or hazel. To grow and harvest the rods for making hurdles required four to six full cycles of the sun.

During the long sunlight of summers, scouts cut down the mature rods and lashed them together into hurdle panels to support and underlay tracks through the worst boggy areas. Over the hurdles they laid a top layer of hardwood planks, usually oak, cut from thick trees growing for generations and selected carefully through the forest. Workers felled the giants with their polished stone axes and split each tree into planks using a stone wedge. They laid the stout planks over the hurdles. It was hard, sweaty work done in stealth while battling swarms of midges. Occasionally the workers silenced their axes while intruders passed by, unaware of them working in the forests. The Starwatchers made a solid track at hidden places through what had been marshy bog.

With dawn, Tadhg found Ardal at work in a coppice and told him what had happened to Airmid. Three scouts had to restrain Ardal else he would have tried to demolish the Invader walls with his bare hands.

It was Boann who assembled the Starwatcher women and brought them before the elders' council. Their women protested Airmid's kidnapping and forced marriage; this was yet another outrage. They had lost another woman of childbearing age to the Invaders, and Airmid was their best teacher of herbs and medicines, their most adept healer.

"What do you intend to do?" they demanded of the elders.

Oghma mumbled into Daire's ear, who sat next to him. Since his stroke, the young man helped him dress and eat, walk through the village and visit the mounds, and meet with the elders. Daire steadfastly nursed Oghma, while studying the stars. Oghma grew more weak with each season of the sun, still he hung onto life for his people. He had yet to complete the mounds' kerbstones.

Daire announced what Oghma said. "We shall put out the intruders' eyes."

Ardal and Tadhg led many stinging attacks on Invader warriors who were feckless enough to be caught outside their walled camp in the dark, spying.

The intruders' fear of the Starwatchers came to the fore. Their assailants seemingly disappeared into the night. The Invaders deemed it magic. They gave up trying to track the Starwatchers and remained inside their high walls at night. They feasted and told stories of the big fellow who eluded them by changing his shape, and the little people who danced under the moon.

The sun sped through its seasons, solstice to solstice. Their Boyne camp, the intruders called *"Bru na Elcmar."* Boann continued to live within the camp with Elcmar. To her surprise, Elcmar did not take other wives, and he remained coldly courteous to her. She circumvented him to visit the Starwatchers and young Aengus. She continued to serve as an emissary from her people and interceded whenever possible, often without his realizing it.

Boann waged her ongoing struggle with Elcmar and Ith. Their ban on the mounds did not prohibit Starwatchers from watching the skies. The mounds showed neglect, sadly, but the astronomers kept to their practices and taught their children. She worked with the Dagda to save her people from cultural annihilation. Their delicate equinox observations carried on in secrecy to pinpoint the Northshift. None of the Invaders, who would be hard-pressed just to locate north in light or darkness, had any idea that the great mounds had been laid out across the landscape from shore to shore according to a plan with the skies. Any notion she might have of sharing information that Ith wanted so badly had been overcome by his ongoing disrespect of her people.

Constant pressures distracted Elcmar; his levy on Eire's wheat, milk, and cattle had not met his needs. His men had not located the mountain stream of gold nuggets but the Starwatchers there always found his warriors. After the loss of Creidhne, Lein grew powerful in his role as master smith in the southwest. Elcmar allowed it, giving him free rein at the Lake mine so that Lein would stay on Eire. He tempted Lein, sending him to scour the mountains where Elcmar picked up gold in the stream long ago. Taranis now firmly controlled that area, so Lein's messenger told him. That ended that. Lein returned to the southwest to concentrate on keeping the copper mines operating, and seek gold there, while Elcmar fortified his base at the Boyne.

Opportunities vanished before he had seen them. Strange it is, Elcmar thought, your man Taranis no longer pursues me for payment. Unchecked by anyone, Elcmar freely ordered goods and livestock sent to him from the Continent. He owed for lost cargoes in addition to goods that made it safely to Eire, but he didn't add up the total.The suns seemed to pass ever faster.

Ith pursued arcane studies of the carved rocks at the mounds. He traveled to Fourknocks, a surprising discovery with rich carvings resembling carved stones on the Continent, at a bay not far from Taranis' port. Ith perceived similarities at Loughcrew with the three Boyne mounds. He knew by this time that rituals happened at each mound at different seasons. With no extra men to go with him chasing after stone carvings rather than gold, his studies slowed. The symbols' meanings eluded him like slippery, darting fish.

A full eclipse of the sun, predicted correctly by the Starwatchers, got Ith agitated. There had to be a connection between the sun and sun metal, he told Elcmar. With Bresal, he tried to produce gold by heating smelly concoctions of minerals and blood and bones with quartz pilfered from the central mound, and with stones that resembled sun metal; but without success.

At seeing their initial failures to make gold, Elcmar let his two advisors experiment without him, suspecting that shamans' usefulness lay in helping control the rowdy warriors but not in making metals. Elcmar and Ith ceased poking into and dismantling the mounds. The Invaders found no gold inside any of the Boyne chambers. For spite, Ith had structures built close to the mounds, flimsy wood and wicker huts at the west mound and the central mound and a circle of wood posts at the west mound. He tried to entice the Starwatchers out in the open for their sun worship. But even Ith avoided Dowth, the eastern mound damaged by warriors with Bresal.

In those years, Elcmar's luck as a warrior continued in that none of his wounds from various skirmishes disfigured him and he held onto his position as *ard ri*. Connor visited the Boyne occasionally. He had used his severed hand in trickery to claim an area in the north, where he sought gold. His old grudge developed into a wary respect for Elcmar; the *ard ri* had learned to lead the warriors and had fashioned a working settlement on his own terms. Maedb refused to live in the north and Connor left her living at the river Boyne, since for him that made far less trouble.

Food and supplies moved through the bogs with Starwatchers.

Where fair Aengus grew and trained, many Starwatcher youths joined the warrior training. When Elcmar brought his warriors there, the competition took an edge and held danger: the older boys faced off with hardened men using real weapons.

Midhir took good care of Aengus and ensured that the boy incurred no disease. He made Aengus train the hardest so that no wound destroyed his chance to one day become the champion. Fuamnach, wife of Midhir, stood back from the boy. She allowed Midhir to make all decisions regarding Aengus, for fear of Elcmar. The boy's education consisted of more than the Invaders' footraces and wrestling and sparring there at Bri Leith.

His mother's visits occurred while Elcmar traveled elsewhere on the island. Midhir released Aengus for long walks with Boann without the hindrance of an escort, and mother and son talked freely of many things. Boann returned from her walks with Aengus with a lighter step and a trug of medicines gathered for Midhir's people.

Thus it was no surprise to silver-haired Midhir when Boann arrived bringing with her the Dagda. Midhir chose not to attend them, although invited, as the Dagda indicated that they planned to walk to the hills some distance away. Midhir made sure they had a safe-passage stone and bade them safe journey. Their trip would keep young Aengus away over several sunrises but Midhir did not inquire further.

Boann held Aengus' hand in hers as they set out. "Our journey with the Dagda takes us to the west." He grinned in excitement. She went on, smiling back at him, "We'll be staying on the ancient high place known as The Storied Hills. The mounds built there are much older than our Boyne mounds."

As Aengus skipped along, he said he hoped that he would find star symbols that no one else understood any longer, or a tool from the ancients that he could keep as a reminder of this trip. "You let me pick up old stone balls around the mounds at Fourknocks, and perhaps I'll find more of those."

"Our journey to The Storied Hills is a long walk for a boy of nine suns," Boann said.

He touched her cloak. "You travel some distance from the Boyne to see me at Bri Leith." Throughout their long walk, Aengus did not complain.

They climbed to the highest point in the grouping of three summits. From there Aengus could see all the way to the mountains in the southeast, and to distant blue slopes to the north. Rivers and streams shimmered below them through lush valleys, for great rivers flowed from this place including the Boyne. The three settled onto fur mats on a warm granite platform overlooking the valley and *Bru na Boinne*. They could even see Teamair beyond in the south.

The Dagda spoke clearly for an old man. "This is your first lesson with me in our knowledge from the skies. The dome above us contains many mysteries. Our people have unraveled some of these mysteries by being patient and watching the skies for generations beyond memory. If you listen well, Aengus, then we shall have another lesson. In time you may follow Starwatcher ways."

Aengus nodded, spellbound at the Dagda's deep voice.

The Dagda began. "The ancients learned when to plant and when to harvest, from watching the skies. You know that there are many upright stones at high places in the lands around Midh."

Aengus nodded again with a serious countenance. The Dagda was older than any person he had seen, and said to know the sky like the back of his hand. A thrill closed his throat to have this special time with the Dagda and his mother.

"Griane set the first marker stone. Over generations, the tall stone showed our people that there were four equal seasons in the sun's journey along the horizon, from north to south and then back to the north. When I say equal, I mean that within each season the sun rises the same number of times. But you know yourself, Aengus, that during the winter lunates the sun travels very slowly along the horizon. Our people saw that the sun pauses during the winter season, it almost stops in its movement along the horizon for around ten risings of the sun. This standstill marks the longest darkness between winter sunrises. That is when you were given to us, Aengus! Then the sun accelerates day by day along the horizon as it travels toward the spring. From sunrise to sunrise, the light becomes longer and longer until daylight is equal to darkness. We celebrate this time at our spring equinox ceremony. This is the time to plant the fields. Your mother will show you what to look for in the night sky to verify the planting time.

"Are you with me so far? The sun continues rising toward the north and graciously gives us more light from sunrise to sunrise, until the sunrise on the longest light of the year. We call those days, Bright Sun. Again the sun has slowed and reached its most northern point on the horizon, at summer solstice. The sun picks up speed again after this summer solstice, the time of longest light from sunrise to sunrise. Soon it races toward the south in its risings and settings along the horizon. The light is leaving with the sun to the south. Soon the sun's light is equal again with the dark. This shows the time for harvest. Your mother will show you what to look for in the night sky at this harvest equinox as well.

"Then as the sun moves even farther south, the longer darkness begins. When it stops at its most southern point of sunrise and sunset, we are back to when you were born. That is when the light slowly returns. This journey of the sun along the horizon from south to north and back completes what we call a solar cycle, with two solstices and two equinoxes. Each solar cycle has a set number of days, and each of its four seasons." The Dagda stood, leaning on Boann's arm, and invited Aengus to stand up also. They all walked to wooden pegs that she had set into the ground: a tall peg at the center with four shorter pegs set to the west of it.

"Aengus, this is one of the mysteries. It is the mystery of the seasons shown clearly to us in the sky. We have learned to mark all four seasons of the light. At sunrise, that tall marker casts its shadow to the west. Those four smaller markers each represent one of the seasons. Remember that each season has the same number of sunrises. To capture the shadow from the tall marker stone, the four season markers stand at unequal distances from each other. This is so even though there are an equal number of sunrises in each season. This understanding is a gift to us. It is our calendar from the sky. But we had to learn to be patient and truly see before we understood the gift. From what you hear today, you can construct this calendar of light anywhere. The sun will tell you what is the season."

Aengus felt the earth beneath his bones and the movements in the skies above and his bond with both earth and sky, a sense of complete belonging. He wanted more moments like this.

The Dagda paused. "We do not fully understand why this is so. It is our astronomers' task to watch the skies patiently and record the movements accurately. We do not question the mysteries. We follow the logic of what we see, for otherwise the hunger would be on us—or we would be lost in darkness." He watched the boy's face and, satisfied that Aengus understood, the Dagda turned to Boann. "It is proper for your mother to tell you about the directions given to us from the sun to find our way."

Boann walked to the central marker peg. "Each of us contains a shadow that shows itself during the light of day. All shadows act in the same way as the sun moves through the sky. By observing the shadow and the sun, you need never be lost."

"You learned today that the ancient one rises at different points on the horizon through the four seasons of light. Its path overhead also changes during its cycle. The overhead path varies according to the season. We will explore this more in the coming lessons. For now, I think you already know that every day there is a period when the great sun is directly over your head and you cast very little shadow onto the earth."

Aengus nodded, apparently glad to hear there would be more lessons. The Dagda suppressed a smile, obviously proud of Aengus' attentiveness despite having spent so long among strangers here in Midh. He was not even fidgeting.

"Our people verified in different ways that between sunrise and sunset, there is a place where the sun is 'highest' above the horizon in the dome of the sky. This happens at midsun, and that place is south, no matter where you are. When the sun is at south, then you will see the shortest shadow. This place does not change no matter what is the season of the sun. The place in the sky called 'north' also does not change. The sun marker will also show you north when it is the shortest shadow in the day. North is opposite to south on a straight line from the sun through the shadow of the marker. Because the Sun fixed the directions of south and north in the sky, this gives us two halves of the sky dome, south and north. We can choose other directions to show us the way. Long ago our people decided that it is best to divide the sky dome into four equal parts.

"How were we to do this? The answer was again to be found in the sky. Twice in each solar cycle the sunrise and sunset show us the directions of east and west. As the sun travels along the horizon, it shows us the line running straight from east to west that divides the sky dome exactly halfway between north and south. This line happens at sunrise and at sunset on the equinoxes. The equinox from the sun fixes east and west no matter where you are on this island. The sun again helps us to measure and understand our world, south to north and east to west, as it completes the cycle of light. This is the second gift from the sun."

Boann wondered, shall we tell Aengus that he must not discuss these things with Invaders? But that caution could wait until their journey home, she decided.

She finished, seeing that young Aengus had heard enough for his first formal lesson with the Dagda. "One of the chambers here at Loughcrew has an old carved backstone that receives a shaped beam of light at the equinoxes, spring and fall, and later you and I shall explore that chamber and read its symbols. Our people also use certain star patterns in the dark sky of night to verify these things told to us by the sun. I will show you the secrets from the moon and the stars later, with the Dagda. For now, remember that at the equinoxes you will see the time to plant and the time to harvest. And that is also when true east and true west are fixed for us by the sky.

"Now, the Seafarers use the night stars to find their way across the great waters. Can you think why this is so?"

Aengus answered instantly, "Because on a boat the Seafarers do not have fixed stone markers to help them!"

Boann and the Dagda beamed now at his absorption and understanding. "Yes, exactly. The Seafarers also learned through their generations that the best time for making sea travel begins and ends at the spring and fall equinoxes and which stars rise and set with equinox."

She fell silent, thinking with a wrench of Cliodhna, and Cian, and the rolling ocean. And the smith Creidhne, gone without a trace. Her fingers laced tight around her astronomer's cord, clenching the smooth beads.

"Mother! Are you all right?" Aengus came to her side, his hazel eyes searching her face.

She smiled at him. "Yes, I'm fine." She stroked his shining head of hair. As long as her lessons with Aengus could continue, then she would hold onto that even as the sky shifted above them.

Many seasons of the sun might pass before she learned of Cian's fate.

The silver apples of the moon,
The golden apples of the sun.
Song of Wandering Aengus, W.B. Yeats

A Fire in the Head

CIAN AND ENYA waited for a propitious season to travel to the
Boyne from the Loire, while his true passion absorbed him: the
sky disk.

Cian had never forgotten his dream, his vision while staying with
Gebann on the Seafarer peninsula, a disk divided into four quadrants
like the sacred directions under the sky's dome. His disk would be
portable. It could alter starwatching forever.

He had several small disks produced by his Loire smith, trying
various metals, dimensions, and finishes to give a surface like the
sky. His trade prospered and Cian could afford to have the disk
prototypes cast in bronze as well as copper, if not solid gold. Bronze
held symbols etched upon it better than did copper. Bronze, the
stronger metal, proved superior for his purposes.

A local sage having astronomy skills helped experiment with
various configurations on the disk. Cian wanted a design that would
be accurate for sightings no matter where one used the sky disk. His
helper took a disk here and there, far inland and along the coasts,

and reported back that over any great distance the markings proved inaccurate. To perfect a universal disk Cian needed an expert astronomer from his people, but he lacked access to one. He persevered, trying various designs using what he learned of sun and stars in his youth.

Taranis, despite his self-absorption, appreciated knowledge and said he enjoyed seeing the disk take shape. He entered Cian's workshop one muggy midsun for a chat about their trading. There his son-in-law and a smith tinkered with a bronze disk.

"I always know where to find you, Starwatcher." Taranis held his nose. "What is that awful smell?"

"Rotten eggs. We smear the disk's surface with them and it changes to deep blue like the night sky," Cian answered.

Taranis waved his arm, expansive. "Your invention shall be the toast in great halls from the Cymru coast all the way south to the river Tagus, and as far east as the snowy mountains. What shall you charge a buyer for your disk?"

Cian glowed at the praise, but didn't have a ready answer.

"You must demand an amount for your sky disk that is, shall we say, astronomical." He wagged his forefinger. "Meanwhile, see to it that you and Enya produce an heir."

Cian took part of this advice to heart. To his surprise, the first disk fetched him a good-sized bag of gold from its eager buyer.

He increased the disk's size and varied its purpose. A sky disk could show the sun's seasonal journey between solstice or equinox positions, or align with particular constellations. He shared what he was doing with Enya whenever she ventured into his work area.

"Your sky disk has both beauty and function, and word of it spreads among those elite who know astronomy. But what of those who would misuse the starwatching disk, frighten others with it or pretend it has some magic?" she asked him in private. They had just witnessed most of a midsummer spectacle, put on by Taranis for his people, that included dancers and a juggler. The two left before the bear-baiting that would end with putting the animal to death and displaying its bloody entrails, head, and claws. Now they sat on a bench among her fragrant flowers.

"Your question is wise, as always. That danger concerns me greatly. I hope that sharing this tool with those who seek understanding will overcome those who would use it to spread ignorance or do evil," he answered. "I would rather not restrict the sky disk to any self-proclaimed elite. But I cannot be sure who will lay hands on one."

Cian's workshop went on to deliver custom sky disks, brought to the buyer's location and finished there. For those journeys, he usually sent his astronomer with an itinerant smith to finish the disk rather than traveling himself, as he preferred to keep his staid routine.

He prayed with sun and stars, ate sparingly of plain foods, and worked on the sky disk. He took ritual baths, exercised, cropped his dark hair, and wore simple clothing. In the marketplace, strangers misjudged the quiet and modest big fellow to be someone slow-witted rather than Taranis' partner.

Season after season passed while Cian busied himself with refining the sky disk, and overseeing the gold trading along with Taranis. They also sent prospectors after more tin to increase the supply of bronze.

Better weather, warmer and stable, resumed along the Continent. Enya devoted herself to gardening and enlarged the gardens at the hall of Taranis, sheltering them with lines of tall yews. The yews embraced into a thick defense against storms, just as Cian and Enya remained the best of friends. They spoke of the return voyage to Eire. Cian knew his disk was ready, but a favorable time for him to embark on that trip did not arrive. The tenuous peace held at the Boyne, and Boann and Aengus were safe; or so Sreng assured him in messages.

Given my situation, he told himself, it's better that Boann know nothing of me.

He ignored his fear of the ocean swells when he took short voyages on behalf of Taranis or with the sky disk. Cian heard of Creidhne's disappearance, and had long resigned himself that Cliodhna had been lost to the waves. There had been countless others drowned when shipments to and from Eire sank. Rather than leave it to shamans he presided over each departing vessel, praying with his hands aloft for the stars to guide the craft safely. He grieved for lost mariners and ensured their families were provided for and their memories honored at cairns along the coast.

Nevertheless his gold trading continued. His gold artisan in Eire, formerly an apprentice to Creidhne, trained another artisan, then another. Starwatcher goldsmiths embellished their gold jewelry, etching very fine parallel lines, solid or composed of minute dots, onto the sheet-gold neck lunulae and other jewelry pieces. Eire's intricately tooled jewelry became the rage in all the northern islands and coasts. The Starwatcher smiths elaborated on the early styles. As gold became more plentiful from the mining they made heavier items. The goldsmiths began to make curved lengths of hollow gold tubes into stunning torcs and bracelets and large fasteners for fabric. Their fabulous jewelry reached the Continent's central plains and into its far corners and set the fashion wherever those items traded.

The tin source he found long ago had held up, some seasons more of it available than in others, but it enabled the Loire to produce costly bronze. Cian prospered mightily with Taranis, beyond their wildest dreams when they made their first bargain. He now lived a hundred times better than that rascal Bolg whom he met long ago. He gave Taranis loyalty in all their dealings. Nevertheless, Taranis complained from time to time, "Why haven't you and Enya given me an heir?"

Then Cian's thoughts, his desires, invariably strayed north with his impossible dream of returning to Eire. Elcmar would kill for gold, Sreng and Lir warned him.

Matters came to a head when news of troubles reached the hall of Taranis. A messenger in salt-stained leather arrived in dark and rain and asked for an immediate audience. "Elcmar confiscated an entire gold shipment! His warriors hold your ship and most of the men captive. Lir got word and sent me on to you; he waits at the northwest to cross the Channel on your instructions."

Taranis' expression darkened. Sporadic "taxes" on the gold by Elcmar's agents had been merely annoying. Elcmar's sudden levy of a whole shipment, and taking of hostages, caught his full attention. Before dawn he dispatched men with the messenger, who voyaged north with Lir all the way to the Boyne estuary with his demand for swift return of the ship, men, and gold. Elcmar ignored that demand. Over the following season of the sun, his silence infuriated Taranis.

A pacing Taranis summoned Cian to his chamber. "We don't want to see Sreng's men and our own mariners discouraged by being potential hostages of Elcmar. The covert mining and the sea travel have perils enough. Men trained in these arts are few and far between," Taranis growled, his voice gravelly and face lined under his groomed curls. "We need to send Elcmar and his Invaders a message they understand. I'm not so old that I couldn't visit your island, Starwatcher, and show your man there what's what."

Cian proposed sending weapons, enough metal weapons to let the Starwatchers reclaim Eire and their gold. Taranis squelched that idea; arming the locals could only endanger his trade network, his own supremacy. Soon the chief brought up the missing shipment again during an evening meal though he disliked unpleasant topics while he ate.

He looked down the table, at Cian sitting beside Enya, and his own sons who offered little conversation, their consorts bedecked and coiffed in the latest high style. On this evening the family enjoyed a first course of toasted thin meal cakes rolled up with pureed chestnuts and chives. Taranis licked a finger and finished, a slave waiting at his elbow to whisk away crumbs.

This delicacy graced his table from the Basque who stayed on as his inventive chef. While Taranis waited, a slave carried in a steaming roast suckling pig marinated in fermented cider, its crisp skin studded with herbs, on a bronze platter. Bronze skewers of roasted roots and apples, their skins likewise bronzed, completed its glory. He inhaled deeply over the platter and signaled to the slave, who commenced carving and serving onto polished wooden plates. No one speared hunks or gnawed bones at Taranis' table. His manner of dining gained favor among the coasts' very elite like the gold lunulae they avidly sought from him. His source of gold, his prestige, must remain secure. Taranis turned back to Enya and Cian, who looked to be holding hands under the table.

"Well?" he rapped on the tabletop, scowling. "Our missing gold?" He regarded the couple fondly across piled fruits and nuts on the honey-hued oak planks.

"Perhaps it is time to send weapons to our men in Eire?" Cian suggested again. He realized how dangerous Elcmar would be if cornered, like a wild beast that had only ever known fighting for survival.

Enya's brothers volunteered to take their warriors over the waters to Eire but Taranis waved away their offer. "No need to spill blood to bring one man in line over trading. That would set a bad precedent."

Enya nodded at Cian, who spoke again. "As you say, Elcmar's actions pose a grave threat that must be countered. I cannot myself return to the Starwatcher island, or I would have done so. That *ard ri* bears me great enmity as it is; I wouldn't be the person to persuade him.

"With your blessing, Enya and a party of armed guards of your choosing shall journey there. We can call her guards diplomats and call this a goodwill mission to further the gold trade—from the Starwatchers. Let Elcmar levy his taxes but in a reasonable amount. Enya will negotiate that amount with him once and for all, and have

Elcmar return this gold. Your ship must of course be returned in sound condition, and all the hostages."

"Enya to go, alone!" Taranis turned to his daughter. She had borne no children and he despaired of ever seeing a grandson from their union. But he had sons who gave him heirs, and who chafed at Cian's prominence. At the risk of losing Enya to the ocean, he well knew that if she wanted to go on this journey it was pointless to tell her otherwise. Even now, her posture indicated her firm decision in accord with Cian. She was certainly capable of reining in Elcmar and having him release the captured gold, the ship, and hostages. Taranis had great faith in his newest strong plank boat for her safe journey to Eire and back.

"I give you my blessing in this, Enya. Ten strong guards, and gifts to the *ard ri*, shall accompany you there. But we had better not send sails edged in gold."

They toasted the decision with copas, rare footed cups in shiny black pottery from a far southern coast. The diners ate in lingering bites and made plans for her journey to Eire. At the end of their dinner the family dabbed themselves with scented water from burlwood bowls and wiped their hands using linen woven fine as mist in a hot land they had never seen.

Enya's necklace of variscite and antler beads caught the light from oil lamps as she rose from the table, and reminded Cian of a particular constellation. He watched, appreciating her graceful exit from the hall. Knowing Taranis expected him to retire with her, Cian excused himself from the table.

He went to stand under the stars. Enya had insisted, despite the difficult journey. The voyage fell during good weather, but if she did not return, Taranis would blame him for her death and her brothers would gladly kill him. Neither could he persuade her to stay behind at the Loire while he contended with Elcmar. He trusted her abilities, and so agreed to her plan.

His own dying mattered little to him. The sky seemed closer with every season that passed. So long as he could tinker with his sky disk, he would be content living in a little stone hut. His gold trade sustained his people far away, his Starwatchers. He ensured they were spared the privation that befell other coasts. He had so far thwarted Elcmar from enslaving the Starwatchers. Owning no slaves himself, he lived comfortably in his own skin. Any notion of his happiness lay well out of reach, left behind.

As Cian dreamed that night, he saw rowers crossing the dark waters. The oars' spray turned into the foamy white river in the sky. He saw Boann in the bright northern stars while the other stars wheeled around them. He dreamed of the boy at her side in the glittering heavens.

On the Starwatcher island, traders from the Continent arrived more frequently. The improving climate loosed a demand for gold and traders brought men who knew how to prospect. The ancient sea routes to Eire for exchange of stone beads and axes and astronomy now flowed with metals trade. On the Continent, a Starwatcher had become a force to be reckoned with, the favorite of powerful Taranis. This much Boann knew from recent arrivals on Eire who came to pay homage to Elcmar, even before the elegant woman stood before her in the great hall.

The foreign woman appeared without notice and with a contingent of robust guards who insisted she have an audience with Elcmar. Boann answered that Elcmar had gone riding. The woman indicated she would speak only in private; Boann dismissed the attending slaves and Invader sentries from the hall. One slave, she sent off to fetch Tadhg and Cermait.

Boann felt awe before the height and well-groomed looks of this woman, at her wide sea-green eyes and full lips. Thick brown hair with golden highlights flowed down her back. Jet earrings framed her perfect face and her pleasing form was adorned by a necklace of sparkling jet plaques and beads, over her sweeping tunic dyed purple-red. Glistening fur lined the woman's skin cloak, spotless despite long travel. As she heard the words introducing this woman, Boann regretted her own lack of adornment, her plain tunic of dark undyed wool. Her hair was neat but as usual she had not bothered to stain her cheeks or lips.

"I present Enya, daughter of mighty Taranis, and the wife of Cian," the woman's guard announced.

A familiar deep longing filled Boann; her ears rang and she took to her tall-backed chair. She composed herself and with detachment indicated a chair for the woman Enya to be seated before her. Only then did Enya bring forward a man of average height and build but who limped noticeably on his left leg. He too wore fine but foreign garments. His determined steps evoked memories for Boann of valiant Sheela, and she took care to indicate a seat for him.

The woman Enya and the foreign man traded pleasantries with Boann. Tadhg and Cermait arrived, and sat near the stranger while Enya began to relate news from the Continent and more specifically, of Cian. Boann listened as Enya spoke, her words dispelling the tortured silence from Cian's long absence. She touched the ocean-blue stone she still wore under her tunic.

Elcmar bounded into the hall after a time; a warrior must have gone looking for him. He appeared displeased to see that two Starwatcher men attended this audience. Boann knew Elcmar could not breach Invader rules of hospitality by countermanding her to send the Starwatchers away. He ignored them, and the foreign man.

Enya replied to his curt greeting with measured words. She resumed talking, her muscular guards staying close behind her chair, Elcmar saying little. After a time, she broached the hostage situation and mentioned the latest "levy" by Elcmar's men. Enya did not retreat under Elcmar's hard stare while she made several points to him about his situation with her father Taranis. "We trust this incident shall not be repeated in future," she added.

He made no reply. Boann apprehended that under his mask, he had no response suitable for Taranis. How vulnerable, how self-deluded Elcmar had been while he tried to control Eire. She could almost feel sorry for him.

From the folds of her garment, Enya removed a soft pouch holding gold jewelry: a wide etched lunula and matching armlets. "These are tribute to you from Cian," Enya said to Boann. She placed a net bag of gleaming nuggets on a small table beside Elcmar, inclining her head toward him. "From Cian."

Elcmar leaped to his feet. "Gold! Cian trades in gold at the hall of Taranis!"

The two women rose, drew shoulder to shoulder, and faced him. Tadhg and Cermait stepped forward with Enya's guards. Elcmar did not dare to seize the gold jewelry. He banged his fist splitting the tabletop, left the bag of nuggets where it fell, and swept out of the hall with eyes ablaze.

Boann picked up the bag of nuggets and put it on his chair. Then she saw to her guests.

They ate and drank well, and spoke freely. Enya's guards replaced Invaders except one sentry whom Boann kept busy bringing food and drink, for she barred all the slaves save her Seafarer woman. After initial unease at being in the great hall, her Starwatcher guests relaxed over food and drink and heard Enya with great interest.

Enya described aspects of gold trading. "Starwatchers shall share openly in this trading now that Cian's involvement is clear. He keeps little gold for himself. Cian has been providing seeds and goods to Eire through the lean years." Boann gasped, and Enya pretended not to hear it. "He helped our allies on Cymru as well, and tribes farther north. As I indicated earlier, Elcmar built up debt for some time, a large debt that he could now erase by turning over the ship, its crew, and the gold."

The stranger interjected, "He would do well to accept your father's offer."

Enya smiled. Boann did not know whether to laugh or cry at Elcmar's predicament and that he should be cornered by this proud and beautiful woman, the daughter of Taranis and wife of Cian.

"We heard afterward, of others starving during the bad harvests. Cian has kept us alive through many suns," said Tadhg, and Cermait agreed. They invited Enya to meet with the elders before she would depart, so that the Starwatchers might learn from her lips the amazing works of Cian on far shores.

"I carry a gift for the Dagda," she remarked, and the three Starwatchers leaned forward eagerly but she told them no more about it while they dined. She turned to the stranger, who told them of far-ranging travels that brought him to the great Boyne in hopes his injured knee would have healing.

"The river Boyne might not be the best," said Tadhg. "If it's warm waters you want."

The stranger appreciated the humor and said he would indeed try anything for his knee. "And I could not travel so far west and north without seeing your island of copper and gold, and your center of star knowledge," he told them. "All the coastal peoples speak of your island. I had to see if it was real, and the Starwatchers."

"Real enough for us," said Tadhg, but Cermait jumped in.

"You haven't traveled, how would you know. This might be the Otherworld!"

Time slipped by with their easy banter, and fascinating tales from the traveler, who came from a faraway tribe. Then the Starwatchers departed, saying they would meet again at the mounds.

For lack of suitable guest quarters, Boann put herself out of her bed for Enya's rest, and had the slave pile furs over rushes outside of the sleeping chamber. Before Enya retired, the two women spoke in private inside the chamber.

Enya surprised Boann. "I see that your beauty and wisdom, of which Cian told me, have only increased over the suns." With a faint smile she continued, "I wish to speak of some matters that concern only the two of us. I shall speak frankly and hope to put your mind at rest.

"Unknown to anyone, Cian and I live as we had prior to the marriage, that is to say, we never consummated our marriage." Enya's voice dropped and quavered. "Cian would come home, here to the Boyne, but he has had to remain at the Loire to appease my father. Cian suffered for you all this time, and for love of another I suffered also. That is what binds us, that and our deep friendship. We have no children, no heir. For that my father Taranis would kill us both— if he understood."

"Please tell Cian that I carry him in my heart forever, shining and constant as the heavens above." Boann suppressed tears.

"I hope you can forgive us. Cian remains devoted to his people, selfless. He did not set out to hurt anyone in this life, nor did I," Enya said, her eyes welling with Boann's. "And you have Aengus, your son. Now tell me more of fair Aengus, so that I can tell Cian all about him."

They talked on, unhurried. At Enya's request, Boann removed the ocean-blue pendant and put on the gold jewelry. She gave the pendant to Enya, who took it serenely and put it into a pouch in the folds of her garment, saying that she would return it to Cian.

While they were alone, Enya opened an exotic wood case and took out a large metal disk. Cian's promise echoed the moment Boann saw his starwatching disk: you shall know this object when you see it. Gold stars shone against the upper surface. She held it until Enya put it away once more.

She resumed her role as hostess to this notable guest. "Brave daughter of Taranis, what may I obtain for you or do on your behalf?"

"Nothing, nothing at all. Though you did not know the truth of things, you showed impeccable hospitality to me. I share in whatever contentment I can give to you.

"And my journey on your island has been delightful, such gentle and charming people. I have seen and learned much to tell Cian, and my father. Tomorrow however, I must return with my guards to the southeast, to the dark-pooled river's mouth. There my ship lies waiting. Let us see if the stolen ship and gold arrive to cross the waves with us." She paused. "Cian does not like ocean voyages. Tell Elcmar that is why he sent the daughter of Taranis!"

Both women smiled, making light of the dangers each faced whether on the ocean's swirling waters or along the silver Boyne.

That night Enya's guards and the male guest slept huddled around the hearth in the great hall, and Boann kept her loyal slave woman sleeping at her side, but Elcmar and his warriors did not return to trouble them.

On the following morning, Boann rose to watch the sun rise. She stepped out onto flagstones; she had had those installed to stop muck coming into the hall on warriors' footgear. Cian would hardly recognize the Boyne camp. He would see that the Invaders had put up more permanent buildings inside their enclosure. Their horses and livestock were now penned outside the banked palisade. The smelting, Boann had moved to a site near the cooking pits. She ordered the camp cleaned of debris and had areas re-sodded. Boann had managed to bring order inside the great hall, scrubbed now and having a dignity of sorts.

She thought of her frantic search long ago for her grooved antler pin, still lost to her. Much had been lost; lives lost or wasted, and for what exactly? That Cian chose to live an ascetic life brought her no consolation. She would not have begrudged him the satisfactions of the flesh; flesh was easy enough to satisfy. She could forgive the portion of happiness Enya said they shared as companions. With a pang, she thought of Enya's ships waiting to the south, a voyage that could reunite her with Cian. The stranger would be staying on, then journeying to Cymru, he said, to its fabled bluestone quarries seeking a cure for his leg and metal ores for trade. From there he planned to travel south to the great stone circle. Boann wondered if she might take his place on the vessel that brought Enya. And if she did voyage to the Loire, if she could be reunited with Cian, then what? Certain death for all from Taranis, it appeared.

She stiffened her spine to hide misery. She would remain here at the Boyne, to see to it that Aengus came into his own, his birthright. Her people needed both Aengus and her.

Her people survived, thanks to Cian. They still had starwatching, she had seen to that. Though Cian would not be pleased by the stone circle Ith erected around the central mound. Invaders put up a circle of upright boulders, and enlarged that clearing to better observe who was coming and going. A wooden hut had been built close to the mound entrance, now sealed by a tall slab. The mound's untended quartz bank slipped and tumbled over the kerbstones. Starwatchers observed the solstice elsewhere. That Invader stone circle appeared to be useless, it had no alignment with the skies. Within it, Ith and Bresal held ceremonies to sacrifice animals and divine the entrails. Around the west mound, Knowth, the Invaders erected a double circle of wooden posts and they held grisly ceremonies there as well.

Stay away from those mounds, her people quipped, or you'll find yourself sacrificed. These open-air displays were the shaman Ith's idea, an obvious ploy to borrow prestige from the mounds. Boann noted it all with contempt.

Changes. How easy to change things it was; how very difficult to improve them.

Ith, the one Invader who perceived he could learn from the Starwatchers; but like the rest it was only to take advantage. He would be with Elcmar now, plotting together. She felt the gold jewelry on her neck and arms as she gazed east toward the rising sun. Elcmar behaved badly toward Enya and the foreigner. She winced to compare him with what she had learned of Cian.

The sun's first light showed that it would be a fine day, but she frowned to think what Elcmar and Ith might be plotting. She wondered where she might hide well this gold jewelry, and also the heavy disk of bronze. Her daydreaming abruptly ended. She and Enya must see the Dagda, straightaway. Her elders must hide the starwatching disk as soon as possible. The sun caressed her face and lifted her spirits.

The two women washed and dressed quickly, and the elderly slave helped each to arrange her hair. On seeing the intricate braids looped around a bun, Enya said she was delighted. They shared a breakfast of stirabout with fruit, soft white cheese, and hot infusion of mint and blackberry leaves.

Boann assured Enya they would stop but a moment at the Starwatchers' village on its swath of green lawn. "We shall ride there on horses if you prefer. Horses travel faster than walking and I know you wish to depart with midsun." Guards helped Enya mount, the heavy disk concealed under her rich cloak. Two guards rode with them; the others stayed behind with the foreigner, who needed to rest his leg.

They stopped at each of the three great mounds set in the bend of the shining Boyne. Enya marveled at the mounds' size and construction. When they reached the central starchamber, Enya took care to dismount and to walk the stations of the cursus, and Boann's admiration for her grew. The Dagda awaited them with all the elders and astronomers. Starwatcher scouts had ejected the Invader sentry.

The daughter of Taranis walked with Oghma to view his most elaborate kerbstones. She did not pretend to understand the symbols, though she said they reminded her of the Morbihan carvings. Resting her hand upon his arm, she gave Oghma special greetings.

"Your time with Cian was well spent. Please accept his gift for the Starwatchers."

Oghma looked into Enya's eyes. "We have waited long."

The elders exclaimed when she produced the astronomy disk. Hands eager, the Dagda stroked the glowing disk. They all watched as he sighted along the solar horizon with it, then each elder held the disk as the group murmured satisfaction.

So it was that Cian sent to his people what he promised.

The Dagda spoke. "At last, something useful has been made of this, this metal."

Oghma drew himself up on his staff to stand straight and proud. "From the hands of our own Cian, comes this tool of understanding."

With that sunrise, Elcmar left Ith's quarters where the two had talked deep into the night. Ith reasoned with the champion, who paced and raged.

"Enya's guards threatened me with a ridiculous amount that Taranis is after claiming I owe him," and Elcmar swore that he wouldn't pay, not any of it. He overlooked Enya's role altogether.

"You cannot send his daughter back to him empty-handed." Ith persuaded Elcmar at length to show restraint and release the hostages, the ship, and most of the confiscated gold to Taranis. "You'll keep Eire that way."

Elcmar fled from Ith's dour face, after capitulating. He'd have to pay the venerable Taranis. Or was it Cian who would benefit? That possibility galled him no end.

He had a horse readied for riding. Taranis, the one man on whose good graces he must rely, his strongest link with the Continent. He had given the gold smuggling a tacit wink, not inclined to interfere when he heard Taranis was behind it. Elcmar's men succeeded from time to time in collecting a share of gold—when they could find it being loaded onto ships, that is. All the while he tried to locate the gold's source for himself. The amount of gold leaving and its exact route from the eastern mountains remained a mystery, one that had long irked Elcmar. It irked him as much as the damp and creeping bogs on Eire.

When a party of miners had left the Lake copper mine, he suspected those men went off to mine gold. Somehow, the missing Gebann had had a hand in all this. Elcmar recalled sending another agent, after losing Creidhne to the sea, to retrieve Gebann from the peninsula. That agent did return, but empty-handed. The man reported that the impaired Gebann was no longer fit for walking much less prospecting, and grieved still for his daughter. And his spy claimed that Cian had vanished along the coasts.

Where have the suns gone since I banished Cian? Elcmar thought it over. He survived on the copper trade and by taking a portion of the Starwatchers' livestock, grain, and milk. He had an occasional windfall by grabbing some of the outgoing gold, where and when he could. Connor settled himself into northern lands, though he claimed to have never found gold there. He had left Connor to his own survival in the north.

I might have untold riches by now if I'd stayed on the Continent, but sure, haven't the gradual shipments of this and that over the suns bettered things here in the camp?

Invaders had more breeding livestock, including more horses. On this morning he rode a sleeker, taller mount. He'd occupied himself quite happily in the breeding and training of horses over the suns. The spring warrior competition now included horse races, in addition to foot races and a form of hurling. He gave his horse an affectionate tap on the rump with a white hazel switch. He admired himself, his finely woven cloak held with a large bronze brooch. So what if Taranis tallied it up and would make him pay for all the breeding stock and costly goods. Still, he had his horses.

His other pleasure was Aengus, and he rode regularly to see the lad at the warrior training camp on Midhir's plain. On this dawning, his visit had one distinct purpose. Aengus had sixteen suns as of the past solstice. Elcmar urged the horse into a loping canter, smoother than its jarring trot—trotting always provoked his old rib injury. His head on fire, he wanted a good long look at Aengus.

He pulled up on his horse before the rough plank-and-wattle hall that housed the young fighters, and dismounted more carefully than he might have in younger days.

On this clear morning, as it happened, Aengus was just falling into bed. He had been out watching the sky through the night.

The astronomy lessons continued for young Aengus since his trip to the Storied Hills, and he applied himself earnestly. He took his turn at stargazing, enduring significant discomfort on chill and damp nights. When he could have been carousing or sleeping like the other adolescent warriors, Aengus stayed out under the sparkling stars shivering under a robe pulled shut over his leather leggings and tunic. Sometimes his layered clothing gave warmth enough, but if the night were very cold, his limbs ached. He had no option of lighting a big fire for warmth, as that would impair night vision. Midhir showed him to bring heated stones in pouches tucked under his clothing, and to layer them around his feet, and many a night that saved his vigil.

The astronomy taught to Aengus came in steps that brought him into the realm of abstract concepts, and their use of symbols. He shared the Starwatchers' connection with the sky and like them, dedicated himself to studying the natural world. He too struggled to make sense of the planets' wild rides through the night. Did the sky dome move, or the stars? Did the earth move, or the sun and moon? What was a shooting star? He did not know if he could crack any secrets of these motions, but he did not shirk the challenge. The younger, sharp-eyed astronomers still studied the Northshift; Aengus helped his mother and Daire attempt to measure and understand it.

His training as a warrior developed Aengus into an impressive young man. His shoulders grew broad, his arms powerful and long, and his chest deep. It was said his legs were the most magnificent ever seen on the island, legs thick as trees but sharply defined in the muscles of thigh and calf. He had his father's stamp on his strong body, bright hazel-green eyes, and his mother's thick auburn hair and elegant nose, her curving lips, and graceful hands. It amused the elders to see Aengus pass through a group of young women like a scythe through tender grass, the slightest glance from him felling one and all. Aengus was renowned to be deeply interested in the Swan constellation that arced in winter skies, so that some of the young women fancied dressing up as swans to disrupt his nighttime vigils. He could have had any one of them, but it was said that he displayed reserve and had not lain with a woman.

He showed courtesy to all Starwatchers, and without the hard edges and talking in circles of Elcmar's people, Invaders. Young Aengus was highly esteemed among the Starwatchers. They watched him and collectively held their breath, looking to him for signs of their future on Eire. Aengus, the one choice, they began to say of him, Boann's son.

A friend shook Aengus by the shoulder just as he drifted asleep in his hay. "Get up, lad. The *ard ri* arrives, outside, now. Get up, will you!"

He threw off his sheepskin bedcovering, and doused himself with cold water as Elcmar strode toward him down the line of box beds in the hall.

"Is it up late you are?" Elcmar boomed.

Aengus grinned and covered his face with a bast cloth to dry himself, and escaped the penetrating stare. After he had dressed and eaten a slab of cold meal cake washed down with mead, the two walked out to the sparring grounds.

While Aengus trained with the other young warriors, Elcmar watched from nearby on a rush-seated stool quickly fetched for him by the camp steward. He noticed a fair number of the trainees were Starwatcher boys and that did not displease him. The more young males recruited to become warriors, the better. He could fend off warriors sent by Taranis or anyone with these able and fearless lads; that thought lingered to tempt him.

Elcmar scrutinized Aengus' chiseled face and body. *It's a fine physique he displays, sure. And he's tall enough. My son?* The question repressed for so long tormented him now. He would stay on at Midhir's hall on the plain, until he fixed his opinion on this question about Aengus. That also avoided his having to deal with problems at the Boyne during that time, always an attractive option.

He observed Aengus practicing on the field over the next sunrises. Elcmar truly enjoyed this time with Aengus, whether at meals, sparring, riding, or trouncing each other at board games played with polished stones. Like him, the lad had an eye for horses and handled them well. Aengus also had a quick mind; if he heard something once, he had it.

Elcmar knew finally that no matter how it might be decided from appearances, he regarded Aengus as his son. *Look at him out there, he's the coming champion, sure there are no other contenders. No one has an edge on him for power and agility. He'll never be defeated in a contest, not by any of these lads. Soon he might think himself ready to replace me.* Curiosity got the better of him.

"Aengus, what would you do if you held the Boyne camp?" Elcmar asked him as they ate a good cut of forest boar, the two sitting apart from the other trainees.

Aengus chewed in silence, then answered. "If you let me have the Boyne camp through a night and day, I shall show you," he said in the Invader tongue that he took care to use with Elcmar.

"And so you shall!" The response pleased Elcmar. At least the lad hadn't answered the question with another question, unlike his irritating mother.

The two agreed that on the coming Invader feast, Aengus would ride into the Boyne camp at nightfall.

Aengus soon regretted the arrangement set with Elcmar. He'd answered as well as he could. Trading, cattle raids, and contests of strength did not interest him. He had not considered being *ard ri* or what that might entail. He liked astronomy and did not mind that others compared him with the Dagda. From childhood, occasional teasing from other boys about his clouded status bothered him. Midhir taught him to deflect and rise above their taunts. And, like his grandfather Oghma, to think before he would speak. When he mentioned his wager with Elcmar to Midhir, his foster father sighed and shook his silver head.

The worst of it was, that Invader feast night coincided with an important starwatch. At his very next lesson with the Dagda, Aengus learned that a lunar eclipse was imminent. The coming eclipse was known, explained the Dagda, as follows:

"The crescent moon lines up with the Seven Sisters once every decade. Look there, we see the moon and stars nearing alignment. But the moon on this night is only a sliver. At what moon phase must any lunar eclipse occur?"

"Only during full moon," Aengus answered at once.

"Correct," said the Dagda. "For this event the Seven Sisters align during the waxing crescent moon, then after seven risings of the sun the lunar eclipse occurs. Now, look again. Who can tell me how many more sunsets until we have this particular eclipse?"

Daire checked his bone marker strip and figured out when full moon would arrive. The Dagda congratulated him. "The rest of you, show me the answer using your markers."

While the others reached the same answer, Aengus groaned inwardly. The eclipse would overlap the Invader feast. He could not explain that to Elcmar, nor renege on their agreement. Elcmar would hold him to that date. He would have to rush from the eclipse to the Invader camp.

Aengus asked Midhir for the swiftest horse kept at the warrior camp, and he gave Midhir a lump of sun metal sent to him by his mother. The island had gold coming slowly into circulation and Midhir looked happy enough to exchange a nugget for his horse. Aengus made it a point to ride and train this horse during the time remaining before the eclipse.

The appointed sunrise came for his return to the Boyne. He took leave of the other young warriors with his horse standing ready, when Midhir took him aside.

"Aengus, I bring you hard news. Oghma has passed from us to the Otherworld."

His breath caught and he hung his head to hide tears. When he looked up again at Midhir, his eyes saw with a man's wisdom. Aengus said, "I shall remain at *Bru na Elcmar*."

Midhir nodded assent, hands on his shoulders. The time had arrived to confront Elcmar, who had yet to acknowledge Aengus as son and heir. Midhir embraced his foster son, then Aengus rode away, strong and true, from Bri Leith straight to the Boyne.

He arrived at the mounds in advance of the eclipse, just as the children of his mother's village finished bundling reed torches for after the starwatch.

The Dagda had decided to observe this eclipse at Knowth, in celebration of the skywatching disk. In the western passage of Knowth lay the body of Oghma, and the Starwatchers intended to honor Oghma as well. They gathered discreetly, without firewood.

The astronomers and apprentices including Aengus waited in darkness outside the mound on its eastern side. Soon enough, the rising moon developed a curved shadow on its lower edge.

The moon turned dark red where the rounded shadow slowly covered it, an intense hue the elders had never seen in an eclipse. Then on the clear still air, the observers heard telltale hooves, many horses coming at them from the Invader camp. Elders, with the women and children, left the mound immediately, fleeing into the forest.

At the feast Elcmar announced his offer to Aengus and he took umbrage when Aengus did not arrive promptly at nightfall. A breathless sentry ran in to announce that Aengus had ridden to Knowth, and Elcmar rose and ran with Ith and warriors to the horses' pen. Elcmar followed his darkest suspicions in a gallop to the mounds. He saw Aengus' own bridle on a horse tethered close to the western mound, just before the full moon's light faded. It turned fully to a deep copper color above them. His blood hot, Elcmar swung his legs over his horse's neck and ignored the pain as he leaped off. He ran with his warriors toward the small knot of Starwatchers who remained defiantly watching the eclipse. Bright rage followed Elcmar like a comet's tail.

Aengus left the Starwatchers and tried to stop the onrushing warriors. Elcmar pushed him aside as warriors chased the quiet ones, some of whom escaped into Knowth's dark passages.

"Why are you here? Go see to your mother and our guests!" Elcmar shouted as he ran to join the fray.

"I am a Starwatcher!" Aengus shouted back.

Elcmar turned on him. "By Lugh, I don't know who you are."

Aengus wavered, then rode off under the ruddy moon to the great hall. He would advise his mother of the troubles here. Then he would win *Bru na Boinne* from Elcmar. He would take it without violence.

Bresal remained inside the camp and worked up hysteria over the reddening face of the moon. Boann presided at the feast, though wishing that she might watch this eclipse and honor Oghma at Knowth, and hoping that Aengus could observe it all. She listened to the growing clamor of the crowd outside the great hall. Shouts derided her, as always. She no longer feared the noisy warriors, no more than being wary of a wolf that howls from a safe distance.

Her guests diverted themselves with tall tales over the laden table, and she waited. At last Ith might see for himself that an eclipse is a natural occurrence of the moon, she told the foreigner who stayed on after Enya left. He nodded. He had toured the mounds and spent much time with her elders, sharing secrets of metals and smithing as they shared starwatching with him. Shall we, he said to her, and they stepped out to see the eclipse.

Hearing steps rushing behind them, Tadhg turned to face their pursuers. His reed torch dimly lit the east passage. He gave the torch to the Dagda, urging him, "Go into the chamber!" while he grabbed the Dagda's macehead and stuffed it under his belt. He crouched and pried up a paving stone.

Ith and two warriors slammed into Tadhg as he leaped up in the darkness. One Invader swiftly pressed a long copper knife at his throat.

"The Dagda! Take us to him—I know that he is here—I see light within!" Ith's eyes bulged and his thin lips pulled back from weasel-like teeth. The warrior pulled Tadhg's free arm behind him to the point of breaking. His captor dragged him down the passageway toward the torchlight but stumbled on a stone sill. Tadhg knocked the warrior in the groin, hard, with the paver and the man's knife clattered to the floor. He grabbed the knife and now it was Tadhg who dragged the moaning warrior down the passage, knife at his throat, as Ith pushed them all toward the inner chamber.

They arrived at the inner recess, where the Dagda stood firm. Lifting the torch, he showed Ith the lunar map on a great stone, and carved waveforms on another. "All these carvings relate to the moon and its cycles," he told Ith. "Here we keep track of the moon. This carving on the interior backstone replicates the carving on the entrance stone but poorly." As it happened, Cian's work at Knowth had been hasty despite Oghma's patience and encouragement.

The Dagda showed Ith the symbols, "Over many generations, the Starwatchers learned the moon and sun and star cycles and when there would be an eclipse. There is no magic to the moon's eclipse and nothing to fear."

Too impatient to puzzle out the Dagda's words about motions of moon and sun, Ith grabbed the torch for himself and briefly looked around in the passage. He could see a serpentine form on one of the tall slabs, and many concentric circles. He found a carving of a dagger on another passage slab and frowned at the dagger. Something about those wily Seafarers on the Continent suggested itself, and inflamed Ith. He had no way to verify the intent of these carved symbols; more deception, probably. This might be the mound that concealed stores of gold. He could not tell if that large stone mapped the shadows on the moon's face, and if it did, so what?

He didn't trust what the Dagda was telling him. The quiet ones might have caused this eclipse, how else could they know it in advance? In all his seasons among the Starwatchers, Ith had not learned the secrets of these mounds. He sought in vain the Starwatchers' calendar. Rumors from the Continent reached him, rumors that the heavens were shifting, and he suspected these quiet ones understood this cosmic change. He craved the new object that a trader from the Loire spoke of, the sky disk. No doubt his rival the Dagda possessed such a bronze disk right here under his nose at the Boyne. He understood Elcmar's fury that a Starwatcher had Taranis' favor. His own desires eluded him for too long here.

Ith returned to the inner chamber. All the men smelled of the sweat of fear, except the Dagda and himself.

"Master of great knowledge! Show me the disk that tells the stars," he snarled. The Dagda stood silent. "Show me the sky disk," Ith demanded. Still the Dagda said nothing. Ith stepped forward and plunged deep his cold bronze knife.

With a growl, Tadhg thrust the knife he carried into the shaman Ith, who collapsed. The warriors leaped at Tadhg and he knocked them senseless with the paving stone. He ran out from the passage. Elcmar and his other warriors were not to be seen out in the open. Tadhg gathered those Starwatchers who could run and sent them to the village for aid. He ripped thick moss from under a tree and ran back inside Knowth.

Ith's warriors had fled and left their shaman behind.

The Dagda lay on the stone floor and Tadhg knelt there holding moss on the wound until help arrived. The Starwatchers did not move the frail Dagda, but lit a fire of strong herbs in a bullaun stone. They gave him a stimulant brew, but it did not revive him. He lay in the dimly lit inner chamber, his life bleeding steadily from him.

"All things change, making way for each other." The Dagda's eyes faded. "You may look back, but you must not stare, at the past."

As the full moon recovered its brightness outside Knowth, the spirit of the Dagda rose from the Boyne, above the central plain and surrounding mountains, and up to the stars where he hid his face among them.

Tadhg and Slainge crossed the Dagda's arms over his chest and placed pebbles on his eyelids. No one knew how old was their Dagda, but with him an age expired. What was the way forward without him, their Lord of the Light? Who would take his place? No one could speak for grief at this loss.

They prepared to remove his body to their village when Tadhg heard heavy footsteps coming along the passage. He looked around, and tossed the Dagda's red stone macehead to the right behind a slab in the inner chamber. It went into place with a slight clatter, it must have fallen into a crevice but Tadhg had no time to check on where this treasure lay. The Starwatchers jumped up to face Elcmar and three warriors pushing into the inner chamber.

"We come for Ith." Elcmar's voice echoed in the passage and chamber. Tadhg pointed to where Ith lay inert but breathing. Then Elcmar saw that the Dagda lay dead. He lowered his knife and motioned for his warriors to do the same. Elcmar approached the body. Eyes glowing, he abruptly demanded to have the Dagda's head.

"No!" And Tadhg made for Elcmar, but the other Starwatchers held him.

Slainge spoke. "That is not our way. What this Dagda knew, remains with us. We teach on the mountain, we tell the ages of the moon, we show the place where the sun goes to rest.

"We teach our children, that our knowledge may be saved and not lost with death." Slainge stepped in front of the body. "You would have to take all our heads. We all hold the Dagda's power."

Elcmar halted, but his eyes glowed at the dead shaman of the Starwatchers. *A noble face and head. A worthy life, and by one who was not a warrior.* Suddenly he wondered what, indeed, his Aengus knew from these Starwatchers, and how he should deal with the lad.

He replied in the Starwatchers' tongue, surprising them, "There are enough of us here to remove the dead and wounded to where they can be tended."

Tadhg spoke before Slainge. "We accept, but there shall be no mutilation of bodies."

"It shall be, so."

Nevertheless, Tadhg and Slainge made sure that the first removal from Knowth was the Dagda to their village, so that his body remained unmolested. Ith went out next, to be slung over an Invader horse that a warrior led back to their camp. The men removed those who lay dying, and next those having lesser wounds, before removing the other dead, Starwatcher and Invader, as the moon steadily lowered.

This night of cooperation following the deaths at Knowth might have produced lasting peace at the Boyne. But it did not.

Full many a war shall be
on Eochaid of Meath because of thee:
there shall be destruction of elfmounds,
and battle against many thousands.

From: *The Yellow Book of Lecan*, 14th Century CE

Teamair (Tara)

ELCMAR, EXHAUSTED AND covered in dried blood, returned to the camp far into the night of the lunar eclipse. He found Boann talking with Aengus in the great hall. Aengus sat in the *ard rí's* chair, so Elcmar stiffly seated himself opposite Boann. The remnants of a fire flickered in the hall's gloom. Both mother and son gaped at the bloodstains on him but before they could ask, he announced the losses among Starwatchers and Invaders.

"The Dagda, your Lord of the Light, lies dead. Ith is after being mortally wounded." Then he turned his piercing eyes fully upon Aengus. "What were you doing there at the mounds on this evening?"

Boann buried her face in her hands. Aengus, shocked by the sudden loss of the Dagda and on the heels of Oghma's death, could not speak. He returned Elcmar's intense gaze, neither wanting to give way. A black silence settled around them all as dawn glowed in the east.

Through the ensuing day, Aengus busied himself with helping to care for the wounded warriors. He helped the foreign guest depart with others bound for the coast. In passable Invader spoken with his strange accent, that man wished Aengus a long and successful life at the Boyne. Elcmar stood at a distance.

After the sun had set on that day, Aengus sat together with his mother again at table. Elcmar leaned back, watchful, listening. He made no offer to appease Boann for the latest violence at the sacred mounds. At last he said, "Aengus, this night and day that have passed, have hardly put you to the test. I am willing to give you another night and day if you wish."

"Father—," Aengus' young voice cracked.

It startled Elcmar to hear the lad call him father.

"Father, you gave *Bru na Boinne* to me for all eternity, for all of time is made up of night and day."

Blood pounded at his temples, his jaw clenched. Aengus used the Invader tongue and Elcmar could claim no misunderstanding or trick played on him. The two waited for his response.

"Very well, Aengus. You shall have the Boyne. For all eternity." He turned to Boann. "And you won't mind having new quarters at Teamair? Now that we are carving up Eire." His hand gripped a knife. Her eyes avoided it.

Elcmar saw her clearly for the first time since he had seen Boann dreaming under the sun in a meadow. She was wearing her good white linen tunic and an overdress of green, soft wool with a saffron sash: green, white, and gold, the colors of a summer's day. She wore the gold lunula from Cian at her throat. He could reach over and slit her neck just so above that shining crescent, but he did not move except to cut his joint of beef and eat it.

She bent her head toward him, her voice gentle. "I have never seen you so thoroughly outwitted, Elcmar, yet already you have another scheme to control Eire."

"Damn you! You have the gold—you have Aengus—you shall not have this island!" His blade flashed at her neck to summon her old fear.

Aengus stood, knocking over his chair. Elcmar jumped up, knife raised.

"No!" Boann threw herself between them.

He sat down, breathing hard, and she pulled Aengus away. They left him in the deep lavender shadows of the empty hall.

Elcmar remained at the table late into that night, thinking. Hidden wounds bothered him now, and he had many. He had a slave bring one of the jars of sour red wine from a far coast, and drank all of its contents without watering it. The gold he had kept back, Cian's gold, could pay for more wine.

Elcmar never returned to Boann in their sleeping chamber, nor that in the new great hall where she moved with him at Teamair. He turned his ambitions to Tara, lying not far from the Boyne.

The Invaders had long coveted the prominent rise in the landscape to the southwest of *Bru na Boinne*. Tara's elevated and sizable grassy sweep presented a focal point for building a grand assembly place. That one Eochaid, a Starwatcher, occupied this area and that Starwatchers had an ancestral passage mound there, did not concern the Invaders in the slightest.

The small camp nearby that Muirgen and her husband started many suns earlier, filled with newcomers from the Continent to help build the great new fort. A huge oval enclosure, one hundred strides at its widest point, rose quickly upon the Hill of Tara. This temple-fort consumed three hundred oaks for its stout posts and retaining wall. Stately oaks toppled where they had grown for hundreds of summers before felled by Invaders' copper axes. The Invaders polished and embellished the new walls, unlike the rough logs surrounding their old Boyne camp. Within the fort, they built a hall of imposing dimensions.

It was to this shining new hall upon Teamair that Elcmar moved with Boann, still his wife in name if not in habit. She kept an eye on Elcmar's doings while she continued to spend much of her time with Brighid, whom she still called Airmid. Rumblings inside the new camp came to Boann's attention.

Why be devoting resources to glorify Elcmar when he failed to find gold here, the warriors complained. It was rumored that Connor's men at last found gold in northern mountains and had no intention of sharing it with Elcmar. Disgruntled warriors returned to the Continent. She passed word along to Tadhg of all that occurred inside the new walls.

Aengus remained in charge of *Bru na Boinne* and the Midh plains. He held the Boyne with young Starwatchers trained by Elcmar's own men and methods, and he waited.

The shaman Ith died of his wounds from the clash at Knowth but his parting words established his name forever: Ith declared that there was a high tower on the Continent from which a man could see Eire, and from there more Invaders would come to claim these shores.

His prophecy quickly gave rise to jokes among the Starwatchers. These Ith jokes referred to persons who believed the earth to be flat. Starwatchers, who compared astronomy with growing numbers of mariners reaching Eire, agreed the earth must be rounded under the circling sky dome.

The Seafarers said, "The north stars change position before us as we progress north." If the earth were flat, experience taught them, then the stars would appear fixed. They saw also that the other stars wheeled in motion around the north. And the domed appearance of the sky itself suggested that the shape of the earth was rounded, an orb like sun and moon; like an apple, said the Starwatchers.

With Ith dead, the Starwatchers openly used the bronze sky disk. Their use of the three Boyne mounds resumed though the passages were sealed.

Each side accused the other of interfering with the peace process.

Tensions boiled over in the dispute over the Dagda's final resting place. The aggression and violence at Knowth sorely reminded Starwatchers of the troubles at Dowth during Sheela's reburial. For the Dagda's resting place, the Starwatchers wanted his cremated bones far from *Bru na Boinne*. The elders chose the less conspicuous mound atop Teamair. Meanwhile his bones rested temporarily in a secret place.

This mound at Teamair had received bones over many generations, and Eochaid said that it would be an honor to have the Dagda interred there. Though it had less than a third of the height and width of the Boyne mounds, the sacred landscape included a cursus that would be adequate for their final procession honoring the Dagda. The Starwatchers planned also to erect a stele near that mound to honor the Dagda.

Elcmar and his warriors opposed burial of the Dagda so close to their new enclosure. To make their point, the Invaders hastily dispossessed Eochaid's settlement. This eviction came at a most difficult time, for recent damp and rains on Eire left little food reserves. Other villages could not feed Tara's displaced inhabitants while they struggled to feed their own. Invader warriors repelled with unrestrained force those homeless Starwatchers who attempted to hunt game in the oak forest between the Boyne and Teamair, what forest remained after Invaders felled hundreds of its trees for their new enclosure.

The evicted Starwatchers turned from grazing herds and tending crops, to waging constant guerilla warfare against Invaders. At Tara's mound, their scouts dismantled a circle of stones put up by Invaders, a brazen move returned in kind. Bitter resentment divided quiet one from intruder.

The shadow of hunger deepened across the island.

Elcmar issued an edict: no Starwatcher could possess a metal weapon. No Starwatcher could possess any horse other than old mares beyond foaling. No Starwatcher could practice as a shaman, healer, poet, artisan, or lawgiver. The edicts proved difficult to enforce and stimulating to ignore.

Heartened by Cian's success at securing their gold against the intruders, the Starwatcher elders deliberated. Could they retake Teamair? They counted the number of their young and old men who were fit enough to fight in a pitched battle. They counted the metal weapons at hand to them, now a sizable cache including those that lay well hidden with the bronze sky disk. Still more metal weapons would be needed.

Sreng lit a mighty bonfire on the eastern coast to signal for long knives and halberds from the Continent. The message passed to Cymru, down small islands, across the channel and on to the Loire. The Starwatchers' share of the gold, held back for so long, left on five swift boats to chance the waves.

Annoyed at gold flooding his market, Taranis balked, but after hard bargaining he gave in to Cian and Enya. They sent the Starwatchers more metal weapons than requested. Cian paced at the Loire waiting for boats returning from the northern isles, desperate for any news.

At the Boyne village a messenger arrived from Lough Gur: those people concurred. The same message arrived from Carrowkeel, from the Wicklow mountains, and from the Lake mine. Men crept through from the north of the island, bypassing Connor's camp. Ready at last, the Starwatchers would have a rising of all the people. The time had come; they were all of one mind. They felt invincible. Whispers turned into a roar that issued first from Tadhg.

"Stand up! Stand with us! Stand up and fight!"

Thousands of dispossessed, hungry, quiet ones—men, women, and children—marched toward the great hall on the hill of Teamair. Its towering oak timbers, stripped of bark and polished, gleamed in the early morning sunlight.

Invader sentries beat on bronze from inside their new camp. The alarm bounced feebly off the dark mass of people coming to do battle. The inhabitants of the great hall and its camp barely had time to pick up their arms against the flood of quiet ones advancing over the now-treeless plain toward Teamair.

Starwatcher scouts showed lean muscle from seasons of hiding in bogs or on mountains. Led by fighters trained in Invader camps, their fledgling warriors carried smuggled weapons from Taranis: bronze knives and copper daggers. Some had curved yew bows, wristguards, and arrows topped with leaf-shaped flint or copper arrowheads. Fighters from Lough Gur brandished their own copper and bronze weapons. Ordinary Starwatchers armed themselves with stone axes or sharp wood pikes and with their common resolve.

Muirgen and her husband joined in at the front of those marching, and with them their sons and daughters, rousing all for battle with frightful cries.

Airmid watched with Boann from a platform high inside the Invaders' new walls. They cried out to see her son Ruadan, not yet age twelve, carrying arms with the Starwatchers. Boann put her arm around Airmid's shoulders. Airmid pointed and she recognized Ardal in the distance.

Boann glimpsed Elcmar striding out with his warriors. Then she saw Aengus, tall and grave among the marching Starwatchers. Her heart sinking, her eyes turned to the sun in a silent entreaty to spare Aengus.

The weapons flashed like lightning from the gathering storm of people. Boann trembled with Airmid at the terrible beauty forming below them on the plain.

The opponents met on the grassland and laid into each other using metal and stone. They hacked without shields, without art or cunning. Caught up in a savage fury, teeth bared, they trampled the injured. They did not regroup or form lines or clever wings, nor would they retreat to fight another day. Only the long bronze knife and the halberd gave an advantage, lengthening the arm's reach and slashing easily through leather. Those who knew from warrior exercises to duck and bob and weave, lasted only a few breaths longer than the novice on this fighting field.

Sreng fought alongside Eochaid, and when he saw Eochaid felled like a mighty oak, Sreng leaped and hacked off the warrior's arm that had done it. Not far away, Slainge and young Daire each wrestled and shoved and struck blows for their lives against skilled Invaders.

Midhir joined in the fray against the Invader warriors. Showing far more valor than strength, at his age he could not spin round quickly between foes. By now the gore on the field made the grass slippery.

Aengus caught sight of Midhir as the elderly one faltered. He muscled his way through the crazed fighters, struggling to reach his foster father and take him off the battlefield. A tall figure happened upon Midhir and swooped, raising a long knife. Midhir faced Elcmar of the killing eyes as he sliced open the old man.

From far away, a woman screamed: Fuamnach.

Aengus saw Midhir crumple. Midhir, who showed him many kindnesses, who kept him safe from all harm, who shared the stars' secrets, lay dead under the harsh sun. Just five paces' distant stood Elcmar, amber eyes glowing, a blade in each hand, looking for his next kill. Aengus froze in that moment, oblivious to the sights, the sounds and smells raging around him, except the figure of Elcmar. Elcmar half-turned but did not react as if seeing him.

He does not know me, thought Aengus. His body snapped awake and he charged with his knife. The blow caught Elcmar unaware. Horrified, Aengus leapt away, threw Midhir's corpse over his shoulder and left the swarming field on his massive legs.

So it was that Elcmar fell at the hand of Aengus the shining one.

The disorderly battle strewed the plain with casualties. The earth there reluctantly drank its first blood of human carnage. Survivors limped and crawled away from the ghastly scene. There followed a deep and awful silence, broken only by moans and the screeches of carrion birds who circled above the dead and dying.

Boann found Elcmar on the plain below the Great Hall. A Starwatcher knife handle protruded from his lower gut.

He looked at it then slowly up to her. "We should have known this would happen, so."

A shudder of pain shook him. He turned with effort to look upon her face, still lovely.

"Boann...I... I have always admired your courage." He told her the truth. She would not expect him to declare love for her. A contest of wills, he saw too late; nothing to do with love but she held his head in her lap while he lay unblinking.

He saw a large black bird above him, then it resembled Muirgen, then one bird became three black birds, three hags mocking him. He fumbled with one hand at his belt. During the battle his small carving of the death-hag must have gone missing. Pain clouded his mind. He saw himself as a child on his own, and his wandering far and away leading him to this island. To Boann, and beautiful Aengus.

"Where is Aengus?" he demanded, raising his head then falling back.

Boann watched as his spirit struggled to hold on to Eire. Elcmar died soon and without complaint, the strange glow not leaving his eyes though his spirit had gone. He smelled of sunlit grass and flowers, and not of horses or combat. His body lay straight and pleasing and for the last time, he stirred her senses.

They had never surrendered to each other, in love or in war. Something inside her gave way to see Elcmar lying dead before her, ending their battle. Boann felt aged and weary. She left the field of gore and the hovering, shrieking birds.

She was not so ready for death, but was herself badly wounded. Boann lay for many days in the high stone chamber of the *Bru*. She longed to see Aengus. He did not appear, to her sorrow, but she was relieved that her Aengus was not found by the mourners who removed the dead and injured from the battlefield.

Those friends who survived the battle attended her, giving herbs brewed into the drink of sleep. Her old dog Dabilla lay watching at her feet. Over the course of an afternoon, the young healer at her side noticed that Boann's pulse slowed.

Boann waited for the full moon to enter in crossing the milky stream above. When the moon laid its silvery hand on her brow, she motioned for Tadhg to bring his face next to hers. She sighed. "Old friend," she whispered with a little smile. Her eyes closed.

Later she stirred, her fingers brushing at the air above. "It was all so beautiful!"

Tadhg took her fitful hands in his. "Rest for the journey. Your work here is done. Soon you'll be seeing your mother, and Oghma. And Sheela—." His tears flowed.

Time collapsed into a blur of light. She rose toward it, hoping to find Cian.

Instead she saw Eire's shores, the waves bringing great ships. More piles of riches and more troubles. More battles, tribe against tribe and father against son. The living breathing land divided like a carcass.

Boann inhaled, breath rattling. Their landscape desecrated, the ancestors forgotten. Chaotic, dreadful visions but she could not turn away, swept along as time bent, looped, folded into itself. She felt so tired. The light beckoned, brighter than any sunrise. She would walk with her ancestors. Cian would find her.

Three spirals: light, dark, eternity. She whispered, "Darkness has come to us. The people must find the light again, or we shall all suffer."

Thousands of stars shone in the void. Boann slipped away with Dabilla into the white river of stars.

Epilogue

THE SUN PASSED FAR above them in the sky, shining on the verdant island and its soaring birds and leaping fish. The white quartz glittered upon the mound of Newgrange along the sweet plains of the Boyne. Tara lay to the southwest, a motorway whizzing with traffic hard by its buried remains and over battle sites of long ago.

"Do you follow me so far?" the museum docent asked his listeners.

"Oh, yes. It's a brilliant story." A tourist sat spellbound. Her leather notebook that recorded years of her travels along Atlantic coasts lay unopened, just there on the table where he surprised her hours ago by joining her to have his tea.

Two students leaned forward from their adjacent table in the elegant tearoom.

The docent smiled kindly and concluded his tale.

"Many important figures fell that day on the battle plain, Invaders and Starwatchers. The elders decided that fire should summon those who yet lived to attend the mass interment. They lit a great ring of fires around the mound on Tara in the empty sockets of the stone circle they'd removed. Afterward, the elders took special care to cover the ashes of Elcmar and his bronze dagger, damaged by the flames of his pyre, with a collared pottery urn. They interred Elcmar's bones inside the mound, where the Dagda also lay at last, upon the hill of Tara.

"We can only speculate where Boann's mortal remains lie. When you see the Milky Way in northern skies, think of Boann.

"In retaliation for the battle, Connor rode down from the north and burned Bri Leith, the house of Midhir. In the flames and carnage there at Bri Leith, the people said, young Aengus disappeared.

"Connor ignored Maedb at Tara and carried Midhir's daughter, Blathnat, back to the north with him. Connor re-invented himself over the coming years in the north, insinuating himself into mythic proportions despite having been caught red-handed in Sheela's murder years before. Maedb reincarnated as well, grabbing for power, appearing and reappearing over the centuries.

"Airmid lived on to be reunited with Ardal. Her son Ruadan survived the fight, as did Muirgen and all her family, and Sreng, Cermait although badly wounded, Daire, and others.

"After the great battle over Tara, the survivors from both sides joined together out of necessity. It was truly the Least Time. Their harvest had been depleted and there were too few survivors to gather in any harvest. Starvation threatened, and plague swept the island. Cian's agents sent food to the Boyne from Wicklow. Cian sent seeds from across the ocean, and encouraged peace on the island so that agriculture—and the gold trade—could resume. The living slowly mobilized to produce food again, and in the next growing seasons the survivors were rewarded by the natural richness of Meath's green plains. Once more their cattle and sheep grew fat and grains hung with full kernels at harvesting.

"Gold flowed from Eire. All men of property carried a copper dagger or a long bronze knife. Eire's smiths made copper axes by the hundreds, and in new styles that found their way overseas.

"A story circulated that Aengus drowned at the mouth of the Boyne, leaving for the Continent. A later story said that Aengus dwells forever in the golden hall of *Bru na Boinne*."

Cian's myth has it that he was killed, stoned to death, by Enya's brothers. He left no known descendants with Enya. His ashes received burial close to the Loire, in a modest passage mound with a few gold artifacts and one treasured blue-green bead.

For all the status and riches Cian achieved in the hall of Taranis, he never gazed upon the sun without seeing fair Aengus. He never saw the milky river of stars without seeing Boann. He still had not found what he was looking for.

Cian's bronze starwatching disk has not been located along the Boyne nor any place on Eire, this fair island.

The museum guide's rambling story ended. No one moved.

The young man asked the inevitable, "How long were the mounds in use?"

"As long as sun and moon and stars do shine," came the answer.

"What happened to Cian's astronomy disk?" asked the young woman.

Mischief sparkled in his hazel eyes, crinkling at the corners with his little smile.

"Tell us," they cried, and he indulged them.

"To make a long story longer, thieves unearthed an astonishing bronze disk around the dawn of the 21st century, close to the town of Nebra in eastern Germany. Archaeologists and police recovered the stolen disk, dug up by modern thieves along with ornate bronze knives. From the knives' design and hilt decoration, these early bronze weapons could have been made far to the south, along the Mediterranean. What about the disk?

"The bronze disk weighs around two kilograms or four pounds, and is the size of a dinner plate. To find out when and where this sky disk was made, micro-analysis of the bronze indicates that its copper and tin came from northern Europe. Golden symbols of the sky gleam from its upper surface that had been treated—perhaps with rotten eggs—to have a rich blue background. The crescent moon shines forth from the disk, cradling the night on a field of stars. The disk shows several alterations made to it over time.

"Could this be Cian's bronze sky disk? The gold shapes appear to be later additions after casting of the original disk, from a microscopic scan of its surface. There are thirty-two stars on its surface including a prominent grouping that resembles the Pleiades, the equinox stars of ancient renown. Experts debate this unique disk's symbolism. Clearly, it was a venerated object. It is the only such disk found to date.

"Consider the man who traveled with Enya to the Boyne, the one now called the Amesbury Archer, a man of status despite his injured left knee. He merited burial within the Stonehenge ritual landscape, a prestige burial with weapons made of Iberian or Breton copper, and gold jewelry. Such an important trader would have ordered a bronze disk from Cian and sent it back to his homeland. His teeth—isotopes—tell us he came from central Europe."

"Other objects have been found from our story. Bolg's pleated linen shirt, made in the Nile valley. The dazzling gold cape, discovered in north Wales in the nineteenth century CE, its pieces now reassembled. The masterful gold cape speaks for itself.

"What archaeologists found here in Ireland is telling, for our purposes. The mound upon the hill of Tara contained dense burial deposits and grave goods. Elcmar's cremated bones and his scorched dagger were exhumed at Tara. Burials continued there for a time after the early battle for Tara. The hill remains important into this millennium. Your children must see to its future.

"Creidhne's gold disc earring, lost at the Ross Island mine in Kerry, was found and carried off but lost again in the northern reaches of ancient Eire. That gold earring lay undisturbed for thousands of years until excavated in county Down by modern archaeologists, who called it a 'Portuguese type.' Its design resembles the very disc that inspired Cian so long ago on the Seafarer peninsula. You see its quadrant design echoed in early Irish crosses.

"An archaeologist discovered the Dagda's exquisitely carved macehead inside the crevice in Knowth thousands of years after

Tadhg stashed it there. The sinuous carving and intense color of its polished stone combine in testimony to a consummate artisan. The Dagda's mace is one of the treasures from that era, the Starwatchers.

"Boann's antler shawl pin carved by Oghma was found at Fourknocks mound, just where Boann lost it as an eager apprentice learning astronomy.

"The bones of a young male were exhumed close to Newgrange mound thousands of years after he fell in battle near Gabhrah, the plain of the white horse. That burial included a gold torc made of thick Irish gold wire, twisted perfectly into a spiral along its length." The docent paused. "This male descended in a line from Aengus or should I say from Boann, many centuries after them. You can see his fine torc here in the museum. He could read the Starwatchers' carved symbols at *Bru na Boinne*. But he was the last person who could read them." The docent fell silent for several moments, then resumed. "Isn't it always the way? The victors create the myths to suit themselves.

"The gold ear disc, the Dagda's carved macehead, and Boann's carved pin; each tell us the Starwatchers' story. These objects and the traces of dwellings, the burials and stone carvings and mounds, are for us to decipher—and to respect. It may never be possible for later peoples to grasp what these ancients observed and applied to their world over their millennia of starwatching.

"The great menhirs still lie shattered at the Morbihan in Brittany. Another area of stone alignments that were pushed over and buried there around 2000 BCE, is presently being excavated. This excavation may help to explain why so many Atlantic megaliths were abandoned during the time of Boann and Cian. Hundreds of sites and carvings in stone remain to be analyzed along what is currently called the Atlantic fringe."

The docent finished the telling and he rose from the table. He looked at the middle-aged woman from the States. It had been grand, she having her coffee while he had his tea, there in the museum's tearoom. Beyond in the majestic exhibition spaces, the gold lunulae and torcs, the gold earrings and bracelets, and the little gold boat with its delicate gold oars and mast that had been fashioned long after Cian's voyages; hundreds of gold objects gleamed in their cases. Pottery that showed traces of firing in an open pit, polished stone and copper axeheads, the Dagda's fantastic carved macehead, and even a cache of ossified hazelnuts; these artifacts all rested within the marble columned halls. Waiting, as if their owners might return.

Does archaeology help us to understand myth or is it myth that shapes archaeology, he could ask, and in any event whose myths and which archaeology do we choose to believe?

He could tell the museum visitors a great deal more, but on this turning planet it was late in the day.

"Ach, sure. Glad you enjoyed yourself with my tale. But I do believe the museum is soon to be closing. I'll show you out, so. Don't forget your notebook, madam. Follow me—and you youngsters as well, if you would."

The two students rose sheepishly from their adjacent table. They had started out whispering, hidden behind their hands, while the old man held forth.

"Lein's Lake Of Many Hammers!" whispered the boy, amused.

"That's where O'Brien excavated the copper mine," she told him.

"Flann O'Brien, was it?" He smirked.

"No, eejit. William O'Brien. The archaeologist. A major find, that was."

They eavesdropped during the docent's entire talk while he captivated this older woman, probably a tourist. Like her, the students stayed to listen while the august docent spoke, and took no break despite their drinking several cups of tea apiece.

"I wonder what time it is," the girl said as they stood and stretched.

"I wonder what millennium it is," the lad answered.

The docent led the visitors past where hidden wee faces peered out at the gold, waiting until the museum emptied of all intruders. Staff switched off lights, footsteps echoing in the exhibit halls.

Under the entrance rotunda, a wild-eyed vagrant, Mad Sweeney, scuffled with gardai and it took a third policeman to subdue and escort him outside. The visitors passed by unaware of the commotion.

Coming out of the great doors onto the high-columned portico of the National Museum, the two students were quiet, reflecting on all that the docent told them. They stood at the edge of a twilight mist, its lavender shadows curling around the semicircular steps. Damp air limned the stone pavement.

A thin place in space and time, the tourist murmured.

The young man heard it and understood. He felt seamlessly connected with earth and sky, conscious as never before. He thought to thank the older man, to seize his hand and sincerely thank him. His companion looked around her as well. Their eyes met. Not seeing the guide's cap and dark suit among the people leaving the museum, they turned to ask the tourist, "Where is your man from inside?"

"That wonderful docent? He was just here a moment ago!"

The students and the tourist trotted after the tall figure vanishing into the soft grey. They all turned the corner onto Kildare Street, where his dignified bearing could just be seen ahead in the fading daylight. Soon he would be absorbed into the throng rushing along Stephen's Green. The young man called out.

"What is your name, sir, to properly thank you for the story?"

The answer resonated through the mist.

"I am called Aengus."

Author's Note:

Technical points, and not letting the facts ruin a good story

Copper to early bronze age: This story condenses, or telescopes, a few centuries of big changes introduced during the Chalcolithic or early Bronze Age along coastal northwest Europe. The mounds, megaliths, carved images, and objects (including the green skull) mentioned in BENDING THE BOYNE date to that period, they do exist, and can be viewed in Ireland, Wales, Brittany, and northern Spain. Clothing and hairstyles reflect Beaker-era burials, Bronze Age bodies preserved in bogs, and items found with Oetzi the Ice Man.

Linguistics problem: Academics debate whether metal use and trade, embodied as the Beaker people, the Invaders in this story, introduced a proto-IndoEuropean language. The native Starwatchers' language and culture did not necessarily disappear circa 2200 BCE with the Bronze Age, nor later at around 600 BCE with the Iron Age and so-called "Celtic" culture named for that language group. Archaeo-geneticists, linguists, and others will gradually untangle this.

Dwellings at the Boyne: The Starwatchers' stone houses resemble those on Orkney (northeast Scotland) and at Carrowkeel (county Sligo, Ireland). Dwellings have not been excavated at the Boyne to date, except that Knowth mound overlaps the foundation of what may have been an earlier dwelling. The Beaker-era structures located around Newgrange mound probably consisted of plank and wattle walls, as described in this tale, but there exists little academic concensus about the roof materials nor exact use of a given enclosure (i.e., whether used as an animal pen, dwelling, ceremonial space, or workshop).

Fire inside the mounds: There is scant evidence of using fire inside the mounds but sufficient air does flow into Newgrange passage or Knowth's passages for use of torches or a small fire inside. Same re: Boann's herbs burned for Sheela inside Dowth mound.

Bonfires: Eire's people continued to use bonfires as signal messages, for example after the fatal shooting of an AngloIrish landlord in the nineteenth century.

Astronomy at 2200 BCE: Positions of the sun, moon, Milky Way, constellations, and certain planets would be visible using just the naked eye. To verify their positions at 2200 BCE, a web-based program was consulted.

Schools of thought about Irish/Welsh mythology: BENDING THE BOYNE echoes older literary sources including the *Dindshenchas, Lebor Gabala,* and other texts. The plot draws from myth though its physical setting strives to be factual. Those interested to read further will find various approaches to the ancient mythology, the oldest in western Europe. These approaches fall into one of the following camps:

1. the medieval-era monks altered the myths in transcribing oral tales from old Irish or Welsh to Latin, and added Judeo-Christian elements (and even doodled in their vellum margins); thus the myths are at best unreliable legends, or at worst are useless for any purpose

2. the myths are "Celtic" fantasy tales of fairies and leprechauns

3. the transcribed myths give a false chronology of various "invasions" of Ireland up to when "Milesians" allegedly arrived from Spain (per those auld monks' anachronisms re: the Biblical Flood, Egypt, etc.; see 1, above), or, in some instances were revised to set forth a contrived genealogy for political purposes

4. the Iron Age myths borrow from Eire's earlier, indigenous oral history

5. the myths contain metaphors and pnemonic devices which pass along an important store of empirical knowledge, namely, astronomy; e.g., Aengus represents the reborn sun, Boann embodies the Milky Way, etc.

The author happily combines elements from all the above, with simultaneous affection and caution as to the astronomy camp. A definitive interpretation of the carved symbols at the Boyne, or those in Brittany, or in Spain/Portugal, has yet to be made. Also, not every bump or old track in the landscape reveals to us the ancients' astronomy. *Caveat emptor*.

Nothing in this story foreshadows "Celts" or endorses that term, especially not the pervasive nineteenth-century label "Celtic" that is routinely misapplied to the mounds (or to Stonehenge) and the people who built them. North Atlantic peoples shared a culture well prior to the Iron Age and long after that era. People of the isles did not call themselves Celts until recently. In time, a more viable construct will replace "Celtic".

The Starwatchers' astronomy practices carried on to St. Patrick's era. He condemned "those miserable wretches who worship the sun [and who] shall surely be punished", and St. Patrick lit his own competing bonfire.

The author's literary use of elements from the myths in no way supports pseudohistory, occultism, astrology, neopaganism, or any specific religion.

Two final points:

First, as of this novel's publication date, the National Museum in Dublin does not have docent guides. The 1916 Rising exhibit does now have a different venue.

Second, recent analysis of Irish gold artifacts suggests another source of ancient gold did exist, in the Mourne mountains—despite what Connor told Elcmar. Regarding the precise location of gold in county Wicklow:

that is still a secret.

For discussion group questions, and a partial Bibliography of sources consulted in writing BENDING THE BOYNE, please see the author's website at: www.jsdunnbooks.com .

PRONUNCIATION OF CHARACTERS' NAMES, MYTHIC ORIGINS, AND ROLE *(in italics)* IN BENDING THE BOYNE

AENGUS, OENGUS (an gus):
Bright One, Youthful Son; personification of one day. A figure with Boann in early solar references in myths of the *Bru* (Newgrange mound – *Bru mac ind Oc*). Pre-Indoeuropean?
Son of Boann.

AIRMID (Ahr mid) renamed BRIGHID (bree id):
Goddess of herb lore, healing, wisdom.
Friend of Boann; the Invaders change her name to Brighid.

ARDAL (ar dahl):
Bear, fury, valor.
Starwatcher scout, lover of Airmid.

BASAJUAN (bah sah whan):
Basque, ancient smith.
The Basque smith who collaborates with Cian.

BOANN (bo ahn):
Goddess, personification of the river Boyne and also the Milky Way, the "Bright Way"; and her totem animal of "White Cow." Not found in later myths. Pre-Indoeuropean?
Astronomer, daughter of Oghma, wife of Elcmar, mother of Aengus, and a symbol.

BOLG (vulag):
Deity name. Also, Fir Bolg ("Men of the Bags").
Trader on Iberian peninsula.

BRESAL (bres ahl):
Pain. Early shaman figure in myth cycle.
An Invader shaman at their Boyne camp.

CIAN (kee uhn):
Derivation unknown, "ancient," "enduring." Pre-Indoeuropean? Also in Persian: Kian = Generations. In Irish myth, said to have been born with the caul on his head; also said to be a shapeshifter.
The missing apprentice to Oghma, and a symbol.

CLIODHNA (clee uhna):
Goddess of beauty. Derivation unknown, ancient name. Pre-Indoeuropean? A version of her tale as taken down by Lady Gregory, says she got into a currach that had a stern made of copper.
> *Captive of the intruders, Gebann's daughter, Seafarer potter, friend to Boann.*

COLL (cull):
"The Sun"; ancient name, said to be a god of the Tuatha de Danaan.
> *Ancestor, grandfather to Oghma's mentor in stonecarving.*

CONNOR, Ir. CONCHOBHAIR (con nor):
Figure from Ulster cycle of myths, Conchobhair of the Red Hand.
> *Miscreant Invader.*

CREIDHNE (cred nuh):
Ancient god of goldsmithing.
> *Smith at The Lake Of Many Hammers (: Ross Island mine, Lough Lein, county Kerry.)*

DAIRE (dah ruh):
"Oak grove" or "fertile"; early fertility or bull god. Pre-Indoeuropean?
> *Apprentice astronomer, Starwatcher scout.*

DAGDA (dagh da):
"The Good God," "Lord of Great Knowledge." (Ir.: *Ruad Ro-fhessa* – Lord Of All Knowledge or Deirgderg, Red Eye); said to occupy the Bru of Boann (and alleged father of Aengus). Pre-Indoeuropean?
> *Elder, astronomer, mentor of Boann, and a symbol.*

ELCMAR (elk mar):
"Lord of the Horses," minor figure in myths about the Tuatha de Danaan, husband of Boann.
> *Husband of Boann, Invader champion.*

ENYA, Ir. ETHNIU (en ya):
Said to have married Cian according to early myth; also, "she who causes envy."
> *Wife of Cian, visits Bru na Boinne from a far shore.*

EOCHAID (oh kad, or, ughy):
Horse rider, lightning god, sun god. Possibly another name for the Dagda. Also, an early king of Midh.
> *Leader, Starwatcher elder at Tara.*

FUAMNACH (foo ahm nahk):
Wife of Midhir, foster daughter of Bresal in mythology of Tuatha de Danaan.
Wife of Midhir.

GEBANN (ge ban):
Smith, de Danaan, father of Cliodhna.
Seafarer, father of Cliodhna, master smith and mining supervisor.

GRIANE. (gri uhn):
Sun god. Pre-Indoeuropean?
Ancestor of Starwatchers, earliest astronomer.

ITH:
Early intruder on Eire, slain there according to myth.
An Invader shaman at their Boyne camp.

IUCHNU (iuk nu):
Figure who leaves by boat with Cliodhna; per myth Cliodhna is lost off the coast of present day Cork.

LEIN (lehn):
Ancient smith figure in south Cork/Kerry.
Smith at the Lake Of Many Hammers with Gebann and Creidhne.

LIR (le ir):
Personification of the sea. Pre-Indoeuropean?
Seafarer of the Atlantic coasts.

MAEDB (mev):
"Intoxicates." Goddess figure, with reincarnations in later myths. Associated site –
Cruachain at Roscommon (Rathcroghan), mythical burial place of Maedb.
Wife of Connor.

MIDHIR (my dir):
Fairy god in Tuatha De tales; said to be Lord of the Sidhe (fairy mound) of Bri
Leith, daughter Blathnat taken as "consort" by Connor of Ulster.
Starwatcher, foster father of Aengus Og.

MUIRGEN (mur ghen):
"Born of the sea."
Seafarer captive at Invaders' Boyne camp. She later appears as the Morrigan.

OGHMA (oh mah):
God of writing; myths describe as a Fomorian; a half brother to the
Dagda in some myths.
*Starwatcher, astronomer, father of Boann, master stonecarver at the
Boyne, and symbol.*

SHEELA (shee la):
Derivation unknown. Pre-Indoeuropean?
Starwatcher, friend of Boann, and symbol.

SLAINGE (Slane):
Early name for area around Teamair (Tara).
Scout and elder of the Starwatchers.

SRENG (shreng):
A fighting man of the Fir Bolg.
Miner, Starwatcher scout, ally of Gebann and Cian.

TADHG (tige, or teig):
Derivation unknown. Pre-Indoeuropean? Also had a twentieth-century usage.
Starwatcher scout, friend of Boann and Cian.

TAIRDELBACH (tahr lak):
Old Irish. Tairdelbach means, roughly, "one who assists or aids."
A snitch on the Starwatchers.

TARANIS (tahr annis):
Breton version of Tuireann. God of thunder, and change (later personified with
a wheel). Father of Enya. One myth says that his sons killed Cian.
Chieftain controlling trade at the Loire.

TETHRA (teh ra):
Per myths, a Fomorian, a magician and chief of an "underground army". Pre-
Indoeuropean?
Starwatcher, friend of Dagda and Oghma, elder residing at Carrowkeel.

GLOSSARY OF TERMS

ARD RI
  chief, champion

BANJAXED
  destroyed

COMHLA BREAC
  speckled gate

CULCHIE
  countryside-dwelling person,
  a rustic

CUMAR
  female slave

CURRACH
  hide boat with wood frame

CYMRU
  Wales

DOWTH, Ir. DUIBADH
  Dowth mound

EIRE
  Ireland

EUSKALDUNAK
  Basque people

FLAHOOL, Ir. FLAHULACH
  profligate, generous

FULACHT(A) FIADH
  cooking pit(s)

GEIS
  ban, bad luck

KNOWTH, Ir. CNOGB
  Knowth mound

LIFFEY
  the river Liffey, "black-pooled"

LUNATE
  one lunar month

MACC
  horse, specifically a horse for
  riding; the term may predate or
  be unique to Celtic among the
  Indoeuropean language groups

MURIAS
  one of the four mythical cities
  of the Tuatha de Danaan, "rich"

NAOMHOG
  sleeker and larger hide boat
  than a currach

SHEELA NA GIG
  carved image of a naked
  woman in a distinctive pose.
  Irish: Sheela na gCioch

SIDH(E)
  "fairy mound(s)"; the passage
  mounds. Later, a term used for
  the fairies themselves

TEAMAIR
  Tara, county Meath

TUATH(A)
  tribe(s), unit, clan

UISCE
  water

Acknowledgments
The author is indebted to many persons for kind assistance during almost a decade of research and travels, including:

PAUL BARNES, TRANSLATOR, GIJON, ASTURIAS, SPAIN.
   Re: M. de Blas Cortina article.

JUAN FERNANDEZ BUELGA, GEOLOGIST – *como mi hijo* – OVIEDO, ASTURIAS, SPAIN.
   Re: the ancient mines of Asturias; Idol Pena Tu.

NEIL BURRIDGE, CRAFTSMAN OF BRONZE AGE TOOLS, CORNWALL, UK.
   Manuscript review.

PETER CLARK, MIFA, DEPUTY DIRECTOR, CANTERBURY ARCHAEOLOGICAL TRUST, CANTERBURY, UK.
   Manuscript review.

ADAM GWILT, CURATOR, NATIONAL MUSEUM OF WALES, CARDIFF, WALES.
   Re: ancient Wales.

MARK FROST, SENIOR ASSISTANT CURATOR, DOVER MUSEUM, DOVER, UK.
   Re: early boats.

BERNARD KAVANAGH, POTTER, KILKENNY, IRELAND, for insight and encouragement.

VINNIE KINSELLA, EDITOR, PORTLAND, OREGON, USA, for editing with uncommon valor and good humor.

The staff of the NATIONAL MUSEUM, DUBLIN, IRELAND.

WILLIAM O'BRIEN, PhD, DEPARTMENT HEAD, ARCHAEOLOGY, UNIVERSITY COLLEGE CORK, CORK, IRELAND.
Manuscript review.

MARTIN RICHARDS, PhD, UNIVERSITY OF LEEDS, LEEDS, UK.
Re: archaeogenetics.

EDWARD RUTHERFURD, author,
for his early encouragement of this project.

S. MARK SWANSON, M.A., USA,
for his enthusiasm and technical research re: astronomy details, and the maps.

CLARE TUFFY, Director, *BRU NA BOINNE* VISITOR CENTER, IRELAND.
Re: Red Mountain.

And with special thanks to:

CYRIL LYNCH, GRAIGNAMANAGH, IRELAND,
for many journeys Home.

Also: GAEL JOUNEAUX, Allo Carnac Taxi, the Morbihan, BRITTANY, FRANCE. NOEL SMITH, BC Taxis, IRELAND.
And to the UNKNOWN DRIVER, DONOSTIA-SAN SEBASTIAN, SPAIN, who graciously drove far into the mountains, then hiked up and up with the author to find the majestic site of Oianleku.

PERMISSIONS

1. *Lebor Gabála*, translated by R. A. Stewart Macalister, quoted with permission of the Irish Texts Society, Dublin, Ireland.

2. *Facing The Ocean: The Atlantic and Its Peoples 8000 BC to 1500 AD*, Barry Cunliffe, 2001, at page 219, quoted with permission of Oxford University Press, Oxford UK.

3. *Metrical Dindshenchas*, translated by Edward Gwynn, 1903, at page 35; republished 1991, School of Celtic Studies of the Dublin Institute for Advanced Studies, and quoted with permission of the Royal Irish Academy, Dublin, Ireland.

4. "The Wooing of Etaíne" translated by Osborn Bergin and R.I. Best, in *Ériu*, Vol. 12 (1938), pp. 137–196 at page 159, and quoted with permission of the Royal Irish Academy, Dublin, Ireland.

Author Biography

J.S. Dunn resided in Ireland during the past decade, and from there pursued a keen interest in early Bronze Age culture and marine trade along the Atlantic coasts of Spain, France, Wales, and Ireland. In 2006, the author attended the Dover Boat symposium regarding the earliest known Atlantic plank boat found at Dover, Kent, U.K. The research for BENDING THE BOYNE yielded many friends in diverse fields including archaeology, geology, and Bronze Age tool-making. The author is an attorney, and holds a master's degree in psychology, and has been published in those fields.